Proximity-fused **_____**
the nearest _____

My faceplate blacken_____ _____, then the
shock wave hammered the sled. Shrapnel crackled off
my armor like tin rain.

The ridge's backside was a cirque, the bowl from
which a glacier begins. I tumbled through space, beyond the bowl's vertical end cliff. Below me, boulders
on the ice looked smaller than spilled pepper.

The sled spent its momentum, so I hung momentarily in the sky, like a holotoon coyote.

The 'Puter slurred its last words. "Recommended
maximum altitude two feet. Current altitude two thousand six hundred twenty feet."

Silence turned to wind howl, louder and louder as
I fell, until I heard nothing. Just as well. I screamed all
the way down.

Praise for the Jason Wander Series

"Heinlein would have enjoyed this...The near future
he paints is as believable as it is terrible."
    —JOE HALDEMAN, **author of** _The Forever War_

"Fast, sharp, this future war tale rings with the authority of a writer who knows the Army from the inside
out. Amid all the military SF, this one gets it clear,
straight and right."
    —GREGORY BENFORD

BOOKS BY ROBERT BUETTNER

Orphanage
Orphan's Destiny
Orphan's Journey
Orphan's Alliance
Orphan's Triumph

ORPHAN'S JOURNEY

★

ROBERT BUETTNER

orbit

Orbit
Hachette Book Group USA
237 Park Avenue
New York, NY 10017
Visit our Web site at www.orbitbooks.net

Orbit is an imprint of Hachette Book Group USA, Inc. The Orbit name and logo is a trademark of Little, Brown Book Group Ltd.

Printed in the United States of America

First Orbit edition: April 2008

10 9 8 7 6 5 4 3 2 1

For Mary Beth,
For everything,
For ever

Patton, himself, pinned my Purple Heart on my pillow today. I told him our Shermans were coffins. Undergunned, underarmored. The gasoline engine makes them rolling bombs. Still, I took on a German Tiger. My boys burned alive. I cried, and I thought he'd slap me. But he patted my shoulder and whispered, "Son, the Army's a big family. But command is an orphan's journey." Then that SOB cried with me.

— Tank Commander's letter from France, December 1944

ORPHAN'S
JOURNEY

ONE

TEN YARDS SEAWARD from where I stand on the beach, the new-risen moons backlight our assault boats, outbound toward six fathoms. Beyond six fathoms lies hell.

Wind bleeds oily smoke back over me from lanterns roped to a thousand gunwales. Fifty soldiers' churning paddles whisker each boat's flanks. The boats crawl up wave crests, then dive down wave troughs, like pitching centipedes. For miles to my left and right, the lantern line winds like a smoldering viper.

I'm Jason Wander. Earthling, war orphan, high school dropout, infantryman, field-promoted Major General. And, on this sixth of August, 2056, accidental Commander of the largest amphibious assault since Eisenhower hurled GIs across the English Channel.

New century. New planet. Old fear.

An assault boat's Platoon Leader stands bent-kneed amid his paddlers, waving his boat's lantern above his head. He shouts to me, "We gladly die for you!"

I salute him, because I'm too choked to shout back. And shout what? That only fools die gladly? That he'd better sit down before his own troops shoot him for a fool? That someone should shoot me for one?

At my side, my Command Sergeant Major whispers, "They won't shoot him, Sir." I blink. Ord has read my mind since he was my Drill Sergeant in Basic.

The Bren may not shoot one another tonight, but the first Bren proverb we translated was "Blood feud is bread." For centuries, Bren has suffered under the thumb—well, the pseudopod—Slugs are man-sized, armored maggots that have no thumbs—of the Pseudocephalopod Hegemony. Still, every Clan midwife gifts every male baby with a whittled battle axe. Not to overthrow the Slugs. To whack human neighbors who worship the wrong god.

But if the newly unified Clans fail at sunrise, the Slugs will peel humanity off this planet like grape skin. Because we four Earthlings arrived.

Did I say "unified"? Ha. We should've segregated every boat. Mixed Clans may brain each other with their paddles before the first Slug shows. The final toast at Clan funerals is "May paradise spare you from allies."

Packed into twenty square miles of beach dunes, the Second and Third Assault Waves' cook fires prick the night. Smells of wood smoke and the dung of reptilian cavalry mounts drift to me on the shifting wind, along with Clan songs.

Yet twenty-two miles across the sea, the Slugs sleep.

Actually, no human knows whether Slugs sleep. But I have bet this civilization's life that tonight the Slugs have left the cross-channel beaches undefended. It seems a smart bet. No boatman in five hundred years has crossed the Sea of Hunters at full moons, and lived.

I chin my helmet optics. Two heartbeats thump before

I get a focus. A mile out, faint wakes vee the water. The first kraken are rising, like trout sensing skittering water bugs.

Sea monsters mightier than antique locomotives are about to splinter those first boats, like fists pounding straw. But troops that survive the crossing should surprise the Slugs. Surprised or not, the Slugs will still be the race that slaughtered sixty million Earthlings, as indifferently as mouthwash drowning germs.

Waves explode against boat prows. Windblown brine spits through my open helmet visor, needling my cheeks. My casualty bookie says that, even before the moons set, four hundred boats and crews will founder. Because I ordered them out there. The brine hides my tears.

Is my plan brilliant? Hannibal crossing the Alps? MacArthur landing at Inchon? I swallow. "What if I blundered, Sergeant Major?"

Ord nods back his helmet optics, then peers through binoculars older than he is. "Sir, Churchill said that war is mostly a catalogue of blunders."

Ord told me exactly the same thing as we lay in the snow of Tibet, three years ago. If I'd listened, this rat-screw could've been avoided.

TWO

"SLIDERS, SIR!" Ord gripped my elbow and whispered over Himalayan wind as thin and sharp as ice picks. We lay together, hidden belly-down behind a storm-scoured boulder, as he pointed. A half mile below us, six Chinese hovertanks slid on their air cushions out of the tree line that bounded the Tibetan valley.

I shuddered, squeezed my suit temp up a degree against the gusts, then boosted my helmet optics' magnification. Each Chinese hovertank's commander swayed waist-deep in his open turret hatch. Chin high, each Slider's commander was goggled and masked against snow fog billowing from each hovertank's skirts as it slid across the snow.

I said, "They're unbuttoned!"

Ord snorted. "In thirty seconds they'll regret that."

Engines droning like distant bumblebees, the hovertanks slid down the narrow valley single file.

I looked ahead of the armored column to where the Free Tibet Forces rebels we were advising lay hidden beneath snow-piled tarps. In fifteen seconds, the hovertanks' light-armored flanks would come in range of our rebels' old-but-deadly Rocket Propelled Grenades. When the ambush sprung, the infantry squad inside each hover-tank would charge out, and our little Tibetan rebels would hose their Chinese tormentors with small-arms fire. Just the way we taught them.

Ord thumbed his old binoculars' focus, then swore. "They're riding high!"

I jerked my optics back to the hovertank column. The Chinese Leopard is just a bootleg-copied Lockheed Kodiak with a cheaper, manual cannon. Like the Lockheed, and every other Nano'Puter-stabilized hovertank, a Leopard slides over snow, swamp, or prairie faster than old, tracked tanks ever could. Like the Lockheed, the Leopard's ass-end droops when its infantry squad is aboard. These sliders didn't droop.

My heart skipped. "Then where are their—?"

Ord was way ahead of me, as ever. He pointed behind our rebel ambush party. Scurrying gray against the snow, dismounted Chinese infantry popped, one after another, over the knife-edged ridge behind the unsuspecting rebels.

On my advice, the rebel commander, Tensing, hadn't covered his troops' rear. Why waste combat power? The ridge's backside dropped away in half-mile cliffs that I assumed were impassable. Like the Romans assumed the Alps were impassable to Hannibal. Like North Korea assumed the Inchon mud flats were impassable to Mac-Arthur. I shook my head. "With an adviser like me, Tibet doesn't need enemies."

Somehow, the Chinese had seen our rebels preparing our ambush, and had dropped off the Chinese infantry behind our rebels to ambush the ambush.

Officially, it wasn't "our" ambush. Since mankind won the Slug War, global unity hadn't crumbled back to "Cold War," but U.S.-China relations were frosty. Within the borders of what China laughingly called the Tibet Autonomous Region, Ord and I supplied clandestine advice and back-channel equipment to Tibetan rebels. But combat participation was forbidden. Officially.

The hovertanks stopped short of the kill zone.

I chinned my radio to our rebels' frequency. "Mouse, this is Ox—"

Nothing but static.

Hovertank turrets swiveled toward the hidden rebels.

"How did the Chinese know—" I asked.

Ord craned his neck at the blue sky. "Overhead surveillance. Must be."

"The Chinese don't use overhead 'Bots."

Ord sighed. "So the Spooks claimed."

Chinese hovertank cannons chattered, but the rounds thumped high and wide of the rebels.

Hidden beneath their tarps, our rebels returned fire with RPGs.

I pounded my fist on rock. "No! They aren't close enough!"

The ancient rockets died fifty yards short of the hovertanks, then burrowed into the snow.

The RPGs' back blast flapped the tarps and geysered snow, revealing our rebels' positions.

Cannons twitched as hovertank gunners adjusted aim toward the firing signatures.

The rebel commander already had his troops up and running. Clanking rocket tubes slung across their backs, they ran crouched behind a snow drift that concealed them from the hovertanks. At the drift's end lay secondary firing positions, close enough for our rebels' RPGs to reach the hovertanks.

The hovertanks' second volley thundered harmlessly into our rebels' emptied foxholes.

Ord pumped his fist. "Good boy, Tensing!"

But Tensing still hadn't seen the infantry slipping ever-closer behind our rebels. The Chinese outnumbered his band six to one. He was brave and bright, but he had been the village schoolteacher until six months ago.

In minutes, the Chinese infantry would scramble far enough downslope to slaughter our rebels before they could get off a shot.

"Mouse this is Ox. Over." Static answered.

I swore. "Why can't we smuggle them decent radios, Sergeant Major?"

Ord blinked.

A handy thing about rank is subordinates have to answer your rhetorical questions. During the second that Ord was distracted, I levered myself up on one elbow, and locked my rifle into my GATr's weapon bay.

"Sir? You can't—"

Crack.

A cannon round whistled toward one rebel lurching behind the drift. Smiling Lobsang had always been a step slower than the others, limping on an ankle broken in childhood.

Whump.

The Chinese round bored through the snow drift, struck Lobsang's chest, a Golden Beebe of a shot, then exploded. Lobsang became a twelve-foot-wide red-fog umbrella, drifting slowly on the wind.

My head snapped back inside my helmet, so hard that my optics blurred.

I breathed deep.

Ord whispered, "When I buy the farm, I want a quick sale, too."

I thumbed the cover off my GATr's starter button.

"You can't go down there, Sir. We're not legally in-country."

"Let them die? Because I blundered?"

"War is a catalogue of blunders, Sir."

"Tensing's wife is pregnant. Did you know that?"

"Tensing knew the risks just like we did. He could have stayed home drinking buttered tea with his wife. But he chose to fight."

"When I quartered with Tensing, he and his wife drank their tea without butter. I found out later they gave it all to me. Now I return the favor by doing nothing?"

A half mile below, the Chinese infantry unslung their weapons.

Ord laid his hand on my Plasteel forearm gauntlet, and shook his head. His gray eyes softened, but didn't blink. "I understand. But we can't, Sir. Rules of Engagement."

"I know the Rules. No shooting. Unless we're shot at first." The first shot of the Slug War killed the remaining half of my parents. If the Chinese killed Tensing, and identified his body, his wife would be reeducated. After graduation, the heads of reeducated Tibetans showed up on roadside poles. Was I going to let Tensing's baby become an orphan, too?

I pressed my GATr's starter, then twisted the handgrip. Instantly, instead of lying on my belly on a Plasteel slab in the snow, I was floating on that slab above Ord, and above the rock that had hidden us. I looked like a body-armored kid, belly-flopped on the sled from hell. The GATr's 'Puter bleeped in my earpiece, then said, "Maximum recommended altitude two feet. Current altitude seven feet."

A Special Operations ground-effect assault transport rides on an air cushion, just like a recreational ground-effect toboggan a teenager might rent at Aspen or Malibu. Nano'Puter stabilization revolutionized ground-effect vehicles, from toboggans to hovertanks, like headlights revolutionized night driving. But a GATr is lots more. With its supertuned engine, Carbon9 chassis, and ThinkLink, its price would buy a pre-Blitz condominium.

GATrs also run as silent as field mice, unless the operator bypasses the suppressor. I toed the bypass, and my sled bellowed like a rutting moose. The roar echoed clear off the cliffs across the valley.

A GATr skims the ground, presenting a, well, alligator-low target silhouette. But that supertuned engine can blast enough downforce to bounce the sled into the air for a couple seconds, like a pronking antelope.

I blipped the throttle again, and pronked again.

Below, a slider turret traversed, away from the rebels, toward me. Its cannon snout lifted.

I swallowed hard.

Crack.

I flinched, even as the round screamed past, so high that it exploded against the cliff five hundred feet behind us.

I stuck my head over my sled's side and forced my

eyes wide. "Sergeant Major! Those bastards just shot at us!"

Ord, lying on his own GATr, just shook his head and muttered something that included the word "fool."

I throttled forward, downhill. A GATr's silhouette is so low that at full throttle over snow, the sled's own snow spray masks it. The enemy has no idea where it is. Of course, that means the driver behind the windscreen has no idea where he is, either. The GATr Mark II would correct that, but, military production being military production, the Mark II was six months behind schedule.

I shot downhill, my chin a foot above the snow, as blind as justice—but faster.

The 'Puter bleeped. "Maximum recommended speed, eighty miles per hour. Current speed one hundred nine miles per hour."

I squeezed the handgrips tighter.

With my rifle clamped in the weapon bay, I could fire wherever the GATr pointed. All it took was depressing a trigger in the right handgrip.

I slowed enough so the windscreen cleared itself. Tensing's rebels had spotted the Chinese infantry, and now ran for their lives. But our rebels were picking their way across a boulder field. The Chinese infantry above them loped over a smooth, wind-bared downslope, and were gaining.

Tensing's rebels raced on toward the distant trees.

I raced through the Chinese GIs close enough to see their wide-eyed faces.

My light-brigade charge slowed the Chinese as it carried my sled almost to the ridge top.

Meanwhile, Tensing's rebels beat feet for the trees.

My GATr's 'Puter scolded, "One hundred twenty-three miles per hour."

Drive-by-wire Nano'Puters made all-terrain hover vehicles possible, but 'Puters can't overcome physics, or human stupidity.

I peeked backward over my shoulder, to locate the Chinese.

When I looked forward again, a fridge-sized boulder jutted from the snow ahead. At eighty, even ninety, I might have steered around it.

Pow.

The ground-effect skirt clipped the boulder, and the GATr corkscrewed skyward. A ground-hugging GATr is unhittable. But an airborne GATr becomes a clay pigeon for a slider cannoneer.

I cranked back the throttle, but the GATr floated on above the ridge line, barrel-rolling for endless seconds against the clear Tibetan sky. The slider gunners down in the valley adjusted aim, and fired.

Proximity-fused cannon rounds detonated, the nearest forty feet behind me. My faceplate blackened against the flash, then the shock wave hammered the sled. Shrapnel crackled off my armor like tin rain.

The ridge's backside was a cirque, the bowl from which a glacier begins. I tumbled through space, beyond the bowl's vertical end cliff. Below me, boulders on the ice looked smaller than spilled pepper.

The sled spent its momentum, so I hung momentarily in the sky, like a holotoon coyote.

The 'Puter slurred its last words. "Recommended

maximum altitude two feet. Current altitude two thousand six hundred twenty feet."

Silence turned to wind howl, louder and louder as I fell, until I heard nothing. Just as well. I screamed all the way down.

THREE

FOUR MONTHS LATER, I sat in my private room at New Bethesda Naval Hospital, while my Rehab chair flexed the hip and knee joints at both ends of my repaired femurs, and a nebulizing tube circulated antibiotic mist through my regrown lung. Eternad armor kept the fall in Tibet from killing me, Ord kept the Chinese infantry from killing me, and the State Department, of all people, sprung me from China before socialized medicine could kill me.

Things were looking up. Until my therapist decided I was well enough to receive visitors.

My *second* visitor was Lieutenant General Nathan M. Cobb. General Cobb was my commanding officer. For the second time in my career.

The first time had been fourteen years ago, during the Battle of Ganymede. Then, a Slug round had left him naturally blind, and had left me in temporary charge of saving the human race.

The last four years, tied by his wounds to a Pentagon desk, Nat Cobb dispatched me, and others under him at

Army Advisory Command, to romantic foreign climes, all of which smelled like urine.

There we trained partisans—and regular troops—aligned with American interest. Meaning we fomented or unfomented revolutions, *coups d'état*, or insurrections, wherever the United States deemed justice needed serving. Proving that justice was blind, though Nat Cobb now read faster with his Virtulenses than a naturally sighted English major.

Before General Cobb arrived, my *first* visitor was a Quartermaster Colonel. Thin and bald, he wore a chestful of non-combat ribbons. He inquired after my health, then commented on the weather.

I said, "What's up, Colonel?"

He sat down, flicked on a lap display, and kept his eyes on it. "General, you are Commander of the Fourth Military Advisory Team (Detached)."

I nodded. MAT(D)4 was actually Ord and me, but it sounded like the Army of the Potomac.

"Sir, before you enplaned en route to Nepal—"

"Tibet." I pointed at my slowly flexing legs. "All this happened after the Zoomies pushed us out over Tibet."

"Tibet is part of the People's Republic of China, Sir. You weren't there."

I rolled my eyes. "Whatever. I don't suppose you know what happened to a Sherpa named Tensing, then?"

"I have no information on Chinese Nationals, Sir." The Colonel whispered a recall code and a document flashed up in the air between us.

"Tensing thought he was a Tibetan, not a Chinese National."

"At all events, before you enplaned en route to—shall

we say, your previous duty station—as MAT(D)4's Commanding Officer, you thumbed for the standard equipment load." He pointed at a scrolling form.

"Sure. That's my name under my thumbprint."

"As you know, what a Commander can't sign back in, he reimburses the Army for. Normal wear and tear excepted."

"So?"

The Colonel squirmed in his chair, then red-clicked a serial-numbered document line. "The Inspector General's office has brought to our attention that a ground-effect attack transport signed out to you may have suffered abnormal wear."

I tried to shrug. "If you call cliff-diving abnormal "

He scowled.

I said, "It was a combat loss."

"You were non-combatants in a non-combat zone."

My eyes bulged. "Me? Pay? You know what GATrs cost?"

"To the dime."

My monitor beeps sped up, as I pointed at the IV tube curling from my forearm. "You want my blood? Line up. The test orderly already sucked today's pint."

The Colonel switched off his audio recorder. "Take it easy, General. Show's over." He leaned forward, elbows on knees. "I had to give you the lecture. Now listen up. Sir." He was twenty years my senior, but I wore stars. "As of now, you're thumbed out for that GATr."

"I never denied that."

"It won't officially show up missing until you thumb MAT(D)4's load back in, and the inventory turns up light."

"So?"

"Where MAT(D)4 goes, that equipment goes. As long as MAT(D)4 is field-deployed, Quartermaster never inventories. Just keep MAT(D)4 in the field for a year and a half."

I rolled my eyes. "Stay of execution?"

"Better. The first GATr Mark IIs are already coming off the production lines. In eighteen months, the Mark I you wrecked will be obsolete." He waved a hand, and his display vanished like a magician's rabbit. "Once the GATr Mark I is declared obsolete, we'll write its book value down, and declare 'em all surplus."

"That's stupid. They'll still be top-drawer weapons."

"Of course. But Military Advisory Command is authorized to resell surplus abroad, cheap. India will buy anything, if it's cheap enough. India badly wants Tibet as its Himalayan buffer from China. So India will buy, then quietly resell, the GATrs, at India's cost. Which is?"

"Cheap?"

He smiled. "Who to? To those Tibetan rebels you're so concerned about. Result? Your rebels will get top-drawer weapons. Coincidentally, your bill for that wrecked GATr will drop to less than a week's pay."

I cocked my head. "Why are you doing me favors?"

"I've never been shot at. I respect soldiers who have. The Army's a big family, General."

"We are a family. Sorry I got pissy."

He pointed at my rebuilt legs, and smiled. "I'd get pissy too."

I smiled back. "I respect what you put up with, too, Colonel. Paper pushing's the hell of command."

He stood with his display, then raised his eyebrows.

"Really, Sir? I'd have thought the hell of command was ordering your family to die."

An hour later, my therapist led General Cobb in. He sat in a padded turquoise hospital chair across from me, Class-A's crisp across his thin shoulders, chin high, lenses humming as they echo-located. "You look good, son."

After four months on my butt, I looked like unbaked bread.

"Spoken like a blind man. Sir."

Nat Cobb chuckled. "Both of us are high-mileage units now, Jason." His smile faded. "Leave us, please, Lieutenant."

General Cobb spoke to the room, but my therapist nodded, fluffed my pillows, and warned me to avoid sudden movements and emotional upset.

She stepped out and pulled the door shut behind her.

Nat Cobb adjusted his lenses.

Then he sighed. "What were you *thinking?*"

"Sir?"

"Are we at war with China?"

"Americans don't know how China raped Tibet for the last century. Or we might be."

The general turned his head to the ceiling. "Americans know Greater China is two billion people. People who build 76 percent of our cars, and 94 percent of our holosets! Did Congress delegate its war powers to you?"

I swallowed. "I guess you're not here to pin a Purple Heart on my pillow."

"*Your* pillow?" He stood, turned, and stuck out his butt, bony as ever under his uniform trousers. "Last six months, the Foreign Relations Committee's chewed this ass nine times. It's *me* should be sitting on a pillow!"

I gulped. Nat Cobb was a plain-spoken GI's general. I'd never heard him raise his voice to a subordinate before.

"The Chinese shot first, Sir. Ask Ord." I leaned forward. "I heard he—"

"He's fine. Except for the case of Dumbass he caught from you. He told me you provoked the Chinese."

I studied a bandaged finger. "Sort of."

"I didn't pair you with the best Non-Com in the Army so he could dig you out of some hole I can't even pronounce."

"*Bergschrund*. It's the crevasse where a glacier pulls away from its head wall."

"Whatever. If Ord hadn't held off the Chinese, you'd be wolf shit now."

"What kind of shit am I now?"

General Cobb stabbed the air in my general direction. "Don't get smart!" He sat back, then sighed again. "Jason, what do I do with you now?"

"We both know I'm not General Officer material. I'm a mediocre Company-Grade officer, with rank for show."

General Cobb pointed between my eyes. "Moose shit! I had you snuck into Command and General Staff College twice. You weaseled."

"My aptitude scores—"

"Are so high you can define *bergschrund!* You just think administration and logistics are boring."

"No. I just think they're hypocrisy. You wouldn't believe the scheme some Quartermaster weasel laid on me an hour ago."

"I would. You're not the first pup I've had that weasel bail out."

"Oh."

He sighed again. "Yes, command requires bureaucratic hocus-pocus. And you're half right about your rank. You kept your field promotion because the world owed you—"

"The world owed the soldiers who died, not me."

"And because a hero Major-General Adviser impresses Host Advisees. They usually get a middling Captain."

"Which is what I really am. So let me keep doing what I'm suited for."

"Suited for? Peru?"

"He was a butcher."

"Kazakhstan?"

"They were going to stone those women to death."

"That shoot-out in Sudan?"

"Okay. Maybe I'm not suited for advising."

"The Pentagon thinks you've cowboyed up once too often. They think you're suited for forced retirement."

I stiffened. Most people would think retirement on a Major General's pension would suit a thirty-something bachelor. But the Slug War had cost me my family, the woman I loved, and more friends than I could count. The Army was the only family I had.

I leaned forward. "No!" Something hissed in my chest. I coughed, which felt like gargling tacks. The monitor howled.

My therapist tore the door open, like a first-grade teacher policing a food fight. She pointed, first at General Cobb, then at me. "The taxpayers paid to regrow that lung once. You two juveniles buy the next one."

She backed out, eyes narrow, then slammed the door.

General Cobb waved his hand, palm down. "Easy, son."

"Sir, you know the Army's all I've got. I'd die to save another GI."

"That's exactly your problem."

"I should have let those Sherpas die?"

He leaned forward. "If that would have saved the mission. For which they chose to bet their lives. Yes." He stared down into his hands. "You've heard me say that rifleman is the world's hardest job. The truth is, sending riflemen to die is harder. But more vital. Jason, the Army may be a big family, but command is an orphan's journey."

"I know about being orphaned."

General Cobb pressed his lips together. Then he said, "So you do. That's why I convinced the brass that you were worth salvaging. They approved an alternate assignment. An old friend of ours actually requested you. It's a slush tour. Just buying you time to grow up, and buying the Army time to sweep your private wars under the rug." He tugged his Chipman from his uniform jacket, and keyboarded faster than a Stenobot while he talked.

"What if I never want to grow up and throw GIs into the meat grinder?"

"The Army doesn't want Peter Pan. Neither do the soldiers who depend on their commanders to spend their lives wisely." He shook his head. "This is no debate, Jason. Grow up. Or ship out. Besides, this posting's where you and Ord can't get into trouble."

Old Nat had saved what remained of my ass! I nearly smiled. "There's a place left on Earth where I can't get into trouble?"

General Cobb downloaded the orders he'd typed onto

my Bedside Reader, then patted my arm as he turned to leave. "No. Oh, no."

In the doorway, he nearly bumped my therapist, then he pulled her head close to him and whispered.

She stepped back into my room.

I asked, "Did he tell you to re-break my legs?"

"No. He told me to tell you something he forgot to mention."

I frowned.

"He said to tell you, 'Tensing, wife, and baby are fine.' Good news?" She smiled.

"Excellent." I smiled at her. She was very pretty. "You should take special care of me. I'm really a pretty good guy."

"Actually, the General said all that, too."

Over the next two months, I worked up a monster crush on my therapist. The morning Bethesda discharged me, I asked her to dinner. She shook her head, patted my cheek, and said she thought of me more as a brother.

The last pretty girl who had told me that was the first person I spoke to when Ord and I got to our new duty station.

FOUR

THREE DAYS AFTER my therapist harpooned me, I stared at the Himalayas again. From twenty-three thousand miles up, through four inches of quartz porthole, Earth's mightiest mountains were just brown-and-white wrinkles, with the blue Bay of Bengal shining to the south.

I flexed fingers that had death-gripped my armrest since takeoff. I liked spacecraft. I just hated space. I suppose that was because the last few times I traded a perfectly good planet for space, some disaster had shot me out into cold vacuum. Once explosively decompressed, twice shy.

Ord, in the seat beside me, tapped the rigid shoulder beneath my civvies. He pointed forward. "Almost there, Sir."

I looked up, then sucked in gardenia-scented cabin air. Holo shows couldn't do justice to New Moon. It revolved against black space, enormous, carrying the weight of its five thousand inhabitants, but as delicate as three side-by-side bicycle tires. And so white that I blinked. Cocooned in the tires' center turned their common axle, the elongate, blue-black spider that was the Firewitch.

The attendant floated down the cabin aisle, dealing red silk arrival kits left and right. As she floated, she repeated, alternating Chinese and English, "Thank you for choosing New Moon Clipper."

I smiled. Some choice. I felt fine. But New Bethesda wouldn't guarantee my regrown lung against military-launch G-forces, yet. Therefore, the taxpayers had flown Ord and me up commercial, like the plush vacationers with whom we shared the Clipper's eight seats.

Across the aisle sat a tycoon and his wife. He had spent the flight puffing the attendant how he owned all the Empress Motor dealerships in Western Pennsylvania, while she smiled and nodded.

The tycoon shook his head at his wife, as the Clipper drifted toward its mooring. "Look at that! Our room's subsidizing half that boondoggle."

Ord raised his eyebrows to me.

One of New Moon's three rings was the Great Happiness-Hyatt New Moon. Its small rooms *were* strictly tycoon posh. But even the overall naming rights, for which Sino-American Lodging had paid The Brick, didn't cover New Moon's light bill.

Neither did the revenue generated by bike tire number two, the Multi-Use Ring. Multi-Use housed Holo Bouncers, overhead imaging, electronic snoops, vacuum-optimized manufacturing, medical research and rehabilitation, and a protruding observatory called the Hubble Bubble, named after a pioneer-days telescope.

No, mankind's first permanent outpost in intralunar space existed strictly because of the alien war prize that formed New Moon's core. That captured Pseudocephalopod

Fighter-Escort, UN phonetic designator "Firewitch," would teach mankind to fly to the stars.

Or so the Intel Spooks persuaded Congress. America, in turn, funded New Moon under the table, via the United Nations Space Force.

U.S. tax dollars subsidized New Moon's commercial window dressing, not the other way around. The deadbeat Chinese handled Firewitch research participation just like they handled technology development of everything from last-century submarine propellers to Drive-by-Wire Hover Nano'Puters. They let America finance the discovering, then tried to steal the results.

Therefore, New Moon crawled with more MSS agents than the Chinese Spook academy. This meant that the Firewitch, and bike tire number three, a.k.a. the Spook Ring, to which the Firewitch was joined, were off-limits to Happiness-Hyatt's guests. As if they cared.

The tycoon's wife shuddered. "I hate seeing that Slug thing."

"You won't. I sprung for outboard views. But we should visit the Memorial." The tycoon shrugged. "History and all."

His wife shuddered again. "I hope it's just history."

He patted her hand. "It's been sixteen years. Even that kid general must be over thirty. Wonder where he wound up."

The wife rummaged through her silk arrival kit, and fished out a real-glass lotion bottle. "Look, dear! *Lily de Chine!*" She cocked her head. "I'm sure he found a nice girl and they had a family."

We passengers nodded forward as the Clipper bumped New Moon's mooring collar. The nicest girl I ever knew was also the best pilot anybody ever knew. She would have flown the Clipper in without a nudge. But she died. No family.

Once the Clipper moored, and New Moon's rotation gave us weight, Ord went to claim baggage.

I walked through the disembarkation tube directly into the Happiness-Hyatt lobby. Across the lush bustle, through a quartz inboard wall, the Firewitch loomed. Its forward mag rifles were in-folded like alien squid tentacles, and it gleamed as blue as bruises. Breathtaking, if you like reminding about a war that killed sixty million people.

I shuddered like Mrs. Tycoon.

"Jason!" Sharia Munshara-Metzger ran across the lobby, then hugged me as hard as a four-foot-ten Egyptian woman can. If she's a former infantry soldier, that's hard enough to pinch a regrown lung. I winced.

She sprang back, eyes wide. "I'm sorry. You looked fine."

A hospitality 'Bot glided by. I snatched free champagne from its tray and gulped. "You look better than fine." Her eyes still shone huge and brown, her olive skin remained smooth, and she fit her tailored suit just as well as she had eleven years ago. I waved my glass at the hanging orchids and lacquered tables. "You all live fat up here, Munchkin."

Munchkin shrugged. "The Spook Ring's more like base housing."

I glanced around. "Where's my godson?"

She stared into the carpet. "He didn't come over with me."

"Howard keeps him busy?"

Munchkin pointed to a tube signed "Shops and Entertainment" as she took my arm. "I'll show you around. We'll talk later."

I frowned. When Munchkin postponed talks, what came later was always bad.

FIVE

MUNCHKIN LED ME DOWN a boutique corridor where tourists browsed space-themed trinkets, as well as ordinary goods made extraordinary by shipping them twenty-three thousand miles.

I had shared foxholes with Munchkin, patched her wounds, served my best friend as Best Man when Munchkin married him, and delivered her first and only child seven months after the Slug War widowed her. I knew Munchkin better than a brother knew his sister. Whatever was wrong with Jason Udey Munshara-Metzger, I would hear about it only when she was ready.

At a kiosk in the corridor ahead of us, the tycoon from the Clipper and his wife eyed a zucchini-sized model Firewitch. The model's stand held a blue-black cinder in a transparent vial.

The wife bent and read the tag. "It says it's a real fragment from the Pittsburgh Projectile."

The tycoon snorted and dragged her away. "At that price it should be real."

I bent and whispered to Munchkin, "Does anybody remember the real price, anymore, Munchkin?"

Munchkin gripped my hand. "We asked the hotel not to sell souvenirs. But it's been sixteen years since the Blitz. Everybody knows the Slugs bypassed Earth. Or they're all dead."

Munchkin waved her wrist ID at the wall, a hatch irised open, and we stepped into an unlabeled tube Cap.

"Where does this—"

The hatch closed.

Munchkin said, "To the Spook Ring."

I nodded. "Howard doesn't need a toy space ship. He's got his own life-sized Firewitch to play with."

The Cap shot through the tube and we both floated for a second.

"He shares his toy with eight hundred other geeks."

"Who all report to him."

We stepped out of the Cap, and a live MP Corporal who looked too young to be wearing the sidearm on her belt—and too petite to be an MP—checked our ID. She looked back and forth at me, then at my image, then patted me down.

Munchkin led me through another hatch into an admin bubble in which a slim man slouched, intent on his screens. Bubbles were paperless offices, but Howard's bulged with ancient books that swung open like chipboards, charts, and scraps of rock and bone that he'd packratted, even into orbit.

Sixteen years had changed only Colonel Howard Hibble's rank. He was the same wrinkle-faced scarecrow I met at the height of the Blitz, when he was a new-minted

Intelligence Captain, and I was the Army's most expend-
able trainee.

Howard's uniform bagged over his bones, and he still
wore turn-of-the-century plastic vision lenses. Wire replaced one missing temple piece. Before the Blitz, Howard had been a Professor of Extraterrestrial Intelligence
Studies. Since only nuts believed in extraterrestrial intelligence, Howard's job was as relevant as clog danc-
ing. Then the Slugs greased Indy and Cairo faster than a
sneeze.

Howard sprang from his chair, arms wide, as the
screens retracted. "Jason!" He tugged the tooth-dented
yellow stub of an antique wooden pencil from his mouth
and waved it sadly. "The only smoking on New Moon's
the Cigar Lounge in the hotel."

"They wouldn't let me start now, if I wanted to."

He frowned. "New lung?"

"And Plasteel femurs. I've got enough Carbon9 in me
to make a racing bike."

Howard winced. "You up to a tour?"

"I've been resting for months. Lead on." The truth
was that just flying up on the Clipper, then following
Munchkin around for a quarter hour, had left my knees
trembling.

Howard waved on a holo in the compartment's center and conjured a shimmering image of the Spook Ring,
surrounding a floating Firewitch. The display stretched
longer than an Electrovan.

Howard pointed to a tube that connected the Ring to
the Slug ship, like a bike wheel connected to its hub by
a single spoke. "We breached the hull here, amidships,
four years ago. The Exit Tube was completed a year

later. Wonderful engineering. The Tube's both structural and umbilical. What we found once we got inside amazed us."

I raised my eyebrows. "It hasn't amazed the public."

"If we publicized results, we'd have to publicize costs. You know how politicians get about costs."

"Not to mention how taxpayers get."

Howard crooked a finger and led me away from the holo compartment. "Besides, there are minor risks I'd as soon not dwell on."

Hair stood on my neck. "The last minor risk you didn't dwell on almost extincted mankind."

"Nothing like that."

"Of course not."

Howard waved his hand as he led me past row after row of admin bubbles. Within them rank after rank of his technicians labored. He smiled and waved. They ignored him. As a full-bird Colonel, Howard had the command presence of dryer lint. But nobody on Earth knew Slugs like he did. Not even me.

Howard stopped beside a lock-down hatch stenciled "Firewitch Portal. Cav 512 Monitors required beyond this point."

Howard unhooked three orange chest badges from a wall cabinet, handed one each to Munchkin and me, then clipped his own to a pocket flap.

I clipped mine on, then asked him, "Cav 512?"

"The atomic number's a convenient fiction. It's not really an element." Howard passed his wrist across the entry plate, the hatch hissed open, and chill wind slapped my face.

I shivered, but not from the cold. At the tube's end lay

an oval cross-section passage, barely tall enough to stand in. It corkscrewed away for fifty yards, suffused in purple light.

Howard said, "How long since you boarded a Pseudo-cephalopod ship?"

"Not long enough."

SIX

————

MUNCHKIN POUTED. "This thing still creeps me out."

Howard strode down the passage toward the Slug warship. "Oh, come on! The most dangerous thing in here now is the employee lunch cart."

I slid one foot across the threshold, fingering my orange badge. "What about this Cav 512?"

"There's nothing dangerous about properly shielded Cavorite."

My jaw dropped. "You're joking."

Munchkin frowned, her face lavender under the Slug lighting. "Cavorite's a joke?"

I said to her, "Cavorite's a nonexistent mineral H. G. Wells thought up. It blocked gravity, so his characters could fly to the moon."

Howard grinned. "Catchy name, huh?" He index-fingered his chest. "My idea."

"That's how the Slugs could approach light speed? A gravity shield?"

Howard frowned. "More a graviton sponge. But that's the least puzzling part of it."

Howard must have been the only one in his kindergarten class unpuzzled by graviton sponges.

The passage widened into a chamber bigger than a concert hall, with walls as lumpy and purple as stomach ulcers. From the chamber floor's center, a spot-lit stalk twisted upward thirty feet, then flattened and widened like a metal toadstool. All around the stalk, Howard's geeks had erected a spiraling Aluminex scaffold.

Howard motioned to me to follow him up the scaffold's stairs. "We've identified this as the control ganglion. Pilot's seat, if you will."

In the twilight spill around the stalk a hundred admin bubbles, with empty chairs and dark screens, lay in a ring. Hard wire bundles fatter than fire hoses ran across the floor from them to the stalk.

We climbed toward the ganglion's top. Our boots' clatter echoed in the chamber's emptiness. "Where are all your people, Howard?"

Howard glanced down at Munchkin. "There's nothing left to do in here. For the moment."

"Meaning?"

"We need cooperation." Howard reached the metal platform atop the stairs, knelt, and panted.

"From what?"

Howard pointed at the stem's top.

I stared down into the toadstool's cap. Its blue-black center dropped down in a depression. Within the depression an upholstered day-glo orange pilot's couch was welded to Aluminex girders that suspended the couch in the middle of the depression. A control yoke curved in front of the couch.

I nodded. "Okay. You fabricated a human interface.

A pilot's couch, so we can replace a Slug pilot with a human." I sniffed disinfectant. "Was there a dead maggot in the seat when you got inside?"

Howard shook his head. "We just did routine cleaning. Virtually nothing organic remained in the hull."

I shuddered. "A ghost ship?"

"Nothing supernatural. The Pseudocephalopod maintained symbiotic disposal bacteria to deal with organic waste. In the four years after we captured the ship and before we got inside, the bacteria consumed all the organic matter, notably the crew's corpses. When nothing else organic remained, the bacteria consumed each other, until the last few starved. Our microbiologists identified the residue."

"The Slugs got eaten by their recycling toilet?"

"Basically. Turns out a Firewitch maintains itself. Like a car that changes its own oil and hammers out its own dents." Howard pointed forward. "This section was battle-damaged and transparent when we captured the ship. By the time we started building New Moon around the ship, the section was repaired and solid."

"How did the Slugs fly this thing?"

Howard tapped a blob that looked like a metal liver. "This converted visible-spectrum light to infrared for the pilot."

I nodded. "Slugs see infrared." Every schoolchild knew that.

Howard nodded. "But evidently, the Pseudocephalopod found infrared light inadequate for interstellar navigation."

Howard called Slugs "the Pseudocephalopod," because they were a single organism with physically disparate parts.

Howard stroked the couch. "Unfortunately, even though human vision bypasses the visible-light-infrared conversion, we haven't been able to achieve an interface."

"You've owned the car four years and you can't turn the key?"

Howard shook his head. "A cockatoo has a better chance of starting a Cadillac. We've laid sixty-one different astronauts and test pilots and six custom-designed 'Bots in this couch. The Firewitch never responded."

"Then we can't make this monstrosity fly?"

"I didn't say that. We think the ship is programmed to respond only if an organic pilot demonstrates adequately quick reflexes. Like the alcohol lockout on the family Electrovan."

"Reflexes?" I looked down at Munchkin. "Jude?"

She nodded.

My godson was the only human conceived and born in space. More specifically, conceived in a troop ship bound for the orbit of Jupiter. Jude was the gifted offspring of a supremely gifted pilot and a smart, sharpshooting female GI. But more than that, by age four Jude was quick enough to 'round on a fastball nanoseconds faster than a major-league shortstop. Arachnids do it too, detecting phenomena in the physical environment before other animals, or even 'Puter sensors, can.

Why could Jude do it? Mutation. "Empty" space teems with heavy metal ions. Earth's atmosphere soaks them up before they can pass through human embryos. But in space, those ions zip through a ship hull's atomic fabric like dust through a window screen. New Moon had shielding, even the Clippers have shielding today, but the first troop ship of the Slug War didn't. It had been as naked as an old-time space capsule. Astronauts used to see the ions, tiny light streaks flashing through their cabins.

The Spooks figured an ion sliced one of Jude's DNA strands *in utero*. The rest was natural history.

I asked Munchkin, "How'd the Spooks talk you into this?"

Once the Spooks deduced Jude's "Apparent Precognition," he became Space Medicine's must-have toy.

Unfortunately for Space Medicine, Munchkin wouldn't let them use her only child as their lab rat. She had been winning the tug-of-war since Jude turned five.

She stabbed her finger at Howard. "Ask him!"

Howard unwrapped two nicotine gum sticks at once. His fingers shook a little. "I just offered. I objected to the rest of it."

Munchkin pointed at Howard. "Objected? You were a spineless, devious dork!"

Howard straightened. "I was never spineless!"

Munchkin sniffed, then said to me, "I turned Howard down. So the Army 'discovered' that I was six months short of requirements to keep my pension and Metzger's dependent carry-forward. But if I accepted a civilian contract up here under Howard for six months, and by-the-way brought my minor child along, they would tack on the time. All forgiven."

"That's extortion. Get a lawyer."

"I did. Well, I asked Judge March. He said any decent lawyer could beat the government on it."

I shook my head. "So why—"

"I thought it over. Then I just thumbed the contract."

She dropped her eyes and stared down into the Firewitch's lumpy deckplates. "Jason, Jude needed a change."

"Change what? He's a great kid."

"You haven't seen him for three years. He's sixteen, now. Suddenly, adults are all—" She paused. For former infantry, Munchkin cursed rarely.

"Puggers?"

"Every fifth word is the 'P' word. Even around girls." Munchkin rolled her eyes. "And the girls he was hanging around..."

"Ah." I nodded. Metzger had saved the human race, and he'd been my best friend since preschool, but at Jude's age we had both been jerks bound for nowhere good. "His father and I survived sixteen. And then we found nice girls."

I bit the words off. Even after all the years, it was as bad a joke to Munchkin as to me.

Munchkin swallowed, blinked, then shook her head "Maybe. But he won't listen to me."

"He's your minor child. Tell him he'd *better* fire up this ship. Or he doesn't get to fire up the Electrovan on Saturday night. That always got my attention, even if it ticked me off."

Howard frowned. "It's not as simple as physically starting the family car. Pseudocephalopod control systems are more like brain link robotics, extrapolated to next century."

"He has to *want* to drive this van?"

Howard nodded. "But he won't even talk to any of us. Not even my younger techs."

I smiled. "He's always talked to me." The shrinks said

Jude saw me like a father. Of course, they said I saw Ord that way, too, which was bent.

We walked toward the Firewitch's midships, down another oval corridor. Howard smiled back. "That's what we thought."

I stopped, and held up my hand. "What we?"

"Me, the psychologists, and Nat Cobb."

"I got pulled off important military duty for this? To manipulate a teenager?"

Howard chewed his gum faster. "This *is* important. The Firewitch project's stopped dead, but the meter's running. New Moon's daily operating budget exceeds Finland's. Besides, Nat said your people skills needed work."

I hung my hands on my rebuilt hips. "The Army can make me fight. But it can't make me manipulate my own godson."

"Just think it over." It would never occur to Howard that I had no right to think it over. Unlike sixteen-year-olds, soldiers obey lawful orders. But it occurred to me.

Howard cleared his throat, then waved his arms at the ship around us. He was a geek, but he knew how to change subjects. "You never saw this aspect of a Pseudocephalopod vessel, Jason."

I stared. I'd crawled through an inbound Projectile during the Blitz, and a Troll-class incubator ship four years later, but always with Slugs chasing me.

The passage widened. Not only was a Firewitch as big as a domed stadium on the outside, it was as open as one inside. I couldn't have hit a nine iron to the far end of the chamber we now stood in. At the chamber end opposite us grew another lump, like the pilot chamber we had left. It took us five minutes to walk to the opposite lump. "Why all this empty space, Howard?"

"Buffer zone." Howard handed each of us dark goggles that hung on a rack placed alongside a passage into the lump, then in we wriggled.

The passage widened into a chamber like the inside of a fifty-foot-wide purple egg. At its center floated a thirty-foot-tall glassy sphere, which seemed to be filled with boiling ruby fog.

Howard stepped under the sphere, reached up, and rapped it with his knuckles. "That glowing miasma inside this shielding is raw Cavorite. An unprotected Pseudocephalopod warrior would have dropped dead before it entered the passage we just crawled through."

"Howard, *we* aren't protected."

"No need. Shielded Cavorite has no discernible effect on humans. Though you wouldn't want to swallow any. But Pseudocephalopod tissue we preserved after the Ganymede campaign decomposed like fat in a blast furnace at this range."

He pointed at panels that curved across the sphere. "Open a shutter, and unshielded Cavorite weakens gravity in that direction. The mass of the universe pulls the ship in the other direction. Simple. Elegant. This chamber's size keeps the poison at arm's length."

"Slugs don't have arms," I said as Howard led us back into the main chamber.

Howard said, "People do. Which brings us back to your stubborn godson."

"Manipulating people isn't a GI's job."

Munchkin said, "Leading people is a General's job."

"I'm not that kind of General. And when did you jump on the government bandwagon?"

"When I realized we can't leave until Jude makes Howard's stupid chair light up." Munchkin pointed at the big toadstool.

Behind us, a mechanical whine rose and echoed in the Firewitch's vastness.

I turned and saw Ord, pointing this way, then that. Behind him lurched a Cargo'Bot caravan, like spidery Sherpa porters.

Howard said, "Your baggage is here."

Munchkin turned her chin up like a snippy little sister, and pointed at Ord. "Why don't you ask your Command Sergeant Major what kind of General you are?"

I pointed at her. "I will!"

I did. I wished I hadn't.

SEVEN

I WALKED TOWARD ORD. Within twenty yards, my long-unused thigh muscles burned, even at Orbital Weight. By the time I reached him, he had decrypted the anti-tamper on a Plasteel crate, and two 'Bots were lifting out a V-Range's holo generator.

This assignment had as much to do with military advising as frogs had to do with fireworks. But General Cobb, bless him, had issued orders to Ord and me together as the Fourth Military Advisory Team (Detached). I hadn't signed any gear in or out, so the lost GATr remained officially unlost. And I remained officially unbankrupt. But the taxpayers had shipped four tons of useless equipment to space like tycoon luggage.

Ord saluted. "This is the only Pressurized Volume on New Moon large enough to deploy the Small-Arms Firing Simulator. Colonel Hibble suggested the location, Sir."

The sole resemblance between a Sergeant and anybody's mommy is both can do six things at once. In the time it had taken Munchkin to walk me from the hotel through Howard's tour, Ord had recovered our equipment from the Clipper, consulted the Spook Ring's Commanding

Officer on where to set it up, hired 'Bots, moved the gear, changed from civvies into pressed Utilities, and polished his old-style boots so they shone like glass.

Ord held out a Chipboard and pointed to icons on the screen. "You thumb here, here, and here, Sir." Ord had also completed our disembarkation forms, billeting vouchers, detached-duty *per diem* authorizations, and enough other documents to sink the *Bismarck*.

I thumbed where he told me to.

The Small-Arms Firing Simulator flickered as the 'Bots calibrated it. Once the SAFS was calibrated, Ord and I would be equipped to teach any lay civilians with IQs higher than bacteria to aim and fire any infantry weapon sold aftermarket anywhere on Earth at any time in the last century.

But why uncrate the SAFS? I smiled inside and nodded to myself. Sane soldiers slept, overate, or chipped home during free moments. Ord low-crawled around the firing range, testing antique firearms he restored on his own nickel. This he misnamed fun.

Sacrificing a few inconsequential hours of the SAFS' useful life to satisfy Ord's soldierly perversions didn't bother me. I would commend any other soldier who was that devoted. But opportunities to rib Ord for anything, no matter how minor, had been few since the first day he roasted me in Basic.

I looked away so he couldn't see me smile. "We offering the tourists target practice, Sergeant Major?"

"You missed your Annual Live-Fire Small-Arms Qualification while you were hospitalized, Sir. The qualifying standard allows Virtual-Range makeup exams. But your deadline is midnight, tonight. I don't think your taking the test will detract from this…important mission."

"Oh." Well, someday I would catch Ord in a screw-up. But Ord's last remark puzzled me. It was as close as I'd ever heard him come to bitching about lawful orders.

"Wondering how you and me playing tourist defends the United States, Sergeant Major?"

He shrugged. "General Cobb always has his reasons, Sir."

"Sure. I think it sucks, too. Colonel Hibble just told me what it's really about. The Army shanghaied Commodore Metzger's sixteen-year-old son up here." I looked up eighty feet, to the Slug-metal ceiling. "The Spooks think Jude's the only human who can switch this monstrosity on."

Ord raised gray eyebrows. "Interstellar travel's quite a prize. If the young man's a chip off the Metzger block…"

"At the moment the chip's acting like a teenage dick on the first day of Basic. His godfather's supposed to talk him out of his attitude."

Ord knelt beside another Plastcel crate, thumbed off its anti-tamper, and lifted out an assault rifle, while he narrowed his eyes and nodded. "I did agree with General Cobb that this assignment could give you time to mature."

I snorted. The Pentagon made Byzantium look transparent. Not only had Cobb and Hibble cooked this up behind my back, Ord was an unindicted co-conspirator. "So you think I'm a lousy officer, too?"

Ord concentrated on the rifle. It was a decrepit Kalashnikov AK-47, but so taffy-appled in Cosmoline preservative that I barely recognized it. "Sir, war means people die until somebody wins. Once our country puts us in it, the way home is win it. A Commander too focused on saving his troops, and not on the mission, doesn't win. In the end, defeat kills more soldiers than compassion saves."

"I'm too soft?"

"You're human. And young."

"And twisting my godson's arm will age me?"

Ord held out the gooey AK-47 in one hand, a Laser Simulation Adapter and cleaning kit in the other. "First things first, Sir."

"You expect me to qualify with *that?*" I stared. The year before we left for Tibet, I made my Annual Qual on a range in the Pentagon subbasement. An Orderly helped me into goggles and earmuffs, then handed me a zeroed, white-glove-clean M-40. I rattled off a few rounds. I handed back the rifle, the Orderly handed back my coffee and my upchecked Qual form. I sat back down in my General's swivel chair twenty minutes after I left it.

Ord smiled. The last time he smiled at me like that, I had ended up scrubbing a Basic-barracks latrine with a manual toothbrush. "Sometimes we learn our best lessons the simplest ways, General."

We were a two-soldier unit, so Ord was my judge and jury for field-administered testing, just as I was his. If he downchecked me on Small Arms, I'd be stuck with six weeks' reorientation. Even though I wore stars, and he wore chevrons.

I sighed, then grasped the tar baby and started cleaning.

Insurgents still choose the century-old *Avtomat Kalashnikova* Model 1947. It's inaccurate, even with 2050s optics, but cheaper than rocks, unjammable even if it's dragged through yak dung, and it makes human meat just as well as an M-40. However, an AK is wood and steel, and weighs more than two modern rifles.

Ord made me low-crawl between stations, like a rookie. I still fired expert, even dragging that old blunderbuss.

I lay on the deck wheezing while Ord eyed the score screen. "A couple more runs should do it, Sir."

"What? I hit seventy-six of eighty!"

"I've seen the General fire seventy-eight."

Two hours of crawling over Slug metal later, my knees and elbows throbbed and looked like pizza. But I fired seventy-nine.

Ord rewarded me by downloading the Rehab PT schedule that Bethesda had 'mailed up. I slapped the Reader. "This isn't Rehab. It's sadism!"

Ord relocked a tamperproof, eyeing my noodle-soft forearms. "As you say, Sir. Would the General care to join me for his prescribed morning run?"

No was not an option. "Okay." I rolled sideways, so I could stand without using my knees, then slouched toward the exit tube. "I'm gonna shower, Sergeant Major."

Then I was going to visit the only person aboard these hamster wheels who felt sorrier for himself than I did.

EIGHT

I FOUND THAT PERSON somersaulting around the Airpool.

Once they've gawked the Earthviews, the only thing people can really do in space that they can't do dirtside is fly.

New Moon tacks people to its decks with rotational gravity, so tourists can't even enjoy flying in the 90 percent of Pressurized Volume that makes up the outer rings.

New Moon's specs describe the Airpool as pure utility, the auxiliary atmosphere reservoir. But those swooping, smiling models in the holo ads sure sell vacations.

Suspended from a hollow transfer tube that runs inboard from the hotel ring to the centerline, the Airpool dome is wider and taller than a dirtside hockey rink.

And more fun. On New Moon's dead-centerline, everything weighs zero. Even at the Airpool's rotating edge, a person weighs ten pounds. Give average goofs arm and leg paddles, helmets, and lessons, and they soar through the Airpool like eagles. Well, turkeys, at least.

I buckled my rental helmet while trophy wives jiggled overhead. In designer synlon that couldn't have increased their weight one ounce. No wonder a sixteen-year-old male spent hours here.

Above the rental counter, a hundred helmeted novices flailed. Above them coasted two dozen experienced fly-ers, barely twitching custom-painted paddles.

Above them all, Jude soared and barrel rolled from one perch to the next. His father's athleticism showed in every flip and rebound.

He looked down, spotted me, and waved me up.

I shook my head and shouted, "Doctor's orders." It was only half a lie. The last thing I wanted to do was jump a hundred feet up and crack an aching knee or elbow against some tourist's paddle. Heights scared me even when I didn't feel fragile.

"Wuss!" He grinned, then folded back arm paddles air-brushed with skull-and-crossbones. Then he plunged two hundred feet like a swooping Peregrine falcon. He flared his paddles at the last nanosecond and shot through a semi-private lesson group. Jude didn't even mess any-body's hair, but a woman screamed. Then my godson touched down beside me.

The group instructor glared at Jude and held up his index finger. "One more! One more and you're gone, Metzger!"

Jude flicked a different finger at the instructor. "Pug-ger." Then he turned to me and grinned. "You should have seen the losers I scared yesterday. That bozo sounds like Mom. 'Jude! Language, please! Jude! Language, please!'"

"Your mother said you clipped somebody last month."

"Utter pugger. He was in the wrong layer."

In fact, my godson's recklessness had broken an old

man's arm. So far, Jude hadn't been banished to dirtside Juvie only through repeated interventions by Howard's JAG officer. I began to share Munchkin's parental pangs.

We bumped knuckles. I hadn't seen Jude in three years, but sixteen-year-old thug-wannabes don't hug.

I said, "I brought us real bacon." I hadn't known when I overpaid at duty-free, but the hotel sizzled up Genu-Swine on its breakfast buffet as lavishly as Fakon. Years ago, frying overloaded ship ventilation, so bacon was a delicacy, off-planet. Now, just pay Climate Offsets, certify you've added null-gravity diet supplements, then fry up a storm. What was space coming to?

"Mom'll *love* that." Munchkin hadn't practiced Islam since the Slug War. What kind of God lets big snails slaughter sixty million people? But childhood habits die hard.

I pointed at Jude's helmet decal. It showed a clinically detailed Het couple doing rudies, with paddles on. "Does she love the hat?"

He tugged off his helmet, and grinned. "She says it's disgusting."

At Jude's age, his father and I actually *would* have loved the hat, but I wasn't about to tell my godson that.

Under his helmet, Jude sprouted his father's strawberry-blond hair, too. But Jude's hair had overgrown into a last-century afro, with peach-fuzz muttonchops. And he had dyed it green, like his face.

Before I joined the Army, when I was Jude's age, I shaved my head and lasered skulls onto my fingernails. But that was beside the point. "You look like broccoli."

"I look bump. Check the 'zines."

I sighed. "Why do sixteen-year-olds mimic every

sixteen-year-old within a thousand miles—and call it individuality?"

Jude swung his hand at the middle-aged vacationers crowding the exit lobby. "Jason, look around. I'm the *only* pugging sixteen-year-old within *twenty-three* thousand miles."

I slid my paddles back to the rental attendant, while Jude lockered his. "Fair enough. That sucks. You want back dirtside? Do what Howard says."

"Hibble? Give me one reason I should listen to a bag-face nicotine addict. He's never even heard of *Raging Phlegm.*"

It seemed to me that last was a great reason. But I said, "*Colonel* Hibble served with your father."

Jude snorted. "Bag-face? He's a Spook. My father was a pilot."

"If Howard hadn't fought Slugs on the ground until he broke his rifle stock over one, your father couldn't have saved the world."

Jude snorted harder. "Tug me, Jason."

"I was there."

We waited in the emptied lobby for the next Cap, in silence. The Moon gleamed through the Panoramic, silver against spangled black.

I hadn't lied. In fact, I had so told the truth that I had to blink back tears. Howard was no more hero than I was. But when it comes down to it, GIs don't fight to save the world. They fight for each other.

As Jude stared out at space, he twisted his finger ring. Munchkin had it made from Metzger's Distinguished Flying Cross, Posthumous. Jude cleared his throat. "Mom says he loved flying. Not this Airpool stuff. Real flying."

I nodded. "Since he could walk. It wouldn't kill you to try it."

Jude blinked at the Moon.

Then he grinned, and punched my arm. "If it does, Mom will *so* whack you."

NINE

TWO DAYS LATER, in the Spook Ring's amphitheater, twenty feet below Howard, Munchkin, and me, Jude lay in a Firewitch control chamber mock-up, complete with toadstool, hardwired cables, and bubbles filled with staring, chattering technicians.

Howard leaned, elbows on the railing that ringed the test bay, sucking a lollipop in lieu of a cigarette. "It took life three billion years to leave Earth. Less than a century later, here we stand on the threshold of the first step toward leaving the Solar System."

Munchkin frowned. "It's still too long. Jude's already missed soccer season. SATs are next month."

Howard said, "Tomorrow we go live. He lies down in the real couch. The Firewitch powers up. We take readings. Then we shut down. You and Jude will be on the afternoon Clipper."

"And then?"

"We'll analyze the data. We'll replace the rigid tube that you've been coming and going through with an umbilical that can be disconnected from New Moon, so the Firewitch can move. All that will take two years. Then, and only then, if we still need him, Jude will come back up here. At that time, we think we might actually get the Firewitch to move a couple of feet. Baby steps."

Munchkin was spooled too tight. I poked her. "Come on! It's just rocket science."

Howard said, "Actually, rockets have nothing to do with it. Reaction propulsion is too slow to fly us to the stars."

I waved my hand. "You already told me. We need anti-matter drive."

"No. Anti-matter drive's just another reaction propulsion system. Slap anti-matter against matter. Squirt the explosion out the ship's back end."

"You said Cavorite was anti-matter."

"No. I said Cavorite wasn't even matter. Not as we conceive of matter as occupying the four dimensions of space and time that define this universe."

"Oh." I leaned back against the rail and crossed my arms and ankles. Ord's PT had rejuvenated me enough to risk a round of Hibble baiting. "Then what *is* Cavorite?"

"A piece that broke off of what's beyond the end of the universe. Obviously."

"Why obviously?"

"Because it consumes whatever it contacts in this universe. Especially gravity."

"Howard, there can't be something beyond the end of the universe."

"No. There can't be nothing."

Munchkin rolled her eyes.

Below us, the hourly break chime echoed. Techs stood and stretched.

Enlisted Zoomies lifted away the control yoke that

sandwiched Jude against the mock-up. He sat up, shook his head at me, then wiped sweat off his forehead.

Howard said, "Jason, he's a changed kid."

Jude and I had finally cruised the Airpool a couple of times. It scared the crap out of me, but it was good PT, and it helped with my fear of heights. I helped him with homework, at least the non-math stuff, and we went to a holo together. Unbidden, Jude cut his hair pilot-short and washed out the green dye. He spoke when spoken to with minimal profanity, and hadn't heard, "Jude, language please!" from his mother in days.

More important, he regularly showed up for his "job," which consisted of being taped with electrodes, then poked and prodded by Spooks.

I said, "He's the same kid. He wants to go home. There are girls his age down there. You remember girls, Howard?"

"Still, I credit your influence."

"I want to go home, too."

The break chime sounded again, and Howard's minions strapped Jude back in. Today's cycle had four hours to run.

Munchkin stepped away from the rail, arms folded. "So, tomorrow we leave. What are you doing tonight?"

I smiled, then I scuffed the deck. "I thought I'd visit the Memorial. I dunno. Is it too hard to take?"

She stared down, too. "I wouldn't know."

"You've been here five months."

"Then I guess it's hard."

"It's time. For both of us. We'll go together. We've done harder things."

Munchkin looked up, her eyes glistening, and nodded.

Few Earthlings ever actually see the Ganymede Memorial.

But then, few Earthlings ever saw the ten thousand men and women who actually fought on and above Ganymede, either. We trained and embarked in secret. We were gone six years. The battle ended before most of Earth knew it began. Only seven hundred of us lived to come home aboard the relief ship.

There were parades, but no loved ones welcomed or mourned us. The volunteers of the Ganymede Expeditionary Force were chosen from among orphans who had already lost their families to the Slugs.

The Memorial abuts the hotel. Tours end at noon. But veterans can visit in silence, 24/7.

It's just a hollow marble cylinder, not much bigger than a dim-lit horse barn. That's enough wall to carve 9,700 names. The clear window at the cylinder's end looks down on the Firewitch, and on space.

Our breathing echoed in the chamber.

Munchkin's lip quivered, then she stepped to the wall and touched the first name. "Abazan. Airman Second Class. I didn't know many Zoomies."

We both knew two. I touched the letters. "Hart, Priscilla O., Cpt.; UNSF; Medal of Honor; Distinguished Flying Cross; both Posthumous." Pooh Hart had been Munchkin's Maid of Honor when Munchkin married Metzger. Munchkin never got to return the favor for Pooh and me.

Munchkin turned away, her head shaking, and sobbed. "I can't." I touched Metzger's name for her.

She buried her face in my chest and we cried together. I don't know how long.

I dried her tears with my lapel. "Come back to my cabin. There's an old friend there who'll cheer you up."

My cabin befit a General, meaning I had a room with stall shower, fold-down bunk, and desk. And a robot cockroach, hanging from the ceiling.

I opened the hatch and whispered, "Company, Jeeb."

Jeeb wasn't part of the furniture. I held his title chip. He was an obsolete Tactical Observation Transport, bought at DOD auction.

Jeeb had once been brain-linked to a name on the Memorial Wall. Ari Klein; SP6; UNSF; Medal of Honor; Posthumous. Ari had been a TOT wrangler. More important, he had been my friend.

I bought Jeeb for scrap. If a Wrangler dies, or his linked TOT gets fried, it's prohibitively expensive to rehabilitate the other. Really, I had adopted an orphan.

"Jeeb!" Munchkin squealed.

Jeeb flew into her arms like a thrown football. If footballs had six legs. J-series TOTs still had eye-shaped optics, and radar-absorbent fuzz for skin. Compared to puppies, TOTs creep people out, because they look like roaches as big as turkeys. But compared to cold modern Tacticals, Jeeb was an anthropomorphic teddy bear.

Jeeb folded his wings, then backflopped on my bunk, six legs flailing. Munchkin scratched his belly, and his diagnostics hummed.

That's just the way it looked. It's true that even an old TOT like Jeeb has more cognitive power than an Enhanced Australian Cattle Dog's brain. But 'Bots were animate machines, nothing more.

The stuff about TOTs acquiring personalities from their

wranglers was nonsense. Or so Jeeb's technical manuals claimed.

Munchkin drew her finger across a scratch that diagonaled across the radar-absorbent fuzz that coated Jeeb's back, and frowned. "He's older."

I rocked back. If Jeeb was old, I was old. "He's old, but he's combat-fit. If you want to map a battlefield, eavesdrop a thousand conversations at once, or learn Mandarin overnight, Jeeb's still a TOT ready to trot."

Jeeb rolled his whining carcass over, mooching a back-scratch from Munchkin. It just looked that way. The J-Series was programmed to preen its radar-absorbent skin against any non-abrasive object.

She stroked the scratch and smoothed it away. Jeeb purred.

Munchkin said, "I should have just taken a Mandarin lesson last night."

I raised my eyebrows. "Last night? Do tell." Munchkin got lucky rarely. Me even more rarely. Unfortunately, I was the only one of us two who was trying.

"Not that. I had a bad dream. About tomorrow."

"Tomorrow's cake."

She shook her head. "Maybe. But after this, they can take my pension. Jude's not coming back up here."

"But Howard—"

"Howard's a devious idiot."

"Howard's not really dishonest. He's a smart kid who's covered up to fit in since kindergarten."

Munchkin raised her eyebrows. "Since when did *you* start having motivational insights?"

Including forcing my surrogate sister to face the reality that her husband was dead.

I cocked my head. Since, I guessed, Ord and Nat Cobb sent me up here for a cram course in family.

I chucked her chin. "I'll be there tomorrow, too. I'm not an idiot."

"You have your moments."

Unlike me, Munchkin already had insight. It's in female DNA. But, though I might have my idiot moments, history can't blame what happened next on me.

TEN

HOWARD SCHEDULED THE LIVE TEST for dawn. In geosynchronous orbit, the sun still rises just once each day.

The only reason for Ord and me to remain on New Moon was Jude. After this morning, Jude would be gone. Surely, General Cobb could bury MAT(D)4 somewhere else harmless. If not, and I had to face the music over the lost GATr, so be it. I had Ord book us on the Down Clipper.

I slept late, then overspent *per diem* on a hotel breakfast.

By the time I reached the Firewitch's big bay, Ord already had a 'Bot gaggle poised to haul our gear to Clipper check-in. Jeeb, who never slept, perched on a crate.

"All accounted for, Sergeant Major?"

He saluted. "To the last MUD, Sir."

I sighed. "A deployment without Meals Utility, Dessicated is a day without sunshine."

Ord stared toward the control room's bustle. His gray eyes unfroze. "Soft deployment, true. But I rather enjoyed being part of it, Sir."

I raised my eyebrows. "Who's soft now, Sergeant Major?"

Ord shrugged. "When I was a boy . . ."

My eyebrows ticked up further. I had assumed Ord sprang from the womb in pressed fatigues, forty years old.

He continued, "We had discovered that the rest of the Solar System was cold rocks. Not worth a human trip. After Ganymede, I never thought I'd live to see mankind reach for the stars."

It's not that people ignore historic moments. It's that they don't know they're in them. I said, "Shut down the 'Bots, Sergeant Major. Starting a starship's engine's a pretty short reach. But let's go watch."

Ord actually smiled at me.

When we got to the control chamber portal, the petite MP Corporal who had checked me and Munchkin in on my first day was working security. Even after six weeks of carding me daily, she rotated my ID in spotless, white-gloved hands. Maybe I fit the Chinese-Agent profile. Then she handed my ID back stone-faced, with a perfect salute.

Ord's kind of gal.

Over the past six weeks, she must have carded Ord as often as she had me. But when he stepped up, her eyes lit, and I noticed they were blue.

She whispered to Ord behind her glove, "They accepted my App!"

Ord grinned at her, then shook her hand. "Outstanding! You'll love it."

She still carded him.

As we stepped through the portal, I asked Ord, "What was that about?"

"I recommended the Corporal for Drill Sergeant's School, Sir."

"Funny. She seemed so normal."

Ord smiled at my joke. Two smiles in ten minutes broke his record. Maybe this tour really had grown me up.

I patted my breakfasted-but-solid-again belly.

Nothing could spoil a day that started this well.

ELEVEN

INSIDE THE CONTROL CHAMBER, every admin-bubble row glowed like strung pearls. Supervisors hovered behind each row, their eyes for once on Howard. Two hundred voices rumbled like an idling MagLev.

The vents were cranked to teeth-chatter cold. As the day wore on, two hundred tense bodies would make the chamber steam.

Howard stood in a hydraulically elevated basket that was raised up even with the empty control couch, like he was an orchestra conductor. Somebody had even pressed his uniform.

Ord and I stepped alongside Munchkin, who stood hugging herself against the chill. I poked her, then whispered, "Where's Jude?"

Howard pointed to a side hatch. He said nothing, though he wore a lapel mike. Two Zoomies opened the hatch.

Suddenly, the only sound was vent whisper, and Howard's breathing, magnified through his mike.

The figure who entered wore pilot coveralls, with "Metzger" stitched above his heart. Strawberry-blond, arrow-straight, with a fighter jock's swagger.

My jaw dropped.

Ord said, "The resemblance is—"

Munchkin sobbed.

I swallowed, so I didn't.

Jude stopped at the base of the stairs that led to the Pilot Couch, then lifted his arms while techs wired him.

Howard nodded. Jude climbed, and as he corkscrewed around the pedestal, he faced us.

He winked. Not arrogant, just supremely confident, like his father had been.

Twenty minutes later, Jude was hidden from us, down in the pedestal. The techs scurried off the platform and into the shadows.

Ord asked, "Now what?"

Munchkin whispered, like a mother watching her son at a high-school gym foul line, "They clamp Jude into the couch, so the Firewitch senses an organic presence. Jude performs an operating sequence. If the Firewitch senses a pilot with reflexes that won't crash it, its systems activate. The Spooks record everything. Then Jude climbs out, the ship shuts down, and we get to go home."

Munchkin's scenario was boring enough.

I put a hand over my mouth to cover a yawn. Nobody said it, but the other possibility was a bigger snore. If Jude was too slow, absolutely nothing would happen. Jude would just be one more princess the pea couldn't feel.

And Howard would think up Plan B.

Meanwhile, Howard pointed at a bubble bank.

The toadstool's top whined and vibrated. Silver clamp wings enfolded Jude.

Two hundred people held their breath.

Thirty seconds passed. People started to exhale.

Nothing happened.

Thirty seconds more without result, and technicians started muttering.

"Son of a bitch!" I whispered. The Army put up with Howard Hibble because his hunches about the Slugs were always right.

But this time Howard had been—

The chamber went black.

TWELVE

THEN THE VENTILATORS THUNKED, and stopped.

Munchkin lurched forward in the dark. "Jude?"

I grabbed her arm. "Don't just go—"

The lights flickered back on. The ventilators whumped to life.

Then the walls glowed purple, then red.

Techs in the bubbles craned their necks.

Beneath my boots, the floor trembled.

Munchkin gripped my arm.

The toadstool had twisted and thrust itself toward the Firewitch's bow. The platform that held Jude had thrust Howard's cherry picker aside, and Howard had turned and faced the chamber wall that was the Firewitch's bow.

The whole forward hemisphere of chamber wall disappeared.

Beyond us, five hundred yards dead ahead, the Airpool dome hung like a lollipop on a stick. Beyond the dome lay black space. And beyond that, stars.

"Holy moly!" Howard's amplified whisper boomed in the chamber. "Were the 'corders back up? Did we get that?"

I realized that I was clinging like death to a stanchion. I waited for tornadic decompression to suck us all into space through the hole that now gaped in the Firewitch's bow.

But nothing tugged at me except Munchkin's fingers.

Jude had brought the Firewitch's alien machinery to vibrating life. The forward wall was intact. It had just turned transparent to visible light.

All around us, along the opaque sections of the ship's skin, blue light veins spread and pulsed. Animated light spangled the control chamber, floor to roof, as though the place was an ancient disco club.

Someone cheered.

Then applause spattered the chamber, first a drizzle, then a deluge.

His face spangled reflected blue, arms upraised, Howard jumped up and down in the cherry picker, so hard it shook.

I said, "Wow."

Ord whispered, "Wow."

Munchkin said, "My son did this!"

Ten minutes later, things settled down.

Howard faced a different bubble row, and his voice boomed again. "Commence shutdown."

In the opposite bubble row, techs whose jobs were done for now stretched, shook hands, and back-slapped.

I would have liked to high-five Howard, but he would be playing band leader all day. So would Jude. I would see my godson dirtside soon enough. And I could holo Howard anytime.

I eyed my 'Puter. "Guess that's a wrap, Sergeant Major. Let's wake those Cargo'Bots." I took Munchkin's arm and turned her toward the exit, while the ship's blue veins pulsed. "Come see us off, Munchkin."

Munchkin, Ord, and I stood ten yards behind the nearest tech row.

I heard the row Supervisor say, "Reboot and retry." Pause. "Well, do it again."

I glanced around, toward the control stalk. Silhouetted against newly visible space, dappled in the wall veins' pulsing blue light, the cherry picker's arm had moved alongside the stalk. Howard's basket at the arm's end quivered, empty.

From below, all I could see of what was going on atop the toadstool was a waggling shock of mussed, gray Hibble hair.

"Jason?" Munchkin turned back toward me, then sucked in a breath.

Crap. She saw it too.

I made it to the stairs at the toadstool's base in five strides.

Munchkin ran a step behind me, sputtering Arabic. I caught the word "Howard." From her tone, I think the rest would have embarrassed an angry camel herder.

I clambered onto the platform alongside the pilot couch. Opposite me, Howard bent over Jude's reclined body.

Munchkin elbowed past me. When she saw Howard and Jude, she dove on her son. "Jude!"

Howard said, "It's all right. He isn't—"

Munchkin ran her hands over my godson. "Oh God! Oh God!"

"Mom! Take a breath, huh?"

Munchkin straightened, her hands shaking. "You're all right?"

"Fine."

As a machine gunner, Munchkin was the coolest soldier I knew. As a mother—well, I'd never accuse her of underreacting.

"Mom, I'm just stuck."

The Spook-engineered couch clamps fit Jude's form like cosmic modeling clay. He shrugged as much as he could. "It's no big deal. Like being buried in the sand at the beach."

So far. I frowned at Howard. "He can't lie there forever. How long before you can unbury him?"

"We're working on it."

I pointed at the pulsating and still-transparent walls. "But until you spring Jude, the motor keeps idling?"

Three Zoomies in orange-and-yellow firefighter Eternads dragged a toolbox onto the platform. Two were Airman Seconds, and the third was a Tech Sergeant.

One of the Seconds—I am not making this up—took out a bar of soap and started rubbing it along the junction between Jude's shoulder and the couch clamp. He looked down at Jude and said, "See if that loosens you up."

My godson had become an orbiting cat stuck in a tree, firemen and all. I rolled my eyes at Howard. "I bet this never happened to NASA."

He made a face and waved his hand. "Improvisation is the soul of—"

A rumble echoed through the chamber. The toadstool shook so hard that Munchkin stumbled against the guy rubbing soap on Jude.

The rumble's pitch rose, and became the squeal of bending metal.

A Supervisor on the Chamber floor screamed up through cupped hands. "We have displacement!"

I bugged my eyes at Howard. "Displacement? This thing's moving?"

Howard shook his head at me, his brows knit. "It can't move. It's tethered to the station."

Howard thought the Firewitch couldn't move, but it was sure trying. A row of admin bubbles slid across the chamber floor, caught an edge, and cartwheeled like a crashed snowboard. Somebody screamed.

Cables snapped, sparks fountained. Consoles toppled. In moments, smoke blanketed the chamber floor, and the smell of charred insulation filled the bottled air.

Behind Howard, through haze, and through the transparent wall, the hotel ring inched into view as the Firewitch's nose swung.

I pointed over Howard's shoulder. "Can't move?"

Howard turned. "Holy moly!" He frowned, then scuttled around the platform until he stood beside me. "Jason, this may be bad."

Munchkin grabbed Howard's lapels and shook him until his glasses popped off his nose. "May be? *May* be?"

I pushed her away from him. "Worst case, Howard. Quick."

Footsteps thundered on the deckplates as techs ran screaming toward the Exit Tube. Someone tripped. Squirming bodies piled one upon another.

Howard pushed his glasses back onto his nose, then stared down at the melee. "Worst case? The Firewitch will pull at this mass until New Moon's orbit destabilizes. Finally, the umbilical tether'll fatigue and separate. The Firewitch will break free. But New Moon has no maneuvering capability to restabilize itself. Its orbit will decay. Finally, it will enter the atmosphere, and burn up."

"How long?"

He shrugged. "Depends. How far and in what direction will New Moon be displaced? It could take days, or weeks. But New Moon could incinerate within hours from now."

I shook my head. "You can't risk five thousand people. Tell management to abandon ship."

Howard looked away.

I squeezed my eyes shut. "No. Don't tell me."

He said, "They could jam fifty into the Clipper, if they skip cargo. The Emergency Pods can take another three hundred, total. The design worst case was a one-ring loss."

I winced. "Unsinkable. You rebuilt the *Titanic*."

Jude lay immobile and unsmiling, his eyes shifting between my face and Howard's.

Munchkin clawed her son's shoulder. "Get him loose!"

Below us, the Exit Tube's emergency lights glowed red through the smoke. Where there had been a thrashing arm-and-leg haystack, a single, coughing line now marched, hand-on-shoulder-in-front, into the Exit Tube. Something had transformed panic to evacuation.

"Single file! That's better!" On one side of the human line, the transforming something bellowed, hands-on-hips. Ord pointed at the shuffling technicians. "My uncle Elmo moves faster than that! And he's dead!"

The line sped up.

The little MP stood opposite Ord, penning in her side of the line, white-gloved hands windmilling the evacuees along like a traffic cop. Unfortunately, the people Ord and the MP were saving were evacuating onto a sinking ship with no lifeboats.

I turned back to Howard. "Is there a *best* case?"

"Two cases, actually." He pointed at the Exit Tube. "If the tube gave way sooner, New Moon would stay in orbit. The Firewitch would—well, I'm not sure."

"But at worst, we'd save five thousand people. Case two?"

He shook his head and looked away. "There is no case two."

I grabbed his lapel and spun him toward me. "Goddammit, you just said there was!"

He coughed, then sighed. "If the Firewitch didn't sense a pilot, it might shut down immediately."

I pointed at Jude and the three firefighters. An electric saw whined and sparked, but the metal around Jude held fast. "It senses a pilot."

Howard dropped his eyes. "A *live* pilot."

The Tech Sergeant paused, listening to us. He wore a sidearm.

Munchkin's eyes widened. So did Jude's.

I said, "You're right. There is no second option."

Howard pointed to the Exit Tube again. Fifty people besides Ord, the MP, the firefighters, and the four of us remained in the Firewitch. The fifty were crawling, now, to stay under the smoke.

Howard said, "But there's no first option, either. That umbilical's engineered to withstand hours of worse flexion than this. If the tube doesn't snap in the next thirty minutes, New Moon will be irretrievably unstable."

A red beam sliced through the smoke. Ord must have dug a laser designator out of our gear, and set it to mark a path to the Exit. So MAT(D)4's equipment had been some use, after all.

The smoke thickened. Jude coughed.

The saw screeched, then died. Its smooth-worn chain glowed dull, defeated red. Under the firefighters' head-lamps, the clamp metal reflected barely a scratch.

The Tech Sergeant nodded his head from his two assistants toward the laser beam. "Go."

The other two Zoomies stared at him.

He told them, "You can't do dick here. There'll be casualties in the station that need treatment."

"What about the rest of you, Sarge?"

"This ain't a debate. Move!"

They turned away, heads down, then clattered onto the scaffold.

Electrical fires crackled in the darkness, while the four of us knelt alongside Jude.

The smoke boiled higher, curling around our feet.

The Tech Sergeant strapped a respirator from the tool-box on Jude, then handed respirators to the rest of us.

The Tech Sergeant pressed the side of his helmet, over his ear, with one hand. Then he spoke from behind his Eternad's visor. "Damage Control says orbital velocity's dropping."

Howard asked, "How fast?"

The Tech Sergeant said, "She'll start losing altitude in thirty minutes."

Howard shook his head. "Once that happens, there's no turning things around."

After three minutes, four respirators whirred while we stared at one another.

The Tech Sergeant cleared his throat. "General Wander, you're the senior officer here. Colonel Hibble said New Moon's got a chance if we can make this ship shut down—" He fingered his pistol.

Eyes watering, Munchkin sobbed behind her mask.

Jude struggled against the clamps. Nothing budged.

The undulating Exit Tube, by which the Firewitch was dragging five thousand people to their deaths, groaned louder. But it didn't break.

I shook my head and muttered.

The Tech Sergeant cocked his head. "Sir? I didn't catch what you said, General."

"Nothing." I lied. I had repeated what that Quartermaster Colonel had said to me back in my hospital room at New Bethesda. The hell of command is ordering your family to die.

THIRTEEN

I POINTED AT THE TECH SERGEANT'S antennaed helmet. "You got contact with New Moon?"

He nodded.

I turned to Howard. "If the tube breaks soon enough, the station will stay in orbit, right?"

Howard said, "Jason, I told you! It won't break soon enough."

"So break it!" I turned to the Tech Sergeant. "New Moon's got maintenance equipment. Tell the staff in the Rings to wheel some Plasma cutters to the other end of the Exit Tube. Tell them as soon as they get all the evacuees into Pressurized Volume, cut the Exit Tube at their end."

The Sergeant frowned and shook his head. "Heavy equipment storage's in the Multi-Use Ring."

"So move it out of the Multi-Use Ring, Sarge. Fast."

"Sir, soon as this hit the fan, all Pressurized Volume on New Moon locked down. Nothing passes between the public rings and the Spook Ring."

I nodded. "Sure. Airtights. Override 'em."

Howard said. "They can't be overridden. Jason, the

lock-down program's anti-espionage encrypted. Nothing in or out for four hours. To prevent technology loss."

My breath hissed out between my teeth and I clenched my fists. Knowing why Howard behaved like a paranoid Spook didn't make me like it.

Munchkin hissed through clenched teeth. "If I'd brought my own gun, I'd shoot you, Howard!"

I sighed. An infantry soldier feels naked without her weapon, even years later. Then it hit me. "Munchkin, what did you say?"

She said, "I said I'd shoot this pugging pugger with my own pugging—"

Jude's mouth formed an "O." "Mom! Language, please!"

I said to Munchkin, "Before that."

"If I'd brought a gun—"

I leapt onto the scaffold stairs, slid down the handrails like they were playground equipment, and crashed onto the deck.

I scrambled to my knees, limping, and felt my way through the smoke.

It seemed like I stumbled across the Sahara before I felt the first equipment crate. I voiced the Cargo'Bot that held it, and the 'Bot's forward manipulators whined. The 'Bot tore back the crate top as easily as a child popping a Coke Plasti.

I rummaged. Obsolete radios with blanked serial numbers. "Dammit!"

A hand touched my shoulder, and I jumped.

"Sir?"

"Sergeant Major! We need—"

"The breaching charges are in crate sixteen, Sir."
Ord voiced a different 'Bot, and it unpiled crates until it
lifted out number sixteen, yellow-stenciled "DANGER:
EXPLOSIVES."

There was no point asking Ord how he knew we had to
blow the connecting tube off ourselves. Every Non-Com
speed-reads his officer's mind.

I lunged for crate sixteen, and tugged out the first Sem
tex packet even while the 'Bot was peeling back the crate
lid. I told Ord, "We've only got twenty minutes. I don't
know if you and I can wire that many charges—"

"Delegate, Sir." He voiced two more 'Bots; they whined
to life and began uncoiling det wire.

Through the red-tinged smoke, three human figures
stumbled toward us. Munchkin, the Zoomie Tech Sergeant, and Ord's MP.

I asked Munchkin, "Howard? Jude?"

She jerked her head toward the toadstool. "Howard's
still working on Jude up there. Howard figured out
what you were doing. I can wire charges faster than
you ever could."

Ha.

Over the scream of the flexing Exit Tube, Ord shouted
to the MP, "Status?"

"Last of 'em are on the way down the Exit Tube, Sergeant Major." She arced her arm at the five of us and at
Howard and Jude, as she shouted back. "Nobody else left
in here but the seven of us."

If we could blow the Firewitch loose in time, those
two hundred evacuees, and anybody else who could
make it down the Exit Tube into New Moon's main

structure, would be safe. Anybody left in here remained imperiled.

Four 'Bots spidered up the chamber walls, planting explosives that would clean-cut the Exit Tube from the Firewitch, at the Firewitch end. A fifth 'Bot unreeled a det wire spool.

I repeated, "Seven of us. That's three more people than we need in here to voice the 'Bots." I pointed to the Corporal, the Tech Sergeant, and Munchkin. "You three, down the Tube."

Nobody moved.

I glared at the Tech Sergeant, like I was a real Major General. "This ain't no debate, Sergeant."

He straightened and saluted. But, sweating behind his helmet visor, he didn't look happy to be leaving this party. Neither did Ord's MP. But both faced about and ran, crouching, toward the laser-marked path.

Munchkin stood, neck-deep in swirling red smoke, feet planted, arms crossed. "Pug off. I'm a civilian."

"We don't need you here."

"My son needs me. I won't leave him. I won't leave you. I won't even leave pugging Howard."

Ord knelt alongside a detonator control unit, and glanced at his wrist 'Puter. "Sir, I could use your help here."

I rubbed my chin, so I could get close enough to my uniform mike to voice a 'Bot, without Munchkin noticing. After I whispered, I said, "Munchkin, you said it's a General's job to lead people."

"And it's a mother's job not to abandon her son."

Behind her, the 'Bot I had voiced crept close on four

legs. Its two forward manipulators unfolded, like a spider after a fly.

"He's my godson, Munchkin. I'll take care of him."

She pointed at me. "We. We'll take care of him."

I said, "I'm sorry."

Munchkin narrowed her eyes. "What?"

The 'Bot grasped her around the waist, with manipulators gentle enough to pack Ming vases but strong enough to lift a taxicab.

Munchkin screamed, tore at the encircling manipulators, then looked up at me, eyes wide. "You! Make it let me go!"

I shook my head.

The 'Bot elevated her off the deck, while she screamed, and she kicked the smoke until it swirled. The 'Bot turned and crabbed toward the Exit Tube, like King Kong clutching his bride while she beat her fists against his chest.

"Jason, you dick!"

I shouted after her, "I'll bring him back to you! I swear!"

Then I knelt beside Ord, and fastened wire leads to the Detonator's old brass screw posts.

Ord said, "Well done, Sir."

I said, "We'll see in twenty minutes."

"Five." A thin hand touched my shoulder.

I looked up. "Howard? Did you get Jude—"

Howard shook his head. "He's still stuck in the couch. Fine for the moment. Jason, the Firewitch is pulling stronger. We don't have twenty minutes. We have five."

"We can't have five. It takes ten just to run through the Exit Tube to the Spook Ring." I glanced at Ord.

He held up the detonator. "It's wired. We're good to go, Sir."

I snatched the box from Ord's hand. It was just a generator that you hand-cranked like a pepper grinder, until it stored enough electric charge to spark off caps at the opposite end of det wire, when you thumbed the trigger. Old but reliable, like Ord.

I ran to the Exit Tube's mouth, cranking the generator as I ran, then peered down the Tube.

The Tube's air was barely fogged with smoke, compared to the clouds inside the Firewitch. Through the haze, so far away I could barely make them out, the last evacuees clambered through the opposite hatch, into the Spook Ring's temporary safety.

Two hundred evacuees down, three to go.

Halfway down the tube ran the Tech Sergeant and the MP.

The 'Bot carrying Munchkin skittered behind them. I had voiced off its governor, so it had already made up their head start. It clanked up the Tube's sidewall, and onto its ceiling. With Munchkin kicking and screaming in its jaws, the 'Bot skittered upside down above the human runners, and passed them faster than a roach caught under a flashlight beam.

Ord and Howard came alongside me. Howard panted. "Now."

I held my thumb still on the detonator trigger, and my eyes on the three figures moving down the tube. "We still got three runners."

Howard frowned. "Two minutes. Maybe less."

Ord grabbed Howard and me by the backs of our belts,

and tugged us ten yards back from the Exit Tube lip, inside the Firewitch.

Alongside us the remaining Cargo'Bots idled, manipulators folded, their work done. A web of old-school det wire stretched from the charges in the floor and ceiling back to the trigger I clutched.

Howard craned his neck at the charges. "When those blow, the decomp sensors will lock down this hatch in a half second."

I swallowed. It had better. When the charges blew, the Exit Tube would expel its air into space like a popped balloon. Anything inside the tube, such as us, would be sucked along for the ride.

I had seen human beings explosively decompressed. I had nearly been one, more than once. Fifteen screaming seconds to remember your life is too short.

Ord handed me a synlon cargo sling. "Around your waist, Sir. Then through the floor tie-downs."

"Huh?"

"It's going to get windy in here for a moment, Sir."

The 'Bot carrying Munchkin slowed as it neared the far hatch.

Howard said, "Now, Jason!"

I shook my head. "Couple more seconds."

Munchkin's 'Bot reached the far hatch, lifted one leg at a time over the sill, and she and the 'Bot disappeared into Pressurized Volume.

Howard grabbed my shoulder. "Now! It's too late, already!"

My heart thumped. Ord's little MP and the Tech Sergeant ran for their lives, still a hundred yards from safety.

I pointed at them, and shook my head. "That's two living human beings down there, Howard."

"For God's sake, Jason!" Howard said.

"Two against five thousand, Sir." Ord placed his hand over my thumb, and squeezed until the trigger snicked loose.

The rotor whirred, then vibrated in my hand.

FOURTEEN

WHUMP. WHUMP. WHUMP.

I squeezed my eyes shut against the flashes as the charges exploded in three opposing pairs.

I opened my eyes, and the Exit Tube was still there, still flexing like a python's gut, but intact.

Then metal moaned and echoed.

A tear opened along the Tube's left side, with a boom that made the charges sound like popcorn.

A ring of black nothing opened all around the hatch margin, and red, smoky air howled out into space. Wind slammed my back and threw me across the deck toward space, as the Airtight began scissoring shut across the Tube mouth.

I slid on my belly toward the too-slowly-closing hatch, clutching the cargo sling I hadn't looped through the tie-down ring. "Crap. Crap, crap, crap."

Ahead of me, sandwich wrappers, dust, screwdrivers, and Kleenex got sucked into space. Through the narrowing opening between the closing hatch segments, I saw the Tech Sergeant and the MP tumbling head-over-heels, back up the severed tube toward us, as the air outflow sucked them to the breach.

Air rushing from the Firewitch hurled me against the lower hatch segment, then rolled me up and across the closing lip.

I pulled myself back inside, until I clung, spread-eagled, across the hatch opening, while the wind tore at me.

The MP hurtled toward me, now close enough that I could see her bulging blue eyes, and count the white-gloved fingers on her flailing hands.

The hatch segments seemed to close in slow motion. My hands, then my feet, slipped, until just fingers and toes held me back from spinning out into the vacuum. Wind roared around me as loudly as if I had fallen beneath a speeding train.

The fingers of my left hand slid off the hatch lip. "Oh, no."

Something grabbed my waist and held me.

The airtight hatch lips joined and sealed.

Wind howl stopped as though chopped by a cleaver, and I hung in mid-air, safe inside the Firewitch.

Thump. Thump.

The hurtling MP and the Tech Sergeant bounced off the outside of the closed hatch.

With luck, the impacts knocked them unconscious. Before my heart could beat, they became debris adrift in frigid nothing, along with the Kleenex, dust, and screwdrivers.

Behind me, the Cargo'Bot that Ord had ordered to snatch me back from the brink whined and lowered me to the deck.

I shivered, as much because the air remaining in the Firewitch had turned thin and cold as from shock.

The decompression had snuffed the fires and cleared the smoke. I got to my knees, shaking, and turned away from the closed hatch.

I lay with my cheek against the floor plates, panting.

Ord knelt beside me. "You all right, Sir?"

"I couldn't do it."

"Sir—"

"You had to pull the trigger for me. I couldn't even subtract two from five thousand and get the right answer."

Ord touched my shoulder. "We're past it now, Sir."

I shook like an out-of-tune Electrabout. "Is it cold in here, or is it me, Sergeant Major?"

Ord rolled me onto my back, tucked a crate plank under my feet to elevate them, and covered me with my uniform jacket. "Mild shock, Sir. Your replacement parts aren't quite up to this yet." He tugged the end off a syrette with his teeth, then rolled my sleeve up to expose a forearm vein.

I shook my head. "No drugs, Sergeant Major."

Ord patted my cheek. "Sir?"

I shook my head again. "Put the syrette away. I just need to catch my breath."

He smiled. "You've been out two hours, Sir."

I flexed my arm. Better. I rolled onto an elbow and sat up.

Twenty yards away, Howard stood, knees shaking, silhouetted against the Firewitch's transparent bow plate, thirty yards in front of him.

He breathed, "Holy moly."

In front of him, where the Airpool dome had dangled

from its connecting tube, the Firewitch's six forward-pointing arms, tipped with Mag Rail cannon, had unfolded like an inverted umbrella frame.

Dead ahead of us loomed a white, pock-marked disc. It grew larger and larger, until it seemed to fill the bow plate.

The disc flashed past us to starboard. Ahead now lay only blackness and stars.

I said, "What was that thing?"

Howard turned to me, his eyes wide. "The Moon."

FIFTEEN

I SHOOK MY HEAD. "No. Howard, the Moon is, like, a quarter million miles from us. Three days away if we were boosting like a Clipper. And we're barely moving. Where's New Moon?"

"No. It just feels like we aren't moving."

Above us, something clanked on the Aluminex scaffold.

"Jason!"

I looked up as Jude clambered down the scaffold stairs on shaky legs.

Howard, Ord, and I ran to him.

Howard said, "What happened?"

Jude shrugged. "I saw the big thing coming at us. I steered left. Next thing I knew, the clamps released."

Howard nodded. "That big thing was the Moon. Obvious."

I rolled my eyes. "Yeah. Obvious."

"The Pseudocephalopod sees in the infrared spectrum. We see in what we call—appropriately for us—the visible spectrum. The pilot couch mount stretches into the forward dome so the pilot has a clear view. He reacts to visible-light images of objects in the Firewitch's path."

"Then why is Jude walking around down here?"

Howard said, "The ship wouldn't release Jude while it was near Earth. Planetary gravity pulls in too much floating junk. The ship requires a pilot close to planetary masses, like a sailing vessel requires a harbor pilot. Clear sailing now that we're past the Moon. No pilot required."

Jude jerked his thumb toward the ChemJon bank, behind MAT(D)4's crate pile and the employee lunch cart. "Then I can go pee?" He didn't wait for an answer.

I walked to the bow and laid my nose against the transparent Slug metal. The surface was cool, vibrating as faintly as an old-fashioned wind-up watch. I craned my neck. Through the clear dome, I had to admit, I saw no sign of Earth, or of New Moon, or of the old one.

I turned back to Howard. He ransacked an admin bubble's wreckage, then straightened up, holding a salvaged drive as big as stacked pancakes.

I said, "When I floor my car, I get slammed back against the seat. When the Clipper boosts, the tourists weigh six hundred pounds for a couple minutes. If we just went from zero to a hundred twenty five thousand miles per hour, we'd be squashed against the rear bulkhead like tomato paste."

Howard waved his arms at the hull pulsating all around us. "That's the elegance of it. When we started moving, the vessel channeled Cavorite's properties all around us."

"We're in a gravity cocoon?"

Howard nodded. "We're so insulated from G-forces, we don't even feel that we're moving."

"So, how fast are we going?"

Howard shrugged. "No idea, really. We did Earth-to-Moon in under two hours. I'm sure we're still accelerating. But we'll never exceed light speed, of course. So we can't go fast enough."

Pop.

I turned toward the sound. The therm tab on the wrapped Burrito in Jude's hand poked up red, where it had popped. My godson sauntered back toward us, Jeeb perched on his shoulder.

I asked Howard, "Not fast enough for what?"

He shrugged. "To arrive wherever this ship is programmed. Before we starve."

Jude paused, steaming Burrito halfway to his lips. "Where are we programmed for?"

"I don't know." Howard extended his elbow like a falconer. Jeeb telescoped out his wings and fluttered from Jude's shoulder to Howard's. "But Jeeb can help us find out."

Jude asked through a mouthful of queso, "Why would we starve?"

Howard walked toward the bow, then dropped his shoulder and Jeeb fluttered to the deck. "Even if we're going two-thirds light speed, we're decades away from the nearest star with a planetary system. Probably farther still from any habitable destination."

Jude said, "Can I turn us around?"

"I don't know. But if you could, we'd need to know where we wanted to get back to." Howard felt around Jeeb's belly until he popped Jeeb's output access panel and sprung it. He hardwired the drive to Jeeb, then stood back as Jeeb bugged out his opticals. "Jeeb will record star positions as we travel. If we ever figure out how to turn around, we'll have a road map."

Fourteen days later, we found out that a map was the least of our worries.

SIXTEEN

WE SPENT THE FIRST FOURTEEN DAYS of our ride to no-where discovering surprises.

Howard was a paranoid geek, but he was still a genius. He used Jeeb's optical spectrometer to calculate Red Shift as we sped away from certain stars. From this, Howard estimated that, by Day Two, we had settled in at a cruising speed of a hundred twenty thousand miles per second.

The Firewitch's six splayed, forward-facing tentacles were more than just gun mounts. They leaked enough Cavorite influence forward to make an invisible umbrella in front of us. This buffed aside the rare debris of interstellar space. Without that umbrella, at that kind of speed, collision with debris smaller than a lima bean would blow the Firewitch into rubble.

In the lima bean department, Ord determined that between the preservable stores in the lunch wagon, which was provisioned to feed two hundred people, plus MAT(D)4's Meals Utility, Dessicated, the four of us could survive for months. The ChemJons recycled what our bodies didn't need any longer into potable water, and the Firewitch seemed to manufacture fresh-enough air.

The difference between our situation and a life prison sentence was that a convict could always dream of parole.

Our problem quickly became morale. That meant I had to keep my troops busy.

Howard and Jude worked together each day, trying to refine Jude's flight skills, get the Firewitch off autopilot, and turn it for home. So far, no dice. But it kept them busy.

We also devised less weighty diversions. Ord broke out the SAFS and taught Jude marksmanship. A firing simulator was really a glorified hologame.

Ord also taught Jude hand-to-hand combat. On Day Fourteen, in the central bay, Ord, silver drill whistle between his lips, refereed Jude's pugil stick bout with a Cargo'Bot.

Howard now released Jeeb from astrogation duty one hour of each forty-eight, so Jeeb could perform self-maintenance. Jeeb perched ringside on a crate, extending and retracting antennae while he wiped them with his forelimbs.

On paper, no clumsy Cargo'Bot can last even a round with a Vegas Kick'Bot, but I wouldn't bet against the Cargo'Bot Ord had reprogrammed. The 'Bot could grip the padded pugil stick in its two forward manipulators but still stand stable on three legs—and sweep at its opponent with the fourth.

The only sounds echoing in the vast bay were the clack of pugil against pugil, the rubber squeak of Jude's slips across the deckplates, and the electric whine of the 'Bot's motors. The air smelled of sweat and 'Bot-joint Synlube.

The 'Bot thrust its stick at Jude's jaw. My godson

dodged easily, but in the same instant, the 'Bot's right center ambulator kicked forward, so fast it blurred, toward Jude's padded kneecap.

I'm fair with a pugil, even with all my replacement parts. But that leg sweep would have caved my knee joint like a hammer whacking a drinking straw.

I said "toward" Jude's kneecap because the 'Bot leg swept through empty space.

Jude sidestepped, lunged, and thumped the 'Bot's carapace with his stick end.

Ord tweeted his whistle. Then he stepped in, touched Jude's shoulder, and announced, "Point. Match."

Jude grinned and wiped sweat with a wristband.

I swear Jeeb's optic lids drooped when his dumb but muscular cousin went down for the count. Synlube is thicker than water, I suppose.

I jerked a thumb toward the control chamber and said to Jude and Jeeb, "Howard says break time's over."

Jude nodded, still grinning. "You see that? Want next?"

I shook my head.

Ord and I watched Jude meander toward the control room, peeling off pads and strewing them on the deck. Jeeb clattered behind on four legs, plucking up the sweaty laundry with the remaining two, diagnostics clicking like a fussy nanny.

The Sergeant Major shook his head. "Never seen anyone so fast, Sir."

"Come see him in a soccer game. He—" My stomach tightened.

Activity helped me forget where we were. But when I remembered, the nearest soccer goal was still dropping a hundred twenty thousand miles further behind us every second.

Ord crouched alongside the inert 'Bot, and flipped up its program panel. "Care to tangle before I wipe the fighting program, Sir?"

I shook my head. "What's the point? I could plug in to Jeeb and learn a language, too." Overnight, a TOT could teach even a grunt enough of any language to get into brothels and out of *coups d'état*. A TOT could even decipher a language it didn't know, as easily as it cracked codes in signal intelligence it intercepted.

Ord said, "If anybody can turn this ship around, it's Colonel Hibble, Sir."

I nodded. "He's suited for his job." Whereas I sucked at mine.

Ord paused, cocked his head. "Sir, the detonator hesitation was nothing. A split second."

I sighed, and waved my hand. "It doesn't matter any more, does it? I'll never have to command anybody again."

Howard's voice crackled from my uniform mike. "You two better get up here!"

SEVENTEEN

ORD AND I HIT THE CONTROL CHAMBER entrance on the run, panting.

Jeeb had resumed his station front-and-center in the ship's transparent bow, Howard kneeling beside him. Above us, Jude swung a leg into the toadstool, then disappeared as he lay down in the pilot couch.

We jogged to a stop alongside Howard, and I asked him, "What?"

He pointed at the stars with the antique yellow writing pencil that he had taken to chewing in lieu of cigarettes. The stars along our flanks were no longer the points of light we had become accustomed to over the past fourteen days. They stretched out in elongate streaks.

Dead ahead, the stars were gone.

Howard pointed at the discarded pugil pads mounded above Jeeb's thorax like an inverted pyramid. "Get all of those we have up here."

Ord voiced a 'Bot with his lapel mike, and it scurried away.

"What's going on, Howard?" I said.

"You remember I said we were moving too slow?"

"Yeah."

"We're accelerating."

"That's why the stars look stretched out?"

"No. Their light is being bent."

"By what?"

Howard pointed at the black void in front of us. "That."

The Spooks had always assumed the Slugs transited interstellar space by short-cutting through Temporal Fabric Insertion Points, places where the gargantuan gravitation of collapsed stars tacked folded space together.

"We're so close that black hole's bending light?"

"Sucking it like gravity sucks water down a drain."

I swallowed. "Us too?" The central mass of a black hole packed matter bigger than the sun into a golf ball. I didn't want to die as a piece of a golf ball.

Ord's Cargo'Bot dumped a pugil-pad wad as big as a mattress at Howard's feet.

Howard said, "I think this ship's designed to transit the hole by skirting the central mass so fast that the ship slingshots out the other side."

I eyed the toadstool. "Jude?"

"The closer we get to the central mass, the more inbound matter, like the ship itself, the ship has to avoid. Jude's reactions to what he sees in the visible spectrum will dodge the ship around anything too big for the bow array to deflect."

"Why the pads?"

Howard hunched on hands and knees, spreading out a chest protector across the deck plates. "Jude will make the transit in a form-fitting, reclined couch. But insertion-point gravity may be so strong that, even in a Cavorite cocoon, an unsupported human body would be crushed."

I pointed at the pads, so flimsy that they nearly floated in air. "And those will help?"

Howard shrugged. "I dunno. It's my first time. We might get squished anyway."

Ten minutes later, I lay flat on the deckplates, my body's hollows shored up by air bubbled into petroleum-based plastic. Nothing shored up my confidence. Howard and Ord lay alongside me, and above us Jude lay in the toadstool couch.

The stars were all gone, now. Their light was being sucked parallel to us, into a cosmic garbage disposal that whirled us closer every second.

The Firewitch, massive as it was, shuddered.

I gasped; it felt like the bar had dropped on my chest during bench presses. Howard cautioned that the slight est movement risked serious injury and told us to stay as motionless as possible during the transit.

That was like putting up a "Wet paint—Don't touch!" sign, for me anyway. Naturally, I tried to lift my little finger. It was just an organic prosthetic that dated back to a wound during the Slug Armada days, and it dislocated.

I've never been an orange, so I don't know what it feels like to get juiced. But now I have a pretty good idea.

I think I felt the ship juke a time or two, but that could have just been one of my joints popping.

According to Howard, at this point, the ship's Cavorite was pushing back against the gravity of the densest mass in this universe. One of the four basic forces of this universe was battling dead-even with our power plant, something that tumbled in here from a universe next door, across the eleventh dimension.

I sweated. Or maybe water was just being squeezed

out of my tissues. Howard predicted that the transit would be "elegantly simple." Maybe when a Slug crew flew this ship off the showroom floor, that would have been true. But Jude was our only crew, and he didn't even have his learner's permit. And Howard's Spooks had been tampering with the Firewitch for years. What if they had broken something?

If—if—everything worked, the ship would retain just enough angular momentum to slide around the core mass with sufficient oomph to pop out in what Howard called "new space."

"New space" was apparently not the same as breathing space, because, much as my chest tried to expand, I took no air in.

Howard never said whether gravity would get so strong that light sponging would blind us.

So when everything went black, I didn't know whether I was blind—or just suffocated.

EIGHTEEN

WE TOTED UP THE DAMAGE NEXT DAY. The net cost to us of transiting a temporal fabric insertion point, as Howard called it, was one dislocated finger (mine), intermittent blood passed in urine (Howard and Ord), and thirty Fakon, lettuce, and tomato braninis squished when a lunch cart tray buckled.

Plus everybody, even Jude, popped enough eyeball blood vessels that we could have passed for ten-day drunks.

Sometime during the first post-transit day, the stars returned. Well, not *the* stars. Some stars.

Two days after the transit, Howard calculated that we had resumed cruising speed of a hundred twenty thousand miles per second. We didn't know where we were going, but we were making great time. He stood in the bow, stargazing, bloodshot eyes aglow. "Fabulous."

"How is nearly killing five thousand people and press-ganging us onto this *Flying Dutchman* fabulous?"

Before us, a band of stars swept like spilled diamonds. Howard said, "I'm not even sure this is the Milky Way, Jason! No man ever dreamed of seeing this!"

Howard had had no luck turning the ship around before we shot through the hole in space. Now, even if we turned around, there was no certainty we could find the hole again, retransit safely, or come out where we originally went in. "Howard, why do I care what stars I'm looking at when I finally starve?"

He said, "That's the downside." He touched the screen wired to Jeeb, looked at it, then raised his eyebrows. "Holy moly!"

I had given up trying to teach Howard to swear like a proper grunt. "What is it?"

Howard pointed dead ahead. A star among millions seemed brighter than the others, yellowish, and swelling bigger each second. He fingered the screen to display the position of his marker stars from the prior sampling compared to current. He said, "Don't worry about starving."

"Why not?"

"I still don't know where we're going, but we're slowing down. We'll be there before lunch tomorrow."

NINETEEN

HOWARD WAS WRONG. We sped through the orbits of the outer planets of the big yellow star's system. Then we trailed along behind the fourth planet out from our new sun, following in its orbit. Not just before lunch, but before Ord even finished his morning coffee.

From space, the planet looked Earthlike, blue with white cloud wisps and polar caps and brown landmasses. As we closed in, we saw that the largest continent was actually one, a landmass connected by a narrow isthmus, like North and South America rotated from North-South to East-West, to lie along the equator like a dumbbell.

One crater-pocked moon orbited the planet's equatorial belt line, in the plane of the ecliptic. If you think of the planets that orbit a sun as spinning like tops while circling the sun like meatballs around a tray, that tray is the plane of the ecliptic. All the planets and moons of the Solar System we had left behind spun in the plane of the ecliptic. According to Howard, most stars and their systems were arranged the same way.

The planet's other moon was smaller, the bright red of arterial blood, and marble-smooth. Stranger still, it orbited slowly, north to south, over the poles. As Howard would say, its orbit was perpendicular to the plane of the ecliptic.

Howard and I stood side by side on the toadstool's platform in the bow, watching the scene come closer. I had my Eternad helmet on, so I could use the optics like binoculars. I narrowed my eyes. "We hit an Earth clone on the button. How convenient."

Howard shook his head. "Of course it's convenient. The Firewitch homed on this planet. The Pseudocephalopod would establish itself where it found worlds temperate enough to support life."

"But we know the Slugs can just make a rock Earth-like. They were terraforming Ganymede."

Howard looked away, at a rounded corner of the control chamber. "True. But why terraform if you find an Earthlike planet sitting right in front of you?"

I cocked my head. "But the Slugs *did* sit out on Ganymede when they found Earth. They bombed us from a distance, like a caveman would beat a rattlesnake with a long stick."

Howard kept looking away. His Spook "need to know" paranoia was his least-endearing characteristic. "Rattlesnakes are dangerous, if you get too close."

I narrowed my eyes. "But, Howard, the first time a caveman came across a rattlesnake, he wouldn't have known it was dangerous. So the analogy doesn't hold, does it?"

Beyond the transparent bow, we sped on above the ocean, but the inside of the Firewitch felt as still as houses.

Before Howard could answer me, the Firewitch dipped

into the planet's uppermost ionosphere, and red flames of incandescent plasma blossomed from the leading edges of the ship's forward arms.

Howard pointed at the planet below. "If this were the Pseudocephalopod homeworld, we would have been challenged by now. This ship is going to land in an outpost of some kind."

"Even if it's just an outpost, a hundred thousand warriors will storm the ship and kill us," I said.

Jude frowned up at me. He had clamped in to the pilot's couch as soon as we reentered the traffic jam of interplanetary space.

Howard and I stood alongside Jude.

I asked Howard, "How much have we slowed?"

Howard rubbed his chin. "I'd guess we're down to ten thousand miles per hour."

The huge ship skipped like a stone across the top of the planet's ionosphere, but we felt no motion. We might as well have been standing in the still gallery of an aquarium, watching a flaming ocean flow by.

I said, "So, in a couple minutes, we land. Then we die."

Howard lunged past Jude, and thrust the control yoke full forward.

I grabbed Howard's arm. "Are you nuts?"

Jude's eyes widened, and I looked up, to see what he saw.

The horizon had disappeared. The Firewitch had been cruising like a Clipper reentering Earth's atmosphere, parallel to the ground. Howard had plunged the Firewitch into a kamikaze dive straight down toward the planet's surface.

Howard said, "Four thousand miles per hour. But slowing."

I heard Jude's rapid breathing, felt no motion.

Within two heartbeats, we shot low enough that I saw the rocky ridges of low mountains. In another blink, mossy, jagged boulders and scrub brush became clear.

Snow patches dusted the ground in the shadows under the brush.

I closed my eyes.

Everybody screamed at once.

We were still diving at two thousand miles per hour when the Firewitch splattered against the planet like a gnat against a speeder's windshield.

TWENTY

SOMEONE HAD STRAPPED A SCHOOL BELL to my head, and it wouldn't stop clanging. My cheek was cold and all I could see was rock as grainy and gray as headstones.

Was I dead and buried?

Corpses didn't feel icy wind.

I levered myself onto my knees, and looked around. I knelt on gray sandstone—grow up in Colorado, know your rocks—under gray clouds.

To figure out whether my eardrums had ruptured, I shouted out loud to myself over the ringing in my ears. "It's not the twenty-story fall that kills you, it's the sudden stop."

Not only did I hear myself, I understood what Howard had done. The Firewitch had protected its payload from acceleration to two-thirds of light speed, and from gravity strong enough to squeeze the sun inside a golf ball. So protecting us when we hit a brick wall at two thousand miles per hour had been small beer.

Howard had crashed us on purpose, because he knew a crash was more survivable than a soft landing in a nest of a hundred thousand Slugs.

I looked around. The Firewitch, itself, didn't land soft. Fist-sized Slug-Hull fragments lay impact-blasted across the scrub-covered rock over a radius so large that the fragments looked like poppy seeds. The War had taught us that when a Slug ship blew, it blew into nothing but junk. That's why the intact Firewitch was so valuable. Had been so valuable.

My armor's heaters kicked in as wind scuffed a twig across the rock of my new home. Mine alone?

My suit's audio and 'Puter nested between my shoulder blades, formed into the Eternad underlayer, alongside the battery pack. But the antennae were mounted in my absent helmet. My earpiece was connected, but useful now only to block wind.

I shouted, "Jude?"

Nothing.

"Howard? Sergeant Major?"

I cupped my hands, then shouted over and over, turning through 360 degrees. Only wind screeched back.

I screamed so loud and so long for them that I panted and saw spots. I wore no helmet, but I seemed to be breathing fine. Much on this planet might kill me, though it seemed the atmosphere wouldn't.

But my ears burned, numbed by the wind. I unfurled the weather hood from my armor's neckring, tied the drawstrings beneath my chin, then turned round again.

The rock on which I stood sloped up behind me toward snow-capped mountains, and down toward flat prairie that stretched to the horizon. The Firewitch had blown itself to rutabagas against what on Earth would be called foothills.

I visored my hand over my eyes, scanned the landscape, and wished I still had my helmet optics. But there was little to see.

The watery sun had already dipped below the peaks at my back. Across the prairie, in a sliver of sky between clouds grayer than Earth clouds and the horizon, one of the moons rose, huge and pale.

The sun went down, and clouds snuffed the moonlight. I stumbled in the dark for an hour, calling for the others, as the temperature dropped. Finally, I found a wind-shadowed crevasse between boulders and tucked myself in to it.

During the final hours of our inbound voyage, Howard had Jeeb calculate this planet's rotational period; he got 24.2 Earth hours per day. I recalibrated my wrist 'Puter, assumed the sun had set at eighteen hundred hours, and agreed with myself that where the sun set would be west, where it rose east, and north and south would be at right angles to those directions.

My body ached and my eyelids drooped. Eternads aren't pajamas, but the underlayer is padded. The motion of breathing, and the occasional rollover during sleep, stores enough kinetic energy to recharge their batteries.

I fell asleep cold, and awoke colder, in the dark, when cold sleet stung my cheeks. It rattled off my armor, rico-cheted off rock, and puddled in the bare depressions that pocked my new home. My head pounded from snot that packed my sinuses. The first night sleeping outdoors after a layoff always sucks.

I turned my face to shelter against the rock, then flashed my wrist 'Puter. Zero three hundred.

At three in the morning human biorhythms hit low ebb. It's a great time to catch your enemy napping by mounting a night attack, to attempt suicide, and to feel sorry for yourself.

I thought about my broken promise to Munchkin, that I would return Jude safe to her. I thought about failing once more to put mission ahead of troops, when it came time to blow the Exit Tube charges. I thought about the woman I didn't get to marry, and about too many friends buried.

Mostly, I thought that I was now marooned for eternity, so far from home that I couldn't find the sun if I had the Hubble Bubble, an orphan once again. I hugged my rock pillow, wiped my nose on my gauntlet's snozz pad, and cried.

At four, the sleet quit, the clouds parted and the second moon—the blood-red one—shone down as it traveled among the unfamiliar stars, from north to south. If I was looking at Sol, somewhere among those billion sparks, the light I saw could have left the Solar System centuries ago.

Five A.M. brought red-glowing dawn in the east.

By sunrise, I had scooped puddled sleet into a rock depression, and melted it with meager Eternad exhaust. Alien bacteria *might* kill me, but dehydration certainly would, so I drank until I belched.

I peeled off my armor and washed, shivering, with the remaining water. Eternad padding is anti-microbial, but after a few days, you don't care for the smell of yourself in Eternads. I re-dressed, then I blew my nose like a saxophone until I could breathe through it again.

My ablutions were no hot shower and coffee, but an infantryman learns after many nights on cold ground that if your body feels beaten, your mind does, too.

I stood at the edge of the debris circle that marked

the Firewitch's remains. The circle seemed centered downslope from me. Anything or anyone else that had been saved by the ship's gravity cocoon likely also lay along or within the debris perimeter. I picked my way along that perimeter, stooping to examine every cinder for life signs.

I also broke twigs, laid stone cairns, and generally tried to mark my trail, so that if the others crossed my path, they could follow it and find me.

An hour later, the debris-field edge had turned me east, downslope. The lower I descended through boulder fields toward the plain, the thicker the vegetation grew. To me, the brush looked like mesquite; scrawny twigs with scabrous green leaves withering to brown, mixed among gnarled pines with stunted needles. This far from ground zero, the mesquite had had a few leaves blown off by our explosive arrival, but remained intact enough that I couldn't see through it.

I wove through the brush and swore to myself. Back at the barren spot where I'd landed, I had been able to see clear to the horizon. But here, farther downslope, the head-high scrub kept me from seeing twenty feet ahead.

That meant I could walk right past significant wreckage. Worse, I couldn't see trouble, from Slugs to something that might eat me, until it was on top of me.

I had seen no hint of animate life on this planet yet, but I'd picked up a fist-sized rock for a weapon, anyway. In my thigh pocket, next to my Aid pouch, I carried a single-shot .22 caliber toy of a survival pistol that Advisers joked was issued to allow suicide before capture. I decided to save it for signaling. With no rifle, I felt like a Neanderthal with no spear. And with no helmet audio or optics, I felt deaf and blind.

What happened next shows you how much our species traded away as we depended more and more on our tools.

With a climate-controlled helmet, I could see and hear better. But I couldn't smell much.

Now, without a helmet, I tilted my head back, sniffed the wind, and wished I hadn't.

TWENTY-ONE

VENTED HEADGEAR OR NOT, an infantryman who has survived combat knows the smell of death.

The stench on the wind wasn't like any corpse I'd experienced, but this place wasn't like any battlefield I'd experienced. This stunk like meat that had rotted for a semester.

I followed the scent upwind, no longer snapping twigs or kicking rocks, but my heart pounded so loud that I must have been audible twenty feet away.

I stopped and listened. Close ahead, something buzzed.

I elbowed back a pine bough, and there, in a rock-floored clearing, it was.

Looking left and right, like I was jaywalking through a tennis game, I crept forward until I knelt alongside it.

I'm no hunter, but four years before, I took a course at Ft. Bragg called "Patrol Craft." We spent a whole morning studying spoor. Spoor is crap.

I knelt beside a turd the size of a bed pillow.

Based on a rudimentary gut-diameter estimate, whatever deposited it was twenty to forty feet long.

The buzz I had heard was a cloud of winged beetles.

They hovered over their feast, but hadn't burrowed in yet. So it was fresh spoor.

I poked the turd with a twig.

The brown mass lacked plant fiber, like horse dung had, and was more like pudding in consistency. A carnivore's calling card.

Steam curled up from the blob where I had poked it. *Very* fresh.

Across the clearing, brush rustled.

I backed away from the noise, slowly, clutching my rock, scanning the ground for another, and wondering whether to dig out the little .22 pistol.

Movement flickered beyond the brush, twenty yards from me, and something snorted like a steam engine. The beetle buzz stopped as though cut by a knife.

My eyes on the spot where the brush moved, I backed away until my hand touched brush at the back of the clearing, where I had entered it. My heart hammered. Make my stand here, or run for it?

Behind me, something clamped my arm.

TWENTY-TWO

I BIT OFF A SCREAM as I jumped and pulled away.

I spun, raised the rock in my hand, and saw what had grabbed me.

A man knelt in the brush.

I blinked, looked again. Dirty. Emaciated. But a two-arms-two-legs-one-head man as human as I was.

One gray eye blazed up at me. The other was just a slit in scar tissue. Thin lips were drawn back from clenched, yellowed teeth, and dirty hair tangled down below his ears.

He spun a hand, as thin as mahogany wire, beckoning me toward him, while he hissed something I couldn't make out.

I glanced back across the clearing, then said, "I don't understand you."

He cocked his head, stood and grabbed my hand again, this time with both of his. His clothing was crude-cut hide that covered his torso and legs.

I leaned back away from him.

He took one hand off mine, pointed across the

clearing, then clamped and unclamped his fingers and
thumb, pantomiming snapping jaws.

Something snarled, across the clearing, and I caught
a whiff of animal, in addition to the dung, on the breeze.
The only reason we hadn't been noticed was that whatever predator lurked in the distant brush was upwind from
us. If the wind shifted, we'd be snacks.

Glancing over my shoulder, I pointed in the direction the man was backing, nodded, and whispered,
"Lead the way."

He sprang into the brush, hobbling. A rough wood
stump replaced his left leg below the knee.

On one whole leg and his stump, he zigzagged silently
through the brush as fast as I could sprint.

We ran for five minutes, then he dropped to one knee,
panting, and tugged me down beside him. He cupped his
hands to his ears, turned his head, then moistened a finger
and held it in the air.

We waited another five minutes. There was no sound
but the wind and our heavy breathing. Then he stood,
grunted, and stumped off into the brush.

Five paces on, he turned back to me and spoke.

I shrugged. "I don't understand."

He held up his hand again, this time to his lips, and
made chewing motions. Then he patted the slack belly beneath his hide tunic and smiled. He windmilled his hand,
then walked on.

My stomach growled, and I stood and followed him.

Twenty minutes later, he began side-crabbing, as we
descended a scree slope into a steep valley. Distant rumbling grew.

My one-eyed, one-legged friend made his home alongside rocky rapids through which a creek dropped from the mountains. His home was a shelter woven of brush laid over logs as thick as my arm. It sat on a rock shelf that looked to be above flood stage.

I looked around for a stone pit, or some evidence that he possessed fire, but saw nothing.

He sat me on a flat stone beside the water, scuttled into his hut, then returned with a grainy brown patty as large as a dinner plate. He broke it, and offered me half.

I stared at it.

He broke a bit off his half, chewed it, and smiled.

I said, "Thanks." I tapped my breastplate. "Jason."

He tapped his chest, and said, "Bassin."

I still hadn't bitten Bassin's bread.

He frowned, reentered his hut, and returned this time with a stone two feet long, chipped sharp along one edge. He stood in front of me, and raised the dagger in two hands.

I leaned back. "Easy! I'll try the bread."

Before I could raise the patty to my lips, he stabbed down.

"Jesus!" I jumped, and threw my armored forearm across my face to deflect his blow.

Bassin's blade dug into the ground between my boots, then he dropped to his knees, and dug furiously with the knife.

After thirty seconds, he dropped the tool, and dug with his fingers, until he tugged out, and shook dirt from, a shiny, chestnut brown root as round as a grapefruit. He made chopping motions with his hand over the tuber, then pointed at the patty in my hand.

I tore off a piece of the patty with my teeth, then smiled. "I understand. No additives or preservatives. Very tasty."

It was, if you enjoy hemp rope seasoned with frigid water. My stomach growled.

An hour later, the sun set. Bassin the Assassin beckoned me to share his shelter's matted grass floor.

By the time I snuggled in, he had unstrapped the stump from his left leg, laid it at his side, and snored like a gasoline-powered motorcycle.

I stared up into the darkness and sighed.

I was destined to live out my days in the distant analog of the Stone Age. But at least I wasn't alone.

For the next two days, I watched Bassin enjoy life. Morning consisted of a bracing breakfast of brown rope cakes, followed by standing ankle-deep in the muddy midstream bars below the rapids. I supposed the job was easier because his wooden leg didn't feel water that had been snow forty-eight hours earlier.

Over and over, Bassin bent down and sifted silt through a round twig basket. At most once each day, he would pluck a muddy ball as big as a walnut or an egg from the basket, examine it with his good eye, then toss it on the stream bank.

After a zesty lunch of rope cakes and water, Bassin gathered his day's take, if any, then buried it in a hole he had scraped alongside his hut, which he covered with a flat stone. Seven identical muddy stone balls defined his life's work.

After that, Bassin the Assassin got his sharp stone, and hunted the always-tasty brown root balls. These he located by crawling, nose an inch above the mud, sniffing. After washing the balls in the creek, he strung his harvest

from tree limbs to dry, so he could make more rope pancakes. Apparently, the secret to zest and tenderness was
proper aging.

Then we slept in the dark.

On the morning of the third day, I pointed upslope.
"You've got a great career here, Bassin. But the prospects
for advancement? Not so great."

He stared.

I told him, "I'm gonna go prospect for flint. You will
absolutely love fire."

I walked toward the trees that bounded Bassin's valley.

"Jason!"

I looked back. Bassin shook his head, and made the
chomp sign with one hand.

I made the chomp-chomp sign back. "I know. I'll
be careful."

He pointed at the sun, then pointed at the sky's mid
point, where the sun would be at noon, then raised his
eyebrows.

I nodded, and patted my belly armor. "Don't worry. I'll
be back by lunchtime."

He frowned and watched me all the way into the
woods, crooked on his leg and stump. His stone sifting
basket dangled from one hand.

Two hours later, I had retraced the path Bassin and I
had followed to his hut. The breeze was in my face, I carried a spear I had fashioned by sharpening a fallen branch
against a rock, and now I knew what to watch out for.

I resumed my search along the debris perimeter, mark-
ing my trail as I went, increasingly sure that no Earthling
would ever follow it. It had now been more than three days

since the crash. But I had survived. I persuaded myself that the others could be hunkered down somewhere, too.

At eleven hundred by my 'Puter, I had circled around to the point where the debris field arced back upslope. So far, I had found no sign of life more advanced than a dung beetle, not even a monster turd.

To traverse the remaining unexplored perimeter would take until well past noon. But if I shortcut the search, I'd just have to come back after another frigid night.

I sighed.

Bassin had eaten lunch alone before I got there, apparently forever. One meal without me wouldn't kill him.

I started on around the crash site's remaining unexplored quadrant. The visibility was as bad here as it had been everywhere else.

Brush crackled.

I froze. This sound was no whisper, it was crash-crash-crash.

I clutched my spear, no thicker than a pool cue, and wondered how it would work on something hungry and forty feet long.

My heart racing, I retraced my steps for a hundred yards. Then I mounted a low boulder cluster and scanned the area.

All I saw was a gray-green brush sea, ten feet tall, quaking in the wind that blew toward me, and split by rare clearings.

Again the wind carried the crackle of snapped branches.

I knelt, froze, and stared toward the crackle. It came from the clearing from which I had retreated.

Something bigger than a backhoe bucket rose above

the low treetops. It was an animal head on a thick neck, white and ochre, like a pinto pony.

The head dipped out of sight.

I leaned forward and squinted as the head rose again. It had big, brown eyes, and a broad duck's bill. Leaves and branches mustached from the bill, and the animal's lower jaw ground side-to-side as it chewed. Its skin was hide, tufted not with hair so much as with coarse down. Based on the length of the neck above the trees, this animal fit my size estimate of twenty to forty feet long.

The good news was this giant ate plants. The bad news was whatever left the spoor I had found didn't.

The duck-billed pinto swallowed the last of its mouthful, except for two long, stubborn tendrils.

I stared at them. And blinked.

The tendrils didn't hang from the animal's mouth. They dangled from its nostrils, brown, artificial, and secured with rings. The straps disappeared down behind the brush that screened the creature's body.

I stood, and peered over the brush to see what lay beneath.

TWENTY-THREE

I STARED. THEN I BLINKED. Then I shook my head.

What I saw remained. The pinto stood on massive hind legs, but bent forward on shorter forelegs, with a tail as long as its body balanced behind. I guessed the thing measured twenty-five feet, nose-to-tail.

To dodge calculus, I satisfied the science requirement of my mail-order Masters' with Paleontology. The animal looked like a teaching-holo reconstruction of a duckbilled dinosaur.

In a world becoming loonier by the second, that almost made sense. The flora I had seen, conifers, angiosperm plants, was analogous to what existed on Earth during the late Cretaceous. This planet fell within the same sliver of cosmic creation that Earth did. Similar mass, and close enough to its star to liquefy water, but not so close as to boil it away. It was not so strange that parallel life would evolve in two identical petri dishes.

One fact was strange, however. Men like Bassin hadn't evolved on Earth until more than sixty million years after the last duckbilled hadrosaur died off.

The puzzle grew stranger as I looked below.

Beneath the pinto's great head a figure knelt, head down alongside the path I had just followed, clutching the dangling straps in one hand.

Hand. It was a man. But a man unlike Bassin. This man was black-bearded, booted, and his shoulders and chest were plated in coppery armor. But unmistakably he was another man.

I staggered back against a twisted tree trunk.

The man tugged off an armored gauntlet, then reached down, and rubbed the soil with bare fingers. Where some idiot had industriously left broken twigs, stone cairns, and Eternad bootprints.

The man stood, hands on hips, and rubbed the chin beneath his beard. Six foot six, he wore brown leather trousers thick enough to deflect modest battle axes, and a matching tunic beneath his armor. From each hip hung a holstered pistol so large that its muzzle nearly reached his knee. Two more pistols just as big were strapped to his chest, cross-draw, over his breastplate. A sword hilt diagonaled from a scabbard strung across his broad back. A scar as fat and brown as a nightcrawler creased his nose bridge, and he scratched it with three fingers and the stub of a fourth.

Tough neighborhood.

Blackbeard patted his monster's flank, then drank from a skin bag hung from the beast's saddle. All the while, his eyes traced up the hill, along the path I had followed back to these rocks.

I ducked behind the tree, and peeked out from behind it to watch him.

He stared at the outcrop that hid me. Then he threw back his head, cupped his hands, and bellowed.

Small and distant, another duckbilled head rose above the brush, this one dappled gray. Then another, and another. Human bellows answered.

One minute later, thirty duckbills and riders thundered toward the big bearded man, crashing through brush like armored personnel carriers.

I slid down the outcrop's rear slope, then sprinted, away from Bassin's valley. If these guys turned out friendly, I could always find my way back to Bassin. If they were unfriendly, Bassin didn't need me bringing them home for lunch.

My breath grew ragged as I picked my way over boulders, and wove through brittle trees.

A middling tree to my front splayed flat beneath a monster's foot.

I skidded to a stop, spun left, but that way another tree rustled.

I ducked right, and the barrel-chested, black-bearded warrior on the pinto crashed into sight ten yards from me. His mount reared. He reined it with one hand, drew one of his chest pistols, and I stared down a bore as wide as a carrot.

Blackbeard shouted at me.

I had no more clue what Blackbeard said than I had when Bassin spoke, but by Blackbeard's tone and gestures, "Drop your spear" was a fair guess.

In that instant, a half dozen mounted warriors surrounded me, pistols drawn. Their mounts pranced, snorted, and stomped feet big enough to squash me.

I held my little sharp stick between my thumb and

forefinger, away from my body, knelt, and laid it on the ground. I raised my empty hand, palm out, and said, "Friend."

Six pistols fired as one.

TWENTY-FOUR

FEW ROUNDS CAN PENETRATE ETERNADS. But armor doesn't insulate the wearer from physics like a Firewitch does. Six outsized bullets whacked my chestplate like a blindsiding linebacker, and the impact whiplashed my head forward. Without my helmet, my chin struck my helmet-connection ring, and I dropped like a boxer KO'd by a hard right.

I awoke strapped like a bedroll across a duckbill's butt, face-down behind its rider, with my hands bound at the small of my back. This new guy had hair as coarse as Blackbeard's, but as gray as the plain armor he was wearing—I'd been handed off to one of the lower ranks. He and the rest of the cavalry rode their mounts in un-ornamented, stirruped saddles. I was still in my armor, my face against the beast's dapple-gray flank.

Branches slapped my face. The animal was lumbering through the foothills' thick brush.

If you ever vacation here, bring nose plugs. Whatever I might estimate as a duckbill's gut diameter, it's big enough to ferment gas by the blimpful. And bring bug repellent. Ticks as big as quarters crabbed beneath my ride's feather-like fur, inches from my eyes. I shuddered at what might already have crawled down my armor, then tried squeezing my sore chin against my suit's neck ring to close the gap—but gave it up as a bad deal.

I craned my neck. The sun had sunk so low that hours must have passed.

The duckbill that carried me stopped, but I could hear others crashing through brush, and I heard rock slide.

I was warm enough under my armor, but I shivered at the sound. The cavalry had followed my trail back to Bassin's valley, and now they were descending the scree slope into it.

Bam.

One gunshot.

I squeezed my eyes shut.

Bassin had warned me not to leave his valley. But I was smarter than he was. That simple little man had saved my life, and now my stupidity had cost him his.

An hour later, I heard shouts, then the sounds of snorting duckbills. I craned my neck.

Four cavalrymen spurred their mounts, as they scrabbled back up the valley's steep slope. One man held high a lunch-bag-sized sack that dripped muddy water. They had pillaged Bassin's pitiful homestead, killed him, and had even stolen his meager life savings.

I hung my head and felt a lump in my throat.

Whup.

Something pliant and heavy got slung across my duck-bill's back, forward of me, hard enough that the beast snorted. Probably a sack of muddy stones.

"Jason!"

I twisted toward the whisper.

Bassin lay belly-down across my duckbill, his hands bound behind his back, like mine were, his face a foot from mine. He smiled.

I could have kissed his muddy lips.

I said, "I'm sorry. This is my fault."

One of the quarter-sized ticks crawled across the duckbill's hide, toward Bassin's chin. Before the bug could sink claspers into him, Bassin stretched his neck, bit the insect in two, then spit the pieces into the brush.

I said, "Suit yourself. But protein's part of a balanced diet."

He stared at me. Wherever we were going, it was going to be a quiet trip.

Two hours later, the posse had ridden down out of the hills, and made camp out on the plains.

My rider hefted Bassin off the duckbill, carried him like a flour sack to a flat rock, unbound Bassin's hands, and handed him a water bag.

Then he did the same to me, but staked me down so far from Bassin that we couldn't talk to one another. Segregating prisoners was standard procedure, but our captors evidently didn't know that Bassin and I didn't communicate well enough to escape if we had Houdini's own lockpicks.

Our minder looked older than Blackbeard, and his bushy eyebrows were as gray as his long hair.

I drank, wiped my mouth on my gauntlet's snozz pad, and said, "Thanks."

He scowled, and tapped the sword hilt at his shoulder. "Friend" evidently translated in their language to fightin' words. "Thanks" seemed little better. I shut up rather than press my luck.

He pointed at my leg armor and pantomimed.

I dropped trou and peed, as instructed. I watered the brown grass, inspected my tackle for giant ticks, then buttoned up. My minder re-bound my hands, slung me back on the rock like a duffel, and roped my leg hobbles to a driven stake. I sat up and looked across the twilight at the endless prairie. If I could get untied, where would I go, anyway?

Something flicked across the darkening sky. A bird? I looked closer, and my heart leapt. Jeeb hovered twenty feet away, barely visible, his carapace chameleoned to match the gray clouds.

I whispered, "Return after dark."

The cavalry unloaded their mounts, hobbled them, then set them to graze. Downwind, mercifully.

Someone made a fire, from what looked like dried dino dung patties. The men sat around their fire, talking, laughing, and eating while sparks spiraled up into the cold night. A half dozen hide bags, which one of the animals had carried, the men kept close beside the fire.

Blackbeard tapped three men's shoulders, pointed, and set them out as perimeter pickets.

The smell of roasting meat drifted to me and my mouth moistened. Evidently prisoners got water. Period.

Jeeb's emergency default setting was to track me. But without my helmet antennae to boost my suit transponder's signal, it was little wonder finding me had taken him days. Especially since my transponder had wasted days broadcasting straight up from the narrow funnel that was Bassin's valley.

A TOT chassis will survive a Brilliant Bomb nearmiss that would vaporize a GI in Eternads, and TOT electronics withstand even a nuke's electromagnetic pulse. Still, Jeeb had survived, so the others could have, too.

Finally, Jeeb tiptoed to me through the dark on four of his six legs, and cocked his optics.

How to use him? Tomorrow, when the others might be active, I would send him to search for them.

But for now? A TOT's manipulators couldn't untie knots, even if I had somewhere to go. But a J-series TOT has many talents.

I pointed my hands toward my ear, then nodded toward the conversing horsemen. "Listen. Learn." I pointed at my earpiece. "Teach."

Jeeb scuttled toward the circled men, then hunkered down just beyond the firelight.

I lay on my back, not on my six-shot-sore chest, popped a Sedtab out of my breastplate dispenser, and swallowed it dry.

Within minutes, I felt my eyelids droop. I haven't drugged, not even Sedtabs, since one terrible day, light years away, in Basic Training. But I had a busy night ahead.

By morning, Jeeb squatted six-legged alongside my head. He unplugged, then shut down in the grass, impersonating a local rock.

My minder rolled out of his bed robe, cocked a shaggy-browed eye my way, and muttered, "Sleep well, Fisheater?"

Overnight, Jeeb's Nano'Puters took in, then decrypted, my captors' language, based on frequency and recurrence of eavesdropped sounds and word groups. Then Jeeb had plugged into my communications 'Puter, and force-fed me the download through my earpiece while I slept.

My jailer walked five yards into the grass, turned his back, and peed.

I rolled onto my side and tasked Jeeb. "Find Ord. Bring Ord."

Jeeb telescoped his wings from beneath his carapace, and spiraled up into the clear morning. In a blink, he became a speck indistinguishable from a bird.

I glanced over at Bassin, who sat hobbled to his distant rock, his good leg crossed over his stump. He stared at me, head cocked, like he was making mental notes. When he noticed I was looking at him, he smiled and waved.

Bouncing across the frigid grassland of Bren—that's what these folks called their garden-spot planet— tied to a farting dinosaur's butt is better when you're eavesdropping.

After an hour's ride south, Blackbeard dropped back from the column's head, and brought his pinto alongside my minder's dapple gray.

Blackbeard leaned out of his saddle, rapped my shoulder plate, and said, "What did this Fisheater offer last night, Yulen?"

I twisted so I could watch them talk.

My minder shrugged. "One word, Captain. Gibberish."

"A Fisheater who doesn't bargain? Even when a Casuni may take his life?"

Life? I twisted my wrists inside my bonds.

Yulen, my minder, threw back his head and boomed a laugh. "Scratch a Marini, find a haggler." He paused. "He *is* peculiar. I've never seen such armor."

"He's Marini, all right. Only a Fisheater magazine train could make such an explosion."

Now that I understood their language, I still wasn't

understanding much of what these two were discussing. But I understood that the explosion when we crashed was what had attracted these guys. And I understood that they might kill me.

Yulen fingered his reins. "Fisheater wagons would need a month to travel from the Frontier to the Stone Hills. And where's the rest of this one's Legion? Where's their gun peloton?"

Blackbeard shrugged. "Maybe the explosion sent his Clan mates back to hell."

"Exploded by their own powder? Maybe they were Tassini, instead." Yulen grinned.

It was the Captain's turn to laugh, then he nodded. "A Tassini would defecate in his own yurt. But Tassini are also too stupid to operate cannons. This one's simple-minded even for a Tassini." He jerked Bassin's head up by the hair, then let it flop back down against the duck-bill's flank.

Now I understood a little more. These big guys were part of a Clan, the Casuni. There were two other Clans, maybe more. Bassin, the feral loner, was from a Clan called Tassini. Tassini were primitive. The Marini Clan lived far from here, and were smart enough that they had artillery. My captors thought I was Marini. Flattering, I guess.

They rode in silence for a minute.

Yulen said to his Captain, "Do you suppose the Marini have started poaching Stones?"

"For the first time in three hundred years?" Captain Blackbeard snorted, glared down at me, and sighed. "I hope you're no poacher. For your own sake. Casus roasts Stone poachers in their own armor."

A distant bugle sounded.

Yulen, the Sergeant, drew a curved, hollowed tooth as big as a walrus tusk from his pack, and bugled back.

Blackbeard stood in his stirrups and shaded his eyes. "It's Lieutenant Brendin's Troop."

I twisted to follow Blackbeard's gaze. Far across the rolling prairie, another duckbill-and-rider gaggle strode like monstrous ostriches, trailing a dust plume. Above them a tiny shadow flitted, zigzagging like no bird, and my transponder detection circuit beeped in my earpiece. Jeeb.

I had tasked Jeeb to find Ord. Jeeb wasn't some mutt who could be sidetracked if a rabbit crossed his path. Jeeb wouldn't shadow a cavalry troop unless—

Captain Blackbeard said, "Looks like Brendin found poachers of his own."

Sergeant Yulen nodded, as he visored a hand over his own eyes. "I count three bodies."

My heart sank.

TWENTY-FIVE

TEN MINUTES LATER, Blackbeard's cavalry crossed paths with the distant group.

The other troop's Lieutenant, if I was reading his fancier armor style right, rode forward, grinning. He led a second, riderless duckbill by its reins. Where a rider would have been, there clattered an empty jumble of roped-together Eternad armor segments. I saw my own helmet, two stars on its fascia. I counted segments that added up to two old crimson suits and one modern suit, with three-up-three down chevrons clearly visible on its fascia. And "Ord" stenciled on the breastplate.

I shook my head and closed my eyes.

Blackbeard said to the new Lieutenant, "Find any Stones on the Fisheaters?"

The new Lieutenant, whose beard was brown, shook his head. "None they confessed. They answered questions with nonsense, or silence."

Blackbeard's eyes narrowed. "No Stones at all?"

"We stripped their armor, and searched them lips-to-assholes. Their armor is of new design, by the way. Light as magic. If the Fisheaters have any on offer at The Fair,

I'll trade all three of these poachers for a set in my size."
The new Lieutenant shrugged. "But question them yourself, over the embers."

Embers? I squirmed. But the Lieutenant had used the
future tense. My heart pounded. Maybe . . .

Blackbeard shook his head. "No time. Already, we're
going to have to overwork the mounts. The men would set
us on the embers if we make them late to The Fair." He
turned to Yulen, and pointed at me. "Sergeant, strip the
armor off this one, too. Dump him and that addled Tassini
back with the Lieutenant's other Fisheaters. Just have one
man guard all five. We'll make better time."

Five minutes later, I shivered in my uniform underlayer.
Yulen left me my boots and gauntlets. Without them, my
tied hands and feet would have been frostbitten in hours.

As I lay bound at his feet, Yulen watched Blackbeard
and the Lieutenant's troops trot in column toward the
horizon. The troops' mounts, spares, and pack animals
added up to a hundred, so much tonnage that I felt the
prairie shake beneath my shoulder blades.

Yulen reached into his saddlebag, and drew out a double handful of brown wafers. They resembled Bassin's
patties, but appeared to have been baked, and they actually smelled good. He knelt beside me, tucked them in my
chest pockets, and patted the bulge with a great hand, on
which remained two fingers. "For you and your friends.
It's four days' ride to The Fair. Brendin will starve you,
otherwise."

As six-foot-five barbarians who roast enemies over
embers go, Sergeant Yulen was a nice guy.

"Thanks, Sarge." I bit my lip, because the words

blurted out in my new-learned language, which called itself Casuni.

His eyebrows rose, then he smiled and nodded. "That's more like it. I never met a Fisheater who wasn't clever. And slippery."

"You're wrong. But you wouldn't believe me if I told you. Just thanks for the kindness."

He loaded me and my armor onto his duckbill, then he led his mount toward the lone cavalryman the Lieutenant had left behind. Our new minder, draped in pistols and blades in the Casuni fashion, dismounted and hefted Bassin onto one duckbill among a remuda of five, all grazing head-down. On each of three duckbills squirmed one bound but obviously live Earthling in his quilted Eternad underlayer.

My heart leapt.

Yulen and the minder made the duckbills hunker low, and sat the other three captives upright in their saddles, bound hands grasping the saddles. Then Yulen hefted me so I rode upright, too, in the saddle on the vacant fifth duckbill.

Yulen said, "Kindness? I show Marini kindness when groundfruit is in season."

"When's that?"

He grinned. "Groundfruit is never in season." He slapped my duckbill's rump; it trotted, and he shook his head. "Fat prisoners just bring higher ransom. That's all."

"Crap, Sarge," I said.

He grinned as our five-animal caravan bounced away.

Our new minder paid out twenty feet of rope between him and us five. Then he turned his back on us as we rode, ignored us, and focused on eating his lunch while in the saddle.

After a day's backseat driving, I knew how to steer a duckbill, and to distinguish the girls from the boys. I kicked my mount's flanks, and she trotted forward, alongside Ord, Howard, and Jude, who rode three abreast.

Jude said, "We thought you were dead!"

I smiled. "I thought you were dead." I asked Ord, "What happened?"

"Same as you, Sir, I expect. We survived the crash, found one another, gathered up the gear and anything we thought might be useful. Then we got engulfed by an overwhelming, more mobile force. A firefight would have been pyrrhic."

"Our gear?"

Ord nodded toward the main body we were chasing across the prairie. "The 'Bots shut down and folded. The cavalry loaded them and everything else up on pack animals. I gather from what I just heard that Jeeb taught you their language, Sir."

I nodded. "He'll sleep-teach you all tonight."

"The language barrier didn't keep them from asking questions." Beneath one eye, Ord wore a mouse the size and color of a plum.

"Bad?"

Ord shrugged. "Enthusiastic. Rudimentary."

Jude said, "Jason, these are dinosaurs!"

Howard said, "Parallel-evolved dinosaur analogs. They *aren't* dinosaurs. They resemble them."

I steadied myself with my tied hands against my saddle, and turned to Howard. "If they're dinosaur analogs, there shouldn't be people analogs here for sixty million years, true?"

As we rode, Jude, Ord, and I swung in our saddles like metronomes. Duckbills rode easy once you caught the rhythm. Howard pogo'd up and down in his saddle, wincing and poking his glasses back up on his nose every few strides. "T-true."

"Then who are all these guys that tied us all up and gave Sergeant Ord the analog of a shiner?"

Howard shook his head. "I have a theory about that. But it's a little odd. I need more information."

Ord nodded toward Bassin, who wide-eyed us as we spoke among ourselves in English. "Who's this?"

"Bassin the Assassin. Harmless little guy. I thought he was a caveman. He's a subsistence-level prospector, a cast-off from a Clan called the Tassini. These cavalry, the Casuni, don't like Tassini."

Ord asked, "Sir, you've been listening to the cavalry. What do they want with us?"

"They came to investigate the big bang when we crashed. They think we're from another Clan they don't like. 'Marini.' The Casuni cavalry call Marini 'Fisheaters.' The Marini are smarter than the Casuni. Everybody's smarter than the Tassini.

"The Marini are smaller than the cavalrymen, and they look like us. The cavalry think we're survivors of some Marini raiding party that snuck in here to poach valuables from their Clan. They assume the rest of our party got blown up when a powder wagon exploded. They're taking us to some swap meet. To ransom us back to our fellow Fisheaters."

Jude frowned. "What happens when the Fisheaters don't want us?"

I shrugged. "These guys roast poachers alive."

That night, Jeeb latched onto Ord, Jude, and Howard in turn and dumped each of them a language download. But they didn't get to speak it much, because our minder was always struggling just to keep us in the main body's dust cloud.

According to Jeeb's mapping, during the four days after we Earthlings got back together, the Casuni cavalry traversed the interior prairie of Bren's largest continent, from the Stone Hills to the navigable headwaters of the River Marin.

That was like traveling twelve hundred barren grass-land miles east from the foothills of the Rockies to the Mississippi at St. Louis. Earth horse cavalry of the 1880s couldn't have sustained a third of that speed. In fact, last-century Panzers couldn't sustain that pace.

As we traveled, other Troops intersected our line, from north and south, with their own booty. The total column grew to four hundred in all, cavalry, spare mounts, and cargo duckbills.

We picked up information by eavesdropping as the column traveled. Prisoners like us were rare, especially since we were, obviously to them, Fisheaters. Mostly, the Casuni cavalry collected taxes in kind from Tassini prospectors all along the Stone Hills, then let the little guys go back to work. Poor Bassin became a cropper only because he was associated with us Fisheaters.

The new minder didn't share Sergeant Yulen's appreciation of the need for prisoner segregation. Once twilight, as we rode east, trailing the main body by two hundred yards, Jude said in English, "Jason, we should make a run for it." He nodded at our minder, ahead. "The four of us can take this bozo."

Howard said, "I don't know. The other Clan may treat us better, Jason."

Ord looked to me. "We'd have to retrieve our weapons and armor to sustain any escape, Sir. That would be difficult."

I was pretty sure that the drafters of the U.S. military command structure hadn't contemplated its application outside the Solar System, but everybody here seemed to think decisions were up to the ranking officer. Even though that was me.

I jerked my head back at Bassin. "Whatever we do, we don't abandon my friend back there, if he wants to come."

Ahead, the column halted, and so did we.

Commanders pointed off our left flank.

Five minutes later, three groups of five riders each separated from the column, and ran off at right angles to our line of march, until they disappeared into the darkness. Graceful in their saddles, they skimmed the prairie at an easy thirty miles per hour.

Jude breathed, "Cool!"

I walked my mare back to Bassin, who usually trailed us by twenty yards. He had been hearing snatches of our conversation for days, so it probably didn't surprise him when I pointed at the outriders, then asked him in slowly pronounced Casuni, "Bassin. You know what these men do?"

He squinted ahead. The minder had his back to us, watching his comrades ride out.

Bassin answered in Casuni, "They're flank-security

outriders. Their armor and tack weigh 60 percent of a standard trooper's, for better speed. Tonight, they're thinning out predator packs. A column of five reinforced Troops like this one is as large as a migrating herd. The predators shadow large columns as they would herds, picking off stragglers."

I sat back in my saddle and stared at Bassin like he'd grown horns while I watched. There was more to my prospector friend than he let on.

In the distance, yellow flashes bloomed.

The rattle of the shots echoed across the prairie a heartbeat later.

I stood in my stirrups, but in the darkness, I couldn't see the fighting.

The cavalry pumped fists in the air, and roared like their team had won the World Bowl.

Our minder trotted back to us, jerked his head at me to get back to my place in line, and we moved out.

The outriders dragged back rib slabs so big that it was clear the predators would make short work of four Earthlings in long johns.

I said to Ord and the others, "As for escape, we'd never outrun Casuni regulars, much less the outriders. If we did get away, we don't even know what the predators look like, much less how to fight them. None of us even knows where the waterholes are out here. We sit tight for now."

Ord nodded.

Howard nodded, too. "I agree. What did Bassin have to say, back there?"

I cocked my head. "Not much we wouldn't have guessed. But he said it the damnedest way."

The rib slabs were enormous, and they got roasted and

distributed later that night, but not to the five of us. We
rationed the flatbread Sergeant Yulen had slipped me, and
listened to our stomachs rumble.

The next morning, Bassin's mount went lame, and he
got separated from us.

For the rest of the ride, we escaped rain and snow.
That meant we only got water because my duckbill had a
nose for it, detoured frequently, and dug out subsurface
springs and puddles with her blunt-clawed forelimbs.
She had a hint of strawberry in her bristly mane, so I
called her Rosy.

At sunrise on day five in the saddle, the main body
halted, then fanned out in a line. Trailing as usual, we
caught up at a walk.

The only sound and movement in the chill dawn was
the ting of duckbill bridle hardware as the huge animals
shook their heads, and their snorts of steaming breath.
Riders and mounts stared at the scene before them.

The cavalry was drawn back a yard from the top edge
of an escarpment that stretched north and south for miles,
in the form of a ten-foot rock cliff. The escarpment divided the continent's high prairie from its coastal plain.
It also demarcated the obviously undefended border between the Plains Clans and the Fisheaters.

Below the short cliff, the land beyond sloped away
into a shallow, green basin that stretched to the horizon.
Through the basin's center a broad river curved, silver in
the sun. Forested arcs split meadows in the river flood
plain, and sunlight glinted off flocks of something that
wheeled above the water.

My jaw dropped, but not at the natural beauty of the
Headwaters of the River Marin.

Strewn across the valley like spilled candy were round multicolored cone-topped tents. Hundreds were red, more indigo, many violet. Between the yurts and the river rose hundreds more tents, multi-peaked like sailing ships, striped in yellow or garnet, and hung at their centerpoles with pennants that twisted in the breeze like rainbow pythons. Beyond the peaked tents, on the river, two hundred wooden ships rocked at anchor under scimitar-shaped sails.

Beside me, Jude stared at the vast encampment and whistled. "Now that is what I call bump!"

Down the line, Yulen turned in his saddle and spoke to a cavalryman whose beard was barely more than blond fuzz, and whose armor was as elegant as Blackbeard's. "First Great Fair, boy?"

The youngster nodded, then swallowed.

"Your father says you keep with me." Yulen pointed below. "For one month each year, that's the biggest city on Bren down there. With more wickedness than all the janga dens of Marinus."

I turned and stared at Jude, then stared back across the thousand miles of arid barrens we had just crossed, slashed by frigid winds, patrolled by man-eating monsters, ruled by dinosaur-riding cutthroats. But Yulen thought the pretty scene below held worse peril for a young man. My promise to Munchkin, to protect Jude, seemed more tenuous than ever.

Yulen said to his young student, "If you met a Fish-eater yesterday, what would you have done?"

The boy patted one of his pistols, and grinned. "If you see a snake and a Marini, kill the snake last."

Yulen wagged a finger. "But at the Fair, you nod, and

raise an empty palm, and greet him, 'Peace of the Fair to you.' He'll do the same."

The boy frowned. "Tassini, too?"

Yulen clapped the boy's shoulder, then smiled. "Don't worry. If you see either of 'em after the Fair, you still shoot 'em."

Blackbeard drew his sword, circled it above his head, and looked left and right at his troops. He grinned. "A Stone for any man who bathes in the Marin before me!"

Then he bellowed, spurred his pinto, and I watched four tons of dinosaur lurch forward and try to fly.

TWENTY-SIX

BLACKBEARD'S DUCKBILL STALLION hit the broken scree apron at the cliff base like a snowboarder off a stair rail, rolled on its rear haunch, and came up galloping downhill like there was free beer at the bottom.

Down the line came more bellows and whoops. Duckbills and riders Niagara'd over the escarpment. Our minder dropped our lead and spurred his mount over the edge.

The ground shook as three million pounds of dinosaurs stampeded.

Rosy raised her head, scenting the river—more water than she had drunk since spring. I tugged back her reins and looked north and south. "Easy. There's got to be another way down this—"

Rosy launched herself into space.

"Crap." I leaned forward and clutched the down on her neck like a life preserver.

Rosy feathered a three-point landing on hind claws and tail, then trotted downslope. Ord and Jude, pale but in their saddles, trailed us by ten yards.

Upslope I heard rocks slide, then "Holy moly!" echoed

off the cliff, over and over. Behind us, Howard's duckbill trotted toward us, with his rider crooked in the saddle.

Ahead of us, our captors raced down toward the river, shaking the ground and spraying turf clods.

Our minder waited below, two pistols drawn and trained on us, until the rumble died. Then all four of us reattached our mounts to his lead rope, and he led us forward at a walk.

Twenty minutes later, we reached the Fair's edge farthest from the river, where the Casuni and the other Plains Clans pitched their yurts.

The breeze carried the alcoholic tang of whatever passed for booze here, and of urine and vomit. We rode paths where the meadow grass had been beaten to mud and was strewn with horn flagons that would be missed when their owners sobered up. The paths wound between round hide tents from which buzzed snores, moans, and human flatulence.

Jude said, "Must've been a rager last night."

For ten minutes, we snaked among yurts. Here and there Casunis peeked out from behind tent flaps at us, bloodshot eyes screwed narrow against the sunshine.

We crossed to the yurt city's opposite edge, then continued a half mile across open meadow. There, our captors' hobbled duckbills grazed a meadow already chewed to stubble by earlier arrivals. The saddles, bridles and other tack, our gear, and the hide bags the cavalry had kept close at nights, lay in piles at the meadow's edge, guarded by a half dozen of Blackbeard's finest. Sergeant Yulen had been left in charge.

Yulen motioned us four off our mounts with a drawn

pistol. The other guards cut our wrist bonds but replaced them with sprint-proof rope hobbles around our ankles.

The guards unsaddled our duckbills, then set them to graze with the others.

Yulen lined us four up, then paced in front of us, hands behind his back, armor clanking. "First you clean that tack until it shines. Then you clean it again, till it shines to my standards. Then you'll clean Stones." He looked us up and down, shook his head, then sighed. "Why does God test me with the pathetic likes of you?"

I whispered to Ord, "Do all Sergeants go to the same acting school?"

Four hours of tack cleaning, and re-cleaning, piled upon four days' riding, left us dragging ass enough that Yulen cut us a break. Four women, the first we had seen, walked out from the encampment and brought us flat-bread, skins of water, and pale blue fruit that tasted like limburger peaches.

Well, I'm pretty sure they were women. Each stood a head shorter than the scrawniest Casuni cavalryman, smelled better, and whispered constantly to the others. But indigo robes draped them head-to-ankle, and the eyes that peeked above their face scarves were kept downcast.

I sat on a rock, chewed a blue peach, and asked Howard, "What do you make of this?"

He peered into the half-moon he had bitten out of his peach. "Dicotyledonous Angiosperm."

"I mean this Fair."

He cocked his head. "There must be a quarter million people jammed in here. The ships and peaked tents don't belong to the Plains nomads who brought us here. I'd guess once a year the Plains Clans and the 'Fisheaters' call a truce, and trade. Obviously, it's become a festival."

I nodded. "Brendin talked to Blackbeard about trading us for fancy armor. But what do the Fisheaters get in return?"

Howard pointed at the mounded bags in front of us. "I expect we're about to find out."

Yulen had been sitting on a rock, edging his sword with a sharpening stone. He looked up and snorted. "Now my aching Fisheaters wag their tongues like women. Then you're rested enough to do women's work."

Yulen pointed his sword at the hide bags, which made a mountain taller than he was. Alongside them sat wooden tubs of river water, coarse-bristled brushes, and empty, iron-banded chests. "Clean Stones go in the chests."

He drew his sword back behind his shoulder, one handed, then spun a blue peach in the air with the other, like a juggler.

Yulen's sword flashed, and the peach fell in two dicotyledonous halves. "Steal one Stone, that's your hand. Steal two Stones, that's your head."

Yulen must have known that his demonstration kept Stone washers honest, because he backed off thirty yards, sat with his back against a tree, and propped his helmet over his eyes.

I yanked a pillow-case-sized hide bag from the pile, staggering backwards as it popped loose. "It's like feathers!"

I tipped the bag, and a hundred dried mud balls the size of eggs and walnuts bounced to the ground.

Howard dipped one in a bucket, then sluiced mud off the Stone with a brush.

The rough rock in Howard's hand glittered. I don't just mean like jewelry. It glowed, blood-red, even in the afternoon sunlight, like a plugged-in light bulb. I had to squint to look at it.

Howard lifted his Eternad helmet off the equipment pile behind us, unsnapped the optics headring, and peered through the lenses at the Stone, like a jeweler louping the Hope Diamond. "Holy moly!"

"What is it?"

Howard peeled off his headring and handed the 'ring and Stone to me. I hefted the Stone. "It's like a ping pong ball!"

Howard said, "It just feels that way."

"Huh?" I manual-focused Howard's optics on the Stone's surface. The Stone itself didn't glow. It was a water-rounded cobble of sedimentary rock. Just a naturally cemented sand and silt grain lump, as common as any kid ever picked out of any creek on Earth. The glow shone from transparent spherules, as tiny as pinheads, scattered among the mundane grains.

Jude said, "What are they, Howard?"

Howard paused. Then he said. "Well....A black hole core weighs gigatons. It sucks in light. The material encased in those spherules lightens the rock around it, and it reflects light so perfectly the whole Stone seems to glow. I can only think of one explanation."

"Cavorite? In these little red blobs?"

He nodded. "So this is the natural state of interuniversal Cavorite."

"You said Cavorite came from the edge of the universe. This place is the armpit of the universe, definitely not the edge."

Howard shook his head. "The universes commingle at their interface. The spherules are bits of Cavorite that crossed over, and picked up a coating of material from our side. Somewhere out beyond the edge, there are probably similar bits of our universe in adjacent ones. The Fire-witch powerplant just mimicked one of these spherules, with shutters added to release and direct the Cavorite effect."

Jude said, "But we're not at the boundary."

"Meteorites normally originate within their own star system. But intergalactic bolides are certainly possible." Howard held up another washed Stone, between his thumb and forefinger. "I'll bet a carton of cigarettes that these spherules fell on Bren eons ago, got buried, lithified, then eroded out over geologic time."

Howard laid the Stone he had cleaned in an empty chest. "Spring thaw would erode new Stones from the mountain outcrops." He gazed into the distance. "The Stones are so light that the spring rains wash them down-stream. The Tassini prospectors must mine the placers all summer. That's why the Trade Fair is in the fall."

Ord had already filled one chest with washed Stones. He gazed at the peaked tents, banners now flapping in the afternoon breeze, and at the ship sails swaying beyond them. "Do these river people use these Stones to fly in space?"

Yulen sat up beneath his tree, and cupped his hands. "If you've time to talk, I'll fetch Stones enough to keep you busy all night! Or I could cut out your tongues."

The bag pile's shadow had already lengthened. We all shut up and scrubbed.

We finished scrubbing at dusk, then Yulen staked us

down for the night. He found us an abandoned yurt in the encampment's Casuni quarter.

Our minders stationed themselves in a ring around the tent's perimeter.

Jude ran his hands over the yurt's hide wall, tested the ropes that hobbled his legs, then turned to me. "Isn't it time to escape now? If everybody gets as drunk as they got last night, we could sneak past the guards."

"And then what?" I shook my head. "Tomorrow, Blackbeard's going to trade us to the Fisheaters."

Howard said, "The Marini seem more genteel than the Casuni. We'd probably be better off with them. I vote we stay put tonight."

I raised my eyebrows at Ord.

"We're not immediately threatened, Sir. Our resources are limited. Our intelligence is nonexistent. And we lack an objective."

I tugged off my boots. "Okay. Let's make tonight's objective sleep."

Outside, singing began—throaty, off-key, and destined to worsen as kegs emptied. But after what we'd been through, I drifted off to sleep in minutes.

Yulen and Blackbeard woke us at dawn, made us wash, and dressed us in plain cloth tunics over our underlayer, then remounted us on our duckbills. They and a half dozen others led us back through the yurt encampment, until we emerged onto a grass midway. Awninged tents and stalls cut it up into a rabbit-warren of a bazaar, teeming with people, some mounted like us, most dismounted.

I rode alongside Yulen, eavesdropping while he pointed out passers-by to the blond youngster Yulen had taken under his wing.

I had already learned volumes listening around the campfires on the journey here.

Across the midway, two men wore sun-cheating robes over bodies as thin and brown as rusted wire. Indigo dye stained their foreheads. Yulen grinned as he pointed. "Tassini. The more purple on their heads, the higher their station."

The pitiful Tassini roamed the Plains' arid south. Noble and dashing Casuni raiders routinely burned Tassini encampments. The cowardly Tassini did exactly the same to Casuni encampments whenever they got the chance.

This cycle pretty much described Plains-Politics-according-to-Yulen, for three centuries. The closest thing to a Plains-Clan Constitution was a proverb, "Blood Feud is bread."

The Plains Clans may have been peevish with each other, but they agreed on one thing. They hated the Marini worse.

Yulen pointed at a half-dozen Earthling-sized men and women. The men wore wide-sleeved shirts under brocaded vests and eschewed facial hair. The women walked alongside them unveiled. Men and women seemed to have a skin fold above the eye that made them look sleepy. Yulen said to the boy, "God made Marini look tired because they sleep beside the devil."

Clan Marini, a.k.a. the Fisheaters, were Bren's worldly traders and navigators, and controlled the lush, temperate Coastal Plain. A transfer to the Marini looked like our most promising way forward.

Our bound wrists drew a few looks as we rode, but most of the crowd was buzzed on mead, hungover from same, or bargain hunting.

Rosy, my mare, ignored the first Fisheaters we passed.

But we came up behind one Marini who wore a black-lacquered breastplate and cheek-plated helmet, and boasted rippled forearms. Rosy reared and squealed as we passed him. The Fisheater had a hint of scent about him. But to me, it was nothing to thrash one's tail about.

Blackbeard turned our little caravan down a zigzag alley so narrow that we had to ride single file.

After five minutes, Blackbeard halted us in front of a yellow-and-red awning that fronted an enormous tent, from which music bubbled. Beneath the awning sat a droop-eyed, turbaned Marini. Cross-legged on multicolored carpets stacked two feet high, he clenched the carved mouthpiece of a woven fabric hose between his teeth.

The hose snaked down into the belly of a bubbling, glass-globed water pipe. Beside the man's pipe, a spectacular, dark-eyed woman lay curled like a cat. Unlike our lunch porters of the day before, her costume left no doubt about her gender.

Howard leaned toward me, and pointed at the pipe. "Do you suppose that's tobacco?"

Droop-lids raised his palm to Blackbeard. "Peace of the Fair, Captain."

Blackbeard raised his own palm. "And of the One True God, may He smite those who lie with the devil."

Droop-lids snorted smoke out of the corner of his mouth. Evidently the Fisheaters didn't like being accused of sleeping with devils.

Then the Marini smiled and bobbed his head, counting back up the alley along our line of mounted guards and prisoners. "A dozen for your men, then? And two for

so considerate a commander as yourself, at no charge."
He reached down and stroked the woman's hair. "On my
honor, my girls have copulated only with royalty."

Jude whispered, "Whoa!"

The woman blew Jude a kiss. On her, the droopy Marini
eyelids looked great.

I groaned. When I swore to Munchkin that I would
protect her sixteen-year-old son, I didn't expect it to be
from extraterrestrial hookers.

Blackbeard waved a gauntleted hand at the pimp. "I'm
selling. Not buying. You know the flesh trade. Where can
I ransom these four back to their kin?"

"Ransom is good business." Droop-lids nodded. Then
he snorted. "But Marini don't ransom half-breeds."

"What?" Blackbeard bristled. "These four are as Fisheater as you, old man."

"Not with those eyes. We all look alike to you Plains
hicks, hey?" The pimp made a shooing motion with the
hand that held the pipe tube, and smoke curled from its
mouthpiece. "Get this filth away. They block paying cus-
tomers." Then Droop-lids' eyes brightened. "Of course,
my girls would service them, and your men, with extra
enthusiasm, if you change your mind, Captain."

We couldn't turn around in the narrow alley, so Blackbeard led us on down to its opposite end, cursing as he
rode. He told Yulen, "It's just a matter of finding the right
match. We'll go visiting tonight."

Jude kept turning in his saddle, gawking back at the
woman reclining beneath Droop-lid's awning, and muttering, "Whoa!"

Blackbeard reconfined us to our tent, left our hobbles
on, and made our guards stay inside the tent with us. Yulen

slipped us more flatbread on the sly, and we slept through another party night at The Great Fair.

In the morning, Blackbeard sent Yulen to spruce us up, like the day before. But this morning, more guards crowded into our tent behind Yulen, pistols drawn. Yulen replaced our rope hobbles with leg irons, and, as he locked them around our ankles, he knit his brows. Unpromising.

As we dressed, I asked him, "Hard night, Sarge?"

He shook his head. "I didn't drain one horn. When my Captain's unhappy, I'm unhappy."

"Why's your Captain unhappy?"

"We passed the night going tent-to-tent among the Fisheaters. None will ransom you."

Uh-oh.

I looked at Yulen sideways. "So you're gonna let us go, right?"

Yulen turned up his mouth corner in a failed smile. "In a fashion. To the highest bidder."

TWENTY-SEVEN

A HALF HOUR LATER, Yulen halted the duckbill caravan of us four, the guards, and our gear at the edge of a vast meadow that sloped from The Fair's tent city to the River Marin.

He sat back in his saddle and sighed to the young soldier alongside him. "In a month, we'll strike our yurts, the Marini will sail into the downriver fog like ghosts, and the Tassini will slink back to the desert."

Yulen pointed at two structures one hundred yards from us, close enough to one another that I could have thrown a baseball between them. "But The Pillars and The Block will remain here, like they have for three hundred years."

The young cavalryman squinted at a row of stones set with iron rings. The stones lined the riverbank, each one as big as a sleeping duckbill. Chains as thick as men's thighs branched from the stones, and anchored ships out in the river. The young man pointed at the anchor stones. "My mother said, 'Good boys sail from The Pillars one day.'"

Yulen snorted. "Mine said, 'Rotten boys go on The Block.'"

Given my record, I focused on The Block.

The Block was a three-foot-high cut-stone stage twenty feet long and ten feet deep. Situated halfway between The Great Fair's tents and the river, it squatted in an open meadow that had been trampled to lifeless dirt by crowds. The Block's more complete name, which I had heard around the campfire, was The Slave Auction Block.

That morning a crowd of a thousand spectators and a hundred bidders surrounded The Block. Awnings on poles, placed to protect the crowd, not the merchandise, hung limp, and the sun shone in a clear sky.

When Yulen cantered our caravan up behind The Block, Blackbeard met us. He flicked his eyes to the sky, and said to Yulen, "Sun makes a man open his pockets, hey, Sergeant?"

Yulen shrugged. "For half-breeds? At least they have property."

From my campfire eavesdropping, I knew that the Clans of Bren didn't mind bigotry, chopping one another into lunch, religious intolerance, gender inequality, public drunkenness, or slavery. But the Clans agreed on three inviolable rules. First, no chopping one another at The Fair. Second, once the auction hammer falls, a deal's a deal. And, third, private property is private property.

When a seller offered a person for sale, he had to include as a package deal all property he captured along with his prisoner, down to the captive's last peppercorn. The buyer had to bid for the whole package, too. No cherry picking. In the meantime, the prisoner owned his own stuff (or her own stuff; they were even-handed that way).

It was a fig leaf of decency, because incoming slaves seldom owned more than what they wore. But our four tons of gear, consisting of sealed Plasteel Tamperproofs, four suits of Eternad armor, and our four inanimate Cargo'Bots, were just as much ours by law as some peasant's peppercorn. For another hour or so.

An Apprentice Auctioneer, a Tassini wearing indigo eye shadow, made us unload all four tons of our own stuff from Blackbeard's duckbills. Then the Apprentice looped a long chain through our leg irons, paid it out, and locked it to a ring set in The Block. Then he made us sit in the dirt alongside all our gear. Not quite all. Jeeb hovered high above the spectator's awning, still unknown to the Bren.

On stage, a Tassini girl, maybe eighteen, held a baby. Her dress was coarse cloth that hung on her down to her ankles, and her feet were bare but for wooden sandals. Her hair had been gathered with a carved blue comb. The baby squalled, and she flexed her knees rhythmically, bouncing the child to calm it. Her lip quivered.

The Tassini Auctioneer stood alongside her, his face dyed indigo from the nose up. He pointed his polished wood mallet at the biggest Casuni I had seen yet, a broken-nosed mountain who sat in a raised chair, wearing jeweled armor.

"I have one hundred from My Lord, there. Who will say two?"

The enormous Casuni held a bid fan, but didn't move it.

The Auctioneer looked out across the crowd. "A fine lady's maid here to be trained. See the intelligence in those eyes!"

Someone shouted, "And who feeds the child? Split the Lot. I'll give two hundred for just the girl."

The girl clutched her baby, and tears rolled down her cheeks. They couldn't sell her without her hair comb, because it was her personal property. But they could sell her without her child, because he wouldn't become personal property until he was sold for the first time.

Jude sat alongside me, his eyes wide, shaking his head.

Howard's hands shook. "They call themselves human?"

Ord didn't speak, but his fists were clenched white-knuckle tight.

The Auctioneer turned again to the jewel-armored bidder, whose shoulders were so broad they obscured the chair back. Every Casuni I had seen looked like he could toss a cow through a closed barn door.

The Auctioneer bent on one knee, and stretched his palm toward the bidder. "Come, Sir! Say two hundred! Give the lie to those who say your people are stubborn!"

A woman hooted, "You can always tell a Casuni. But you can't tell him much!"

The crowd roared, and even the big, bearded man smiled. But he didn't twitch his bid fan.

In the end, "The Lot," mother and child, went together to the outsized Casuni, because nobody raised his bid. The girl ran off the stage, the baby clutched to her, knelt and kissed the Apprentice's feet. He toed her aside, then refastened her chains to The Block, on the side opposite from us, where sold merchandise awaited collection.

Then the Apprentice scuttled into the crowd, where a man alongside the seated Casuni counted out coins, and traded them to the Apprentice for a parchment sheet.

I swallowed, and my heart sank. Two human souls had just been sold like beer at a ball game.

Jude said, "I wish we took our chances with the monsters."

I hung my head. Another crap decision by me. Likely the last decision I would have free will to make. We should have gone down swinging against one set of animals or the other when we had the chance.

I looked around. Besides us, twenty "Lots" were on offer, Marini, Tassini, and Casuni. The Bren were equal-opportunity slavers.

I saw one familiar face.

Bassin the Assassin sat cross-legged in the dirt. He was the next Lot behind us. A small hide bag, presumably the Stones that were captured with him, lay alongside him. He wore a Tassini robe, obviously borrowed because it barely covered his knees, and he had been fitted with a hideous glass eye, all presumably to boost his marketability. He nodded to me, but didn't smile.

Blip. Jeeb's low level alert yipped in my earpiece.

I whispered, "Hold." Jeeb knew something was wrong. But unless it had a bomb stuffed in a pocket, a TOT had no capability that would be useful to extract us from this circus. Jeeb had no pocket, much less a bomb.

Six armed and armored Casuni stood between us and our stuff. Whether the stuff was our property or not, I doubted that those bouncers would allow us to decrypt our Tamperproofs, unpack our rifles, load them, and shoot our way out of this.

I looked out in the audience. Alongside Blackbeard stood the Lieutenant whose men had actually captured Bassin. That made the Lieutenant Bassin's seller, just as Blackbeard was ours.

After an hour, the four of us Earthlings got herded from the on-deck circle up onto The Block.

Jude whispered, "This sucks sewage."

I asked Howard, "Can't you predict a solar eclipse or something, and awe the crowd?"

The Auctioneer looked out across the upturned faces. "Four strong Marini, offered as a Lot. Who'll start the bid at the ridiculously low price of four hundred?"

Somebody yelled, "For half-breeds? It's ridiculous all right!"

Laughter rippled.

In the audience, Blackbeard scowled at the Auctioneer. *Blip. Blip.*

I covered my mouth with my hand, and whispered into my throat mike, to Jeeb. "I said 'hold'!"

The Auctioneer arched his eyebrows, as he pointed at our sealed Plasteels. "Who knows what treasures await in those chests?"

Our armor was too small for any male Casuni, and we owned no other property except the Tamperproofs, and the folded-down 'Bots, which looked like iron lumps. Our Seller evidently thought the chests' mystery would romance bidders. Besides, he didn't know how to open them.

"Maybe there's more skinny half-breeds in there!"

More laughter.

So much for romance.

The Casuni who bought the girl and the baby flicked his bid fan.

The Auctioneer laid the back of his hand across his purple forehead, and swayed like he was about to faint. "One hundred? Only one hundred for these marvelous specimens? Even if they survive but one year, they're still cheap at two hundred."

"The play's not till tonight, you purple-faced ham!"

After the laughs came silence, and no bids.

The Auctioneer sighed. "Going once."

The Casuni with the fan smiled.

"Going twice."

Jude muttered, "Slaves. Forever. I don't pugging believe this."

"Two Stones."

The Auctioneer turned toward the voice. "Two *Stones?* That's more than—"

"Three Stones." It was the same voice.

The crowd buzzed.

The Auctioneer craned his neck.

Alongside The Block, Bassin the Assassin stood, his ankles chained. "Four Stones for the Lot. And two more for the next Lot."

The buzz became a rumble.

The Auctioneer pointed his gavel at Bassin and snorted. "You *are* the next Lot! Sit down!"

Bassin bent, drew a handful of Stones from the bag he held, then raised them above his head. The jewels glowed so red in the sunlight that he looked like he held a flaming torch.

The crowd gasped collectively.

Someone shouted, "They're his Stones. Why can't he bid?"

A heckler hooted.

The Auctioneer spun back to the crowd. "It's ridiculous!"

"It's the law!"

The crowd picked up the phrase and chanted. "It's the law! It's the law!"

Howard nudged me. "Look at the Captain. Whatever a Stone's worth, it's a hundred times more than he ever figured to get for us."

Blackbeard was smiling. The Lieutenant who had actually captured Bassin stood alongside Blackbeard, purple and trembling, with his teeth clenched. He must have figured the bidding for Bassin alone would go up to six or eight Stones, once bidders found out what surprising bonus they would get from Bassin's bag. If Bassin's ploy worked, the Lieutenant would only net two Stones. But the Lieutenant couldn't afford to cross his boss, Blackbeard.

The Auctioneer raised his eyebrows at his Apprentice. The younger man turned his palms skyward and shrugged.

Ord said, "Slaves buying themselves! Case of first impression, apparently."

The Auctioneer furrowed his brow.

Bassin reached into his bag a last time, and held another Stone aloft, in his other hand, "And another Stone to My Lord Auctioneer, in appreciation for his services."

The Honorable Dickie Rosewood March told me, when I was young, "If the truth won't set you free, try bribery."

A heckler shouted, "That's more than the old gasbag makes in a year!"

The crowd roared.

The Auctioneer glared at the crowd. Then he glanced first at the bidding Casuni, who folded his fan, and nodded. The Auctioneer shot one more glance at Blackbeard, who beamed.

The Auctioneer swung his mallet. "Sold!"

The crowd cheered.

The Apprentice, shaking his head, unlocked our leg irons, then Bassin's, then prodded the next Lot toward the stage.

Blip. Blip. Blip.

I growled into my throat mike. "It's okay, now. We're fine. Shut up!"

Somebody slapped me on the back, and thrust a full horn flagon into my hand. "I'll buy you a drink on that!"

"Never seen nothing like it!" A man slapped his knee.

People surged around us, shouting. "There's one in the eye for the Slavers!"

"*And* for the Casuni!"

Someone said to us, "You'll celebrate tonight, hey, boys?"

The Apprentice took Bassin's Stones from him, pocketed the one that was the Auctioneer's tip, then shouldered me aside, as he carried the remaining Stones to Blackbeard and the Lieutenant, as their respective profits.

Jude asked me, "Can we go back to the tent with the girls?"

"No!"

Howard stood beside me, shaking his head. "I don't understand. If a handful of Stones is valuable enough to make a man rich, what happens to those piles of them that we cleaned?"

I turned, stood on tiptoe, and scanned the crowd, searching for Bassin. "And who the hell is my caveman friend, really?" Technically, Bassin owned us now, but he had vanished, and somehow a former slave didn't seem like the slave owner type.

Jude tugged my sleeve. "Can I get drunk?"

"No."

"Just one?"

"Maybe."

Blee-Blee-Blee-Blee-Blee.

I tore out my earpiece. "Goddammit!"

Ord stood beside me, head cocked. "What's wrong, Sir?"

I scanned the clear sky. "Jeeb's up there with a fried chip or something. He's been blipping for a half hour. Just now he kicked up to Threat Level Four." I nodded toward the quiet green slope across the river, and snorted. "You'd think a thousand Slugs were gonna charge over that hill any minute now."

I shuddered. I had been to war against the Slugs twice, and even tossing off their name in jest still spooked me.

I rested my eyes on the graceful wooden Traders nodding their sails out on the river. Between us and the ships rolled a green and gold fall meadow. We four were free men, and whatever my missteps, we were suddenly as okay as we could be, so far from home.

The four of us walked back to our gear, the crowd turned its attention back to the show up on The Block, and in the soft, windless afternoon we could finally talk to one another without shouting.

Jude cocked his head. "What's that?"

"Huh?"

"Don't you hear it? It's like, boom-boom-boom, boom-boom-boom."

Howard, Ord, and I looked at each other.

I said, "Uh-oh."

TWENTY-EIGHT

BOOM-BOOM-BOOM.

I heard it, now. My blood coursed cold in my veins, and hair rose on my neck.

Jude was right. He was just a nanosecond ahead of us unmutated humans, as usual.

Boom-boom-boom. Louder still.

Howard's Spooks guessed that Slug infantry could sustain eight miles per hour over obstacle-free terrain, at Earth gravity. Howard's Spooks never guessed why Slugs on the march pounded their mag rifles against their body armor. Maybe to beat cadence, maybe to assist respiration, maybe to scare their enemies. Whatever the Slugs thought, I always thought it scared the crap out of me.

A few faces in the crowd turned up toward the clear sky, puzzled.

A woman near us asked her husband, "Did you furl the tent flaps?"

He told her, "It didn't look like rain."

Mostly, the crowd sunned themselves, or listened to the Auctioneer's sing-song.

Slugs made war on humans the way humans made war

on the common cold virus. Dispassionately and totally. No one who survived the experience forgot, and neither did their children, or their children's children.

I turned to Howard with my jaw dropped. "The sledge-hammer's about to swat the fly, but these people have no idea what's coming."

Howard said, "The Pseudocephalopod's contact with this planet must have happened very, very long ago. Or it's current, but very restricted."

Ord said, "Whatever it was, it's changing." He hopped on one leg as he pulled on his Eternad leggings. I realized that I had begun doing the same thing, reflexively. So had Howard.

"Jude!" I pointed at his crimsons. "Armor up!"

My godson's eyes widened. "Is this gonna be cool?"

"No. Move it!"

Boom-boom-boom.

Now the thunder was so loud that people were turning to one another and scratching their heads. The Auctioneer paused in mid-rant. He looked over his shoulder, shrugged, and resumed

I could have shouted a warning, but what? Anything I said would have been as meaningless as a stop sign to a walrus.

I twisted my earpiece back in my ear, then locked my helmet to the connecting ring. The ventilator clicked, and filtered air feathered my cheek for the first time in weeks.

More important, my visor visuals exploded to life like star shells. I was no longer limited to Jeeb's basic audio feed.

I tasked Jeeb. "Show threat."

As I said it, I chinned my optics to panoramic, and focused on the hilltops that bounded the river's opposite side. "Oboy." It suddenly became unnecessary for Jeeb to flash me aerial images of the threat.

The distant ridgeline slowly sprouted a line of black whiskers, like a holo for beard cream.

Boom-boom-boom. Now the sound rumbled, the way trains did in the years before 'levs.

People in the crowd pointed fingers at the hills, and visored their hands over their eyes as they stared in the direction of the rumble.

Someone shouted, "What sort of show is this?"

"A free one, I hope!"

The crowd laughed.

Zzzzeeee.

"Incoming!" I shoved Jude to the ground, and spread-eagled across him.

Slug weaponry is as simple, and as alien, as Slug physiology. Howard calls it the Pseudocephalopod equivalent of anthropomorphism. Whatever.

The Slugs use magnetic force to accelerate non-explosive projectiles of various sizes along rails to as high a speed as necessary to inflict the damage level they want. The big berthas mounted on a Firewitch look pretty much like the rifles Slug warriors tote, except for size. But size matters.

Ka-boom.

The Slugs hadn't tossed many Heavys on Ganymede, but I recognized the impact thump. Heavys were long-range rounds, as big as a gallon milk jug and as heavy as a wall safe.

Silence. It had been just a single, ranging round.

I raised my head and looked around. "Jeez!" It had been a ranging round, but it had also been a Golden Beebe.

In the center of the field Blackbeard stood, the bag of stolen Stones that had bought our freedom clutched in his right hand.

He stared down at his armored breastplate, his eyes bulging. Where Blackbeard's chest had been there now yawned a steaming hole, as large and round as a meat platter. The distant hills showed through the opening, bordered by the golden remains of his breastplate, as though a landscape painting hung around his neck.

Beneath me, Jude said, "What was—" and raised his head. I elbowed his helmet back into the dirt.

He squirmed. "I want to see!"

"You don't."

The bag slid from Blackbeard's fingers, and the glowing red Stones bounced and rolled across the soil like solid fire.

Blackbeard wobbled on his boots, then toppled backward and lay staring at the sky. A severed artery pulsed a red arc a foot in the air above him. His blood glistened an instant in the sun, then rained back down on his face.

One woman screamed.

Then her voice got lost in a thousand others, and in the rumble of running feet.

The Auctioneer, his eyes wide, jumped from side to side on The Block, pumping his palms downward. "Stop! It's some mistake! Peace of the Fair! Peace of the Fair!"

Boom-boom-boom.

The far ridge was black for a mile in each direction, as thousands of Slug warriors in body armor spilled across the crest and glided down the hillside toward The Fair.

I stood, and Jude scrambled up beside me. He peered through his helmet visor, jumping side to side, and pointing. "They're real! They're real!"

History-chip images taken from HelmetCams, and Holowood special effects, had shown every kid on Earth what Slugs looked like, but Jude Metzger was now the only member of his generation to share a planet with live ones.

Zzzzeeee. Zzzzeeee. Zzzzeeee.

I knelt and tugged Jude down alongside me.

He said, "We have armor on!"

"Armor's good against mag rifle rounds, not Heavys."

The first Slug Heavy volley slammed the meadow. The rounds just plowed dirt.

Slug rounds were as dumb as Napoleonic cannonballs, but the hole in Blackbeard demonstrated that, in war, smart isn't everything.

I looked back at the Fair. At ten-second intervals, volleys crashed into the close-packed wood, hide, and canvas tents. Already, flames flickered where the red hot rounds had started fires.

Ord had voiced our Cargo'Bots to life and tasked them to carry our Plasteels. Now he held my M-40 out to me.

I grabbed my rifle from Ord, cocked, and loaded it, as I looked out to the river. A Heavy volley pounded like driven sleet against the Marini trading vessels. Torn sails erupted flames, then thrashed in the wind, as friction-heated rounds slashed them. Spray geysered as rounds bracketed ships. A mast, snapped like straw, toppled onto sailors rowing a small boat, and exploded it in a fountain of oars and bodies.

Ord, his visor up, held his targeting binoculars to his eyes. "Let's see how they react to the river obstacle."

Beyond the ships, the Slug skirmish line approached the opposite bank.

Ord hardly needed his binoculars. The skirmish line was so close that individual Slugs were distinguishable to the naked eye.

A Slug warrior looks like a puke-green zucchini nearly six feet long, tip-to-tail. A warrior has no eyes, just white patches along its anterior taper that sense infrared light. A warrior doesn't have permanent appendages, either, just a pseudopod that toothpastes out of a hole in its body armor, which the warrior wraps around its rifle. Slug body armor is black, shiny, and segmented, and an M-40 round cuts it like cheese.

Slugs crossing open ground look just like oversized garden pests. When they're scrunched up and oozing, the anterior crest of their armor stands less than five feet tall, and they move as fast as double-timing infantry.

Howard said, "We've never seen how It reacts to water."

A Casuni woman pointed back at the Slugs as she ran away, and screamed, "The Devil! The Devil!"

Howard turned, hands-on-hips, and watched her run. "She didn't say, 'What's that?' She seemed to know."

"Goddammit, Howard! Load your weapon!"

The front rank of Slugs reached the water's edge.

Ranks of half a dozen oozed forward, carrying logs wrapped by their snaky pseudopods, like a rowing team carrying a scull to the water. Each half dozen dropped its log in the water, then the next rank and log oozed along the first, extending a thousand bridges, each one log wide, across the river in minutes. The next rank followed, then the next.

The Heavy volleys stopped, and the only sounds were the crackle of flame, distant human screams, and the splash of water and creak of logs.

I said to Ord, "They've lifted the barrage."

Jude asked, "Now?"

Howard cocked his rifle. "Wait."

Ord had our 'Bots loaded, with the two carrying explosives and ammunition thirty yards behind us, and the two carrying inert equipment hunkered down in front of us like mobile pillboxes. They would move when we moved, screening us from Slug fire.

I knelt behind the 'Bot that sheltered Jude and me, and sighted on the water's edge, a hundred yards away. Behind their 'Bot, so did Ord and Howard.

Jude lay alongside me, his rifle at his shoulder.

I turned my head toward him. "Just like the Sergeant Major taught you on the Simulator. Aim. Breathe. Squeeze. Okay?"

He nodded. "But—why don't we just run?"

"We can't outrun them forever. We fight when we can take out the most of them with the least risk. When I say fall back, you fall back with me. Keep your head down, and keep the 'Bot between you and the Slugs. Reload on the run. Howard and the Sergeant Major will cover us, then we'll stop and cover them. You keep doing that until I tell you to do something else. If I don't tell you, do *exactly* what the Sergeant Major says."

"Why wouldn't you tell— Oh."

A warrior rank dropped a log that touched the river's

near bank, in front of us, then another bridge was completed, and another.

I asked Ord, "Did you clock 'em?"

"I calculate the water crossing slowed them about two miles per hour, Sir. They've always been full of surprises."

They were ten feet from shore, now, all across their advancing front.

Bang.

Jude fired and hit nothing.

I said, "Wait till the first one hits land. Then we'll back 'em up on their logs."

"Jason, I'm scared."

"Me too."

Ord said, "I have a target." His rifle popped, and a warrior splashed dead on the river bank's mud.

Zeeeee.

I flinched at the sound of the first mag rifle round I'd heard in years.

But not the last. For the next three minutes I fired, moved, reloaded, and fired, over and over. A half dozen rounds grazed my armor without effect.

Jude didn't stay behind the 'Bot, as he was told, and took a round full on his chestplate. The blow's force knocked him onto his back, and I dove toward him, screaming.

He came up on one knee, coughing and rubbing the dent in his chestplate. "Pug! That stung!"

We retreated fifty yards, while the Slugs we killed became hurdles that slowed the warrior ranks behind them. Then the rear ranks surged over the corpses. The four of us lay, panting, behind the two Cargo'Bots. The remaining

Slugs, still too many to count, pressed forward, and their rounds thunked as they struck the 'Bots' carapaces.

I told Ord, "Time to break contact." I turned to Jude and pointed upslope. Black smoke from the burning tents oozed across the ground like a great wall. "When we get up this time, run till we're all obscured in that smoke."

Jude said, "But Slugs can see in the dark."

Howard said, "Not exactly. Air that's as warm as bodies moving through it *will* make it harder for those warriors to see us."

I looked one more time at Jude, Ord, and Howard. "Ready?"

Jude grabbed my arm. "But, Jason, what about them?"

He pointed to our left. Fifty yards away was The Block.

Its stage was empty. The Auctioneers had fled moments after the crowd. But a hundred slaves and slaves-to-be remained chained to the iron rings that hung from the stage. Slug rounds cracked against the stone, powdering small clouds into the air.

A half dozen slaves already lay still and bloody. The rest screamed, clawed the ground trying to dig holes to hide in, or tore at their chains. The slight girl with the baby and the blue hair comb bled at the ankles as she struggled to tear free of her leg shackles.

If we turned and ran from the Slugs now, we would make it to the smoke's safety with fifty yards to spare, easy. But the Slugs would slaughter the slaves. If we detoured to help the slaves, we would likely be overrun— and killed—ourselves.

I turned to Ord. "We can't leave them, Sergeant Major."

Ord was already working the combination on a Plasteel balanced on a 'Bot's back. "Thermite sticks should cut those chains, Sir."

I pointed up the hill and told Howard, "You take Jude up there. Ord and I will rejoin you after we get those people loose."

Jude said, "No way. I stay with you."

Howard shook his head at me. "You'll need covering fire."

I looked downslope, where the Slug wave rolled on toward us, and blinked. As a soldier, it was Howard's privilege to spend his life, and my duty to order him to do so. But Jude was no more a combatant than those screaming, bleeding people trapped in chains. He was a child. My child.

Jude said, "Jason, I just want to do the right thing."

There wasn't time to debate. And he was right. I pointed at The Block. "Okay. Keep down, behind the 'Bots."

Ord tossed me a bound pack of Thermite sticks as we ran to The Block. Now the Slugs were close enough and thick enough that I thumbed my rifle to full automatic, and fired as we ran without fear that any shots would miss.

As we approached, the slaves scrabbled back away from us, throwing up their hands, wide eyed, and pleading.

With our visors down, in armor the like of which no Clansman of Bren had ever seen, we must have looked like demons to the slaves. Bren firearms were single shot, but our rifles were spitting seven hundred rounds per minute, like dragon fire. And at our sides crawled iron spiders as big as young duckbills.

No wonder we terrified the people we were trying to save.

I dodged out from behind the 'Bot that sheltered Ord and me, molded a Thermite stick around the first manacle

I saw that had an animate foot in it, jammed an insulation pad under the manacle to shield the foot from the heat and flash. I yanked the starter ribbon.

Whoosh.

A red, forty-five-hundred-degree-Fahrenheit flash severed the manacle. I brushed the red-hot iron away with my gauntlet, pushed the man to his feet, and pointed toward the smoke. "Run!"

Ord had cut three slaves loose in the time it took me to free one.

He knelt beside me, firing, and shouted, "Sir, it's taking too long!"

I said, "Retask the 'Bots. Have 'em break chains with their manipulators."

Ord nodded, and moved out.

Howard and Jude saw what Ord was doing and Howard retasked their 'Bot, too.

I glanced up the hill and counted twenty freed slaves, stumbling and crawling for their lives. Farther up the slope, just in front of the smoke screen thrown by the burning of The Great Fair, was the only other Bren who had not fled the meadow in panic.

On a prancing, snow-white duckbill sat the huge, jewel-armored Casuni who had allowed Bassin to win the bid for us. He pressed a brass spyglass to one eye, watching the battle.

The Slug front line was thirty yards away, now.

A 'Bot snapped the last chain and freed the last slave on the for-sale side of the block.

Three slaves, four counting the young girl's baby, remained imprisoned in the "sold" compound. I ran to them, and wrapped the first Thermite stick.

Ord knelt beside me again. "Sir, we're about to be overrun."

"Tell Howard and Jude to fall back."

"I did, Sir. Colonel Hibble said he outranked me. Jude told me to pug myself."

A Slug warrior leapt across the 'Bot that formed our final barrier, six feet from us. Ord shot him, point blank, then stood and hosed down a half dozen more, nearly as close.

The girl with the baby was the last chained slave. I knelt alongside her as she trembled in the dirt, her eyes as wide and white as hard-boiled eggs. Crimson stained her dress hem, where her ankle had bled as she tried to free herself from her chains.

I wiped blood off her chain, so the Thermite stick wouldn't slip, then said to her, "Look away when I pull the ribbon, and don't touch the manacle. I'll pull it off. Then run up the hill and don't stop."

She stared at me.

I popped my visor, and made my speech again.

She nodded, pulled her crying infant to her chest, looked over my shoulder and screamed.

I spun, slapped a Slug warrior off my back, then clubbed him with my M-40, barrel first.

A GI can always take one Slug, hand-to-pseudopod. But he can't take fifty.

I burned the girl's leg iron, helped her to her feet, and shoved her toward the smoke screen.

Then I turned back to the fight.

Howard had retasked a 'Bot, so it flailed its manipulators like a Lawn'Bot, slicing through a Slug every second. Each Slug's armor split, and green slop exploded onto Howard's and Jude's red Eternads. The two of them looked like Christmas elves from hell.

Ord stood literally knee-deep in dead Slug warriors, while he blazed away with a pistol, his own 1911-model .45 automatic, in one hand. His torso shook as he fired the M-40 he held in his other hand. He had fixed a bayonet to the rifle, and green slug blood dripped from it.

Beyond Ord and Jude and Howard, the ground was black with advancing Slugs. There was no outrunning the wave now.

The smells of burning canvas and flesh, and of cordite, swirled through my open visor. The incessant rattle of our weapons punctuated the unending sigh of thousands of Slug mag rail rifles.

I didn't review my life, or think that we saved some slaves, or even think that my friends, and my godson, would die alongside me within two minutes.

What I thought of were all those oil paintings of last stands, in all those military museums, like Custer at Little Big Horn, or Chelmsford at Isandlwhana. The central figure always stood alone, surrounded, blazing or slashing away at his enemy, some flag flapping behind him, before he and all the troops around him got killed. They didn't have Cam'Bots in those days, so who told the artist what the scene looked like at the end?

Something behind me struck my shoulder and knocked me face-down in the bloody meadow. That didn't conform to the portrait model.

TWENTY-NINE

I TURNED MY HEAD, and saw, six inches from my face, a snow-white, clawed foot as big as my torso.

I rolled onto my back, aiming my rifle, and stared up at the jewel-armored Casuni who had spyglassed our battle, looming from on top of his mount.

The man held a pistol in each hand and his reins in his teeth. His black hair and beard swelled around the edges of a crested gold helmet with a metal nosepiece, and he wore the showy armor he had on at the Slave auction.

Blam. Blam.

The big man's pistols flashed yellow, and two Slugs' anterior armor exploded. The white duckbill trampled three more, while its rider holstered his two spent pistols at his waist. Then he reared his mount back, so it balanced for a heartbeat on its tail, and the huge animal pummeled two more Slug warriors with its hind feet, like a boxing kangaroo.

I scrambled to my knees, and sprayed a half dozen Slugs.

The cavalryman's intervention had opened a tiny

hurricane eye around us four Earthlings, our 'Bots, and himself.

He leaned down, and extended me a gauntleted hand. "Up with you! Be quick!" He tossed his head toward the massing Slugs, and grinned. "God defends the virtuous only while the devil rests."

I looked around. Three more riders had already scooped up Ord, Jude, and Howard, who sat behind them on their duckbills.

Ord already had the four 'Bots quick-marching uphill.

I took the big man's arm, and he swung me—Eternads, rifle, ammo, and all—up onto his saddle behind him like I was a kindergartner.

A Slug round glanced off his helmet, and he snorted. He reined his mount so it turned and faced the Slug that had fired the shot, then cross-drew the two pistols holstered across his breastplate.

As his duckbill reared, the pistols kicked in his huge hands, the armor of the Slug that had fired at him split like a peeled banana, and the bullet killed a following Slug as well. The other shot dropped a third Slug. Then he holstered the spent, smoking single-shot pistols, drew his sword, and slashed a warrior in half as though its armor was paper.

The man frowned. "I would have expected the devil to provide better sport."

Then he turned, and we galloped until we crossed into the smoke and left the Slugs behind.

Five minutes later, we caught up to within a hundred yards of the ragged rear of the fleeing crowds. The big man glanced over his shoulder at the empty countryside we had opened between us and The Fair's wreckage, then reined in his mount.

From our left, the duckbills that carried Ord, Jude, and Howard approached and slowed to our pace. Our 'Bots scurried in their wake.

We halted, and the man swung me down. Then he dismounted and led his frothed and panting duckbill by its reins.

A straggler scurried alongside us, his arms filled with blankets and crockery. He bowed as he passed. "M'Lord."

The big man ignored him.

I said to the big man, "Thank you."

"What?" He held his reins in hands clasped behind his back, as we walked side by side.

"You risked your life to save us."

"Save *you?* I paid good money for that girl! Then you cut her loose!" He shook his head. "A hundred pissed away!"

I turned to him, and my jaw dropped.

He stared, too, then a grin spread out from the middle of his beard, and he threw his head back. He slapped my shoulder so hard I stumbled, then roared a laugh. "You're gullible, for a half-Marini!"

We walked on, as he plucked huge cartridges from a bandolier, and reloaded each of his four single-shot pistols. Then he reached for the M-40 I had slung across my shoulder, and poked it with a finger as thick as a sausage. "Gullible, but a clever salesman. These guns that talk like women would make a Tassini wet himself. You know where I could buy a few, quietly?"

"How few?"

"A shipload."

"Sure. Factory-direct, and cheap. But you won't believe the freight."

He shook his head, and rumbled a chuckle. "You gun runners always play the virgin. We'll talk again."

The others joined us. The big man pointed at the 'Bots, as they trundled along beside us. "Do those eat much?"

I said, "You have questions. So do we. But the devil, as you call the black worms, will be back on our tail as soon as those warriors regroup." I jerked a thumb back toward the smoke plume that rose behind us. "They'll catch up to you before your defenses are prepared. You need to select terrain and dig in."

He snorted. "Holes are for the crap of snakes, and for the Marini who grow from crap. No offense."

I pointed at the refugee throngs in front of us. "If you don't dig in, the worms will overrun those civilians."

"So? They're Marini and Tassini. But, God willing, there will always be more fighting. I'll regroup my Army."

He swung up onto his white charger, then pointed at us and said to his men, "See no harm comes to these half-breeds. Or their weapons."

"Where should we take them, Casus?"

"Where they want to go. But if they choose to go back to the Fisheaters, you don't help them." He spurred his mount, and galloped off, his duckbill spewing a storm of dirt clods.

Casus? Blackbeard had mentioned "Casus." I stood with hands on hips and watched him ride off.

Jude walked up alongside me, adjusting his M-40's sling to match mine. Ord had said Jude was a quick study. Munchkin hadn't raised her boy to be a soldier. Neither had my mom, but suddenly and unexpectedly I had become one. Now events had made my godson a soldier, too.

Jude asked, "Who's that guy?"

"Casus. He roasts poachers alive. He attacks the devil incarnate on a white charger, while all about him flee in terror. And he doesn't care flea snot for any Clan on this planet but his own. The Casuni must be named for his bloodline."

"He's, like, King?"

"A king who can shoot."

Ord stepped alongside us, reached over and tucked in the flapping tail of Jude's sling. "The equipment survived. The rest of us made it through with bumps and bruises. You, Sir?"

"Same."

"Sir, I took the liberty of retasking Jeeb to overfly the area, to assess damage and enemy dispositions."

I nodded. "This was the weakest Slug force I've ever seen. Something's screwy."

An hour later, neither Jeeb nor Casus had returned. When the Slugs had attacked, Casus's troops had cut the hobbles off all the duckbills they couldn't ride. The animals smart enough or lucky enough to run away from the battle had been rounded up by Casus's men later.

So I was reunited with Rosy, who actually honked when she sniffed me, and the other three Earthlings got mounts to ride as well.

Headed uphill this time, we returned to the base of the ten-foot escarpment that divided the barren Casuni steppes and the Tassini deserts, from the green, watered meadows of the Marini. Casus's appointed bodyguards led us to a narrow gap in the long cliff, through which refugees from the Slug blitz still climbed, funneling up and crossing into Casus's wind-scoured kingdom.

I stopped and swept my hand left and right at the north-south barrier, and said to Ord, "Casus should make a stand here. Now we know the Slugs can bridge rivers, but we've never seen 'em fly. This gap's the only way up for miles. A platoon could hold it against a division. Then Casus could cover the rest of the escarpment with a few dug-in troops per mile."

Ord frowned. "Casus and his cavalry aren't built to dig in, physically or mentally, Sir."

I nodded back. "Let's stop at the top of the gap for lunch. If Casus comes back here, I'll talk to him again."

The bodyguards Casus assigned to us did double duty, setting up an aid station for any Casuni stragglers who staggered back. Their first-aid business was lousy. Slug rounds hit hard. Human casualties were mostly dead, few wounded.

The bodyguards also made a fire, and boiled a soup made with what looked like dried peppers.

I walked over to the pot, sniffed, and the odor watered my eyes. I coughed, and shook my head. "Smells great." I patted my abdomen plate and grimaced. "But I'm coming off stomach surgery." Which was not a lie.

He nodded. "Once a man's eaten the janga, he never wants it again."

Evidently, every man within sniffing distance had already eaten the Janga. The pot just sat there and boiled.

The foodstuffs MAT(D)4 carried were finite, but we had plenty of MUDs left. After weeks of eating nothing but groundfruit patties, I had Ord crack open a provisions Plasteel.

The four of us sat cross-legged in a circle, while our bodyguards grazed Rosy and the other duckbills.

I squirted water from a hide bag into the nipple on a MUD that Quartermaster's comedians labeled "Spicy Chicken with Savory Chipati," then waited while bagged glop swelled and warmed itself.

Howard gazed back across the smoke-shrouded valley of the River Marin, and shook his head. "Well, we no longer have to wonder whether the Pseudocephalopod maintains a presence on this planet. But these people seemed astonished to see those warriors, and more astonished to be attacked."

I swallowed a MUD mouthful, tasty after weeks of groundfruit hardtack. "Especially during the 'Peace of the Fair.' Something must've changed recently."

Howard said, "The biggest thing that changed recently on this planet is we four arrived from outer space."

I paused with the packet halfway to my lips, and shook my head. "We're just four more humans. Why assume the Slugs even noticed the crash?"

Even as I said it, I didn't believe it. If Bassin the one-eyed prospector—or whatever he was—noticed the crash, the Slugs certainly noticed when one of their ships went down.

Jude squeezed "Homestyle Beef Stew" into his mouth, then he stared down at the smoke in the valley.

He could only imagine the human carnage it hid, and Munchkin would want me to keep it that way. If it were only Ord and me, and even Howard, I would cowboy up and join the fight on our new neighbors' side. But I had Jude to protect.

I said, "All Casus wants from us are automatic rifles, so he can grease his neighbors. Once he figures out we can't manufacture more M-40s, he won't want us at all. We have our gear. We can hole up anywhere on this continent for months. Our mission here is to survive. Period."

The three of them frowned at me.

Jude whispered, "But it's our fault!"

I stiffened. "No. We didn't expect this. We didn't wish evil on these people."

The three of them kept staring.

I said to Jude, "I promised your mother when I left her on New Moon that I'd keep you safe. Nobody promised we'd save this world. My mission is keeping us alive. That means getting us all away from this mess, and keeping us away. You all want me to take charge? Fine. We aren't getting involved."

Jude said, "You say you're keeping a promise to Mom. Mom said that if a person makes a mess, he should clean it up. Even if it was an accident. We made this mess."

I couldn't have said it better myself. But I wasn't going to admit that if doing so would risk Jude's life.

I stood, crossed my arms, and glared at Jude. "I don't have to decide this now."

The ground shook.

Howard's eyes widened as he stared at the prairie behind me. "Yes, you do."

THIRTY

I TURNED AND STARED. A miles-wide dust cloud sizzled on the horizon as Casus's army thundered toward us. I chinned my optics and spotted Casus, on his white beast, out ahead of his army. He twirled his sword above his head, shouting. Scarlet, gold, and purple banners, borne by other riders, boiled in the dust that churned behind him.

I bit down on my threat-count tab, and my optics began counting individual riders. I turned off the tab when the counter on my display whirred past four thousand, and kept spinning.

Casus, now there was a commander. Literally larger than life, skilled in the arts of war as he knew them, courageous, charismatic. Me, I couldn't even persuade a sixteen-year-old, a geek, and a Sergeant Major who reported to me to save their own skins.

Three minutes later, Casus's great army slowed to a canter, then halted, a thousand yards before they reached the Escarpment lip. His commanders rode from their units to confer alongside him. Casus seemed content to let the Slugs bring the fight to him.

As the four of us remounted, Ord said, "This is bad, Sir."

I nodded. "Casus wants to fight the Slugs out on the plains, where his cavalry can maneuver. But the Slugs'll overwhelm them. Those single-shot Casuni hand cannons shoot dinosaurs out from under opponents fine. But when the rider shoots the first four Slugs out of a hundred, what does he do about the ninety-six left?"

Ord said, "Digging in at the Escarpment is their best option."

I sighed, and shook my head. "I've been talking to Casus. Like that heckler at the auction said, 'You can always tell a Casuni. But you can't tell him much.'"

Howard said, "Show him, don't tell him." He had unfolded a holomap generator, and balanced it across his saddle. The generator popped as its display crackled on. Howard voiced up a direct feed from Jeeb, who hovered high enough above the Fair's flames to show the whole area.

In the river shallows, the smudges of sunken ships showed beneath the surface, or jutted bow or stern up, above the water. Dead Slugs littered the meadow between the river and the tents like spilled caraway seed. Smoke and flame still obscured most of the tent city's wreckage, but too many charred human silhouettes lay sprawled in the ashes. There had to be tens of thousands dead.

Jude gulped, then turned his face away.

The Slugs were visible, too, of course. They maneuvered in a black mass, surging toward the Escarpment. The threat counter identified ten thousand individual warriors.

I said to Howard, "Only ten thousand left? We only killed a few hundred."

He said, "I'll want to review Jeeb's broader survey to

see the big picture. But this is a smaller force than It normally deploys."

Ord pointed to a tree line off the Slug right flank. "What's that?"

Visible from Jeeb's overhead vantage, but screened from the Slugs at ground level by the trees, scores of foot troops and vehicles drawn by animals lay behind rough earthworks. The berms were being improved as we watched, faster than ants could empty a sugar bowl.

I said, "They're not Casuni. Casus says earthworks are for snakes. I'd guess they're Marini."

I overrode Howard's generator and tasked Jeeb. "Oblique close up."

Unnoticed by the combatants, Jeeb dove, flattened his flight line, and hovered a hundred feet from the force hidden behind the trees.

The animals dominated the image Jeeb transmitted. They walked on hind legs, like Casuni duckbills, but fifty feet long, where a big duckbill stallion might go twenty-eight. And these monsters had tumorous, blood-red heads, set with ranks of teeth as large and scabrous as overripe bananas. Their hides were elephant-gray, and their forelimbs like clawed twigs.

They snorted, so loud that Jeeb's audio picked up the sound, and they pawed the ground as they swayed their great heads side-to-side.

Howard whistled. "Theropod carnosaurs."

Jude asked, "T. rex?"

"Same niche. But I can't imagine a tyrannosaur could look that mean."

Iron muzzles clamped the beasts' jaws, the muzzle halves joined by a pin from which hung a chain. The chain, and two more chains that hung from rings that were pinned into each monster's head just behind the earholes, hung in arcs that gathered and ran beneath the beasts' centerlines. Reins.

A rigid harness attached each carnosaur to a two-wheeled cart behind it. A chariot. In each chariot stood two men, one who held the massive reins, and the other whose armor bristled with pistol holsters and a short sword. They wore the same black-lacquered helmets and armor as the Marini whose scent had spooked Rosy yesterday at the Fair.

I muttered, "No wonder she was scared." Those jaws could bite a duckbill in half at the neck.

The Marini infantry wore the same round helmets and armor, but dull blue. They carried rifles so slim that they were as obviously single-shot as the Casunis' pistols. They crouched in ranks, waiting.

The scurrying Marini troops wore brown tunics and helmets, and armor hung with scabbards that held short-handled axes. Squad-sized groups hefted phone-pole-sized logs, ran them forward as precisely as ballet troupers, then fitted them together to form causeways that bridged a creek bed that separated the Marini from the Slugs. Once the causeways were in place, the carnosaur chariots could roll to battle in seconds.

Ord said, "Sappers."

Jude cocked his head. "Sappers?"

"Combat engineers. And good ones."

Their officer stood hands on hips, directing his men. A man stumbled, his group dropped a log, and the officer ducked in and lent a hand. There was something awkward, yet familiar, in his gait.

I tasked Jeeb. "Right five." The image we saw centered on the officer. "Closer."

The back of the officer's helmet filled our image.

He turned, shouted to his men, and I saw that he wore a black patch over one eye. The other eye looked familiar.

THIRTY-ONE

I WHISPERED, "Bassin, you mendacious, one-legged son of a bitch!"

But my former hut-mate's duplicity was the least of my immediate concerns.

I motioned Howard to bring the holo generator, and to ride with me to Casus. Ord and Jude rode behind us.

Jude said, "Casus won't trust you. He thinks we're Marini."

"No. He thinks we're Marini half-breed crooks. He knows we won't cross him, because we want to run guns to him."

When Casus looked up and saw me, he frowned. Then he shooed his commanders back so we could parlay. "You've reconsidered my proposal?"

I shook my head. "I'm here to make you a better one. Free combat intelligence."

Howard had been hidden behind Rosy. He walked his mount out where Casus could see the translucent, holo-generated image.

Casus's eyes bugged, and he paled beneath his beard.

Casus had been surprised at our rifles, our armor, even

our 'Bots. They were next-year's models of things familiar to him. But moving pictures that hung in the air were
beyond any Bren human's imagination.

Casus extended his hand until his fingers touched the
image, then he thrust them into it, wiggled them, and
whispered, "You're not half-breeds! You're warlocks!"

"No. We're your best friends," I said.

I voiced Jeeb to pull back to panoramic. Once he did, I
pointed at the tree line visible in the image, and the Slugs
massed a thousand yards beyond.

I asked Casus, "You and these Marini aren't planning
this together, are you?"

"Make common cause with Marini?" He pointed at the
red head of one of the muzzled monsters, as it flickered in
the air, and Casus snorted. "I'd sooner bed that wronk."

"I didn't think so. But even if you aren't working together, you have a chance to destroy the devil whole, if
you'll take it." I pointed at the floating image. "If—"

Casus nodded, and pointed his finger at the Escarpment, where it appeared on the holo. "Yes! If my army
attacks frontally now, we'll draw the black worms in upon
us. Once they engage with us, the black worms will be
stuck to us like tar. They won't be able to wheel, and defend their flank. Then, if the wronkers attack the flank,
they'll roll the black worms up like a bed mat."

I said. "Otherwise—"

He nodded his huge head, and narrowed his eyes.
"Otherwise, the black worms will concentrate against
two weaker forces in succession, and defeat each of us
in detail."

TOT-link overhead holography might have seemed like

witchcraft to Casus, but he saw a battlefield as clearly as Lee had seen Chancellorsville.

Then he frowned. "But what if we cross the Escarpment, and the Fisheaters don't attack? The worms would drive us back against the cliffs and crush us."

"You can see that the Fisheaters are about to attack the black worms anyway. Why would they hold back?"

"The Marini are in league with the devil. These black worms are the devil reincarnate after three times ten thousand years. This may be a charade to lure my army into a killing box."

"No. Trust me. Us warlocks know who's in league with the devil."

He cocked his head at me, and nodded. "I suppose so, if anyone does."

"So I say attack. Together, your Clans will sweep the black worms from the field."

He pointed at the holo generator. "Your glass foretells victory?"

I took a deep breath, and tried not to blink. "Guaranteed. But you need to move fast, or—"

Casus spun away from me, and remounted his stallion.

He reared the huge white duckbill, and shouted to his army, "Today!"

Four thousand men fell silent. The only sound was banners snapping in the wind. Casus pointed his sword toward the Escarpment's edge. "Today, we send the devils back to hell! Forward!"

Four thousand warriors roared. Trumpets echoed through the ranks. Then the ground trembled under massive footfalls, and the vast army rolled toward us like a living tsunami.

Jude, an eyeblink before the rest of us, turned his mount toward the Escarpment, kicked it to a gallop and yelled, "They're gonna run us over!"

The remaining three of us, and the 'Bots, followed Jude. But the vast cavalry charge swallowed us up as it cascaded over the Escarpment into the impending battle and bore us along like leaves on a roaring wind that smelled of dust and overheated animal.

Howard bounced side-to-side, clutching his saddle. As his duckbill leaped over the Escarpment for the second time in days, Howard shouted to me, "You said we weren't getting involved!"

THIRTY-TWO

THE SLUGS BUNCHED into an armor-touching-armor phalanx, as the Casuni bore down on them.

Galloping two-ton animals occupy lanes wider than Electrovans on a Guidepike. Therefore, Casus's charge couldn't overrun the Slugs in a single, broad wave. The cavalry had to funnel itself into lines, one behind the other, and attack in successive, weaker pulses. And as the rear ranks waited to move up, they milled around, exposed to Slug artillery. Slugs were alien, but they weren't dumb.

Zzzzeee. Zzzzeee.

Slug Heavys tore into the Casunis all around us. Animals and men screamed, as soil, blood, and flesh whizzed through the air around us.

I swung Rosy around until I spotted Jude. This was his first sight of men, not alien blobs, torn into arms and legs and meat by battle.

He raised his visor, leaned off his mount, and puked.

Ahead of us, the leading ranks of cavalry and Slug infantry came within range of one another's direct-fire weapons. Casuni pistols rumbled, and Slug mag rail rifles howled in a collective moan.

Duckbills stumbled, then cartwheeled, tails thrashing, spraying blood. Riders somersaulted ahead of their mounts, until the reins in their hands snapped them to the ground.

Casus's stallion reached the Slug front rank, hurdled the black picket fence of Slug-warrior helmet crests, and Casus slashed left and right with his sword.

Casus's second wave slowed, as cavalrymen jerked left and right around fallen duckbills and riders. At slow speed the cavalry made better targets.

I peered to our left, through milling riders, at the distant trees that had hidden the Marini. If their commanders were all as smart as Bassin seemed to be, they should recognize the opportunity presented by the Casuni attack, and exploit it.

But nothing stirred.

I chinned up my magnification, scanned the tree line, saw nothing but leaves, and muttered, "Come on! Now!"

The Casuni third wave surged forward into massed volleys of mag rail rounds. In sixty seconds, the momentum of the charge would carry Howard, Judo, Ord, and me into the front rank.

"Ahh!"

Alongside me, a helmeted Casuni clutched the stump of his leg, the foot and calf torn away by a Slug Heavy.

Even as he fell, Rosy carried me past him.

I tapped my M-40's magazine to be sure it was seated in the well, thumbed off the safety, and stared one last time at the vacant tree line.

My blunder became obvious. The Marini wouldn't attack. Why would they? They could simply hang back, and watch an old mortal enemy and a new one punch and

counterpunch one another into hamburger. Decades of
fighting Slugs, Buddhists, Atheists, Christians, Muslims,
and assorted lunatics should have taught me that what
makes sense to one culture usually doesn't make sense
to another.

I clenched my teeth. The only thing that made sense to
me, at this moment, was to get Jude, and Ord, and Howard, through this debacle alive. Time enough later for re-
crimination about bad advice.

I spun Rosy until I picked out Jude again, a billboard in
his infrared-cheating crimson armor. I swiveled my rifle
muzzle toward his duckbill. I could shoot Jude's mount
out from under him. Then Jude would lie here in the rear,
nose in the dirt, away from the close-quarters battle. With
luck, the bulk of his mare's corpse would both pin him
to the ground and shield him from stray rounds. In the
chaos, Jude would never realize what I had done.

I aimed at the flank of Jude's duckbill. A three-round
burst would tear her heart out. She would go down in seconds, and die almost before she felt it.

Before I squeezed the trigger, I coughed, and paused
to wipe my eyes.

Bren gunsmiths had advanced far enough that their
single-shot weapons fired unified bullet-and-casing cartridges. But their gunpowder was decades away from
smokeless.

Already, the Napoleonic pall that spawned the phrase
"fog of war" shrouded the battlefield, so thick that its
acrid tang overloaded my helmet ventilator.

"About time!" Ord's voice rang in my earpiece.

"Sergeant Major?" I looked away from Jude, toward
the tree line.

Leaves parted, twelve feet above the ground, as a hundred crimson snouts scented blood.

The Marini carnosaurs stalked into the meadow, crushing saplings and tearing tree limbs like spider webs. Black-armored charioteers clung to the two-wheeled carts that the monsters dragged behind them on rigid booms. Infantry, rifles at port arms, trotted in the chariots' wake.

The carnosaurs stalked only as fast as a man jogs, heads turning left and right. The pins that had clamped shut the iron muzzles now dangled from chains beneath the animals' jaws, and the beasts flashed dripping teeth, and bellowed as they advanced.

"Wronnkk!"

No wonder Casus called them wronks.

The Slug Heavys lifted fire from us, shifted, and rounds began falling among the onrushing chariots. The respite we got was the first dividend paid by the suddenly-two-pronged human attack.

My clenched jaw relaxed one millimeter, and I stopped aiming at Jude's duckbill.

We were upwind of the onrushing chariots, but Rosy reared and squealed when she heard the wronks bellow.

I reined her in, hard, until she settled and stood fast.

Howard's mount squealed and reared as it dashed alongside Rosy and me, while Howard clung to his saddle.

Howard said, "This ends the debate."

"Debate?" I said. About my leadership abilities?

"Whether tyrannosaurid carnosaurs were predators or scavengers." He pointed at the advancing chariots. "They're too slow to chase down prey."

"They look plenty predatory to me." With their lumpy

red heads, slobbering jaws, and teeth like rusty cutlery, they looked as unfriendly as eight-ton buzzards.

"Mean isn't necessarily predatory. Big, ugly, and grumpy scares competition away from a carcass."

The first chariots reached the Slugs' flank.

Green-dripping armor crunched, then flew like crawfish husks. The carnosaurs rolled up the Slugs' lines, openmouthed heads scooping like bulldozer blades. Warriors that didn't get bitten in half got trampled beneath clawed feet bigger than they were.

The Casuni pulled back before the wronks, but humans and duckbills that moved too slow got mangled as thoroughly as the Slugs. So did Marini infantry who came within range of their own carnosaurs' jaws. The beasts were more unguided missiles than smart bombs.

As more Slugs turned to battle the Marini attack, the Slug ranks broke, and Casus's cavalry were able to slash through formations, pistols ablaze. Then the cavalry reloaded, wheeled, and slashed through again.

The only things that slowed the plodding wronks were themselves. Every few seconds, one would pause, drop its great head like a power shovel's bucket, and tear at a downed duckbill, a human corpse, or a limp Slug.

The halted wronk's charioteer would jerk the chains joined to the rings mounted in the beast's skull, and it would growl, raise up, and stalk forward, devouring the next animate object that came within reach.

Within fifteen minutes, the Slugs withdrew. I had never seen Slugs withdraw.

Marini infantry trailed after the chariots, shooting or stabbing anything that twitched.

The chariot force had split as it advanced, bypassing

and ignoring us, and the few Casuni cavalry around us. So a column led by chariots had swept by our position on the upslope side, and another on the downslope, isolating us in between.

Across the barrier created by the advancing Marini infantry, Casus looked at me, twirled his sword above his head, and pumped his fist.

I saluted him.

Ten Marini chariots, these pulled by duckbills smaller than the ones the Casuni rode, peeled off the upslope column, and rumbled toward the four of us, low-drifting gunsmoke swirling around their wheels.

The chariots wove around heaped Slug carcasses and dead Casuni duckbills. As the chariots drew closer to us, they swung wide around a wronk bleeding buckets from a neck wound. The beast lay on its side, its flank heaving, its chariot overturned behind it, with a wheel still revolving slowly in the wind. The monster lunged at the Marini as they passed, and a Marini fired a pistol round into the dying monster's eye.

Ord said, "Sir, those chariots are coming after us."

"Yeah. But why?"

The chariots approached in a line, then circled the four of us, while black-armored marksmen in nine of the chariots aimed outsized pistols at us.

When the chariots had surrounded us, they stopped, their duckbills panting.

We raised our rifles, and I felt the selector switch to be sure I was on full automatic. The four of us were outnumbered, but hardly outgunned. We could easily have mowed down the lot of them, while their handful of rounds would have pinged off our Eternads like beebe shot.

But the rest of the Marini army, not to mention their monsters, were more than we could handle.

I said into my mike, "Hold fire."

The brown-helmeted passenger in the tenth chariot stood, his shoulders crooked, and laid his gloved hands on the chariot's woven wood rail. He blinked his eye, and stroked the black silk patch that covered the other. "May I invite you four to accompany us, Jason?"

"What if we say no, Bassin?"

"You wouldn't get your questions answered, would you? And neither would I." He craned his neck, visored his hand above his helmet, and scanned the smoke-stained sky. "Where is that marvelous insect of yours? Where did your weapons and armor come from? Where did you come from?"

I glanced at Casus, who eyed us across the battlefield through his spyglass. "You may have trouble kidnapping us if Casus wants us to stay. He's curious about us, too."

Bassin shook his head. "Casus knows the law. Someone else outbid him fairly for you, and for your goods. Not even a Clan head who hates the Marini will interfere with the movements of another's property."

"Another? You. The law protects you, even though you Marini sleep with the devil?"

Bassin rolled his eyes. "Yes, even though." He sighed, then motioned to the riflemen in the chariots to lower their weapons.

I nodded to Ord, Jude, and Howard, and they followed suit.

Bassin reached inside his tunic, withdrew a folded parchment, then held it over his head in two hands. He pointed at two of his riflemen, who nodded. "As for kidnapping"—Bassin tore the parchment in two, and let it slip away on the wind—"I owned no slaves before today, and by this Act of Emancipation Before Witnesses, I hold none once again. Jason, you and your friends may accept my invitation—or do as you please."

Jude's whisper sang in my earpiece, as he pointed at the soldiers who still surrounded us. "Some invitation. He's a phony."

Howard whispered, "But I'm curious."

Ord said, "Your call, Sir. The devil you know, or the devil you don't know."

THIRTY-THREE

JUDE WAS RIGHT. Bassin was a phony who had fooled me once. If he fooled me twice, shame on me. But Bassin had also saved me—and the people I was responsible for— once. And that made me as curious as it made Howard. Curiosity won.

I turned to the other three Earthlings, and waved them toward Bassin. "Let's go sleep with the devil we don't know."

I patted Rosy good-bye, then the four of us got loaded one-each into chariots, and Bassin's little caravan bounced downslope toward the river.

The Marini chariots were built of light woven reeds, for speed. Their solid-axle suspensions were for durability, not comfort.

I clutched the side rails as we bounded along, and shouted to my driver, "Why do you carry a marksman along in each chariot? He can't hit anything from a platform this unstable."

The charioteer shouted back, eyeing my unfamiliar armor. "Did you train in a cave? The marksman isn't there to shoot the enemy. He's there to shoot the wronk if it turns. I'd sooner trust a Tassini than a wronk."

Our chariots skirted the Fairground. A few men struggled, loading corpses on wood carts and dragging them to pyres. They wouldn't be able to cremate a tenth of the bodies before the scavengers arrived. Too many fairgoers had been asleep in their tents when the Slug attack fired the encampment. The dead had to number in the tens of thousands.

My driver shook his helmeted head, and asked nobody, "Why would they do this? The Peace of the Fair has held for three centuries."

At the riverbank, Bassin's chariots fanned out among the handful of ships that remained afloat, some listing in the shallows, some beached by their masters to save them.

My driver reined up in front of a green-lacquered vessel a hundred feet long. A man with a close-cropped white beard stood alongside it in the shallows, uniform trousers rolled above his knees, hammering wood pegs into a hull patch with a mallet.

My driver said, "She looks sound. You did well to beach her."

The white-bearded man straightened, and stretched, hands at the small of his back. He nodded. "She'll float the Locks." He glanced back toward the Fair. "If my crew can scavenge replacement canvas, we'll be the first to sail away from this graveyard."

The charioteer said, "We need passage to the coast, Ship Master."

"Suddenly everyone does. Who's we?"

"I speak for the Queen's personal representative."

The Ship Master turned and cocked an eyebrow. "And who might represent Her Majesty this far upriver?"

"Bassin the Engineer."

The Ship Master snorted. Then he threw back his head, laughed and slapped his ship's hull. "Bassin? Bassin's dead!"

The charioteer said, "No—"

"You're blowin' up the wrong trouser! I was this close to Bassin"—the Ship Master held his thumb and fore-finger apart—"when the slavers offed his leg." The Ship Master turned back to his patch job.

"An engineer's faster on one leg than a pirate on two, Wilgan," said a voice behind me.

I jumped, as Bassin limped up alongside me, and I stared at the well-formed prosthetic that had replaced the crude stump below his left knee.

Wilgan the Ship Master froze at the sound, then turned, and wheezed. "Bassin?" His voice dropped to a whisper. "Mother's blood! The slavers took your eye, too?"

Nine hours later, at midnight, Wilgan's patched-up ship set sail down river on the tide that rose with the big, white moon. Four hours after that, Bassin, Ord, and How-ard slept below deck, with our gear and the 'Bots, while Jude and I sat in the prow, helmets off, breathing the river breeze.

Trees walled the riverbanks, and the chirps and hoots of small animals in the trees echoed across the water.

Jude looked up at the second moon. "The crew says the white moon raises the tide, but the red moon never does. That shouldn't be, should it?"

The altitude drop from the Stone Hills to the high plains to the valley of the Marin warmed the air and moistened it, but made two of my fingers throb. I tugged off my gauntlet, and rubbed them. "A lot of what you saw today shouldn't be, Jude."

Rehabilitation Command says organic prosthetics are "indistinguishable from natural limbs." Like Quartermaster says MUDs "taste farm-fresh." In the years since I acquired those two fingers, courtesy of a Slug Viper, every change in weather or altitude made them throb. My hand never let me forget that only the dead see the end of war.

"Today I saw men die, Jason. It made me sick. Does it get easier?"

"If it does, you should be a hangman, not a soldier. It still makes me sick. Every time."

"I should be bump with this. It's like living a holo game. Dinosaurs. Sword fights—"

"Half-naked women?"

He smiled, and looked down at the deck. "Jason, I'm sixteen. I've already—"

"I know. I was sixteen, too."

"But even with all the cool stuff, I—" He swallowed. "This is the longest I've ever been away from Mom. The first night in the hills, when it sleeted, I couldn't sleep. I just looked up at the sky and cried."

A lump swelled in my throat. I had been eighteen when the Blitz took my mother. I couldn't tell my godson to get used to it, tell him that forever was a long time. I touched his shoulder armor. "I miss your mother, too."

"You two get below!" Wilgan the Ship Master shouted from the stern, as the deck planks shook beneath the feet of running sailors. "You're in the way!"

We dodged scurrying crewmen as we lurched back to the hatch ladder, and I paused with my hand on the ladder rail and looked up at Wilgan. "What's going on?"

He let the wheel spin through his hands, then pointed toward a pale red stripe that grew on the horizon ahead. "First light, first portage."

"What does that mean?"

He rolled his eyes. "Did you fall off the Red Moon? Just keep your rifles loaded."

THIRTY-FOUR

AN HOUR LATER, AS THE SUN ROSE, Wilgan put us, his First Mate, and the rest of the crew ashore at a log ramp carved into the river bank. Termites, or Bren's analogs thereto, had swiss-cheesed most of the deadfall that littered the river's banks, but the logs that made the ramp looked, and thunked underfoot, solid and fresh-cut.

The ramp joined a ten-foot-wide trail that twisted across a flat gray rock shelf. Unlike the log ramp, the trail was ancient, worn two feet deep into the rock by the foot traffic of centuries.

The crew split into two groups, one ahead of us, one behind. Every man carried a slim Marini rifle, and had a pistol in his belt. Most had put on lacquered leather armored vests.

Then we marched off downriver, east toward the sunrise. Wilgan steered the ship back into the mainstream and passed us by with a wave, headed the same direction.

Within another hundred yards, the pines thickened around us, until we neither saw nor heard the river.

After two hours' walk, the trail grade dropped away. It switched back repeatedly, and the pines mixed more and more with deciduous trees until we were transiting a multicanopied, temperate rainforest.

The air grew warmer, sweeter with flower scent, and louder with bird cries and a distant rumble.

We had descended a thousand feet when the trail switched back at a bald rock outcrop from which we could look toward the river.

I walked up behind Bassin, who stood at the outcrop's edge. He still wore the wide brown bowl helmet and thick leather armor of the engineers we had seen the day before, and his hands were on his hips. I looked where he looked.

We stood on one rock wall of a gorge that dropped away a thousand feet below us, and rose a thousand feet behind us. To our right, the Marin thundered in a glistening ribbon, its falls cascading a half mile over a red stone escarpment, sparkling in the morning sun. Rainbows pierced the mist clouds that swirled up from the catch pool at the falls' base.

I sucked in a breath as I stared at the scene, then I gasped, grabbed Bassin's elbow, and pointed at the falls. "The ship! Bassin, the ship can't go over that!"

The First Mate, his rifle slung over a stiff leather vest that covered his shoulders, came up alongside us, smiling. Neither Bassin nor the Mate shared my panic.

I looked again at the falls, at insects crawling on the rocks alongside them, then chinned my magnification.

From the top of the escarpment to the catch pool at the falls base, a series of straight, manmade ribbons dropped. Up one set of ribbons crawled a water-filled box bigger than an ocean liner, within which a Marini sailing ship floated like a twig. Down the other set of ribbons crept a similar box, descending at the same pace the opposite box rose. The sprig of lacquered green floating in the descending box that counterweighted the rising box was our ship.

Howard stood alongside us and whistled.

The Mate nodded to Howard and me, as we stood open-mouthed. "I seen The Locks on the Marin six times, and the other Three Wonders twice each. But I still get the chills."

Howard nodded to the Mate. "Astonishing civil engineering. Who built it?"

The man stage-whispered behind his hand to Bassin, and pantomimed a dig in Bassin's ribs, without touching him. "He's having us on, hey, Colonel? Like any sod in this world don't know Bassin the Engineer!"

Bassin turned to Howard. "I had a hand in the design."

Colonel. Bassin, who grubbed rocks from the mud with a flat stone, was not only a commander of combat engineers, he was the architect of at least one of the numbered wonders of this world.

I leaned out over the crag, and peered downriver.

My knees trembled, and I clutched a sapling while I leaned. My Airborne School Ticket reads "Restricted," because the shrinks diagnosed me with Treatable Acrophobia. "Treatable" means "dope-able," and I don't dope. So whenever I had to drop, I just used to squeeze my eyes shut, then order Ord to boot me down the extraction tube. I say this proves my command deficiency. Commanders have no phobias. Ord says true commanders just control them.

The trail below switched back and forth down the cliff,

then threaded along the river bank among the trees, as far as I could see.

I pointed back at the slowly descending ship, where Wilgan rode, and asked Bassin every infantryman's first question. "Why do we have to walk?"

Bassin frowned, then pointed at the catch pool. Around the slowly revolving wheels of the Locks' great mechanism floated curved sticks and twigs. Under magnification, they resolved into the ribs and guts of ships that looked like they had fallen half a mile. "The transit's risky. Only Masters stay aboard."

"Then why even bother? This trail looks like it was here for a long time before you built the Locks."

Bassin turned to me, crossed his arms, and squinted. "Why does a man of your age and intelligence ask a child's questions, Jason?"

The whole truth would have sounded like lunacy or lies. "I'm new here," I said.

The First Mate looked over his shoulder at the trees behind us, then said to Bassin, "Best keep moving, Colonel. Howlers."

I frowned, and rubbed my throbbing phony fingers as we descended deeper and the air got thicker.

The trail into the gorge narrowed, so our column broke down in side-by-side pairs, three yards apart. I wound up striding alongside Bassin.

He picked up our discussion like we hadn't been interrupted. "You know the Queen's full title is 'Deliverer of the Stones, Protector of the Clans of Marin, and Sovereign of the Near Seas.'"

I knew nothing of the kind, but I nodded.

Bassin said, "Note that her charge to Deliver the Stones

comes before everything else. Every year since The Beginning, every child has been taught that Bren delivers or Bren dies. Every year since The Beginning, Stone demand has grown."

The trail traversed a steep section cut through limestone, improved with iron hand grabs corroded by time, and flats cut in the stone where a climber could rest a heavy load. I, much less one-legged Bassin, couldn't descend and have breath left for talking.

What Bassin had just told me linked up some clues. The Slugs were nothing but galactic shakedown artists. Cough up our Cavorite fuel, and nobody gets hurt. For centuries, the Clans had evolved their entire society to feed their visitors' Cavorite habit, even if it meant cooperating with other Clans. But then, why had the little maggots blitzed the Fair yesterday, for the first time in so long that most people seemed to recognize Slugs only as pictures from a book?

Skrreek!

The trail flattened out, and I looked up at the branches that arced overhead. A chittering banana-colored lizard as large as a monkey swung from a vine by a forelimb, and bared its teeth at me.

I waited for Bassin to catch up. Well-formed or not, the prosthetic that replaced his leg made him wince with every step. The leg that Wilgan had said slavers had cut off. I pointed at it. "Bren delivers. Even if the society has to turn to slavery to meet the quota?"

Bassin shrugged. "I'd die on the pyre before I'd live in chains, or suffer another to do so. But Bren has known The Block, in one location or another, for millennia."

"But if you could find a way to deliver the Stones

without slave labor, so it wasn't a necessary evil, then your society could change things. You designed these locks to make slave stone carriers obsolete?"

He shrugged again. "That was one reason. The slavers thought the locks would hurt their business. And they were unhappy with the fellow who designed them. My locks have hurt the slavers. But the few slaves saved were like tears saved from the ocean. Jason, necessity long ago became convenience. Too many men are comfortable owning other men."

I gazed again at the huge scale of the slowly rising and falling locks, then narrowed my eyes at Bassin. A full-bird Colonel like Bassin may be a demigod to a sailor, but the locks were a project for a preindustrial society like the Marini on the scale of the pyramids.

Before I could frame anther question to Bassin, another banana lizard squealed its high-pitched chitter at us. I asked Bassin, "Is that a Howler?"

In the distance, low-pitched screams grew, echoing off the gorge's walls like a fire brigade racing to a five-alarm.

Bassin unslung his rifle, then smiled. "What do you think?"

THIRTY-FIVE

FIVE HUNDRED YARDS FURTHER, the half dozen sailors on point slowed and peered ahead at a place where tree boles narrowed the trail to shoulder width, forming a dim tunnel roofed by leaves. Bassin and I walked first behind them. Jude, Ord, and Howard trailed us, and a half-dozen more sailors trailed them.

The screaming grew to a chorus in the surrounding trees.

The First Mate halted our group with an upraised hand, and said, "Let's get a count."

He raised his rifle, and fired a shot in the air.

The screams swelled until I had to chin down my audio gain.

A living thing sprang into the path between the tree boles. It was a stump-tailed lizard covered in rust-colored feathers, except around a flat face, streaked in red and purple and set with dark eyes. Its forelimbs were longer and thicker than its haunches, and it sprang forward on them, screeching, then hopped back, like an angry baboon, but as large as a gorilla.

A dozen more Howlers sprang into view, some leaping

out into the path, some dangling from overhanging limbs by a single forelimb.

"Bag off!" The First Mate reloaded his rifle, then thrust the muzzle forward at the big one that had appeared first, and shook his head. "Don't make me take that pelt of yours!"

The Howlers just jumped, swung, and screamed more, but when the sailor stepped one foot forward, the big Howler dropped one foot back.

The First Mate crept forward, rifle in one hand, and waved the other hand for us to follow. "Steady on, mates."

Rifles up, we shuffled between the shrieking Howlers, one so close that I could count his teeth, as his spit splattered my visor.

The ones on the trail would leap forward, bare their teeth, then retreat, then repeat the behavior. The ones in the trees would swing down, slap at a helmet, then pull themselves back up onto a branch.

Bassin whispered, "Once they realize that we're only passing through their territory, they'll draw back."

Howard whispered in my earpiece, "Isn't this great?"

Blam.

Behind me, a Howler wailed in a different key.

I spun, and saw a sailor in the rear group clutching his bleeding shoulder. The rifle of the man alongside him smoked from its muzzle.

Both men stared down at a Howler, lying still in the middle of the trail at their feet, like a rusty sack of feathers.

The howling died, and the air became so still that the only sound was the Falls' distant whisper.

The First Mate sighed. "Young male on his muscle."

He glanced around. "That will back them off for an hour." He walked back to the man the Howler had bitten, unwrapping a bandage, and turned to the others. "Right. Rest ten minutes."

The man with the rifle knelt on the trail, drew a knife from his belt, and began to skin the dead lizard.

I walked to the kneeling man, and stood beside Jude. Howard bent, hands on knees, peering at the carcass. "With that pelvis, it's a theropod. More parallel evolution."

I said, "Parallel my ass. Wronks are like Earth carnosaurs. Duckbills are like Earth duckbills. Earth didn't have dinosaur chimps."

"Not parallel to Cretaceous fauna. To primates. This reptile occupies a niche the great apes occupy on Earth." Howard swung his hand at the steep wall the trail clung to. "Besides, do you think an upland species' skeletons are going to get buried in the river as often as fish bones? If we haven't found primate-mimic dinosaurs on Earth, we just may not have looked in enough places yet. You see what this all implies about the people here, don't you?"

I rolled my eyes. "No. Tell—"

Deep in the trees, a single Howler cried.

I looked down at the meat that had been a living thing minutes ago. Was the cry his mother's?

Jude stared into the trees, toward the sound.

I tapped his shoulder, and pointed toward the trail ahead. "Time to move on."

We saw no more Howlers, but six hours later, when we rejoined the ship and Wilgan, we could hear the lizard monkeys far behind us.

This planet scared us Earthlings. But our technology

would scare Bren's natives like we were space invaders. Which, of course, we were.

Therefore, that evening, as Wilgan sailed us on toward the coast, only us four Earthlings and Bassin clustered around the holo generator set up on the forecastle table to review the data Jeeb had gathered in his reconnaissances.

Bassin passed his fingers through the holo image, with his mouth widened into an "O." "It's done with light, then?"

Howard nodded.

Bassin shook his head, slowly. At least he didn't call us warlocks.

Ord switched the display to map view, and there we were, a flashing red icon inching down the River Marin toward its delta, which was straddled by Bren's one great city, Marinus.

Bassin unrolled parchments, borrowed from Wilgan, on the table, weighted their corners with brass map instruments, and looked back and forth between those charts and Jeeb's images.

"Jason, your chart shows the bar we just passed, which was new after the past spring's flood." Bassin tapped the corresponding spot on Wilgan's parchment, which showed blue water. "But Wilgan would have grounded if he relied on the Admiralty's chart."

I pointed at our map. "This is an embellished real-time image. You're seeing the world through the eyes of the flying thing you saw me talking to when we were Casuni prisoners."

"The insect is a machine?"

I pointed at the brass map scale in Bassin's hand. "As much a machine as that thing."

"The machine talks through the atmosphere, as real as my voice. But as invisible as my voice, too?"

"Basically."

He closed his eye, and sighed. "I need a moment to absorb this."

I asked Bassin, "Why are we going to Marinus?"

Bassin opened his eye and said, "We aren't."

He drew his finger across his map, down the river, past the city, to the mouth where the river emptied into the sea. "We're bound for the Sea of Hunters." He turned his finger and traced south along the coastline a hundred miles. "By this time of year, the Queen has taken to the Winter Palace. I'm going there because she prefers even bad news fresh."

I glanced at Howard as I raised my eyebrows. Did Bassin also suspect that it was our arrival on this planet that had brought the Slugs down upon Bren like a dung storm? I said to Bassin, "Bad news?"

"We can't talk through the air, like you can. The Queen will have no news of the Fair until I reach her."

I pointed at a bold red line on the map that paralleled the coast, from a half mile to several miles out to sea, all the way from the north end of the chart to the south end. "What's the red line?"

"Six fathoms."

"Is that a territorial limit?"

The First Mate called down the hatch, "Colonel Bassin, we need those charts back up here, Sir!"

As Bassin rerolled the charts, he smiled. "You could say the Red Line marks territory, yes."

The more I knew Bassin, the better I liked him. Except

that he hoarded information like an Intel dick, based on what he thought was someone's need-to-know.

The two days from that time until we reached the sea were a nice boat ride, punctuated by descents through two more sets of locks. After Bassin's Locks, these locks were boring, with gates into and out of chambers that flooded and drained, lowering our ship in fifty-foot increments.

The ship got towed from chamber to chamber by hawsers attached to bellowing purple and brown draft animals bigger than elephants, with horns that had been sawed off by their handlers. Howard pronounced them analogous to ceratopsian dinosaurs.

So complete had been the Slugs' destruction of the Marini trading fleet that I didn't see another sailing ship on the Marin. But smaller local packets swarmed the river. A few moved under sail, but most of them were rowed by ranks of slaves, twenty-five to a side, like Greek galley rowers.

We ghosted through the Marin estuary in a single rainy night, so all we saw of the city were flickering lights and spots of red glow. Bassin said the glow marked the forges of the weapons foundries, which had burned continuously for three hundred years. Wilgan said the glow was the raging wickedness of places that separated sailors from their senses and their pay.

The next day dawned clear, with the ship already well down the coast. Wilgan and I stood alone on the rain-washed deck, side by side. The Ship Master steered as we ran south before the wind, while below, the others took breakfast. I had laid my armor out on deck to air, and Wilgan and I chewed warm biscuits the cook had brought us.

The shore lay a mile from us, and small boats from fishing villages already dotted the shallows as they put to sea.

A half mile distant, to the east, toward deep water, a smaller ship, black sails full and taut, passed us like we were anchored.

Wilgan glanced seaward at the fast mover and swore.

I smiled. "Are we losing a race?"

"Red Line runners are smugglers, not racers."

"Red Line?" I pointed at the smaller ship. "That's where the depth hits six fathoms?"

Wilgan nodded. "She's bound for the Tassini ports south, with a belly full of rifles, by her draft."

I nodded. "The smuggler stays on the Red Line so the government won't stop him?"

"But if he strays too deep, the Coasties will be the least of his worries." Wilgan glanced seaward again, and swore again. He locked the wheel, then stepped to the rail, where an ivory horn, carved from a tusk as big as an elephant's, swiveled on an iron mounting. Wilgan swung the horn toward the smuggling vessel, blew into it, and a note echoed across the waves.

The black ship ran on, oblivious.

Wilgan blew another note, then pounded his fist on the huge horn, and shouted. "You're too far out, you fool!"

"What's wrong, Wilgan?"

The white-bearded sailor stretched his telescope, and peered through it at the other ship. "Put on that hat of yours with the spyglasses, and you'll see."

I picked my helmet off the deck, dropped it on, and focused my optics on the other vessel.

A couple of crewmen scurried over the black ship's

deck, and the ship's bow rose and fell as it cut the sea. "It looks like nothing—"

"Too late! Dumb bastards."

Seaward of the black ship, a faint wake curled a vee across the waves. I zoomed on it.

At the vee's apex, a fistful of dirty-white snakes broke the surface, fifty yards from the black ship, and closing on it.

White smoke puffed at the ship's bow, then I heard a rifle's faint crack.

The snakes rose further out of the water, and resolved into two dozen suckered, flailing fire hoses, in front of an eye as big and yellow as a stop sign.

Wilgan said, "Kraken."

The hoses wrapped the ship's hull, and as the ship heeled, the monster's body came up out of the water. It looked like a giant squid, but with more arms. The beast was stuffed into the end of a tapered shell fifty feet long, like writhing ice cream in a cone.

The others clambered up from below at the sounds of Wilgan's horn, and the shot.

Howard said, "Holy moly!"

The black ship's masts snapped like straw. A single human scream echoed across the water, then the monster slid backward and pulled the black ship under like a tarantula dragging a beetle into a burrow.

Jude gripped the rail, eyes wide. "What was that?"

Howard whistled. "That's the biggest nautiloid I've ever heard of!" He turned to Wilgan. "Are these top predators numerous?"

"Top predator?" Wilgan snorted. "That pissant?" He rapped on the tusk horn he had blown, which was as big around as my thigh. "This warning horn's made from a rhind tooth."

Wilgan held up his biscuit between thumb and forefinger, and pointed at it with his other index finger. "Kraken." He opened his mouth, then pointed at his tonsils. "Rhind."

Wilgan popped the biscuit into his mouth, bit down, swallowed, then grinned. "Any questions?"

Howard said, "Oh."

I stared at the empty sea that rolled where the smuggling ship had been, as half-chewed biscuit caught in my throat. I gulped, then asked Wilgan, "Could we sail closer to shore?"

Wilgan returned to the wheel, laughing and slapping his thigh. "Top preddy-tours!" He shook his head. "Landlubbers!"

I walked to the bow, where Bassin stood.

I said, "Is a rhind the scariest thing on this planet?"

Bassin peered ahead, where the sun glinted off something atop a distant headland. I zoomed on the glint, which was a turreted complex of white stone that commanded a coastal bluff.

Bassin pointed at the bluff. "Her Majesty will receive us at noon. You may decide for yourself."

THIRTY-SIX

The beast that menaced Howard, Jude and me for our last few hours at sea was neither kraken, rhind, nor Queen.

Ord was not about to allow any troops with which he was associated to go before royalty looking unsoldierly. We polished armor, shaved, cleaned weapons, re-polished, re-shaved, re-cleaned, washed everything that moved and scrubbed everything that didn't. Even Jeeb, who Bassin asked us to bring along so the Queen wouldn't think he was nuts, got his radar-absorbent fuzz groomed, and Jude polished Jeeb's optics.

Bassin changed into a dress uniform that included a broad-brimmed suede hat with one side turned up, and plumes that looked like Howler feathers. He even traded his engineer's axe for a gold one so dainty it couldn't have cut prime rib.

The Captain of the Queen's Household Guard met us at a jetty railed with rhind teeth.

I whispered to Bassin, "Did the Queen pull those?"

The Captain commanded two dozen Householders, who wore polished armor, with helmets crested with purple feathers, and who carried Marini rifles with gold bayonets fixed.

The Captain saluted Bassin, who returned it. "The Queen will receive you in the Morning Room."

The Morning Room of her Majesty's Winter Palace stood far enough above the sea that a visitor climbed two hundred twelve stairs to reach it, with breath-catching intervals along corridors hung with tapestries.

Along the way, we passed fifty more eyes-front House-holders, each guarding a corridor junction or mammoth carved door, each armed with a gold-bayoneted rifle. Not one blinked at Jeeb, who skittered ahead of us, six legs crackling over the marble floors.

We also passed one unsmiling woman. She wore a high-necked, floor-length dress as smooth as her skin, and as black as her skin was white. Scarlet feathers winged each sleeve, and crystalline jewels ruffed her collar and wrists. The dress fitted her so closely that she couldn't have hidden a coin under it, and the material seemed to be leather as thin and supple as silk. Her dark hair swept up, gathered by combs that matched the sleeve feathers, and she carried her chin high and serene.

I didn't know whether she was a Countess or a chambermaid, but I bet on chambermaid, because she dropped her eyes as she passed Bassin.

When she saw Jeeb, her sleepy eyes bulged, but she said nothing. Jude turned to watch her slink away, and tripped over Jeeb. I nearly stumbled into a Household Guard myself.

We made one stop before we got to the Morning Room. Howard, Ord, and Jude were taken off through double doors into a two-story paneled room Bassin said was the

Queen's Library. Then Bassin took me and Jeeb and the holo generator to meet the Queen.

The Winter Palace's Morning Room turned out to be an awninged roof terrace long and wide enough to land a twelve-passenger bouncer, surrounded by rhind-tooth ivory rails. These teeth were carved with battle scenes and inlaid with gold.

Like every proper castle since Beowulf's day, the Winter Palace commanded all approaches to it. Beyond the terrace rails, and beyond battlements along which House-holders marched, spun, and countermarched, I saw all the way across the Sea of Hunters.

On the horizon, like a chalk line, rose the low coast of Bren's other continent. That was a distance of twenty-two miles, according to Jeeb. The water was an epeiric sea, according to Howard. A salt water puddle that would shrink to nothing over the next few mere million years, barely worthy of the name "sea." According to me, with its kraken and rhind, the Sea of Hunters was one more bad neighborhood on a planet lousy with them.

To the north and west stretched green farmland, cut into facets by an irrigation-canal network that watered Marin's southern breadbasket. To the south, beyond the canals, the land remained the wind-scoured red desert of Tassin.

The Captain of Householders announced us, then backed off the terrace.

The only object on the shaded terrace was one bent-wood chair.

Alongside it, her back to us as she gazed across the Sea of Hunters, stood the Deliverer of the Stones, Protector of the Clans of Marin, and Sovereign of the Near Seas of Bren.

The Queen pivoted with her hands on a jeweled cane

and faced us. She stood five foot three, and looked no heavier than two pounds more than a hundred. She also looked no younger than two decades less than a hundred. Her hair was white, her skin pale and creased, but her eyes shone as sharp as gray diamonds. Her dress was cut like the one on the younger woman, but silver, with ermine-white feathers, and brighter jewels.

When she saw Bassin, her eyes widened, and she sucked in a breath.

Then the Queen blinked and extended her hand. Bassin stepped to her, knelt, and kissed it. "Greetings to her Majesty on her seventy-second birthday."

The Queen waved him to stand. "Bassin, never remember a woman's birthday unless you forget her age." She appraised Jeeb, with his faceted optics that looked like onyx eyes, and she arched her eyebrows. "Or you bring her jewels."

Bassin shook his head. "I bring news."

She sniffed. "Bad news, if I know that tone. What's bad enough to raise you from the dead?"

The old woman inched toward Jeeb, in small steps, then bent forward, and eyed him through a round lens she held on a short gold stick.

Jeeb's optics swiveled up at her, like two jeweled Oreos, and he whined.

The Queen's eyes widened, then she straightened, shuffled back to her chair, and rested her hand on its arm. With her back to us, she rapped her cane on the marble floor. "Out with it, Bassin! Bad news doesn't improve with age, and neither do I."

Bassin stepped alongside her and steadied her with a hand on her elbow. "The Receivers crossed the Wall. The

Peace of the Fair was broken. The Fleet was destroyed. So many died that some bodies were burned on pyres, Casuni-fashion. The smoke turned the sky black to the horizon. The Stone Trade is shattered."

A leathery pterosaur glided above the sea and wailed. Wind flapped the terrace awning.

The old woman's shoulders sagged, until she seemed to shrivel inside her silver gown.

Then she straightened, turned toward Bassin, and whacked his ear with her cane, so hard that the crack echoed across the water. "That's a vile joke to scare an old woman on her birthday. I expect better from my only child."

THIRTY-SEVEN

MY JAW DROPPED so far that I chinned my command-circuit audio alarm, and Ord's voice came back. "Sir?" I chinned the alarm off.

Bassin rubbed his ear. "It's true, Mother."

The Queen stepped around her chair, and collapsed into it, trembling and rubbing her forehead. "How?"

"The Fair went like it has three hundred times. Then the Receivers appeared without warning."

"Are you sure—"

"They look like the old storytellers said they look. Worms in black armor. Once the Peace of the Fair was broken, we assembled troops, and counterattacked. Casus himself led a counterattack, simultaneously."

The Queen jerked her head toward Bassin, and narrowed her eyes. "You trusted that slobbering barbarian?"

Bassin glanced over at me, paused, then continued, "Pure coincidence. But the black worms were wiped out. To the last one."

The Queen sighed, and stroked her temple. "For now."

"For now." Bassin nodded.

"Your spy play has brought the end of the world upon us."

Bassin shook his head, and ticked off on his fingers. "No! Mother, *because* of the census, I now know reserves, and I know deliverability. I have calculated percentage leaked to smugglers. Any fool can see it was the right thing—"

"The only fool I see is the one whose adventuring has cost his eye and his leg. You could have ordered...." The Queen reached up and touched her son's cheek, below the eye patch, and her eyes glistened with the beginning of tears.

Bassin reached up, held her fingers, and said, "Mother, surely you never taught me that ordering others to die can be right?"

The Queen stood, and sighed. "It can not. But it can be less wrong."

Bassin said, "Because of the census, I know we've delivered—"

The Queen stiffened. "Of course we delivered! Your grandmother would strike me from her grave if we didn't. And her grandmother before her, and so on, and so on." The Queen's eyes narrowed again. "Then what's brought the end of the world upon us?"

Bassin looked over at me, and waved me toward them.

Crap. Why did this always happen to me? Bassin had brought me along to blame me for the end of the world.

Following Bassin's example, I popped my neck ring, tucked my helmet beneath my arm, and walked over and knelt before the Queen.

Bassin said to her, "I present Major General Jason Wander."

The Queen tapped my cheek. "Stand with me, General."

General Cobb was right. The title got Advisees every time.

After I stood, she stared up at me, then frowned at my half-breed eyelids. "You're—ah—as young as my son."

She rapped her knuckles on my sleeve armor. "I know the forge of every armorer in Marin. Where did your mother bear you, General?"

I sighed, and hoped that, for once, the truth would set me free. "Colorado."

The Queen's eyes narrowed and she swayed. I braced for her to whack my ear with her cane.

Bassin said, "Shall we sit, Mother?"

The Queen rapped her cane again, this time against her chair. Footmen in green silk livery appeared and set a table in front of her chair, and two more chairs alongside it.

Bassin seated his mother at the table's head, and as he stepped around to the table's foot, he motioned me to fill the remaining side chair.

A footman stepped forward with a covered tray, but Bassin waved him off, and motioned for me to set up the holo gen on the table.

I waved it on, and the first shimmering image that popped was an overhead of the Fair, smoke, corpse piles, shipwrecks.

The Queen's eyes widened. "Dreams?" She snorted. "I don't govern by sniffing janga. I leave that to Tassini Headmen."

Bassin sighed. "No, Mother. This is quite real. As

though you were looking through the eyes of the six-legged machine."

The Queen stared at Jeeb, whose hydraulics hummed as he squatted on the terrace beside me and preened his antennae.

"You miss my meaning, Bassin. Dreams can be more real than flesh. And this is no machine." She stared down at Jeeb.

Bassin rolled his eyes. "Mother, its bones are steel. It just looks—"

The Queen looked in my eyes. "The little one belongs to you, General?"

I held Jeeb's Department of Defense salvage title. "Yes."

"And whatever the little one's bones are made of, whatever hardheads like my son say, you believe the little one is alive?"

Everybody knew the notion that TOTs imprinted their Wrangler's personalities was anthropomorphic crap. Only an idiot would admit he believed otherwise.

The Queen didn't blink. "Well, General?"

I breathed deep. "Yes. He reminds me of someone I was close to. A comrade in arms."

The Queen turned to Bassin and sniffed. "You see?"

Bassin threw up his hands. "See what, Mother? I just explained for you how I can rely on what the machine may tell me. No more and no less."

The Queen stared at me. "And I am explaining for you, Bassin, how I can rely on what the General may tell me. A lie would have been expedient. The General, here, told me the truth, even though it made him look a fool. A man who lies about small things will certainly lie about large ones."

She turned back to her son. "Bassin, men only rule machines. Kings rule men. Pay attention. Learn how to do the job you're born to, while I can still teach you!"

I let out my breath.

Not the first quiz I passed by dumb luck. If her Majesty wanted the truth . . .

I cleared my throat. "Your Majesty, the truth is that we came here from another world. In a ship that sails in the sky. We captured it from the black worms. We've fought them before. And, because we know them, we think now you're going to have to fight them, or they will wipe out every human being on this planet, most especially the four of us."

Bassin's jaw dropped, and he muttered.

The Queen shot a look at him, then at her cane, and Bassin clammed up. "General, if you tell me it is so, it is so." Then she leaned forward on her elbows and stared into the holo gen. "You may brief me."

I sat back in my chair and exhaled. Now I was on familiar ground. I'd winged a hundred Advisee briefs, if I'd winged one. Sometimes even to royals doing a ceremonial stint in their country's uniform, though Colonel Bassin was no toy soldier. I began, "As to Mission—"

The Queen waved her hand. "Defer the Mission Statement. Please begin with Enemy Situation."

I raised my eyebrows. Her Majesty was no toy soldier, either. At least, she was no stranger to a logical military briefing format.

I waved the generator to map view. Jeeb's images from

the last few days unreeled, beginning with a pull-back shot from the Fair.

I said, "The Slugs—we call the black worms Slugs, because they look like small animals we find in our gardens—"

The Queen nodded. "My Garden Master kills those with salt. The name is apt."

"These are tougher. We tracked this group back to where they came from."

I scrolled the map back along the Slugs' approach, hundreds of miles north of Marinus, then back onto the fifty-mile-wide isthmus that joined the Clans' continent to the other landmass to the east. The image showed in luminous green the path Jeeb's sensors had identified as the Slug infantry's axis of advance. Slugs didn't normally have an axis of retreat. They always fought to the last maggot. But not this time.

I froze the image, and pointed at the object center screen. "The remnants of their attacking force retreated behind this barrier. They don't usually retreat."

Bassin said, "We call it the Millennium Wall. The Receivers—the black worms, your Slugs—built it long ago, at least a thousand years. And the old stories go that it took a thousand years before that to build it."

I said, "We don't know what your measurements are, but we measure it as seventy miles long across the isthmus, counting the wings that extend out into the sea." I pointed. "Dense as granite, and three hundred feet high, along all five walls."

Bassin frowned. "Five walls?"

I pointed. "Behind the first one, each separated from the one behind it by an obstacle belt two miles deep."

Bassin leaned forward, stared at the fortification, and shook his head slowly.

I asked, "Don't your measurements agree with ours?"

Bassin said, "We have no measurements, beyond this first barrier. No one who went over the wall ever came back."

The Queen stared, too. "We have never seen beyond the Wall. We deliver the Stones to the Gate." She pointed at a road that wound down the isthmus' center spine, then ended against the Wall. "When the Stones have been removed, that is our signal to deliver more."

I scrolled the map east, on across the isthmus, then on into the eastern continent's center. I pointed. "Then you've never seen this."

Centered in a cleared area bigger than the Cairo Crater rose an iridescent blue egg-shaped mountain.

I raised my eyebrows at Bassin.

He turned his palms up as he shook his head. "No."

I said, "We've seen one. It's an incubator ship. We call it a Troll-class. Inside a Troll, the Slugs can grow a new army in ten months."

Bassin said, "We just defeated an army of theirs. We can defeat a new one every ten months forever, if we have to."

I shook my head. "What we defeated was one tenth of a normal Slug assault force. Probably just what could be spared on short notice from the skeleton garrison that has operated this outpost for centuries. Until now, all these Slugs had to do was sit behind the Wall they built to keep you out, retrieve the Stones you left at the Gate, and, probably, load cargo ships when they called to pick up the Stones."

I zoomed in on the Troll, and pointed at the forest belt that surrounded the Troll's mile-wide base, and long, low stone buildings that curved around a stone pad big enough to land a Firewitch. "From the height of the redwoods grown up around it, and the deteriorated surrounding stoneworks, we think this ship's been dug in for centuries. Probably millennia."

Bassin shook his head. "So, the Slugs didn't retreat. They came to get something. My census counters say the Stones at the Fair disappeared. Perhaps the Slugs got what they came for, then left. And that will be the end of it."

The zoomed image of the Troll resembled a swollen beehive. I pointed at openings that ringed its top, and shook my head back at him. "But these vents opened during our overflight. We think that means the Slugs are starting up the incubator. If they intended to let you stay around and keep delivering, they wouldn't need a new army. And they wouldn't have attacked you in the first place."

The Queen nodded.

I looked from Bassin to the Queen. "Let me be clear. We believe those reinforcements will number in the millions. Slug warriors are—" I paused, and cocked my head. Howard's Spook autopsies showed that a Slug warrior was a single-purpose element of one enormous organism, more white corpuscle than independent-minded GI. The Marini barely had microscopes, much less a word for "corpuscle."

I said, "To explain Slug warriors, I need a word you can understand."

The Queen said, "'Evil' will suffice."

I nodded. "Slug warriors never disobey orders. They never complain about the food. They retreat only tactically, and they never surrender. We believe that new army's mission will be to eradicate human life from Bren. And that army won't rest until it accomplishes that mission, or its last warrior is dead."

The Queen closed her eyes, and frowned. Then she looked at me and asked, "Do you believe that army will succeed?"

"If the Clans fight separately, yes."

The Queen tapped a finger on the table. "You speak from experience?"

"I've fought them twice."

"To what result?"

"We killed all of them that came at us, and they haven't come back since."

I didn't say that we had won the war. I had always believed that we had won only in the way that the American Colonies had beat the British, and North Vietnam beat the United States. We were too far away and too much trouble, so the Slugs left us alone.

I continued, "But Bassin tells me all the Clans together number twenty million people. Our world's *losses* alone were sixty million. And, with all respect to Marin's armorers, our weapons were more advanced than yours."

The Queen stood, walked to the terrace rail, and gazed across the impassable sea. It had insulated her land from an enemy that her bloodline had coped with for centuries. "Bassin, join me, please."

Bassin and his mother whispered together.

I glanced down at Jeeb, and tapped my ear.

He whirred up on his hind legs, and swiveled his directional mike toward Bassin and the Queen.

The State Department might have frowned at my

unmannerly eavesdropping. Bad etiquette fills advice columns. Bad intel fills graveyards.

My earpiece crackled. "—trust him, Mother, most certainly. But don't rush."

"Your grandmother's grandmother didn't rush to resolve the Hejus! The Clans still bleed for her hesitation."

"Exactly. Jason will suggest that we ally the Clans. He doesn't know how impossible that is. Casus would eat your heart off the peace table, unless some Tassini Headman cut Casus's out first!"

The Queen sighed. "And I would do the same if God favored me with a sharp knife."

My earpiece hissed silence.

I chinned my radio and whispered into my mike. Nobody really knew what made Slugs tick, but the Army put up with Howard because events usually confirmed his hunches about them. "Howard, why did the Slugs raid the Fair?"

Howard's voice buzzed in my ear. "Jason? I found something down here in the library that you need to know. Do you remember I said I had a theory about the human population—"

"I found something out up here, too. Answer the question."

Silence.

Howard said, "Okay. The Pseudocephalopod sees humans like humans see penicillin. A disease organism that can perform service beneficial to Its health. A virulent new strain of us, the disease, that can travel independently between stars is a nightmare to It. And, suddenly, here we are. If we contaminate the humans on this planet, the disease could spread, and threaten Its life."

"If the Slugs kill all the humans, how will they get their Cavorite?"

"It's decided to eliminate the dangerous middlemen. But It will probably keep Eolithic-level slaves, like the Tassini prospector Bassin impersonated, to perform mining and transportation."

I nodded. "If we four gave ourselves up, would the Slugs leave these people alone?"

Howard said, "We've already contacted this population. To mix metaphors, how much of a tumor would *you* leave in your body?"

I nodded. "So the Slugs will wipe these people out, just to make sure they get the four of us? Howard, how much would you bet that your hunch is right?"

More silence.

Then Howard said, "The farm. Jason, don't do anything until—"

The Queen and Bassin returned, so I clicked off.

Her Majesty looked me in the eye. "General, I have a favor to ask."

THIRTY-EIGHT

"WOULD YOU LIKE MY ADVICE?" I asked the Queen.

"General, in my home, it is customary that I ask the first question."

My cheeks warmed. "Yes, Ma'am."

"Why would you share advice? If this is not your world?"

"I hate Slugs."

The Queen nodded. "These Slugs. They killed your comrade, the one who lives on in the little one?"

Howard's only living relative, his uncle; my mother, and Ord's all died in the Blitz. The War killed Jude's father, all four of his grandparents, and his six maternal aunts before he was even born. And those who had died while they served with me were family, too.

I said, "The Slugs killed lots of people we all cared about."

"Then you have Blood Feud with the Slugs, General."

I shook my head. "I don't so much hate the Slugs. I hate what they've done. So, get together with the other Clans. We'll share any intelligence we have, advise your commanders about tactics, weapons design—"

The Queen said, "General, my counterparts among the Casuni and the Tassini would not follow me into battle, any more than you would follow the Slugs. Centuries of Blood Feud divide the Clans."

This wasn't the first time I had to referee rival tribesmen, even royals. With the really stubborn ones, I even had to threaten to withhold American advice and logistic support. They sulked awhile, but, eventually, they picked one of them to lead, even if they had to draw straws. Then we watched them get on with their mission. I called it my come-to-Jesus speech.

I cranked up my righteous indignation, and said, "Well, with due respect, your Majesty, *some*body's going to have to step up." I poked my index finger into the tabletop. "*Some*body's going to have to talk all of you into following *some*body." I poked the tabletop again. "Then *some*body is going to have to assemble, and train, and command an army, and lead it into battle. Or else, by your next birthday, *no*body is going to be alive on this planet to celebrate, except Slugs, and slaves." I stared into her eyes and didn't blink.

The Queen rocked back and raised her eyebrows.

Royals and warlords always recoiled at the come-to-Jesus speech. Nobody ever told them what they had to do.

The breeze died, and a blue-feathered bird fluttered down to a terrace rail and twittered.

Her Majesty hadn't cracked a smile in an hour, but she beamed at me. "I could not have said it better, General! I thank you. I thank you so very much." Then she laid her thin hands across mine.

I looked across the table at Bassin. He smiled at me.

My come-to-Jesus speech had never worked *that* well before. "Thanks for what?"

The Queen said, "Why, for volunteering to be that somebody."

THIRTY-NINE

CRAP. CRAP, CRAP, CRAP.

I said, "I don't have—"

"Every resource of Marin will be placed under your command."

Ord whispered in my earpiece. "Sir, we need to talk to you."

I said to the Queen, "Might I have a few minutes with my staff, your Majesty?"

Ten minutes later, the Captain of Householders pulled the double doors of the Queen's paneled library shut as he backed out and left us four Earthlings alone.

Howard hung from the upholstered rungs of a sliding ladder attached to the two-story bookshelves, and scooted sideways like a skateboarder, scanning book spines.

"Goddammit, Howard! Get down here!" I stood with my fists stabbed down onto the polished wood top of the room's central table. Ord stood beside me, his hands clasped behind his back. Jude leaned across the table, and snatched something that looked like a pink banana from a gold bowl in the table's center.

I said, "The Queen doesn't want us to advise her. She

wants us to take the rap for the whole war. She wants me to get those other barbarians to dance around the maypole with her. It's ridiculous."

"A neutral commander seems logical under the circumstances, Sir," Ord said.

"Circumstances? Unite barbarians who cut each other's hearts out? So they can fight the scourge of the galaxy with black-powder pistols?"

Howard said, "We probably have at least ten months' incubation time."

I rolled my eyes. "Ten months to do what?"

Jude paused with a peeled banana in his hand. "To do the right thing."

I shook my head. "I've never really commanded more than seven hundred soldiers. And that was on Ganymede. It was more like Peter Pan and the Lost Boys than being a General."

Ord said, "Sir, Jeeb's 'chips carry more know-how than the Army War College and the MIT Library put together. And we have MAT(D)4's equipment."

"That equipment's U.S. Government property, Sergeant Major."

All three of them stared at me. Okay, the government-property argument sounded stupid.

I asked, "What's got into you three? Sergeant Major, you know we can't take over some aliens' war! We can't even shoot at the Chinese!"

"Our present situation is dissimilar, Sir. Our prior formal obligations and loyalties hardly apply."

I nodded. "And we have no other obligation or loyalty to these people, do we?"

Jude, Howard, and Ord looked around at each other, like they were about to mutiny.

The thud of armored knuckles on wood echoed through the library. I walked to the library's double doors, and yanked them open. The Captain of Householders saluted me. "Her Majesty's apologies, Sir. But she asks how much longer you might be, Sir."

I glanced at my 'Puter, and grumbled under my breath. Queen, schmeen. She wasn't pushing me into a decision. I said, "We've only been in here five minutes. Is her bus leaving, or what?"

The Captain knit his brow beneath his chrome visor as he mouthed, "Bus?" Then he said, "Why, no, Sir. Your ship is."

I knit my own brow and mouthed, "Ship?"

"A minute longer, Captain." I pulled the doors closed, turned, and said to my three mutineers, "Am I missing something here?"

Howard frowned. "Yes."

FORTY

HOWARD LAID HIS HAND on a stack of books on the table. "I did some quick reading while you were gone."

"Real quick," I said.

"You remember I said I had a theory about the human population here? But I had to fill in some gaps?"

"And you couldn't tell us before?" Sometimes Evil Spook Howard shanghaied Goofy Geek Howard, like Dr. Strangelove.

Howard asked, "You remember you were surprised to encounter Bassin? Encounter a human on this planet?"

"I'm over it." I shrugged. "Humans evolved faster here." I frowned as I thought about Jude and his cosmic rays. "Is that what's got you puckered? Are we getting mutated here?"

Howard shook his head. "Nothing like that. Remember the Howlers?"

I nodded. "The lizards in the monkey niche."

Howard picked up a book. "This is a dictionary. There's no Bren word for monkey. Or any kind of primate." He waved his hand at the shelves. "In fact, no reference to any mammals bigger than mice, except people."

I shrugged. "It's a big library. Maybe you missed a book. Hell, it's a big planet. Maybe these people still have exploring to do. They evolved from *something*."

Howard held up another book. "This is a history treatise. The Casuni and Tassini split with the Marini over religion."

"From what I heard upstairs, it was three hundred years ago, and they still hate each other."

"The core difference that caused the split dates back even further. The Casuni and Tassini believe God created man in his own image, and placed him in this world in the beginning."

"Most religions believe that. They got kicked out for it?"

"The Marini didn't kick them out. The Casuni and Tassini sects co-existed among the Marini for centuries. Then they felt persecuted, and left."

"Why?"

"Too many Marini came to accept the growing body of conflicting paleontologic, anthropologic, and archaeologic evidence."

"Which said?"

"That the Pseudocephalopod placed man on this planet thirty-five thousand years ago."

I raised my eyebrows. "Man was created by evil giant snails? That *might* be a bitter pill."

Howard shook his head. "It's the simplistic way the Casuni and Tassini see it. But the key word is 'placed,' not 'created.'"

I narrowed my eyes. "You're saying the Marini believe that the Slugs imported people to this planet?"

"Jason, these people aren't merely like us. They are us."

FORTY-ONE

———

I SHOOK MY HEAD. "No. We had carnosaurs, they have carnosaurs. We had duckbills, they have duckbills. You said yourself it's just parallel evolution."

"That's the point. We evolved over millions of years, until modern man emerged about thirty-five thousand years ago. According to the fossil record of Bren, *Homo sapiens* just popped up here about thirty-five thousand years ago, with no evolutionary precursors. We know the Pseudocephalopod traveled between the two planets often enough that our Firewitch came here like a riderless horse to the nearest barn. The circumstances aren't clear, but the Pseudocephalopod appears in Bren's legends from their beginning."

The Captain of the Guard knocked at the door.

I hollered over my shoulder, "In a minute!" I turned back to Howard. "Why would the Slugs import humans from Earth to Bren?"

"The Pseudocephalopod in its exploration of the universe discovered two things at about the same time, on two planets only weeks' travel apart. A rich new supply of Cavorite, and a primitive species that was smart enough, and sufficiently resistant to Cavorite's poisonous properties, to take over the dangerous mining of it. It put Its two discoveries together."

"Slugs didn't visit Earth thirty-five thousand years ago."

"We don't know that. What should we have found? A missing persons report on a cave wall?"

I shook my head. "Wouldn't an organism that can fly between stars have come up with something more sophisticated than enslaving primitive mammals? We would have."

Howard said, "We milk cows. We use cats to exterminate rodents. And I call a system that's worked perfectly for thirty-five thousand years sophisticated."

It explained why the Queen didn't bat an eye when I claimed to be from another world. It was in their lore. Even if Howard was wrong, the Slugs threatened us as much as they threatened every other human on the planet. And we were stranded here, anyway.

Ord and Jude stood beside Howard, with their arms folded.

"You three believe this? These people's ancestors got kidnapped from their parents? Which are us? So we should fight alongside them?"

Howard said, "Unless you have a better theory."

Jude said, "Unless you have a better plan."

Ord said, "It's your call, Sir."

The Captain of Householders knocked on the door again.

Command was an orphan's journey. But, if Howard was right, the journey these orphans had taken made it look small.

I shook my head. "I disagree."

The three of them frowned.

Jude said, "But, Jason—"

I raised my palm as I looked at Ord. "You said our prior formal obligations don't apply here. But Congress declared war on the Slugs six days into the Blitz. There was never any geographic limit on the declaration. No treaty ended the war. Neither you, me, nor Colonel Hibble has been discharged. Mr. Metzger, here, can enlist underage if a parent or appropriate guardian consents. And I do."

Jude grinned.

I looked around at them, sighed, and slapped my palms on the table. "So let's go save the human race. Again."

FORTY-TWO

I'M NO SWABBIE, so I wouldn't know a barge if I water-skied across one, but the Queen's Barge turned out to be nicer than it sounded.

It was a sailing ship slightly bigger than the one we arrived on, but, by my best estimate as we sailed north retracing the route we came by, the Royal Barge sailed twice as fast.

Maybe the Barge was faster because of its sails, which were striped in two shades of silver. Maybe it was the onyxwood hull, which sizzled as it cut through the sea. Maybe it was the crew, so pressed, polished, and square-cornered that even Ord admitted they were okay, for Squids.

The speed couldn't have been helped by the weight of the Queen's traveling library, which Howard inhaled to learn The Natures of our new home world. It couldn't have been helped by The Basket, a rope nest that dangled from the fore spit, from which a rotation of the best harpooners in Marin kept watch. I was told that any kraken that strayed into the submerged kelp forests that choked the shallows inside six fathoms would be dead meat. But

I was glad the Ship Master stayed well shoreward of the Red Line.

And the Barge's speed certainly wasn't helped by the weight of her tableware.

The evening following our afternoon audience with her Majesty, us four Earthlings and Bassin sat around the Salon's onyxwood dining table, while light from the swaying chandelier sparkled off the solid gold plates in front of us.

Howard held up a shellfish on his fork. "On Earth, we'd call this a flexicalymenid trilobite."

Bassin shrugged shoulders now covered by the gold epaulets of the Crown Prince of Marin, then smiled. "Our Chef has sautéed those each first night at sea since I was three."

Howard chewed his forkful. "These should have gone extinct at least a hundred million years ago. Not only should they not coexist with humans, they shouldn't coexist with dinosaurs."

Jude asked Howard, "Why do things go extinct?"

Howard poked his glasses back on his nose. "Rise of competing species. Environmental change."

"Like the comet and the dinosaurs?" Jude shoveled a second helping onto his plate.

Howard nodded. "A bolide impact *did* close the Permian contemporaneous with trilobite extinction. And—"

I pointed my knife at Howard to stop his ramble, and said to Jude, "From Howard, that's a yes." I had ten months to learn what made the Clans tick. Howard could discuss bugs on his own time.

I turned to Bassin as I stabbed my sautéed fossil. "Is this why the Plains Clans call Marini Fisheaters?"

"Eight hundred years ago, the Plague of Men swept Bren."

Howard frowned. "Plague of Men?"

Bassin nodded. "Women suffered mild symptoms, but the male organ blackened horribly, then fell away, entirely. The histories say the plague was carried in these shellfish."

"Paugh!" Jude spit trilobite into his napkin, then stuck his tongue out and scrubbed the cloth against it.

Bassin blinked, but kept his eyes on me. "The church taught the shunning of seafood. When the plague had run its course, the shunning stopped, except among the most religious. Historians date the split of the Clan stocks from that time. The cultures diverged for five hundred years. The flight of the Tassini and Casuni to the Highlands, the Hejus, came three hundred years later. The Clans have been at war since."

Bassin's royal ancestors weren't Abe Lincoln. They preserved slavery, but failed to preserve the union.

I said, "Your grandmothers tolerated religious bigotry. They allowed your society to fragment into perpetual civil war. They made bad decisions."

Bassin smiled. "I can not improve my grandmothers' decisions. I hope to improve their grandson's."

A steward appeared, and Bassin circled a finger at our plates, then stood. "It is customary to take mead on deck between courses."

On deck five minutes later, Bassin, Ord, Howard, and I sipped sweet wine in the twilight, and watched a Master Harpooner teach Jude how to throw a barbed iron, with a bulb that could be loaded with explosives at its tip, into a round, yellow target the size of a kraken eye.

I asked Bassin, "Can a harpooner kill a rhind?"

"Sailors believe they can harpoon everything, after a few cups." He raised his glass, and smiled. "But they also say 'I don't have to outsail the rhind. I just have to outsail the other boat.'"

"Well thrown!" The harpooner clapped Jude on the shoulder, and stared at an iron quivering in the yellow target's center. The harpooner turned to Bassin. "It's in this one's blood, Sir!"

Bassin stared toward the sunset. "Jude's father died a hero?"

"His father saved our world. Jude drags around big expectations."

"I understand. Blood chose me, too."

I stared at the sun as it set in the west, and smelled the continent on the breeze. Somewhere on that landmass were Casus and the Headmen of the Tassini, who had to be persuaded to join forces after centuries of Blood Feud. And that would be the easy part of a job I hadn't even applied for.

Blood had chosen Bassin. Maybe blood was choosing Jude. Whatever had chosen me for command, I had my work cut out for me.

The steward climbed out of the hatchway and tapped a gong with a feathered mallet, to announce the next course.

Bassin stood aside, bowed a notch from the waist, and extended his palm toward the hatchway. "After you, Commander."

I nodded, and stepped ahead of the man who would become king.

The next morning we reached Marinus. In the days

since we had passed through the city, word of the massacre had spread downriver to the city.

The Royal Barge, which drew crowds even in normal times, could barely pull alongside a stone quay without crushing the skiffs—and the river boats rowed by slaves—that bobbed in the estuary. The bank itself was so choked with pedestrians that the crowd forced a dozen people off the quay and into the water. A few people hurled rocks and garbage at the Barge.

I pulled Bassin back from the Barge rail, and said to him, "I thought everybody here was used to war."

He shook his head. "The perpetual relation of the Clans, one to another, is war. But, at least during my lifetime, war has been waged in the form of uncivil talk punctuated by cross-border raids, not genocide. Few people in any of the Clans had no relative at the Fair."

Most of the dockside people didn't realize we had come from the sea, not upriver, and they screamed for news of the missing. A crying woman held up a framed oil portrait of a man in a magenta striped tunic. I had seen a magenta tunic like it thrown on a burning pyre as we left the Fair. Many waved newspapers that looked to have printed front-page casualty lists.

The first great terrorist attack of the turn of this century, and the first reactive wars that followed it, had shocked America. Seven thousand Americans dead from a population of three hundred million. No one would ever know the toll at the great Fair and in the battle that followed, but the Queen's Secretary estimated a hundred thousand dead from a population of ten million, just among the Marini. The wonder was that this shock hadn't collapsed Marinus into its own foundations.

We dropped off Ord and a 'Bot loaded with all the Earth hardware we thought the armorers of Marinus might be able to copy. The Minister of Armaments was supposed to meet us with his carriage, but it took a half hour for Marini infantry to clear a path through the crowds to the quay. It took ten minutes more to convince the Minister's coachman that the 'Bot wouldn't run away if he didn't tether it to the back of the carriage.

A half hour further upriver the Minister of Natures met Howard and Jude at the University's quay and hauled them off to the Great Library of Marin, where Howard would download anything we could use into his 'Puter, and would arrange for a meeting among the Clans, if we could form an alliance.

At every settlement upriver, the crowds lined the banks, but the closer we got to the headwaters of the Marin, the quieter they became. I suppose it was the black smoke from the pyres that drifted above them on the wind. That and the smell of burned flesh.

The Royal Barge's Master didn't care much for taking the Barge up the great Locks, even though his future king had designed them. With the Marini fleet sunk like the Spanish Armada, other large vessels were scarce, and the down lock had to be loaded with rocks for counterbalance. Bassin himself did the math with a little abacus made of shell and bone. But Bassin knew his business, and the trip was uneventful. Even the Howlers seemed subdued.

We anchored at the Pillars after sunset, though the Red Moon already hung overhead and lit the skeletal carcasses of the Marini fleet all around us. Bassin and I stood at the rail, looking out at the ash heap. Jeeb perched alongside me.

Bassin said, "You know, I'm not afraid to accompany you."

I glanced down at his trouser leg, which covered the prosthetic reminder the slavers had given him. "Bassin afraid" was an oxymoron.

I said, "I know."

"Our intelligence stopped trying to infiltrate patrols into the Casuni lands decades ago. The Casuni are excellent trackers, and they shoot first. I had to go in alone, myself, and act the part of an addled Tassini."

"You *had* to go, yourself?" I rolled my eyes.

"The Stone Trade is literally life to us. Our picture of the Trade was decades out of date. Our agents went in, but none ever came out."

"Maybe *somebody* had to go. Did you just want to get out of the Palace, so you could personally whack some slavers?"

He rubbed his eye patch. "That aspect ended badly. Mother complains that I delegate poorly."

I rubbed the plate in my own thigh. "Ord says I do, too."

Bassin stared into the water, sighed, then clapped his palms on the rail. "So. That is why I delegated to you the job of Allied Commander."

We had had this conversation before.

The first thing an Allied Commander needs is allies to command. Half of Bren's human combat power resided with the Casuni and the Tassini. So the first thing I had asked Bassin to do was have his diplomats propose an alliance, maybe by a note in the diplomatic pouch to the embassy in the Casuni and Tassini capital cities. I knew about such stuff. Back home, Ord and I once diplomatic-pouched a copy of a captured parliamentary resolution back to the U.S. Spooks.

However, the Casuni and the Tassini were nomads. They had no diplomatic pouches. They also had no diplomats, no embassies, no capital cities, and no parliaments.

A delegation would have to track down and persuade Casus, and also the Council of Headmen of the Hundred Encampments of the Tassini.

However, if a Casuni, a Tassini, and a Marini were placed in the same tent, the only thing that would prevent them from stabbing each other would be their desire to choke the crap out of one another first. Therefore, no delegation member could be Marini, Tassini, or Casuni.

That drained my delegate pool down to one.

I said to Bassin, "I don't like the way I'm being inserted."

"The herds are migrating this time of year, so Casus moves his encampment daily. We will allow Casus to find *you*. What you must do is walk to the escarpment. I counsel that you skirt the ruins to the north. Better cover, there. Cross the escarpment, let a Casuni patrol pick you up. They will take you to Casus."

"Eventually."

Bassin nodded. "Eventually."

"We don't have till eventually. And a prospective commander shouldn't arrive in custody."

I whispered to Jeeb, and he telescoped his wings, and whirred off into the dark.

Bassin frowned. "Where is the little one going? Jason?"

I checked moons-set time on my 'Puter, then went below to gather my gear.

"Jason, how do you expect me to help you if you won't tell me what's going on, and you won't allow me to do my job?"

Bassin was a good guy. Better than good. But he had been the Crown Prince all his life. Even if he didn't realize it, he was still micromanaging my show, sharing what he knew with me only when he felt like I needed to know. The time to fix the relationship was now, not when the crunch came.

This little charade would put Bassin on the receiving end of micromanagement and of being denied information, but it wouldn't kick up much dust between us. Bassin was smart. He would figure it out, give me breathing space from here on out, and we would still be able to work together.

A few years ago, I would have handled the situation by sulking until I blew up. I was maturing into a commander. Or I was turning into a devious total dick.

FORTY-THREE

THE BARGE'S LONG BOAT put me ashore at the Pillars under the 2 A.M. light from the slivers of two moons. I carried full pack, my M-40 cross-slung, and two snacks in silk sacks that Bassin had the Chef prepare, after I explained my plan.

I stood knee-deep in the lapping water as Bassin reached over the gunwale and shook my hand. "Remember—"

I nodded. "Don't sleep on sand in the desert. The screw worms will crawl up my ass. *You* remember, if I'm not back in eight days, head back downriver. There's no prep time to waste, and Howard and Ord can teach you more than I ever could." I tapped the time display on my wrist 'Puter. "Do I have to make it an order?"

He grinned. "No. But it's going to be interesting to take them from someone besides Mother."

Bassin's swabbies turned the long boat without a whisper and rowed him back to the Royal Barge, and I slogged ashore.

For a graveyard, the Fair was noisy.

The debris was animated by scavenging shadows slinking from corpse to corpse. The night echoed with challenges snarled across rotted prizes, and with cracking as teeth crushed bone. Ash twisted up from the wreckage like whirling ghosts.

In the distance, milling duckbills and other livestock, abandoned in the chaos, bleated.

It was improbable that the Slugs or Casuni had posted pickets to secure this mess, so I maxed my vent filters against the stench and clambered through the ruins.

I saved my stealth for evading Casuni patrols once I crossed the escarpment. I had no time to waste negotiating with patrols, and less inclination to begin a peace mission with a firefight.

A half hour later, I had left the Fair's ruins behind and headed up the grassy slope that led to the escarpment, alongside the tree line where the Marini chariots and the wronks had lain in ambush. My pack weighed me down enough that I had to chin my suit temp down a degree to retard sweating, and my thighs burned.

A tree limb cracked.

I stopped, turned, and nodded down my night goggles.

In the trees, something snorted.

I realized too late that cross-slung on my back was the last place my M-40 should be at that moment. Howard had said wronks in the wild were scavengers. The Fair's stench had attracted every carnivorous freeloader within trotting distance. First would have come the bugs, then the birds, then the rat- and hyena-sized scavengers. A monster as big as a wronk could afford to come late to the party, then scare off the small fry, or eat them, too. An eight-ton buzzard fifty feet away in the bush was the last thing I hoped to hear tonight.

Then a transponder blip flashed on my visor display, above the trees.

"Found her, huh?" I said.

"Yip." Jeeb chirped in my earpiece.

"And Casus?"

"Yip."

Rosy, all twenty-four feet of her, ambled out of the trees, walked to me on all fours, and slimed my faceplate with her tongue. I had bet that Rosy was too smart to be caught by men, or eaten by wronks, and would stay near the river's water supply.

"I missed you, too." I scratched her neck wattle as I looked around.

If skittish Rosy wasn't spooked, the wronks hadn't arrived yet.

I untied the silk ribbons on Bassin's snack bag, and fed Rosy orange turnips, one by one.

An hour later, after moons-set, and at the 3 A.M. low tide of a sentry's alertness, Rosy pattered up a draw into Casuni territory, as silently as a two-ton reptile can with a human aboard. Then she stretched out at a gallop that not even a Casuni patrol could match.

With Rosy's savvy and sense of smell, and Jeeb's overhead surveillance, I evaded two predator packs and one Casuni hunting party camp. We followed Jeeb across the high plains until, an hour before sunrise, Rosy stood, huffing and snorting steam, in a boulder clump that anchored a rise overlooking Casus's camp, a half mile distant by my rangefinder display.

I dismounted, opened the second silk snack bag, and fed Rosy more turnips, while I ate the breakfast the Chef had packed in the rest of the second bag. Outside my Eternads, the High Plains air was so cold it seemed hard as glass. But stars smothered the black sky, the wind calmed, and Rosy, insulated by bulk, body fat, and millennia of adaptation, purred like an antique bus at idle.

I tasked Jeeb to Watch and Wake, set Rosy to graze the slope away from Casus's camp, snuggled down into a crevasse, and darkened my visor to sleep black.

The last thing I thought, as I drifted off, was that I was getting the hang of this place.

Blip. Blip. Jeeb woke me.

The ground trembled beneath my shoulder blades.

FORTY-FOUR

I LEVERED MYSELF OUT OF MY CREVASSE, and looked up at the sun without even checking my visor's clock. I'd slept three hours.

In small groups, and from all directions, two hundred mounted riders approached Casus's encampment.

"Crap!" If Casus was distracted by raiders, not to mention killed by them, he wouldn't make much of an ally.

I chinned my optics. Every rider was Casuni, wearing polished armor. A black cape streamed back from every man's shoulder. But their weapons remained holstered, and each party drew along behind it a duckbill loaded with a cargo of what looked like bundled sticks.

I swung my head to Casus's camp. At the center of a hundred yurts rose one twice as tall and wide as the others. Casus's scarlet pennant snapped in the frigid wind, attached to a swaying pole that stuck up through the yurt's billowing central smoke hole.

In the open space in front of his yurt, Casus stood, hands on hips, and watched the incoming riders. He wore a black cape over his shoulders, too.

The first group of riders reined up in a dust cloud, and its leader dismounted, walked to Casus, and hugged him.

The next group thundered up. Its riders hugged Casus, then hugged the members of the other group.

The scene was repeated as group after group rode up, until Casus's yurt was visible only as a shadow through a yellow dust cloud.

I whistled up Rosy, swung into the saddle, and patted her neck. "Ever crash a party before, babe?"

FORTY-FIVE

CASUNI PISTOLS CAN'T HIT A BLIMP outside sixty yards. So, although I was staring down four hundred drawn pistol barrels as I rode toward Casus's encampment, Rosy and I got within shouting distance without Casus's guests wasting a first shot.

I popped my visor and yelled, "Casus! It's Jason!"

He squinted through the dust. "Who else would it be in that armor?" He waved the others to lower their pistols.

When I dismounted, Casus bearhugged me so hard that my armor's surface stress display winked amber. Then he held me by my shoulders at arm's length. Tears ran down his cheeks and into his beard. "How did you know?"

"Huh?"

"Yulen spoke of you."

I nodded. "Yulen. Sergeant Yulen? He did?"

"He said you were the cleverest idiot he ever met."

"Oh."

"That's quite a compliment from a Sergeant."

"True."

"Yulen was never so complimentary of my own sons. He taught them all, you know."

"I didn't know." Then I remembered the young caval-ryman at the Fair, that Yulen had taken under his wing. Black cloaks. Tears. "Sergeant Yulen is dead?"

Casun stared at the bare ground at his feet. "Soon. He's receiving the balms."

"How?"

"That battle at the Fair. A bullet from the black worms."

It had been ten days, and they didn't call it first aid for nothing. But maybe. I felt for the Aid Kit in my thigh pocket. Over the last century, U.S. Adviser-team medics had made more friends with Plexytose and Penicillin than the State Department had made with cummerbunds and canapés. "Can I see him?"

"Of course." Casus hung an arm around my neck, and walked me toward his yurt.

A Casuni woman as gnarled as driftwood held open the big yurt's entry flap, and Casus dragged me inside.

Through smoky haze drifting off the central fire pit, I recognized Yulen's tangled gray hair. He lay on his back atop a pile of hides two feet tall. His belly was bare, but robes covered his chest and legs. His eyes were closed, and his breathing shallow.

An old woman in bulky Casuni robes sat cross-legged beside Yulen, rubbing a clove of something across his forehead and humming.

A second woman spooned liquid from a pot on the fire, opened his lips with thin fingers, and drizzled the liquid into his mouth.

A third woman knelt alongside Yulen's pale, bare belly.

I stepped close to the old soldier, and asked Casus, "May I?"

Casus waved the three crones back, and their eyes burned at me.

I knelt, set my helmet on the hide-covered floor beside Yulen, and whispered, "How you doing, Sarge?"

Yulen's eyelids fluttered, he stared past me, and his lips quivered. Then his eyes closed, and he let out a thin moan.

I tugged off my gauntlet, and laid my fingertips on his forehead. Hot. I said, "Let's have a look."

I shifted my weight, bent over Yulen's middle, and grimaced. An entry wound as wide as a golf ball had torn Yulen's belly open, three inches left of his navel.

Slug mag rifle rounds are bigger than a man's thumb, and they hit hard. An unarmored body shot usually made a corpse, not a casualty, out of a normal-sized GI. Casuni were big and tough, and that was probably why even a Casuni as old as Yulen was still hanging on.

I felt for my aid pack, my hands trembling. There might be a chance.

I sniffed in the direction of the pot the woman had spooned liquid from. It was the peppery janga broth Casus's man had brewed at his impromptu first-aid station, days ago, back at the escarpment. Then I sniffed Yulen's wound, and the odor of janga overpowered even the rot of infection.

My shoulders sagged, and I stopped fumbling with my Aid Pack.

A primitive triage for intestinal perforation was to feed the patient an odoriferous liquid. If the intestine was perforated, the smell leaked out the wound.

Casus's balm squad had been testing Yulen, and they had found the worst. A GI could save a buddy who took a clean shot through the shoulder or thigh, if the bleeding could be stopped.

But this Slug round had torn open Yulen's intestine. His gut had been flooded with excrement for probably ten days now, and had incubated enough infection to kill ten elephants.

In the history of warfare, gut shots probably killed more GIs than any other single battlefield wound. Ord and I had tamperproofs stuffed with the latest and greatest battlefield meds. If we had known at the time.... But all the antibiotics in New Bethesda wouldn't save Yulen now.

I remembered Yulen, threatening to cut out our lazy tongues one minute, then sneaking us bread the next, and I blinked back tears. I kissed the old man's burning forehead, then stood, and wiped my eyes.

The woman with the clove knelt down again, resumed rubbing Yulen's forehead, and said to me, "This will help your Sergeant's fever."

"My Sergeant?" I nodded. "Yeah, he is."

Sergeant Yulen died just before noon.

Casuni funerals, like those of most cultures, are as much a product of environment as of theology. At spring thaw, the frozen tundra of Bren's High Plains would vomit up corpses buried during her long, bitter winter, if the ground could be dug at all. And during that winter, BTUs are too valuable to waste.

Therefore, at sunset, Yulen ascended, presumably to heaven, in the form of a roil of oily black cremation smoke.

Kindling is as precious as warmth on the High Plains, which is why the mourners who had ridden from all across

Casus's domain brought a tribute of twigs and branches to build Yulen's funeral pyre.

The mourners formed a circle around the roaring pyre, swaying to the slow beat of one hide drum. I stood among them, downwind, fighting back nausea at the smell of burning flesh.

Casus stood on the opposite side of the pyre. He motioned me to circle around and join him.

When I stood alongside him, he whispered behind his hand, "Stay here. The women like downwind because it's warmer, and they don't drink. But the mead tastes better upwind."

The women left the circle, and returned with mead-filled horn flagons, which they distributed one to each man.

The drum stopped, and the only sound was the wind beating across the prairie, and the crack of burning branches.

Casus raised his cup. "Farewell, brave Yulen."

All the men raised their cups, and I followed along. Then they spoke a single toast, with one voice, and drained their cups.

I figured, given observed Casuni propensities, that the funeral's next phase would be for everybody to get hammered like Irish at a wake.

But on the High Plains the nights are too cold for long speeches or parties, mead is hard to come by, and the dehydration caused by alcohol is unwelcome in the cold. So everybody just stood around until the fire stopped putting out heat, and the wind picked up, then they scurried for their yurts.

Casus insisted I spend the night at his place, covered in robes, on a hide pile so thick it would shield a princess from a pea, so the two of us could visit about matters of mutual interest. I figured the topic would be smuggled guns. But across the chamber, he was snoring like an unsuppressed GATr before I could get a word out.

I lay on my side, stared into the fire, and shook my head.

Yulen's funeral left me empty, guilty, and depressed.

Empty for the loss of a good man. Yulen had suffered, though an old soldier like him probably preferred to succumb to a bullet instead of a coronary.

Guilty because, while my emotion for Yulen was genuine, I was going to play this bond with Casus for all it was worth, like some used-Electrovan salesman.

Depressed because in the morning I was going to ask Casus to ally with the Marini and the Tassini in a war. And now I had to do it after Casus had told me, after the toast I had heard earlier in the evening, that it was the same toast that had ended every Casuni funeral for the last three hundred years.

The toast went, "May paradise spare you from allies."

FORTY-SIX

THE NEXT MORNING, Casus and I walked out on the prairie, bent forward against the wind. Low clouds hung a dirty-gray ceiling above us, spitting pellets too hard to call snow that skittered across the frozen ground. I carried my M-40, four 40-round banana magazines, and a sack of groundfruit.

Groundfruit was the brown tuber that Bassin had lived on while he spied on the Stone trade, the one that made the hardtack cakes Yulen had shared with me. Groundfruit grew wild year round, everywhere beneath the High Plains, and Casuni women harvested it, ripened it, then pestled it into flour that made the leathery bread that served as the staple of the Casuni diet.

A groundfruit was the size of an adult human head, but more durable, so it also served as the gold standard for Casuni target practice.

I laid a row of groundfruit on a rock ledge, then we backed off two hundred yards. I tapped a magazine into the receiver, and plinked the gourds forty times without a miss, varying positions prone to kneeling to standing, without reloading. For my last five shots, I swung the optics aside, and, using just the iron sights, popped one fruit five times, so it yo-yo'd across the distant ledge like a rabbit.

I pointed to the selector switch's full-auto position. "This makes it talk like a woman. Useful in close quarters."

Casus stared downrange with his mouth open so wide that ice pellets ricocheted off his tongue, and asked, "May I try it?"

I reloaded while we walked up closer to the targets. I decrypted the grip safety and handed him the rifle. He plinked a few groundfruit, then thumbed the selector switch to full auto, sprayed a burst, and whooped, even though he didn't hit much. "We must have these! What's the price?"

"You understand that repeating rifles would have to come from the forges of the Marini."

He winked, then held up his hand, and rubbed his thumb against his forefingers. "I know this sad song. The price will include a surcharge to cover certain—expenses—to avoid the Bitch."

"I can not only save you the bribes to the Queen's people, I can equip your army for no money at all. Not just with rifles. Stuff you've never even dreamed of. That thing that makes maps in the air? That's just the beginning."

Besides the crash debris that Howard insisted on dragging along with us like the world's second-largest ball of twine, Ord and I carried radios, meds, platoon-level weapons, demolitions equipment, instruction chips for all of them, and for every military subject under our former sun.

Casus wrinkled his forehead as he tossed an M-40 round in his palm, then tapped the bullet's Teflite jacket against his teeth. "Jason, my friend, now is the time for negotiation, not joking."

"No joke. Just use the equipment against the black worms, and it's yours."

Casus paused with the cartridge between his lips like a cigarette.

I took a breath. "So long as you operate in concert with the Marini and the Tassini."

Casus spit the cartridge, and it spun through the air and tinged off a rock. "You said no more jokes."

I picked up the M-40 round, pocketed it, then sat on the rock, and patted the space beside me. "Hear me out."

He frowned, but sat.

A half hour later, Casus stood, folded his arms across his wide breastplate, and shook his head. "Impossible. The Casuni will fight. But the Casuni will fight separately."

"Then the Casuni will die separately. So will every other human in this world. The Queen understands that. That's why she's making a complete commitment—"

"The Bitch doesn't know commitment!" Casus jerked his thumb over his shoulder, in the direction of the escarpment. "I lost two sons in that battle against the worms, already!"

I rocked back. An ash flake from the funeral fire tumbled past on the wind.

Two sons? Just the thought of losing Jude, who wasn't even my blood son, paralyzed me.

I blinked, then stammered, "I didn't know. Casus, I'm so sorry."

I stood, and laid a hand on his quivering shoulder plate, as he wept.

He wiped his eyes, then blew his nose into his fingers and flicked the snot glob downwind. "Yes. My other sons are devastated, as well."

My brow wrinkled. "How many sons do you have?"

Casus cocked his head, and paused. "Surviving, as of sundown yesterday, five hundred six." He ticked a finger against two other fingers, then shook his head. "No. Five hundred eight."

I stared at him. "All those mourners—"

"Who else did you think would attend the funeral of a miserable buzzard like Yulen but his students?"

Casus raised a finger. "In every encampment I conquer, I bed twenty women. I have each son they bear me trained as a soldier. Then, when I levy troops from that encampment, my own sons are among them." He leaned toward me and winked. "Now, here's the clever part. By Law, no Casuni can refuse to fight for someone who commits all his sons!"

"Oh."

Casus picked up the M-40, worked its action, and blew into the chamber. "As one commander to another, I recommend the strategy. It's slow, but the copulation part is excellent."

"Casus, if the Queen has committed her only son to this alliance, that would be all her sons, true?"

"Bassin? They say he was too tough for the slavers to kill." He lowered his voice. "Personally, I think that means he's half Casuni. Though who would have lain with the Bitch is beyond me."

"Anyway, if the Queen has committed Bassin—"

"Yulen was right. You are clever." Casus wagged his finger at me, and narrowed his eyes. "But you aren't asking me to fight for the Bitch. You're asking me to fight for *you*. Therefore, Bassin is irrelevant, and I may refuse." He straightened up, nodded, and crossed his arms.

I sighed.

Casus wasn't opposed to a horrible and bloody war. Especially since he knew it was unavoidable, and in his nation's best interest. He wasn't opposed to taking orders from me, so long as he retained control of his own troops. He just needed to feel like destiny had forced him into doing what he had to do, anyway.

I'd dealt with a few advisees like Casus, guys who just wanted to act as their own barrack-room lawyers. Ord always said they had fools for clients.

If it were up to me, when this war heated up again, I would make Jude a PFC clerk, and assign him to count beans in the deepest subbasement of the Winter Palace, until the shooting stopped. But I knew it wouldn't work out that way. I didn't even think that Munchkin would pull strings so unfairly if she were in my shoes.

I asked Casus, "If a man only has one godson to commit, does that count?"

FORTY-SEVEN

CASUS REINED UP HIS BIG WHITE DUCKBILL, with its forelegs on a natural pavement of red rock slabs crisscrossed
with crevasses, swirled with rusty sand, and studded with
scrub. The rocky plain stretched a mile further south, then
the sand coalesced into a red dune sea that marched across
the horizon.

I stopped Rosy alongside Casus, and the dozen outriders Casus had brought with us stopped, too. In two days,
we had ridden three hundred miles south from Casus's
camp to reach this ragged border of the Tassin Desert, and
the day had become almost warm. But as we stopped, the
sun had dropped near the horizon. The High Plains' thin
air surrendered its warmth fast.

Casus turned in his saddle and faced me as I sat astride
Rosy. "We camp here tonight. The ground ahead suits the
Tassini mounts, but lames ours. Our fire and smoke will
bring Tassini scouts. You'll continue with them."

Once Casus threw in with the Alliance, he threw in all
the way. He insisted on guiding me to the border personally, but his presence any farther south would have chilled

negotiations faster than a High Plains sunset, if it didn't provoke gunplay.

Casus gazed out to the dunes. "You must win them over. The bastards are good riders and crack shots. Besides, I'm not about to weaken my Clan winning a war while the Tassini conserve their strength, then set upon us later."

I stared at the sunset. There was no point in telling my new ally that without the Tassini, and probably even with them, there wasn't going to be a later to conserve for.

Casus hefted a roll of sleeping gear off his saddle, and said, "Now, here is what you must know about the Tassini in order to win them over."

I nodded. "A Brief."

Back home, the State Department used to send us off to the Third World with downloads called Nation-in-Brief. A Brief provided up-to-the-minute data on Gross Domestic Product, manufacturing, health clubs, and approved restaurants within walking distance of Western-style hotels, and a graphic of the country's flag with circles and arrows that explained the flag's colors and icons. Useful when you were squatting in a tent with a Pashtun warlord who was picking his teeth with a rusty dagger.

Casus held up one finger. "First, you must understand that every Tassini is spit from a whore's womb, either a thief or a cutthroat."

I covered my hand with my mouth and coughed. "Any exceptions?"

"None. The cutthroats learn riding and marksmanship, then become raiders. The thieves learn to drink alcohol and smoke janga, then enter politics."

I nodded. "We have the same system at home."

Casus furrowed his brow. "Really?"

I knelt on the broken rock, and busied myself with gear so he couldn't see my face. We unrolled nets woven from groundfruit fiber that wrapped thick wood poles.

Casus said, "You'll negotiate with the Headman of the Encampment from which the scouts ride. He'll smoke the janga, then decide. Once you persuade him, he, being a thief, will present your ideas to the Council of One Hundred as his own, and the deal will be done. Quite simple."

I shook my head. "Simple? I don't know much about this place."

Casus disentangled his sleeping apparatus, two wood poles thick enough to support the weight of two male Casuni. These he wedged deep into crevasses in the rock. Between the poles he strung the two nets, like upper and lower bunk hammocks.

He rapped his knuckles on one of the poles. "Janga wood. Worms hate it. Otherwise, if you sleep on the sand—"

"Ah!" I nodded, and repeated what Bassin had taught me. "The screw worms crawl up your ass."

He grinned. "You see? You know everything about this place already!"

That night, after Casus had told me what else he knew about the Tassini, I swung in the wind in the upper of Casus's hammocks, and fell asleep with my visor open. I awoke with my nose so cold I thought it would blacken and fall off. Maybe that ancient plague Bassin had described had really been just frostbite, and eight hundred years of Blood Feud had begun with a misunderstanding. That was how little I understood this place.

I snapped my visor shut, chinned up the heat, and stared

at a brass-and-crystal hourglass placed on a rock. Casus's cavalry turned it each hour to mark shift change for the pickets. Casus said hourglasses were Tassini inventions, as were calendars, gunpowder, and poetry. Maybe Casus's worldview that every Tassini was either a cutthroat or a thief was just slightly biased.

I sighed so hard that I fogged my visor.

Casus thought I knew what I was doing, and I didn't dare disillusion him. But the truth was I barely understood enough to keep worms off my ass, and Armageddon was rushing at me faster than sand through an hourglass.

I set my jaw.

I would force these disparate allies together by my own sheer will. I set myself an internal deadline of noon, tomorrow, to have them working together.

Blam.

One of our pickets called out, as his pistol shot echoed, "Halt! Or I shoot your purple ass off!"

Crack.

A Tassini long rifle rang.

Bwee.

The round struck rock out on our perimeter, then flashed an orange spark as it ricocheted away.

A distant voice called, "Eat my excrement, you fat ogre!"

I extended my noon deadline.

Rifle and pistol shots crackled like popcorn. I rolled out of my hammock and low-crawled into a crevasse.

FORTY-EIGHT

THE FINAL DAMAGE TALLY for our party's midnight hand-shake with the Tassini Scouts of the Twelfth Encampment was two janga wood poles shot in half; one clean, surviv-able hole through a Casuni shoulder, and a Tassini mount who broke her leg in the fracas and had to be put down.

The Tassini and the Casuni ceased fire to mourn her, then, just after sunrise, I headed south with the Scouts, into the dune sea.

Tassini rode what Howard would call ornithomimes—sand-colored, ostrich-like reptilians half as big as duck-bills, but lots faster. Desert-adapted, they store water in fleshy headcrests that wobble as they run, and webs be-tween their toes let them scamper over sand dunes that would have mired Rosy like a mammoth in a tar pit.

The dunes we had to cross actually comprised only a two-mile wide belt that shifted with the seasonal winds, forming the real physiographic barrier that separated the duckbill-riding Casuni from the Tassini.

Six hours later, a Tassini Encampment Headman and I sat across from one another, cross-legged.

He said, as he tamped moist, shredded janga leaves

into the gold-filigreed receptacle of a water pipe, "I am told the Ogre Prince and the Bitch have forged a single sword. And have chosen you to wield it."

We sat together on striped cushions under an indigo canopy. A rising wind billowed the furled tent sides, as it scudded late-afternoon clouds toward us. They scraped low across the scrubland visible behind the encampment's other thousand tents.

The Headman looked to be seventy, but it was hard to tell because his face was dyed indigo from forehead to jaw. His mahogany skin was visible only where a mustache and goatee would have grown, and the whites of his eyes gleamed against his purple skin like moons in a night sky.

I pounced on his statement. "Momentous events beget momentous responses. Would it please you to know more?"

The Headman's response itself was momentous, because by it he signaled that his visitor could finally talk business. Company came rarely to the Tassin nomads, and their customs were arranged to savor it, as well as to measure a stranger's worth.

We had passed four hours discussing my journey; my ancestry; his ancestry; my livestock, which consisted of Rosy; his livestock; whether the approaching storm would bring rain or only sand, and the mystery of how devil-worshiping Marini whores and pimps could produce liqueur so sublime that it would be served in paradise.

Our four-hour chat had been lubricated by smuggled Marini liqueur, poured hot from a tall brass pot into cups the size of a man's thumb, which my host refilled as fast as I politely drained them.

The Headman lit the janga leaves he had stuffed into the water pipe, striking a flint he held in fingers as gnarled as a janga hammock pole.

In harsh country, from Afghanistan to the Bren Highlands, the few things like janga and groundfruit that didn't kill you found many uses.

The Headman puffed his cheeks around the ivory mouthpiece of one of the pipe's hoses, until smoke curled from his lips. "Tell me what you know, then what you want. Each detail. Omit nothing." Then he lifted the other hose, and held it out to me.

As I reached for the hose, my seat cushion tipped, and I had to catch myself with my free hand. The Headman's smuggled Marini moonshine had left me zogged, as the price of politeness.

I grimaced as I sat back, and my bladder sent its own signal about impending business. Purple Face's liqueur was as diuretic as it was intoxicating, but after four hours wasted on small talk this was no time for a pee break.

I had a regrown lung and no-smoking orders from New Bethesda. But I had more immediate concerns, and refusing to smoke the old boy's janga wouldn't resolve them.

I slipped the hose mouthpiece between my lips, sucked, and choked back a cough as my throat constricted. "Very mild!"

The Headman grinned. "My mother chewed this batch herself."

An hour later, I didn't care what his mother chewed. I was pretty sure I had covered the major points of the proposed alliance, a tentative order of battle, a loose timetable, and an invitation to the first meeting among the heads of state.

The Headman seemed to have grown two more eyes, my skull pounded, my bladder throbbed, and Niagara thundered in my ears.

The Headman's extra eyes were a janga hallucination, but the Niagara was real. Night had fallen, and the Headman's household slaves had dropped the tent sides against the storm, which had proven to be this desert's once-per-year scorpion-drowner.

Rain drummed above my head and trickled through the tent's seams.

The Headman chopped the air with his hand, and said to me, as fuzzily as though he spoke through a pillow, "The risks are too great. The Marini have cities and ships to lose. We have nothing. Perhaps the devil will ignore the Tassini. I must say no."

I said, "The devil—the Slugs—won't ignore you!"

"If God wanted us to fight, He would give me a sign." He squinted into the smoke cloud between us like it was a holo generator, and said, "I see no sign." He shook his head, again, in wide arcs.

Drunk and stoned as I was, I still knew I was losing this war before it even started.

"You have to see!" I pounded my fist into a pillow, then countered his head shake with my own, even broader, one. That was a mistake. The room spun, I pitched forward into my cushions, and passed out.

FORTY-NINE

SOMETIME LATER THAT NIGHT, cold rain dripped on my face, and woke me in dimness punctuated by distant lightning. The storm still pelted the Headman's tent so hard that it cascaded a frigid stream onto the upper-bunk rope hammock into which somebody had slung me. Whoever had put me to bed had also stripped off my armor, so I lay shivering in my underlayer.

I had to pee worse than ever, but I was still so drunk that I didn't dare try to roll out of the hammock to stagger outside.

Through my stupor, I realized that I couldn't have screwed my diplomatic mission worse. The Headman had already turned me down. Now I had passed out in front of him, and had been put to bed drunk, by him or by his slaves. Without the Tassini, the Casuni would bolt. Without the Casuni, the Marini would bolt.

My head spun worse than ever, and I just peed where I lay as I passed out again.

I woke near noon the next day, and looked around. One tent side flap was up again, and a clear day shone through it. A woman, veiled, and covered head-to-toe in a coarse robe, stood at the tent's far edge, hanging a woven rug to dry in the breeze. When she saw me staring at her, she ran away.

My head hammered as I climbed down from the upper hammock. The lower was empty, as was the rest of the tent, but outside I heard the slapping stride of an approaching Tassini wobblehead.

I found my armor, and started dressing. Then the Headman stepped in through the open tent flap, brushing dust from his cloak.

His jaw was set.

I looked down at the tent floor. "I—"

He said, "Well, it's done. It disgusted me, but it's done now."

"I can't blame you. But I really think—"

He chopped air with his hand and cut me off. "The entire Council of One Hundred still must meet. But I rode out at first light and met with two other Headmen, so the Council will be only a formality."

Wasn't it enough that he had turned me down? Did he have to advertise? My blood chilled. No, he didn't. So he had to be talking about something else. I must have broken some taboo I was too blitzed to remember. Had I puked on an altar? Peeked under a woman's veil in my stupor, and now the Tassini were meeting to decide to chop off my hand?

He walked to a low, lacquered chest in the tent's far corner, took out a jeweled sword, and it rang against its scabbard as he drew it.

My heart skipped, and I stood there unarmored. I swiveled my head back and forth, searching for my M-40.

The old man held his sword up between us, and the blade flashed as he turned it in his hand. He stared into its light, and his eyes glistened. "I take no joy in sending my son to war. But as I must, my blade will go with him."

My jaw dropped. "What did you tell the other Headmen?"

He raised his indigo eyebrows. "That the Tassini must join you in this war, as the Ogre and the Bitch have done. Your arguments were stated with reason and passion. I was reluctant, but the sign was unmistakable."

I stopped with one leg in my armor, then sat on a cushion, shaking my throbbing head. After thirty seconds, I found my voice. "Sign?"

"After I put you to bed, I sat up for one turn of the glass, and waited. But God gave me no sign. I smoked another pipe, but still no sign. I shivered in the cold rain. Then I took to my bed." He pointed at the lower hammock. "And I prayed, one last time. And God's rain came upon my face. And I felt His rain, and it was warm!" He raised his eyes to the tent roof and smiled.

If I ever write a Brief for the State Department, I bet they won't let me add a section on winning allies by peeing on them.

The downside of the rainstorm was that it flooded the wadis that separated me from Casus, Rosy, and, ultimately, the Royal Barge. The Scouts—*my* scouts, now—and I were forced to camp two nights, until the water sank low and slow enough that our wobbleheads could wade across.

I spent the first forced layover teaching the Scouts to fire my M-40, plinking targets one shot at a time. Then one of them discovered the full auto position on the selector switch, and sprayed my last magazine across the desert like he was watering a lawn.

He apologized profusely, and promised to make it up

to me by roasting the testicles of the next dozen Casuni he met. I spent the second layover day teaching the Scouts the etiquette of allied operations.

By the time I rejoined the outriders that Casus had left at the Border, reclaimed Rosy, and bid them farewell, I was almost two days behind schedule for my Royal Barge rendezvous. Casus was already en route to the Alliance's first meeting of heads of state. If I missed my boat ride, I'd be stranded upriver while the Clans planned their war without me.

Just in case that happened, I tasked Jeeb to Cruise and Snooze, an overnight surveillance above the Slug Troll. I hoped Jeeb could gather data on incubation progress, so Howard and Ord would have a better idea how much lead time the Alliance had to plan its war.

I rode Rosy harder than I should have, but she never complained and never slowed.

By the time Rosy staggered to the escarpment's lip, we were both panting. And, for all our efforts, sixteen hours late.

Rosy and I looked out across the valley of the Marin. The sun set at our backs, while the Royal Barge dwindled to a speck, disappearing into the downriver mist.

I popped my visor, waved, and hollered, though I knew I might as well have been an ant calling the moon. I sighed. I had been promising Rosy turnips for days.

"Goddam you, Bassin." There was nothing worse than a Crown Prince who had the humility and discipline to follow orders.

Snort.

Almost nothing.

FIFTY

A WRONK STALKED TOWARD US out of a tree clump, head low, tail high, snarling and slobbering in the twilight, up-wind and eighty yards north of us along the escarpment.

The monster looked like its citified cousins, the ones the Marini hitched to their chariots, but thinner, dirtier, and, of course, unmuzzled. A wronk can't run down a healthy duckbill, and is just smart enough not to try. But a wronk sure scares hell out of anything else it meets.

So Rosy reared and squealed, then leapt over the escarpment. I had made the ten-foot leap easily with her twice before, but this time, exhausted and terrified, she landed badly, cartwheeled, and I somersaulted off down the slope.

By the time I scrambled to my knees, Rosy was trying to stand, and the wronk was pacing back and forth along the Escarpment lip, rumbling as it smelled fresh, relatively stationary meat that it couldn't get at. Another thing a wronk was just smart enough to know was that even its massive legs couldn't absorb eight tons landing after a ten-foot jump.

But, in about thirty seconds, the pacing wronk was

going to stumble onto the path down the Escarpment, and come down below to make us into snacks.

No problem, as long as we kept moving. I ran to Rosy, grabbed her reins, and said, "Up, girl. We gotta go."

Rosy bleated, then hobbled on three legs, holding her right rear leg in the air, while her lower leg below the knee joint dangled. The tibia protruded, white and bloody, exposed in an open fracture.

I snapped my head around, looked away, and felt sicker than I had when I smelled the rotten hole in Sergeant Yulen's gut. With a broken leg, Rosy was going to die even if the carnosaur vanished in the next second like an extinguished holo.

Wronk.

The beast found the way down the escarpment, and put a first foot on the path.

Wronk.

I spun and looked in the direction of the second bellow.

The only thing worse than being chased by a slobbering, fifty-foot-long carnosaur is being caught between it and a forty-foot-long one.

While I had been riding the High Plains, every wronk within an area the size of New Denver must have plodded to the ruins of the Great Fair, perhaps attracted by the bird cloud wheeling overhead, certainly attracted by the stench of the biggest putrefacted smorgasbord this world had known in centuries.

The downslope monster advanced up the hill toward Rosy and me, head down and roaring. When it got within twenty yards, Rosy gave up hobbling, and rolled on her back, hissing, and kicking at the carnosaur with her sound hind leg.

The wronk hung back, dodging Rosy's punches, and snapped at me as I stood between it and Rosy. More, I supposed, to scare away an annoying competitor than to catch a snack.

For weapons, I had an M-40 slung across my back for which I had only empty magazines, a utility knife no longer than one wronk tooth, and, in my thigh pocket, clipped alongside my Aid Pak, the single-shot .22 caliber survival pistol toy.

I stood my ground between Rosy and the monster, unslung my M-40, reversed it in my hands, and swung it at him stock first, like a Louisville Slugger.

The wronk lunged, and tried to reward my Quixotic stupidity by biting me in half at the torso.

Whether I stumbled back over prostrate Rosy, or the wronk's breath blew me back across her like a putrescent typhoon, I'll never know.

I found myself on my ass in the grass, with Rosy between me and the big wronk, staring into her huge brown eyes as she screamed.

The beast's snout thudded into her flank, its jaws clamped, and bone cracked. Rosy wailed and thrashed as the carnosaur began to eat her alive.

I fumbled out the survival pistol, pressed it against Rosy's eye socket, and whispered, "I'm sorry." Then I fired the tiny bullet through her eye, into what I hoped was her brain.

I lay face down and still alongside her, trembling, but her body continued to thrash for what seemed like minutes. Finally, I realized the movement was the carnosaur heaving her lifeless two-ton corpse, as it wrenched her hind leg off like a turkey drumstick.

With the wronk preoccupied, I low-crawled away from Rosy's body, dragging my useless M-40 by its sling, freezing in place every few feet, while I waited to feel huge jaws crush my body.

I was ten yards away from Rosy's corpse when the sound of wrenched gristle and cracking bone stopped. A low rumble replaced the noise.

I turned my head. The smaller wronk had lifted its snout out of Rosy's rib cage, and gobbets of gore plopped from its jaws back into her body cavity.

Ten yards to my right, the bigger wronk that had challenged us at the top of the Escarpment thrust its head at the smaller monster, and roared a hiss like a jet engine.

The bigger beast trotted to Rosy, and muscled in alongside the small one.

While the two tussled, I scrambled to my feet and ran like hell, watching over my shoulder.

The big wronk hip-checked the smaller one so hard that the smaller one staggered three paces away from the carcass, then caught its balance and snarled. The big wronk snorted, and turned back to feed.

When the smaller carnosaur raised its head, it saw me, tearing ass downhill, just slower than a wronk could run. It swung its head once more at the big bully, then bellowed and stalked after an easy consolation prize, that being me.

I cross-slung my rifle to free my hands, then shucked my pack, hoping that the beast would stop and examine it, and also to lighten my load. Meanwhile, I ran like my hair was on fire downhill, toward the charnel ground that had been the Fair.

The wronk trampled my pack without a sniff, and kept coming, but it was eighty yards behind me and didn't seem to be gaining.

Plan B was that when I got to the Fair, some rotten morsel would distract the wronk.

Four minutes later, I entered the mounds of by-now skeletal remains, and debris swarming with scavengers. The chain reaction provided by abandoned livestock and scavengers that got themselves killed in the fray had kept the flesh party jumping for days.

Scavengers snapped and snarled at me as I ran by, and I could hear them doing the same to the wronk as it passed them. In the frenzy, fast-moving small fry like me passed through, ignored by those among the scavengers that were strong enough to bite through Eternads.

Five minutes later, I emerged from the obstacle course with the beast still hot on my trail, and now only fifty yards back.

The prof on my Cretaceous-life holo concluded that tyrannosaurs were too big, slow, myopic, fragile, clumsy, and stupid to hunt. I wished he were here. Not so he could reconsider. So I wouldn't have to outrun the wronk, I'd just have to outrun him.

Three hundred yards downslope my salvation shimmered in the sunset. If a web-footed Tassini wobblehead couldn't swim a flooded wadi, a wronk surely couldn't swim the Marin. All I had to do was make it into the river, swim out to deeper water than the wronk could wade, then climb aboard some hunk of shipwreck flotsam, and wait until the dumb brute lost interest in standing on the shore.

But I was running on repaired legs, breathing with a re-grown lung, and hadn't had a good night's sleep in weeks. Adrenaline takes you only so far.

The beast had closed the gap between us to within twenty yards by the time my boots splashed into the Marin. I high stepped out thigh-deep, then belly flopped, and churned my arms and legs like a monster was chasing me.

Eternads are watertight if the vents are sealed. They aren't designed for swimming, but they trap enough air, and are light enough, that a GI can actually swim faster in them than without them. They say a Navy SEAL wearing Eternads swam faster than Olympic Record time for the sixteen hundred freestyle while he was bagged, to win a bar bet. Probably Squid blarney, but the part about being bagged lends credibility.

I glanced back over my shoulder, and saw that the wronk had paused knee-deep in the river. The beast swung its head side to side, and the gap between me and it had reopened to thirty yards. Twilight had deepened, and the paleo chips say tyrannosaurs, based on brain lobe size estimates, could smell dead meat miles away but couldn't see well enough to get a driver's license.

I rolled over and backstroked, wheezing, and catching my breath.

I had lost my pack and gear, but my M-40 was still across my back, and I realized that, if it had come to it, I still had one round, the one that I had pocketed after Casus had spit it out so many days ago. It might come in handy in the survival-mode days to come. Once the wronk wandered off, I'd recall Jeeb, relay word to Ord, and make my way downriver.

Snort.

The wronk sniffed in my direction, then paced out until the water got so deep that ripples lapped its belly. Then the monster flopped into the river, and swam straight for me, eyes and nostrils above water, lashing its tail back and forth like Captain Hook's crocodile.

FIFTY-ONE

THE CARNOSAUR APPROACHED so fast that its snout cut a wake like a speedboat. I couldn't really blame my error on the paleontologists. You wouldn't think a hunting dog could swim after dead ducks, either, by studying its bones.

I swam, windmilling my arms like a shrub-trim 'Bot, but the race would end in two minutes, tops. I stroked with one hand, and fumbled with my waist seal, underwater, with the other.

If I could get the one bullet out of my pocket, hand-load the round into the M-40's chamber, and hit the wronk squarely enough to penetrate its brain, I might survive. A fool's option, but my only one.

The beast was so close now that I saw pupils in its eyes, which were as far apart as my shoulders were wide.

I wedged my hand inside my armor, and my fingers touched the bullet's Teflite jacket.

I snuck one more glance, and the beast had gotten so close, so fast, that its open upper jaw and teeth showed above the waterline. I seemed to be swimming in glue. Something sloshed, and I realized that, with my hand stuffed through my waist seal, I was flooding my suit, and sinking myself.

Something scraped my boot heel beneath the surface. I kicked, and thumped something soft enough to be the carnosaur's nose. I rolled over in the water, facing back toward the beast, prepared to go thrashing and screaming, like Rosy had.

The beast's eye stared into mine, six feet away, softball-sized, black, and impassive. Then the head rotated sideways, so its jaws could open underwater.

After all the firefights and helicopter dust-offs, after amoebic dysentery and pneumonia, after going toe-to-pseudopod with Slugs at bayonet point, six hundred million miles from home, and again here so far from home that I didn't even know the mileage; after surviving crushed bones, a transit through the very fabric of the universe, and a spaceship crash, I was about to die as reptile candy.

Brown water leaked around my faceplate, as I sank below the surface. I squeezed my eyes shut, clenched my jaw, and waited to feel teeth puncture my armor.

Boom.

I opened my eyes and saw a black rod protruding from the carnosaur's eyesocket, an explosive-shredded pod swelling from its barb. Blood and black-powder smoke fountained up from the beast's wound, and then river water exploded in a belch as the carnosaur exhaled, then sagged away from me.

I floated motionless and stunned, then paddled around and looked up.

From the rope basket that dangled below the Royal Barge's fore spit, the Master Harpooner leaned out and reached his hand down toward me. I grabbed hold, and he clasped my gauntlet and lifted me, dripping, out of the river like I was a child.

As water poured from my armor's heel vents, he thrust me back up toward the ship. Bassin and a crewman grabbed me, one on each arm, pulled me over the rail and onto the foredeck, then sat me on a rope locker.

I gasped, popped my neck ring, and let Bassin tug my helmet off.

The Master Harpooner stood in front of me, bent with hands on knees, and grinned. "You all right, Sir?"

I nodded, puked muddy water, and said to him as drops trickled down my chin, "Thank you."

"No, General. Thank you! No other Harpooner's ever stuck a wronk. I'll drink free for a year!"

I turned to Bassin. "You were gone—"

"Actually, I disobeyed orders. We overstayed by fifteen hours, until we almost lost the tide. The Lookout thought he heard one shot."

The Master Harpooner held up his spyglass. "We spotted you, and came about as fast as we could. Fast enough, hey?"

My forearms quivered, and I shivered so hard that my teeth chattered, though my suit heater whirred.

"No," I said. "Too slow. Me, not you."

Then I stood, walked to the rail, and stared out into the deepening twilight. A mile distant, as small as a beetle on dung, the big wronk still bent over Rosy, its head twisting side to side as it tore her apart.

My arms stopped shaking, and my teeth ceased chattering. My breath hissed in and out, in precise cadence, as I unslung my M-40.

Bassin touched my elbow. "Jason? Are you all right?"

I wasn't all right. I shrugged him off, fished the round out of my pocket, and chambered it. Then I screwed the rifle's optics to night passive, and captured the distant wronk in the green glow of the sight picture. I paused, checked windage, breathed, sighted on the monster's eye, and squeezed the trigger.

I watched through the night sight for three heartbeats. The bullet sped downrange, an invisible, supersonic Teflite-jacketed assassin, then struck the wronk's eye. The beast's head snapped up, he thrashed, staggered, then fell.

Heartbeats later, the carnosaur's dying bellow echoed back to us across the valley.

Water lapped our ship's hull.

The Master Harpooner collapsed his spyglass between his palms, then turned to me, his eyes wide, and his mouth agape. "General, that was the finest shot I ever saw. I shall never forget it."

My forearms trembled again, so violently this time that my rifle slipped from my fingers and clattered on the deck. I staggered back until I felt the solidity of the main mast, then slumped down with my legs sprawled on the deck.

The wronk had been acting out its role in the great play, a dumb, magnificent, living garbage disposal. I had killed it in an explosion of vengeful, cold rage, though the animal's death came far too late to save Rosy, or even to spare her an eyeblink's suffering.

I now commanded an army that would grow to a million soldiers, every one as susceptible to inhuman rage as I had just been. It would be my job to stoke that rage, to leash it, to watch it kill too many of them, and then to send the survivors home persuaded that they were still human. It would be even harder to persuade myself that I was.

I said to the Master Harpooner, "I hope I never forget it, either." Then I cried.

The next morning, Bassin and I stood on deck after the Royal Barge had transited the Locks of the Marin. Jeeb swooped down out of the clouds, returned from his Cruise and Snooze. He buzzed the crow's nest, looped around the ship like an albatross, then flared his wings and settled on the deck at my feet. He turned his optics up toward me, whined, then pogo'd up and down on all six legs.

Bassin raised his eyebrows. "You and my mother would say your machine is upset."

Jeeb had reason to be. And his news wasn't the worst of it.

FIFTY-TWO

TWO DAYS LATER, the Royal Barge eased alongside the stone quay at the University. Bassin and I, in fresh uniforms, jumped the last two feet between the deck and the quay, already late for the first meeting of Clan heads in three centuries.

Howard, Ord, and Jude sat in a carriage, its duckbills already turned, and pointed up the hill toward a multi-peaked, bannered tent. The tent stood on a broad lawn alongside a marble apparition of onion-shaped domes and sparkling fountains, the Great Library of Marin.

Bassin and I climbed in, Ord pointed at my lapel, and frowned. I looked down. My Combat Infantryman's Badge was pinned a finger width too high. I fixed it, and said, "I thought we were meeting in the Library."

Ord said, "There were complications."

I stiffened. "Who's missing?"

Ord raised his palms. "Oh, they're all under the tent, now, Sir. Her Majesty and four Marshals. With the Colonel here that will make six Marini. Casus brought five sons. Six Headmen representing the Tassini arrived last night."

Bassin narrowed his eyes. "What happened?"

"The Tassini and the Casuni live in tents. They refused to set foot inside the Library, Sir."

Bassin's jaw dropped. "It's the Third Wonder of the World! They should have been honored."

"That was Her Majesty's reaction. Then Casus said it was a stinking rock pile that she rigged to crash around his ears. Things deteriorated from there."

Ord had resolved Advisee squabbles before. I sighed, then raised my palm. "But we're good to go, now?"

Ord nodded. "I think so, Sir."

I ran fingers through my hair, then said to the others as the carriage lurched forward, "Where the hell do we start?" Maybe Eisenhower said something more confident before the Allies invaded Europe, but he was fighting on the same planet he got born on.

Ord pulled a sword and three rifles from a long leather case alongside him. "Sir, we might start with the tools we have available—and those we can make available. Marinus is the nexus of Bren's arms industry."

I turned to Bassin. I couldn't command what I didn't understand, and I only had a carriage ride left during which to learn. "Why? Fifty words or less."

Bassin leaned forward. "When the Plains Clans split off and settled the Highlands where the Stones were mined, we traded weapons to the Tassini and Casuni for Stones. For the next three hundred years, we spent a third of our wealth to assure that the Stones flowed. Hardly altruistic. It was good business, and the alternative was the end of the world. The Tassini and Casuni fought one another, and we tolerated it so long as the Stones flowed.

Then they thanked us by sacking our border towns, using the weapons we supplied them."

I raised my eyebrows, and said again, "Why?"

"Because they thought we worshiped the devil."

"Do you?"

Bassin said, "We hold a pragmatic worldview."

"I'll take that as a yes. The Plains Clans killed your people. So you kicked their asses to make them stop."

Bassin nodded. "Then the Casuni and the Tassini complained that we were arrogant bullies. So they raided even more."

"Using the weapons you kept supplying."

"We needed the Stones."

"Sounds familiar."

Ord cleared his throat. "Sir, while you were in the field, Jude and Colonel Hibble researched the technologies available in this society. I visited armorers." Ord lifted the sword, which looked like the saber my Tassini Headman friend was going to pass on to his son. "The cottage industries of Marinus manufacture edged weapons that rival Japanese *Koto* in quality, as well as personal armor."

Ord laid the sword down, then Jude hefted it. "Cool!"

"The larger gunsmiths mill steel weapons as well as any gunsmith in America could before the Civil War." Ord hefted the three rifles, in turn. "The smithies make long-barrel rifles for the Tassini, horse pistols for the Casuni, and short-barreled rifles for their own military."

"All single-shot?"

Ord nodded. "At least they've mastered the one-piece cartridge."

"Can we make repeaters?"

Ord said, "I expect a working prototype tomorrow."

I nodded. "Any other rabbits in the hat?"

Howard shook his head. "No infrastructure." He held up the old Earth lead pencil that he chewed as a cigarette substitute. "We couldn't even duplicate something this simple, if we wanted to. No graphite mines for pencil lead. Marini housewives are already donating brass pots to melt down, because the forges can't make enough cartridges. So this ferrule that crimps around the eraser would be impossible. And forget about synthetic rubber for the eraser."

I sighed, then asked Howard, "Have we got our ten months?"

He waved on the holo gen, and it showed what looked like a bowl full of lumpy minestrone. "Jeeb actually crawled down a ventilator to get these. As you can see, the incubator is up and running. Based on our forensics and experience, I'd guess the Troll will start extruding mature warriors within seven months."

Three months training and manufacturing lost. My heart sank.

Bassin asked, "How many warriors?"

Howard shrugged. "Fifty thousand."

Bassin's eyes widened. "Formidable."

"Per week."

Bassin's jaw dropped. "For how many weeks?"

"Until It runs out of humans to kill."

We were screwed. But Napoleon wouldn't admit that if he were sitting in my chair.

I crossed my arms, and looked around at the four of them. "We'll do the best we can with the equipment and the time we have. I think we can train the Clans to fight together. There's cultural baggage to deal with. But, when it comes down to it, they're really a lot like us."

Howard gave me a sideways look.

If he was right, they *were* us. But ancient history was inconsequential just now.

Hoooooo-ooo.

The footman clinging to the carriage's rear platform announced our arrival at the tent with a rhind-horn blast.

The five of us climbed down from the carriage, and two Marini Household Guards saluted, then held open the tent's flaps.

I checked my gig line of shirt front to belt buckle, then ducked under the flaps, alongside Bassin, and with the others at my shoulder.

I raised my head, looked around, and whispered to Ord, "What the hell?"

FIFTY-THREE

THE THREE CLANS' DELEGATIONS sat around an equal-sided triangular conference table.

Casus, flanked by five of his sons, all in ceremonial armor, stared straight ahead, his great hands folded in front of him. Two red scratches slashed his face above his beard.

The Queen, in silver, wearing a tiara set with cabochon sapphires the size of walnuts, sat chin-high across from Casus, her palms down on the table. One silver-enameled fingernail was broken, and the Field Marshal next to her sported a fat lip.

The indigo-faced Tassini sat in a row behind the far table edge, as sullen as a half-dozen shelved eggplants. One's hand was bandaged, and another's ceremonial shepherd's crook was roped together, as though he had broken it over somebody's head.

Ord whispered back, "The Queen hosted a reception last night, but as I said—"

"The Heads of State had a saloon brawl?"

"Their diplomatic skills have atrophied for three hundred years, Sir."

"But they're here, now?"

"I explained things, Sir."

The last thing any trainee in my Basic Platoon had wanted was for Senior Drill Sergeant Ord to explain things to him. But Queens and warlords weren't trainees. "You threatened them with push-ups?"

Ord shook his head. "I assured them that if they didn't settle their differences among themselves, you possessed otherworldly means to have them all assassinated, and would take over their nations and conduct this war yourself."

I rolled my eyes. "They didn't buy *that?*"

"They just needed a reason to believe something bigger than themselves was driving events that they knew were in their best interests."

One rationale for A-bombing Japan instead of invading it had been that the Emperor would have to sacrifice his subjects to the last peasant against a mere *gaijin* invasion, but could yield to a supernaturally powerful force without losing face.

I sighed. "Whatever. What otherworldly means would you have dreamed up if they asked?"

"Oh, they asked. I told them Cargo'Bots would rip their limbs off while they slept, Sir."

I smirked behind my hand. "That's hilarious."

"After reprogramming, it's quite effective, Sir. Just messy."

"Oh."

I stepped to the table head, bowed, introduced myself, and got introduced back. Each participant sat like a sword point protruded from each chair back.

I said, "First, please believe that all I want is to help you save your people from a common enemy. I have no ambition to govern, and possess no magic formula for it."

One Field Marshal rolled his eyes, one of Casus's sons snorted, and a Tassini looked away, smirking.

But I wasn't lying about the lack of a formula. Like Churchill said, the best argument against democracy was a five-minute conversation with the average voter. Anyway, Casus and the Queen both relaxed a hair's width, and we had no time for civics class.

Howard set the holo gen center-table, and waved it on. Every Bren except Bassin, Casus, and the Queen gasped. A couple Tassini Headmen smiled. I suppose a holo looks like what you see if you blow janga for a living.

The Troll's image squatted on the conference table like a translucent blue watermelon, surrounded by misshapen outbuildings in its clearing.

I said, "The good news for us is that this is the only objective we need to be concerned with. If we had the force and mobility to destroy it tomorrow, the war would be over before it started."

A Marini Marshal muttered, "Here, here!"

He didn't know the half of it. If I could have traded Jeeb, who wasn't equipped to carry a firecracker, for a few last-century jets packing dumb iron bombs, they could fry the Troll like a turkey on a platter. But Bren's mineralogists hadn't even discovered bauxite, much less smelted aircraft-quality aluminum.

I sighed.

A turn-of-the-century defense official said you go to war with the army that you have, not the army you want. The army that *he* had then whipped an oppressive tyranny in six weeks, while suffering minimal casualties. Then the oppressed beat crap out of one another for years, and he lost his job.

I looked around at the Allies, who had already been beating crap out of one another for three centuries, and shrugged to myself. Losing this war meant losing everything. Losing this job meant zero.

"The blue mountain is an easy target," someone said.

"Maybe. Getting to it won't be easy."

I waved on a map of Bren's eastern hemisphere. Where we sat, at the Great Library, was on the east coast of the continent that dominated the hemisphere's western half. It joined the eastern continent, Slug Land to me, only by the isthmus that ran east-west, three hundred miles north of the River Marin. The landmasses looked like North America and Europe, shoved close together, and joined by a thin twig. The Slugs' Great Wall straddled the twig.

The Troll winked as a blue dot, four hundred miles east of the Great Wall. The Sea of Hunters, only twenty-two miles wide at the strait south of the Winter Palace, separated the continents.

One of Casus's sons pointed at the Great Wall. "There's the nut to crack!"

"The boy's right." A Marshal thrust his fist forward. "A good barrage to reduce the works, then punch through. Then cavalry straight on to the objective!"

Howard said, "We calculated that if we massed every artillery piece the Marini have now, plus every one you could manufacture in a year, and bombarded the Great Wall twenty-four hours each day, it would take a year to force a breach wide and deep enough to pass cavalry. And that's just the first wall. There are four more behind it."

"Rubbish!" The Marshal yanked a Marini seashell

abacus from a uniform pocket and fiddled. Then he raised his eyebrows—and clammed up.

I said, "On the other hand, if we defend the isthmus from behind whatever fortifications we could erect in the next few months, we think the Slugs would rain Heavys down on us for two months, then break through. Worse, we expose both our flanks if the Slugs could bridge around us as fast as they crossed the Marin. We risk encirclement and annihilation of our entire defensive force."

A Tassini threw up his purple hands. "We can't attack. We can't defend. What can we do? Die?"

I shook my head. "First, we can train our soldiers into a single, cohesive army. So that whatever we do, we make every life count. Second, we improve that army's equipment, for the same reason."

I paused, then looked around. "Third, we attack before the Slugs are strong enough to attack us." I pointed at the Tassini coast, south of the Winter Palace, and drew my finger across the twenty-two-mile strait in the Sea of Hunters, then overland to the Troll.

Casus said, "Jason, you don't understand. In the last five hundred years, no sailor has crossed the Sea of Hunters and lived!"

"And our fleet lies ruined! This route is impassable." A white-mustached Marini in Admiralty powder blue waved the back of his hand at the holo, as he turned to his Queen. "Your Majesty, I recommend we consider a joint command. Led by someone experienced, knowledgeable—"

"And Marini?" One of Casus's sons slapped his gauntlet on the table edge. "Go to hell!"

The Tassini buzzed among themselves.

The Queen raised her hand. When everyone kept yammering, she slapped the table so hard that it quivered.

In the silence that followed, the Marshals, and Admirals, and Headmen, and Warlords, turned their eyes toward the old woman, who sat as straight as a silver dagger.

She turned to me, and said, "Do you believe what these men believe, General?"

I looked around at the others. "No, Ma'am. But I'm betting that the Slugs do."

The Queen inclined her head, and her sapphires twinkled. "Then continue."

FIFTY-FOUR

THE NEXT MORNING, the owner of the biggest gun smithy in Marinus handed Ord and me heavy leather hoods, set with smoked glass eyepieces, which we wore as he led us onto his foundry floor.

All across a room bigger than a Scramjet hangar, golden sparks fountained from anvils as ironworkers, their sweating skin orange in the forges' firelight, swung hammers that shaped white-hot steel billets. Roaring steam clouds boiled up from quenching troughs and washed us with the acid smell of fresh steel. Ord leaned toward me and shouted, "Almost as hot as yesterday's meeting, Sir. But boldness wins wars."

I shouted back, "I'd like to think they bought the plan on merit. Not because somebody threatened to murder them in bed. But I'll take it."

We passed from the foundry into a room where millwrights bent over squealing lathes, working steel into rifle barrels, then into a quiet room where craftsmen planed stocks, then fitted them to finished steel.

The owner lifted two rifles from a bench, handed them to Ord. "Sorry. We couldn't copy the receiver of the example you gave us. It's a stamping. I stayed up last night, and milled one, myself." The owner covered a yawn with his hand.

Ord laid down one rifle, an old, bulky AK-47 exhumed from one of our tamperproofs. The other rifle's stock had the polished-shark-fin look characteristic of a Marini charioteer's single-shot carbine. But its action was like the bulkier AK, and its barrel looked the same bore as a Marini cartridge. The steel hadn't been blued, so the rifle gleamed as silver as a new-minted Twobuck coin.

Ord balanced the new rifle on two fingers, then raised his eyebrows and smiled. "That's fine. The first AK-47s had milled receivers, too. It's first-class work, Gustus."

Gustus the armorer was thirty, pug-nosed, with black curly hair, and Marini eyes behind gold wire spectacles.

He smiled, then frowned. "The repeating mechanism is brilliant. But the first one we completed seized after four rounds."

Ord shrugged. "Black powder residue. We'll work it out. When can you start production?"

Gustus wrinkled his pug nose. "Not so soon. I have to replace a whole crew."

Ord raised his eyebrows.

Gustus said, "My father died last month. After I checked the books, I found that the night shift had been skimming rifles to the Red Line runners for years."

Ord asked, "You turn 'em in?"

"They're mostly good men who went along to protect their jobs and their families. I turned in the ringleaders, but I gave the others the option to enlist, instead." He grinned. "Every one took it."

Twenty minutes later, a carriage hauled Ord and me toward the quay.

I said, "Logistics could lose this war. Or win it, Sergeant Major." They say Eisenhower conquered Europe by piling up supplies, then letting them fall on the Nazis.

"Always, Sir."

"There's not an officer in the Clans that's moved an army across a sea, and then across four hundred miles of unfamiliar ground under fire. What they just absolutely know—that isn't really true—will hurt us more than what somebody new just doesn't know. Gustus seems sharp. Honest. Resourceful. Knows weapons, cares about people. I thought—"

"So did I, Sir. Once his forge completes the changeover to assault rifle production, it'll run itself. I administered his Commissioning Oath myself, two days ago. Subject to your approval, of course."

"Oh."

An hour later, I left Ord at the quay, with instructions to have Tassini, Casuni, and Marini cavalrymen figure out how wronk units could operate with wobblehead and duckbill units without eating their allies.

I could've just told them what to do, but it's better to tell people what needs to get done, then let them astonish you with their ingenuity. I wasn't smart enough to figure that out. A last-century general named Patton said it.

I turned to my newest recruit. "Wilgan, how do I get an army of three hundred thousand soldiers across the Sea of Hunters?"

The old Ship Master smiled through his white beard, then winked, and flapped his arms. "Grow 'em wings."

I told him my plan.

He shook his head. "It's twenty months on the ways to build even one ship like mine."

"We don't have twenty months."

Wilgan led me along the quay to an open wooden boat creaking as it rocked on the river swell. He knelt, and grasped one of the shipped oars that studded its flanks. "A river packet like this one could make the crossing with fifty men, if they wouldn't mind rowing themselves, and if the seas were fair. We've got thousands of these packets up and down the Marin."

"They wouldn't mind rowing. When are the seas fair?" I asked.

"At Full Moons, mostly. 'Course, that's when the Glowies run." He scratched his beard, then smiled. "Which could suit your purposes."

I knelt beside him, put a hand on his shoulder, and said, "Tell me more."

FIFTY-FIVE

Boom.

Three months after Wilgan educated me about amphibious operations, the Winter Palace's stone battlement jumped beneath my feet. Bassin's prototype artillery piece spit a shell toward a target raft bobbing in the Sea of Hunters. Startled pterosaurs shrieked, leapt from their cliff perches, and glided above the waves. Spray fountained, and the raft disappeared.

Bassin and Jude turned to one another, grinning and tugging cotton from their ears. Both wore Combat Engineers' uniform, Bassin's still with Colonel's rank, because he refused a Marshal's baton, and Jude's with the pips of a Provisional Lieutenant.

When I assigned Jude to Bassin's gearheads, I told him they needed his math smarts. They did. I didn't tell him the Engineers also figured to take fewer casualties than first-wave units.

Culture transfer was a two-way street, so Bassin and Jude knuckle-bumped the gun crew the way Jude had taught them, then Bassin grinned at me. "Another fifty you owe me."

Bassin and I had a running bet on his new field pieces' accuracy, which I had lost all seven days since Alliance headquarters moved to the Winter Palace. "His field piece" was a stretch. Bassin's new darling grew from blueprints printed out of Jeeb's memory for a U.S. Civil War 3-inch Ordnance Rifle. It was the only rifled gun Ord could find that both fit the wrought-iron capabilities of the Marinus forges and had a tube light enough to haul in a packet boat. An Ordnance Rifle could hit the end of a flour barrel at any distance under a mile, or fire canister shot at close range into charging Slugs.

Not all our technology had blossomed. Smokeless powder would have to wait until there was a chemical industry capable of making nitrocellulose and nitroglycerin.

Marini industry was years from being able to duplicate radios, even the surplus antiques that MAT(D)4 was allowed to share with its Earth Advisees. We tried to get Casus to use a backpack portable. But the first time my voice trickled out of the black plastic handset, Casus accused the handset of being a beetle that stole human souls.

Once Ord's boogeyman story about the Cargo'Bots spread, not even the less superstitious Marini would go near them. Howard used them to packrat his debris collection.

Bassin and I walked to the landward battlement and looked back across the farmland and hamlets of Southern Marin. Around every hut cluster that swelled where narrow roads crossed, yurt and tent forests sprouted. In every field, wobbleheads and duckbills grazed, or surged in lines back and forth as their riders maneuvered.

From the embarkation beaches south of the Palace twenty miles deep back into Marin, the Alliance's Army grew. Munitions and supplies poured in, rowed along the coast from Marinus in river packets. From the desert Encampments of the Tassini to the tiny upriver outposts along the Marin, even more troops trained, all to funnel to this place by the jump-off date, which seemed to rush at us like a charging wronk.

Bassin laid his hands on the parapet. "The farmers say their land is about to sink in the sea beneath the army's weight."

If it did, they would throw their last life preserver to a cavalryman.

I said, "I heard a village made dinner for two Casuni Troops yesterday. And the Casuni put on a riding display for them afterwards."

Community relations hadn't been so cordial at first, and often still weren't. Casuni Cavalry had trampled farm fields. Tassini had "requisitioned," then roasted, livestock. City boys from Marinus had taken more than a few liberties with country girls. But country girls were good with fowling pieces loaded with salt, as a few city boys had learned the hard way.

I leaned my elbows on the stone and groaned. "I still spend half my day listening to grumpy aldermen and patching broken gates and broken hearts."

Bassin looked up at the sun. "Time for Staff Meeting?"

I sighed, and we walked back toward the Palace. "I'd rather date a country girl with a gun."

FIFTY-SIX

"A SOLDIER SURE OF HIS FOOTING has no need of a mount!" The Marini Infantry Marshal pounded his fist on the conference table. The Casuni and Tassini cavalrymen he was arguing with rolled their eyes.

I rapped my knuckles on the table. "Let's get started, gentlemen."

Bassin sat to my left, Casus and the ranking Tassini alternated to my immediate right. Infantry Marshals, Cavalry Division Commanders, a General of Charioteers, and a Marini Admiral filled out the table flanks.

Ord, Gustus, and Howard sat at the table's end opposite me. I asked Howard, "What about the timetable?"

"Jeeb's last look showed nothing new. The Pseudocephalopod still has warriors postured defensively in the isthmus, behind the wall. And a large force remains dug in around the Troll. Too many to deal with if we attacked now with what we had, too few for It to start offensive operations. As long as we jump off within four months, we have a chance to destroy the Troll before it puts out warriors in overwhelming numbers. I'd like to send Jeeb in for a close look at those outbuildings beside the Troll."

"The Stone storage sheds?"

"That's what they look like, but a worm's eye view could be interesting."

Howard always wanted to chase interesting. But if some Slug closed a door behind Jeeb, he couldn't shoot his way out of an enclosed space.

I shook my head. "Jeeb's the only pair of eyes we have. I can't risk him."

I asked Gustus and Ord, "How's the Tassini cavalry project?"

Even the Casuni agreed that Tassini could outride the wind, but our budding divisions needed Troops with fifty riders each, trained and integrated into the overall battle plan. A Tassini Encampment's largest unit was the Raiding Party, twelve riders organized like a bus wreck.

So we had established Cavalry Basic schools in every one of the hundred Tassini Encampments, and poured in supplies of guns, powder, feed, and body armor.

Ord said, "Plenty of volunteers. And they really do ride like the wind. Supply shortages are retarding training, Sir."

"I thought we were drowning 'em with stuff."

Gustus pushed his spectacles back on his pug nose. "We are. But after the caravans unload at the Encampments, we're suffering 60 percent pilferage."

At the table's end, a Casuni muttered under his breath. "Scratch a Tassini, find a thief."

I raised my eyebrows at Gustus and Ord. "Sixty percent isn't pilferage. It's hemorrhage. Solution?"

Inventory control was a command migraine even back home, with 'Puters. Gustus slid an object the length of the table's onyxwood. It looked like a bone-carved harp the size of a ham sandwich. Ten pea-sized mollusk shells, drilled through their centers, slid along each harp string.

It was a little abacus like Bassin used.

Someone sniffed. "A zill?"

Gustus nodded, and said to me, "Experienced Shopwives run huge bakeries with nothing more than one of these zills and their wits, and never lose a groundfruit seed."

"So?"

Ord turned another of the little harps in his hands. "Each School Commandant spends eighteen hours each day on training. As he should. Inventory control would bury him, even if he were used to it. We have thousands of female Marini volunteers we could train as crackerjack Supply Clerks."

The Casuni Marshal's eyes bugged. "Marini libertines among the Tassini?"

Ord turned to him. "Only after appropriate cultural instruction, Sir."

I did a mental eye roll. The two Plains Clans were at war for their collective lives. If the Casuni and the Tassini had to swallow some trivial women's lib to win, so be it.

"Make it happen, Sergeant Major. Be sure the Clerks keep their head scarves tied." I moved the meeting on to more important things.

Weeks later, Ord slipped into my office, alone and frowning. "Sir, I've caused a problem. The Supply Clerk idea—"

I paused with a handful of Morning Reports. "I thought the Zill Jills were working out."

He nodded. "Quick studies, fine soldiers. Last night a Supply Clerk newly deployed to a Tassini Cavalry Basic unit was killed—"

"But it's a desk job."

"By the Encampment Headman."

"Get the Tassini liaison officer in here. Now."

My Tassini liaison was a former Encampment Headman. He got his staff job because he was a better politi-
cian than a rider.

He sat across from me, crossed his legs, and slicked an
indigo-dyed eyebrow with one finger. "Is this about the
prostitute?"

I leaned forward. "What?" The Earth military history
I'd read reported millions of female soldiers had served
more than honorably. But there were rare tales of indis-
cretion, for example during the Cold-War dust-ups, like
Vietnam. And, unlike the worldly Marini, Tassini consid-
ered prostitution a capital crime. I couldn't just tell him
he was full of crap.

He waved his hand. "Her manner of dress provoked the
accusation. Then her offense was proved."

"Proved?"

"By Boxing."

"The Accused had to fight?"

He shook his head. "Every Encampment carries with
it a wooden box, large enough for a woman to crouch in.
There is a lid, with a breathing hole. At sunrise, the Headman places the Accused in The Box. Then he drops three
Kris through the breathing hole."

I cocked my head at Ord, who stood against my office's back wall, hands clasped at his back, in the position
of At Ease.

"Foot-long scorpions, Sir. Their neurotoxin paralyzes
in one minute, kills in thirty."

The Liaison Officer said, "*Kris* sting only unclean

flesh. The Headman opens The Box at sunset. If she is innocent, she is alive."

I took a deep breath, then let it out. "How long have the Tassini been using The Box?"

"Three hundred years."

"Has a woman ever survived?"

"Of course not. If she isn't a whore, the Headman doesn't put her in The Box."

On my desk I displayed, as a letter opener, a jeweled dagger gifted on me by a VIP visitor. I took its hilt in my fist, squeezed it, and debated whether to stab the fool across the desk, or myself. I had misassumed that I could dismantle centuries of divergent culture by giving an order. A soldier was dead, and it was my fault.

I asked the Liaison Officer, "What if, as Military Governor, I forbid use of The Box?"

His eyes widened. "The Headmen would lose honor. The Tassini would bolt the Alliance."

"Those clerks are helping to win the war. How do you think the Marini will react if this Boxing continues?"

"Like the cowardly pimps and whores they are. They will bolt the Alliance."

Either way, the Alliance would lose the war, and the Slugs would slaughter every human on Bren.

I asked him, "Well, what would *you* do?"

He shrugged. "Quietly pay each Headman a facilitation fee, so he will not use The Box."

"How many Headmen do you think would do such a deal?"

"Oh, 90 percent or more. And don't worry, each would swear for you to the public that no unclean coin had crossed his palm."

I sighed.

As an Adviser on Earth, I had put up with *baksheesh* in all its permutations. One man's bribe was another man's tip. But this was different. I was ordering Allies who had cut one another's throats for centuries to trust each other to do right. They had to trust me to do right, too. If I bribed Headmen, Staff would know. If Staff knew, everybody would know. The Alliance would be doomed to business as usual, with the Clans at daggerpoints.

I sighed, and rubbed my eyes. Then I said to the Tassini officer, "I see. Prepare a proclamation for my signature as Military Governor. It will confirm that each Headman has ongoing authority to use The Box."

He smiled. "Very wise, Sir."

Ord furrowed his brow.

I said, "But it must be used in the fashion that we use The Box where I come from. In my home place, each Headman begins each month by going in The Box. Since the *Kris* sting only unclean palms, we know from this that our Headmen have taken no bribes."

The Officer squirmed in his chair. "A Headman has many civic duties. He might be unable to spare a whole day to go in The Box."

"I understand completely. Where I come from, Headmen often delay their test until year end, without dishonor. They just don't use The Box in the meantime." I smiled.

He frowned.

I said, "Well, that's settled. Can you issue the Proclamation before lunch?"

He did. Sporadic friction continued between Tassini and Marini female soldiers, but no woman, of any Clan, was put in The Box thereafter. Coincidentally, ninety

Headmen resigned just before the year ended. The following month, pilferage in those ninety Encampments dropped to zero, and stayed there.

Ord told me later that I handled the situation wisely. But nine-tenths of wisdom is being wise in time. Ord didn't say that, Teddy Roosevelt did.

Two months afterward I woke at 3 A.M., and looked at my hands. Even in the dark, I saw that innocent girl's blood on them, because I had not been wise in time.

She wasn't the first soldier that died too young while under my command. She was far from the last. Perhaps one day I'll grow so accustomed to such things that I'll wake up and I won't see that blood. On that day I will retire from command.

The next morning, I rode to one of the embarkation beaches for my morning run. I had covered two miles along the hardpacked sand, as the waves rumbled in and out. Another figure loomed out of the ground fog, closing on me from the shoreward dunes, and called, "We need to talk."

FIFTY-SEVEN

JUDE SWUNG ALONGSIDE ME, and matched my pace.

I smiled at him. "Would the *Lieutenant* care for a little race?"

Jude had traded his pips for regular Lieutenant's talons at a promotion ceremony the week before. I had stayed in the back row among the engineers while Bassin, himself, pinned them on.

Alongside me, in the mist, Jude looked as graceful as his father had looked when we ran together on pre-season early mornings. Even Metzger couldn't match Jude as a rifle shot now, and Jude looked as hard and as fit as any soldier in this army.

He said, "I want out of the Engineers."

I frowned as I huffed along. "Take it up with your CO. You know better than to jump the chain of command."

"I already took it up with him. He's good with it. So's Bassin. R and D's done, so the gearheads don't need my math anymore."

"So why talk to me?"

"I'm transferring to the Scouts."

"No." I shook my head.

The Scouts had emerged as our army's fastest riders, best climbers, best shots, and most dashing elite. Rangers, SEALs, Green Berets, all rolled up in one outfit. But boats carrying the Tassini Scouts and their wobbleheads would be first across the Red Line. The survivors would be the first to hit the beaches. Gustus had Zill Jills quietly cranking out casualty estimates for me. They predicted the Scouts would take 70 percent casualties. No other unit was expected to take even 30 percent, unless everything went to hell.

I said, "You're unqualified."

"I can ride a wobblehead with any of them. And I can outshoot all of them."

"Most of the Scouts have ridden together since they were kids. Shoehorning you in will destroy unit integrity."

"I qualified as a Master Harpooner last night. That way the boat carries one more Scout, one less sailor. We waste less weight and space."

Our boots crunched along the sand.

Jude said, "A Fifteenth Encampment Troop Leader broke his arm yesterday. The CO says the job's mine if I want it."

I stopped, panting, with hands on hips. "If you think I'm going to approve—"

Jude faced me in the gray morning, twisting the ring made from his father's medal. "I'm not here to get your approval. I'm just asking you to stay out of it." He toed the sand with his boot. "Look, I know what you tried to do. I appreciate it. I really do. But it's my life. This is on me."

Jude turned, then ran on down the beach, until the mist closed in, and he disappeared.

My sweats hung wet on my shoulders, and I stood in the mist until I shivered. The waves boomed behind me, as relentless as clock ticks.

I said to the place where Jude had stood, "No, it's on me. It's all on me."

The remaining training weeks evaporated into a fog of reports, accidents, arguments, and exhaustion.

Ord's hand touched my shoulder, and I sat up straight and awake on my cot in the darkness. I saw invisible blood on my hands, and my wrist 'Puter read midnight.

Ord whispered, "It's time, Sir."

FIFTY-EIGHT

I SLID MY TORSO PLATES DOWN over my shoulders by flickering lantern light, and asked Ord, "What are the counts?"

I had accelerated the D-Day morning reports. By sunrise I'd have no time to read them, and staff less to write them. And casualties would change the numbers for the worse with every heartbeat.

We stepped from my tent into the night as Ord read a handful of papers by his headlight. "First Wave, 50,262 available for duty. Follow-on waves, support units, and other admin, total, 454,006 reporting. We have 5,233 vessels seaworthy, 36,744 stock watered and healthy, and 620 artillery tubes tested and serviceable."

I stared into the sky. Moons-rise remained an hour away, but the night was still, chill, and full of stars.

I muttered. "Good."

I was talking about the sky, not the counts. A fiction of war is "the weather is always neutral." Wind, high seas, rain, mud, heat, cold, ice, snow—they all favor the defense. This clear weather was a break, and we needed every break.

Ord said, "They're reporting a front at the isthmus, moving south. Fog, sleet. It shouldn't bother us here for three days."

We deployed some of our scarce radios to make a relay net with our diversionary attack force five hundred miles north, up on the isthmus that separated the continents. The isthmus formed the obvious avenue for a human invasion into Slug Land. The Slugs believed that, or they wouldn't have spent a thousand years walling Slug Land off there, like Hadrian walled off the Scots from Roman-occupied England.

To pin the Slug Legions defending the Millennium Wall, and to freeze their mobile reserve divisions two hundred miles north of the landing beaches, we trumped up an "army" of farm carts driven by old men to kick up lots of dust in the hills on the human side of the Slugs' Millennium Wall each day, and light hundreds of "campfires" each night. A few buglers signaled to Brigades that didn't exist, except for cannoneers that stood by every obsolete Marini blunderbuss we could scrape together.

At first light, today, the cannoneers would barrage the Millennium Wall like they were softening it up for the Meuse-Argonne Offensive.

Ord said, "For once, bad weather favors the offense, Sir. The longer the Slugs can't see how little we really have deployed at the isthmus, the longer before they counterattack our beachhead."

"We don't have a beachhead yet, Sergeant Major." I reached inside my armor, tugged out a single, folded taupe page, and handed it to Ord. "If necessary, have the Queen's Secretary release this to the papers."

Marinus and the larger towns had newspapers. We sent

all their reporters up north, with the diversionary force. The *New York Times* would've howled about that, and I've taken bullets defending its right to howl, but free press is no issue in an absolute monarchy.

Ord unfolded the paper and read it. I'd longhanded it the night before, with a dinosaur-feather quill and blue-black cuttlefish ink. It read:

Our recent landings have failed to gain a satisfactory foothold, and I have withdrawn our troops. The decision to attack at this time and place was based on the best information available. The troops did all that bravery and devotion to duty could. If blame or fault attaches to the attempt, it is mine alone.
> —Jason Wander, Supreme Commander, Allied Expeditionary Forces

I couldn't bear to think that up myself. I cribbed it from a contingent note Eisenhower wrote before Normandy.

Ord nodded, refolded the taupe paper, and tucked it into his breastplate pouch.

He didn't tell me that we wouldn't need it.

We wound for a mile through tent clusters spread among the dunes behind the embarkation beaches. We first passed through the late-wave units, the ones that would only make the crossing if we lodged successfully on the opposite shore.

Sweet janga smoke drifted across the Marini charioteers' laagers. The troops weren't getting stoned before battle. Their wronks were being sedated, so they could be chained down in boats to make the crossing.

I shuddered at the smell. We had perfected the sedation

technique now, but, early on, I had witnessed a test during which an underdoped, trussed-up bull wronk kicked the bottom out of a river packet. The boat sank like an anvil, with all hands. I handwrote letters to the family of each soldier lost, and teared up every time.

As we passed onto the beach, the surf boomed. The fifty Tassini Scouts of the Fifteenth Encampment squatted in a ring around a low fire in the sand. They clapped in unison, keeping time with the surf's pulse.

Their boat lay on its side in the sand, ten yards away, between the fire and the sea.

The upturned boat shielded the fire's heat signature from the far shore, but Jeeb's latest reconnaissance flights seemed—seemed—to confirm that the far beaches were sparsely defended.

Howard still hadn't gotten his look inside the storage sheds near the Troll, and we hadn't covered a host of other contingencies that hung ahead of us like swords. But if a commander can give every unit everything every time, he isn't using everything he has.

Alongside the fire, painted orange in its light, the Fifteenth's Troop Leader and First Sergeant hopped side-to-side, feet together, in time to the clapping. They jumped across Tassini swords planted naked-blade-up in the sand.

The Tassini believed the Sword Dance and prayer before battle bought safety. Personally, I'd buy safety with a good helmet and a clean rifle.

When Jude saw Ord and me, he stopped mid-hop.

His troopers stopped clapping, looked where he looked, then leapt up and surrounded me. I shook hands, patted shoulders, smiled, and tried not to think about 70 percent of those kids as tomorrow's casualties.

Most of the Marini Marshals, and not a few offi-
cers on Earth, thought buddying with the troops wasted
scarce planning time and energy, and familiarity undercut
discipline.

But when I was a Specialist 4th, training before we embarked for Ganymede, Nat Cobb was our Division Commander. He had 9,950 other soldiers on his mind besides
my Platoon. But he woke up and heard a blizzard howling
around his tent, and remembered our Platoon was out on
an overnight route march. General Cobb parka'd up, had
a driver drop him beside the road, then slogged in to camp
beside us, bitching at the snow and the wind louder than
any of us.

I never forgot that, and I bet no GI in that Platoon did
either. I'm not saying the Marshals were wrong. I'm just
saying commanders' time spent with troops is more gain
than give.

While Jude's men doused their fire and toppled their
boat onto log rollers to trundle it down to the surf line,
Jude and I stood apart.

He looked out at his Scouts through the open visor of
his crimson Eternads, and said, "They're as ready as I can
make them."

His kids were older than he was, and as lean and tough
as whipcord, but not one of them had ever seen more
combat than a sniping match with Casunis.

I said, "Nobody's ever ready for what they're going to
see. But if you let 'em flinch, you'll give more than you
gain."

His eyes glistened in the darkness. "I could never give
more than you and Mom already have, Jason."

Maybe he couldn't, but I could, and I didn't want to.

I hugged him before he could see my tears, and patted his backplate. He wore the old crimson Eternad armor Ord had fitted him with from the adviser stocks we had brought from Earth. Back home, Eternad crimsons were junk, but they had been enough to protect me and Jude's mother through the Battle of Ganymede.

"Always." Then he pulled away.

An hour later, I stood in the sand with Wilgan, the old Ship Master, and Ord. We watched both full moons rise over the Sea of Hunters.

The full moons' rare combined appearance lit the night like false sunshine, as it had for eons. The false sunshine bloomed phytoplankton as fast as popped corn. Krill, shrimp no bigger than rice grains, rose to feast on the phytoplankton. The krill's bioluminescence painted the sea beyond six fathoms like a pale blue prairie burning.

Ord stood alongside me and whispered, "Never thought I'd see two moons in one sky, and an ocean on fire."

Wilgan said, "There's our Glowies, fine as you please."

Wilgan's Glowies attracted hungry sardine-sized predators. Behind the sardines, and hungry for *them,* swarmed sharks and bony fishes as long as a human leg.

The first wave's boats pitched outbound in the surf, their thousand navigation lanterns winding north and south from where Ord and I stood.

I chinned my helmet optics. Two heartbeats thumped before they focused. A mile out, faint wakes made vees in the water. The first kraken were rising, responding to the bigger fish, and to the drum of fifty thousand oars all beating the water like struggling prey.

The first boats' harpooners would challenge the early arriving kraken that attacked them. The next kraken would attack their wounded siblings as enthusiastically as the first kraken had attacked our boats. The krakens' struggles would bring up rhind by the hundreds. In the frenzy of feeding behemoths, our invasion fleet would slip through, as ignored as I had been when I slipped through the scavengers that battled over carrion at the Fair's wreckage.

Theoretically, our boats wouldn't have to outrun the rhind, they would just have to outrun or outfight the first few kraken.

Theoretically.

Wilgan said, "So far, so good. Just like the test."

But the next minutes could doom the GIs in those boats, and with them this civilization.

I swallowed, and said to Ord, "What if I blundered, Sergeant Major?"

Ord nodded back his helmet optics, then peered through his old binoculars. "Sir, Churchill said that war is mostly a catalogue of blunders."

I chinned my optics. A mile out, the first kraken, tentacles flailing, raced toward the lead assault boat, until the gap between beast and vessel narrowed to twenty yards. The kraken and the boat closed to within twenty yards of one another. The boat's harpooner stood in its prow, and spray dripped off his crimson armor as it gleamed in the moonlight.

My heart pounded, and I held my breath.

Jude raised his harpoon, and sighted on the monster's yellow eye.

FIFTY-NINE

JUDE HURLED THE BARBED BLACK IRON. At the same instant, a tentacle tip wrapped the boat's lantern, then tore the lantern from the boat's prow. The boat heeled and dipped toward the waves, as the Scouts at the oars swayed.

The harpoon vanished into the kraken's great eye, the barb exploded, and tissue geysered into the sea.

Tentacles thrashed, slipping off the boat, and it righted.

Scouts thrust their arms skyward, and pumped their fists, as the waters around the boat smoothed.

I breathed again.

Yards seaward of Jude's boat, a whitecap appeared on the sea, and grew, first into a black knob, and then into a black mountain that towered twenty feet taller than Jude, as he stood tiny and crimson in the bobbing boat.

The rhind's ebony head was wedge-shaped, as though the *Titanic* had surfaced bow-first from the abyss, and silver seawater rivers cascaded from a double row of shark-fin scutes down the beast's back.

In its toothed jaws, the rhind vised the limp kraken that Jude had harpooned, like a wolf that had snatched a spar-

row as it flew past. Seawater coursed off the kraken's tentacles, and ran off the spear-point of its cone shell.

Howard called the rhind "tylosaurs," air-breathing,
aquatic lizards—like crocodiles with flippers.

The rhind's body shot out of the sea until its snout was
forty feet in the air, and its red eye burned down at the
assault boat. The rhind's foreflipper, bigger by itself than
the boat, cleared the water.

Alongside me, Wilgan whispered, "Big feller. I make
him a hundred fifty feet."

I muttered, and pushed my hand at the air in front of
me, like I was brushing back a dangling snake. "Get out
of there!"

The monster toppled back to the sea with its fifty-foot
prize, and its flipper carved Jude's boat in two, like a
cleaver splitting a bread loaf.

"No!" I whispered.

Oars, men, and rifles splintered and tumbled in silhouette across the brilliant moons.

Jude, armored limbs outstretched, cartwheeled across
the sky like a five-pointed ruby.

SIXTY

I PUNCHED THE ZOOM ON MY OPTICS so hard that they retracted. I swore, tore off my helmet, and reset them manually with quivering fingers. By the time I got them back on, the frame in focus showed nothing at the spot where the rhind had crashed back into the sea but debris bobbing on the waves. Elsewhere, all up and down the six-fathom line, rhind and kraken struggled as our boats bobbed and dashed around and through them.

I switched my radio from command net to Eternad intercom, and spoke. "Fifteen Leader, this is Eagle joining your net, over." Screw procedure and chain of command. "Jude? This is Jason!"

I repeated for three minutes, but only static hum answered.

I grabbed Ord's arm. "Can you see him? Did you see—"

Ord lowered his binoculars, and shook his head. "His radio may have been damaged. You know those old Eternads . . ." He paused. "Nothing moving out there now, Sir. Another boat may have picked him up."

The assault boats were to maintain a hundred yards'

separation, and to stop for nothing, double underscored. Ord knew that as well as I did. He had helped me edit the wording when the orders came across my desk for review.

My heart sank in my chest like an anvil.

"Sure. Probably." I stared into the sand, and shook my head. Why had I stayed out of it? Why had I been so foolish? Why had I let a sixteen-year-old who knew nothing of his own mortality spend his life on a fool's errand?

I blinked back tears.

Because if he didn't, some other immortal sixteen-year-old would have died in his place.

The squeal of keels crossing wooden rollers echoed in the night, and I looked up and down the beach. The second-wave boats and crews moved into launch positions.

A Marini Signals runner, kicking up beach sand as he staggered, stopped, then stood to attention in front of me. He couldn't have been older than fourteen. Not so much younger than my godson had been. No, I lied to myself. Not so much younger than my godson was.

Cheeks flushed, the boy saluted, then panted, "Sir, first reports."

SIXTY-ONE

BY THE TIME THE FIRST REPORTS had become second, and third, and fourth reports, the moons had set, and sunrise had become a blinding sliver above the Sea of Hunters.

At the water's edge, I stood beneath a dun-colored woven canopy, with Howard, Ord, and the Marini Admiral in charge of follow-on overwater transport.

Follow-on meant extracting survivors if we failed, or ferrying admin personnel across the Sea if the landings succeeded. The Admiral was the officer who, seven months before, at the Alliance's first meeting, had asked the Queen to relieve me when I recommended an amphibious assault across the Sea of Hunters.

We stood around a camp table, and stared into the hologen's image.

Howard pointed with a chewed yellow pencil at the overhead image that Jeeb was transmitting. A broad area of the sea below Jeeb boiled white, as animals struggled against one another like bucketed worms. Even as we watched, the area shifted north and broadened. Here and there, our boats darted untouched through and around the melee.

Howard said, "The feeding field now extends eight miles in widest dimension. A moveable feast, to borrow a phrase. The rhind and kraken have worn each other out. The smaller fry are pouncing on *them*. We should have forty-eight hours before the predator population recovers and reinfests this area enough to impede our movement."

Ord folded back the top sheets of a sheaf of reports. "With the first and second waves ashore, and the third under way, casualties stand at less than 2 percent, Sirs. Some of those are missing in action, so the final total should go lower. The Scouts made landfall in disarray. But they encountered only half a dozen sentries along the entire landing beach front—and neutralized them all without loss. They've pushed a beachhead inland two miles already, without firing a shot."

I closed my eyes, exhaled, then looked again at Ord.

He stared at me, pulled a single, folded taupe sheet from his breastplate pouch, then crumpled it in his fist. "We shouldn't be needing this, General."

The Marini Admiral stroked his white mustache. "It's a miracle!"

I stared at the balled note in Ord's hand, felt cold, and bit my lip. It would never be a miracle to the families of the dead. For every commander who had to write a condolence letter to one of those families, and for every family who received one of those letters, the casualty rate was 100 percent. But it was a miracle, nonetheless.

We waded out through the surf, and swabbies pushed and pulled us up into the bobbing boat that would finally take us to war.

As the crew loaded our gear, the Admiral tugged an

oval silver flask from his pocket, flipped back its cap with his thumb, and toasted me. "Brilliant plan, Commander! The worst is over now, hey?"

Then he took a pull, and handed me the flask.

It was as empty as his head.

SIXTY-TWO

TEN MILES OUT into the Sea of Hunters, as we skirted the boiling melee of the feeding frenzy, I came eyeball to eyeball with my first rhind.

The exhausted black leviathan lolled at the surface, like a capsized freighter. Its exposed bulk towered twelve feet taller than our packet boat, and by the time our crew rowed us from the rhind's flaccid tail to its snout, we had covered three times the boat's fifty-foot length.

Every few seconds, a fin cut the surface, as a shark darted in, tore flesh from the rhind's heaving flank, then flashed away. The beast's heart thumped slowly, as though a bass drum lay muffled within its ribs, and its red eye, larger than a cannonball, stared down at me as we rowed past.

Perhaps I should have wondered whether this was the same monster that had crushed Jude's boat. Perhaps I should have been outraged, or triumphant, as the rhind floated, dying.

What could the rhind have made of this fifty-headed creature that paddled past, scuttling over the sea in its own inverted shell?

For eons, the rhind and its kind had ruled Bren's oceans.

Neither the Slugs, which Earthlings called murderers, nor the Clans, which Earthlings would call barbarians, had disrupted the natural order of things. Now, in one morning, four Earthlings had inverted and bloodied this world. Once, I had asked Bassin whether rhind were the scariest thing on this planet. Maybe the Slugs were right. Maybe we were the disease, not them.

Howard stood alongside me as we ghosted past the rhind like mice past a cat.

Howard's helmet cam crackled as he snapped images of the beast. "If I didn't see this, I wouldn't believe it was real. The Bunker Tylosaur was a third this long."

"New planet, new reality. Just be glad reality didn't bite your ass." I mag'd my view of the landing grounds ahead of us. Boats, troops by the tens of thousands, cavalry mounts, cannon, and supply wagons jumbled on the beaches. "Yet."

SIXTY-THREE

_____

AN HOUR LATER, I planted my feet in the sand of our expanding beachhead, and a handler brought up the dapple duckbill I would ride. As I grasped its reins, Casus thundered toward me on his white stallion, cape flying, and reined up.

I squinted up at him, and asked, "You reform your Divisions yet?"

He shook his head, pointing toward the dunes that bordered the beach. "Each Troop dashes inland as soon as its mounts recover from the janga."

I sighed. "You have no command and control of your units?"

Casus stiffened. "We discussed this. We agreed!"

I had been terrified that our troops and equipment would pile up in a restricted beachhead, where the Slugs could cut them to bits with heavy fire. The "miracle" of Dunkirk, and of the British and French that the German army had surrounded on its beaches, was that the Allies won the war in spite of it. Dispersal had been my obsession, if we got ashore.

"I know. You're right." But I hung my head, and

sighed again. "Keep pressing, but try to organize things on the fly."

I assigned Casus to command the dash across the three hundred open miles, from the beaches to the mountains, that lay between us and the Troll, precisely because he had more speed than judgment.

He would press his soldiers mercilessly forward, wringing out their last sweat drops, because speed could win this war. Casus wouldn't press because he was a bastard, though many of his soldiers surely would think he was. Caring about soldiers didn't mean indulging them. A commander should always prefer live soldiers' hatred over the affection of mothers who tell him their dead sons loved him.

A century before, Eisenhower trusted an ivory-handled-pistol-toting, GI-slapping public-relations disaster to boot the Nazis across France. Patton routed the Germans so magnificently that his armies outran their gasoline trucks.

I asked Casus, "Do you even know where your point units are? Whether they need supplies? Do they know whether our overhead imagery shows Slugs ahead of them? Or friendlies on their flanks?"

Casus shrugged. "My men are like their mounts. They smell the way home, and it's forward."

Command is choosing the right horse for the right course, then letting it run. But with a light hand still on the reins. Casus was the right horse for this course, but . . .

I swung up onto my duckbill. "Change of plan. My headquarters will move with yours for a couple days."

A couple days turned out to be four weeks. The weather front from the north slammed us one morning later, then sat for days. Snow turned to rain, rain made mud, and

Casus's great dash forward stalled. Worse, the Slugs figured out where our main thrust was, and shifted their mobile reserve south to block us.

Tassini Scout units made first contact with overwhelming Slug forces at night, in a driving rain. Light-armored and inexperienced, the Scouts got mauled, and fell back through Casus's cavalry units in disarray.

When first contact came, most kindergartens would have had better command and control than we did.

Marini infantry hurled into the breach finally stabilized the front, thanks to Gustus's assault rifles, a few Company-level commanders' tactical brilliance, and, as a Marini infantry sergeant reminded me, "A few bayonets wif' guts behind 'em!"

The Slugs, who did always seem to go to school on human tactics, settled in to a mobile defense, blocking our front, jabbing, then defending every terrain obstacle until we flanked them. Then the Slugs gave ground, retreating behind the next obstacle. I felt as frustrated as Sherman marching south toward Atlanta.

Unlike the Confederates who delayed Sherman, time was on the Pseudocephalopod's side. The Slug army grew by fifty thousand warriors every week. Our army just grew weaker every day, as our supply lines stretched and frayed.

The wobbleheads and duckbills ate whatever they found growing in front of them, which actually eased our logistic headache compared to, say, a diesel-powered Panzer army. Gustus devised a system of prepackaged cargo loads identified by manifests that cut supply wagon turnaround time in half.

Nonetheless, Gustus's wagoners rumbled forward twenty-four-point-two hours every day, through mud and sleet. The wagoners' round trips lengthened two miles for every mile our point units advanced. The resultant exhaustion and haste meant point units sometimes tore tarps off prepackaged wagons and found saddles when they were short of bread, and bread when they needed cartridges.

The Slugs weren't winning, but they didn't have to win. They just had to give us time to lose.

Fifty-four days after we hit the beaches, Casus, Howard, Ord, Bassin, and I stood among field commanders, studying the holo gen map view in a tent that was still three hundred miles from our objective.

Casus stabbed the map with his finger. "The Scouts will position themselves here, along the riverbank." He glanced up at the Tassini Scout Commander. "Make a big show, as though you were an army."

The Tassini nodded. "Many campfires. Much patrolling."

Casus turned to the Marini Colonel of Charioteers. "Position your chariots and my cavalry here, in the woodline of these hills along the river, downstream from the Scouts. The morning fog will hide you even if the trees don't. The Slugs will believe our Scouts are our entire army. So they will advance across your front, along the river, toward the Scouts." Casus slid his finger upstream, in the direction of his Scout decoys.

Bassin nodded and smiled. "Ah! When the Slugs are strung out along the riverbank, the Chariots and cavalry will charge downhill. They will crush the Slugs against the river, like a hammer against an anvil."

Casus nodded.

I smiled. War waged without flying machines hadn't changed much over the centuries. Casus never got within light years of the Command and General Staff College at Ft. Leavenworth, but he had just diagramed the tactics Hannibal used to annihilate the Romans against the shores of Lake Trasemine in 217 B.C.

The Pseudocephalopod was as logical as the Romans, but more naive. I suppose if Howard was right, and the Pseudocephalopod was just a single being, it would never understand that the other guy might try to fool it.

Bassin said, "Then my sappers will push pontoon bridges across the river immediately."

"And my men will put them to good use," Casus said.

The next morning, I hid in the mist that wrapped the pines upslope of Casus's planned killing ground. Arrayed to my left and right were so many cavalry and Charioteers that the nervous scuffing of heavy claws made a constant buzz.

This would be the first time many Tassini and Casuni units that had been fragmented on the landing grounds rejoined. Two hundred thousand of us, two hundred thousand Slugs. It was our chance to break the stalemate of indecisive probes and Slug retreats that had tilted the campaign against us. It was also our chance to lose everything.

Boom-boom-boom.

I heard the Slugs, though I couldn't see them, and they couldn't see us. I flicked my visor display and in front of me I saw through Jeeb's passive infrared optics the marching Slugs below him, their Legion stretched out alongside the river in a thinned black line.

A bugle echoed, and the cavalry buzz became a rumble. Upstream, the Scouts charged the Slug column's head, and collapsed it back into the Slug main body. Downstream,

Casus's cavalry swung in behind the Slug column's rear, and drove it forward into the Slug main body.

Another bugle sounded. Wronks and duckbills thundered down the slope through the mist, into the Slug traffic jam below, as soldiers and monsters roared.

I held my duckbill as he pranced. He was younger than Rosy. Younger and more prone to stick his nose where it would buy trouble.

Like Jude. My heart sank. The constant movement, and the detail of running an army of nearly half a million, had submerged the pain of loss. But every now and then the pain spiked to the surface like an attacking rhind's snout.

The rattle of assault rifles and the zing of answering mag rails echoed to me live through the mist, while I concentrated on the visual of the battle unfolding in my visor display.

An hour after the bugles began the battle, the mist burned off, and I watched live as well as listened. Casus's plan unfolded flawlessly, and his troops executed it magnificently. The Slug elements that his troops backed against the river could do nothing but wheel, fight, and die.

I switched my view to panoramic. Wronks trampled armored Slug warriors like roaches. Tassini on wobbleheads slashed in and out among the warriors. Casuni hacked—and fired point-blank automatic bursts at—packed-in Slugs. So many dead Slugs lay in the muddy shallows that their green lifeblood curled out into the stream and changed its color.

The Slugs rushed reinforcements from their rear up to the opposite bank. Slug Heavys pot-shot Bassin's pontoon bridges, and the spans shattered and sank, as his engineers struggled to bolt their sections together.

But, for once, Gustus's logisticians got it right, and new bridge sections appeared from our rear faster than the Slugs could sink them.

By afternoon, the first Tassini Scouts dashed across the first completed bridge span, while Marini infantry massing along the near riverbank cheered.

The Slugs pulled back, and our rout of them resumed. Eisenhower said, "Relentless and speedy pursuit is the most profitable action in war," and Casus was proving it.

I stood dismounted at a bridgehead as Marini infantry followed the Casuni cavalry that rumbled across the water. Our mercifully few dead would travel with us, until we could inter them honorably, but the Slugs cared less than we did about their own casualties. Slug corpses lay so thick along the river's banks that already, scavenging inland pterosaurs circled high above the battlefield, anvil-headed gliders whose angular wings spanned nearly forty feet.

I had seen similar, smaller gliders skim the sea at the Winter Palace. More awkward reptile than bird, they had to pick their way up the cliffs on which the Palace stood, then launch themselves on barely flappable wings to swoop down on fish at the sea's surface. But even those little coastal versions had plenty of teeth.

One soldier pointed at the river with his rifle, at water transformed by the blood of Slugs, and called to me, "You should change the name, General!"

I did. On this new continent, our maps identified terrain features by number. But any GI would prefer to tell his grandchildren how he won the Battle of Emerald River, not the Action at Water Obstacle No. 89.

For the next weeks, we repeated the pattern, driving the

Slugs back across river after river. The Slugs would shoot up Bassin's bridges, then his Sappers would bring up a spare bridge. The Slugs would shoot it up, and Bassin's boys would haul in another spare. Each time, the Slugs ran out of fight before the Sappers ran out of bridges. Each time, the infantry watched the show, then finally streamed across.

The first hills the Slugs fell back to were limestone, honeycombed with caves. Some of those caves might have made flat, shortcut passages to the other side for infantry, easier than climbing over the hills.

But from bitter experience, I knew the Slugs liked to set ambushes in caves, or hide out in them until we passed, then attack our rear. I warned Casus.

Boom.

I stood alongside a Marini artillery battery, hands over my audio receptors, and watched as a three-inch Ordnance Rifle bucked back on its wheeled carriage. A mile away the shell crashed into a cave mouth, stone collapsed in a gray dust cloud, and the opening vanished.

A mud-caked infantryman, hunkered on one knee alongside the battery, turned to his buddy, and sighed, as his potential shortcut disappeared. "Well, now we got a stinking day of climbing ahead!"

His buddy jerked his thumb toward the engineer column behind them. "Nah. I bet Colonel Bassin carries a spare tunnel wif' him."

The weather had been dry, and we made a good run from the Emerald River to the Limestone Hills.

But every good run ends.

SIXTY-FOUR

THE NIGHT AFTER WE REDUCED the caves in the Limestone Hills, after security was set, stock watered, and supplies distributed, I left Ord at the Headquarters tent, poring over forms by a lantern's yellow glow, while I made campfire rounds.

I tried to get to everybody, but with a third of a million troops scattered across a foreign wilderness, I was lucky to see a couple units each night.

By the time I started my visits, most troops had taken to their tents. A half dozen Tassini Scouts squatted around their fire, and when they saw me emerge into their light, they sprang to their feet.

I waved my hand, palm down. "At ease! What's keeping you all up?"

One scout frowned. "General, somebody said we're gonna have to carry those fat Casuni up the mountains tomorrow."

Troops hear the most ridiculous crap, and they take it seriously until somebody tells them otherwise.

George Washington's Colonials astonished Von Steuben, their Prussian teacher, by insisting on knowing why.

Like the Colonials, GIs in combat want truth even more than hot meals, and good commanders move mountains to give them both.

I squatted next to the Scouts, and ticked off the facts on my fingers. "It's only thirty miles up and over the mountains to the objective. But it's a hundred miles to get around to the objective if we keep advancing across the flatlands. Your wobbleheads can pick their way across the mountain ledges, but the rest of the army can't. There's forage for the cavalry mounts on the plain, but above tree line the mountains have barely enough lichen to feed a few wobbleheads. We've been successful on the Plain. We don't know what might happen in the mountains. So what would you do?"

One said, "Don't split us up, Sir. The whole army should advance across the plain."

I smiled.

Ord was already drafting this unit's order for tomorrow, to do just that.

"Okay. We'll forget the mountains for now." I looked around at their shoulder patches. "You're Sixty-Third Encampment. Hear anything about the Fifteenth?"

A soldier dead wounds his family. A soldier missing tears a wound that never heals. Everywhere I went, I asked about Jude's outfit, about a lieutenant in crimson armor.

Another Scout shook his head. "Some say men whose boats went down swum to other boats, Sir. But nobody I know's seen one, yet. And, meaning no offense to the General, I seen better-organized pub brawls than the beach landings. There's men mixed up in every unit. I'm really with the Ninetieth, myself. But the Fifteenth? They all went down the first day, I heard, Sir."

I nodded, as a lump swelled in my throat.

In all the units I had visited, nobody had heard different.

I stood, turned, and stared into the night, toward the plain along which we would advance in the morning.

It was on fire.

SIXTY-FIVE

IN THE NEXT MORNING'S DAWN, I stood alongside Gustus, Ord, Bassin, and Casus on a low rise. Around us, hundreds of duckbills and wobbleheads cropped low vegetation, while their riders struck tents and prepared to advance. Ten miles ahead, to our left and right, sheer cliffs rose two thousand feet.

The valley to our front was miles wide, and as flat and suitable to pass an army as the three hundred miles of ground our army had crossed so far. One hundred miles up that valley lay the Troll fortress that we could win the war by destroying.

But smoke grayed the valley floor, and where the wind tore away the smoke, the ground was ash-black. The stink of embers blew back across us.

I punched up Jeeb's overhead. For twenty miles up the valley, not a grass blade remained unscorched, and the Slugs had deployed units that could torch the rest of the valley in increments, if we advanced.

Gustus handed Ord back his binoculars, and replaced his spectacles. "There's no forage for the animals anymore. We'll have to forage in the rear, then bring fodder forward in the wagons. That'll siphon off our transport capacity. We'll barely be able to provision and arm the troops." Gustus turned to Casus, and shook his head. "Now, we can't support advances of longer than eight miles each week."

Ord said, "And that's if the Slugs leave us alone, which they won't."

Casus snorted. "I could crawl that far!"

I ground my teeth.

The little maggots had outwitted us again. They had done it on Earth, twice, on Ganymede, and, here on Bren, at the Fair.

The Slugs had slowed our advance up the valley by destroying our animals' forage.

Now, by the time we advanced within range for our artillery to stand off, and blow the Troll to hell, the Slug incubator would have cranked out a fresh new army of Warriors, almost twice the number of the troops we had left, to add to their existing force. If we did nothing but slog slowly up the valley, we would lose the campaign, the war, and the world. We had to be shelling the Troll within a few weeks.

I mag'd up on the distant mountains. They were fault block mountains, a series of high, gray cliffs that rose and faced us, then dropped away in shallow slopes down the far side, to the base of the next cliff. Crossing them would be like riding a thirty-mile long roller coaster, with each upslope a vertical half-mile high. Most of our army couldn't make it over those mountains.

I asked Bassin, "If Casus pinned the Slugs by advancing up the valley, could your Sappers advance the guns across the mountains in a couple weeks?"

Bassin peered one-eyed through his spyglass at the first

cliff wall, then he grinned at me. "We move sailing ships up a half-mile high waterfall in the wilderness every day."

I turned to Casus, and put a hand on his shoulder armor. "The main advance up the valley will be your show from here out. My HQ will now move with Bassin."

Casus grinned. "When you get those guns up on the heights, look before you fire. We may reach the blue mountain before you."

"I'd like that," I said.

That night we caught another weather break. In a dark, cold, obscuring drizzle, half the Tassini Scouts slipped away from their positions across the miles of width and depth of our army. Bassin's Sappers hitched the Scouts' wobbleheads to equipment wagons, and to the limbers of wheeled Ordnance Rifles, and they and the Scouts moved out on foot.

We reached the scree slope at the base of the first mountain cliff in rain and darkness, and the Sappers disassembled Ordnance Rifle barrels from carriages and wheels, so each could be drawn up the cliffs with blocks and tackle.

In the meantime, Scouts scrambled up the cliff face in the oily rain like spiders, coils of guide rope wound around their torsos. As the Scouts reached ledges, they dropped guide ropes that the Sappers attached to the blocks and tackle, which were wrapped in tent cloth to muffle them from clattering against the rock face. The Marini Sappers and Tassini Scouts coordinated their movements with silent hand signals, scarcely visible in the dark, rather than risk the sound of a shout.

The Scouts made the pulley assemblies fast, then pressed silently upward to the next level of ledges.

Through my night snoops, I watched one kid who had made it up three ledges reach out to grasp a rope that flapped in the wind. Whether rock crumbled, or he slipped in the rain, only he and his God know. But in an instant he was gone, a rag doll tumbling through the green glow of my night vision field. In all the last three hundred feet he lived, he never uttered a sound.

The Marini Sappers gathered around his body as it lay in the scree at the base of the cliff, and wept in the rain for him. There could be no funeral fire, so they buried him in the loose rock, Marini-style.

One Marini lifted a stone, and whispered to his buddy, "Can we give rites to a Tassini?"

His friend said, "Tassini? He's one of us, now."

At dawn, Casus pressed forward, and drove the Slugs back, so they wouldn't notice a few distant flies dangling eight hundred feet up a distant wall.

I leaned over Bassin's shoulder, as he sat on a rock in the rain and clicked the beads of his zill.

"What's the math for?" I asked.

Bassin rubbed his forehead. "Each gun barrel's the heaviest single load. The ropes were strong enough, but the rain's weakened them. The weight is close, now. But everything should hold."

Bassin's Sappers had rigged a rope sling around an Ordnance Rifle's tube as carefully as if they were swaddling baby Jesus, though they had no idea who that was.

Bassin shot them a thumbs-up. A Sapper grasped the reins of a wobblehead harnessed to the pulley assembly and marched the beast away.

Foot by creaking foot, the first gun tube ascended.

Forty minutes later, the gun tube dangled seven hundred

feet above us, nearly at the first way point of Bassin's vertical railroad.

The rain stopped.

A dozen feet above the gun, something small and black thrust out of the cliff face, like a dagger through a curtain. I zoomed on it and saw teeth.

The pterosaur peeked out of its nesting cavelet, looked down at the intruder creeping up toward it, and pounced.

I said, "Crap!"

The reptile spread its forty-foot, dirty-gold wings, as it dug its claws into the rope sling, and pecked at the iron burglar.

The upper pulley groaned, as the squawking pterosaur and the gun tube swung like a pendulum, and the gun tube clanged the rock wall.

Even a pterosaur as wide as a small house is as fragile as a kite, and barely outweighs a man. But the weakened ropes popped, first one, then all, and the reptile and the cannon plummeted seven hundred feet.

The gun tube hit the scree muzzle-first, crushed the pterosaur's wing like rice paper, and bounced down the slope, fifty feet to my right. Straight for Bassin. He stood frozen with his back to me, waiting a heartbeat to learn the batoning gun tube's trajectory.

I screamed, "Bassin!"

He leapt. Almost fast enough. Bassin dodged his torso around the gun, but the barrel crushed his leg, and Bassin, the gun, and the screeching, flapping pterosaur slid in a rotating heap down the loose rock of the scree slope.

Sappers and I ran to Bassin, and the first man to reach the heap of them put the broken reptile down with his Sapper's axe.

Bassin lay on his back.

I knelt and touched his face. "Bassin?"

He smiled, and sat up. "That was close!"

My jaw dropped.

Bassin reached forward, cut away his uniform trouser leg with his Sapper's axe, and unfastened his prosthetic leg. He left the ruined appliance crushed beneath the cannon tube.

Bassin said, "A rare advantage of the amputee!"

The fall bent the gun tube out of plumb enough to render it scrap.

Bassin strapped on a spare prosthetic, looked up at the cliff, and said, "I figured 5 percent accident breakage. I just didn't figure it all at once. We'll have to be careful the rest of the way."

I signaled a Tassini Scout down from the cliff, made sure he wasn't the only Tassini on Bren who couldn't shoot, and assigned him to plug the next critter that flew near our rope highway.

Then I rubbed my temples, and muttered to myself. "At least it can't get worse."

My Tassini sharpshooter stood alongside me scanning the cliffs. He said, "You going up free-climb or roped, Sir?"

"What?"

He pointed at the two-thousand-foot acrophobe's nightmare that rose in front of us.

I stared at the dangling climbing ropes, and slapped my forehead. How had I expected to get to the top? Fly up in the Supreme Commander's helicopter?

I said, "Crap."

SIXTY-SIX

IN FACT, I WASN'T THE ONLY PART of this expedition that was afraid of heights. The surefooted wobbleheads would be invaluable on the narrow ledges to come, but the Sappers had to sedate them, rig a basket, and haul them one at a time up the vertical face like flour sacks.

I rode up dangling in the same basket, but I didn't sniff any janga, first. I cursed myself, trembling, every foot of the two-thousand-foot journey for skipping it.

Fortunately for command and control, since I was a literal basket case, operational command was really Bassin's. The mélange of two thousand Tassini Scouts, the Sappers, and pretty much everybody but me and the last supply carts was gone down the first backslope by the time I reached the mountaintop.

When I arrived up top, I didn't kiss the granite, but I did kind of hug it with quivering arms.

Over the next few days, I repeated the funhouse experience four times, once for each new cliff. Then I low-crawled silently, alongside Bassin, through brush to a rock lip, just over the military crest of the peak our task force had just ascended.

Bassin tapped my shoulder, then pointed ahead at the next mountain, two miles down a forested slope to our front.

It was iridescent blue and alien, and I nearly wept for joy.

SIXTY-SEVEN

I LOOKED DOWN ACROSS FORESTS to the Troll and the
cleared land around it, and relaxed. All that remained of
this war was the end game.

Thirty-five thousand Slug warriors, according to Jeeb's
last reconnaissance, made up the defense garrison dug
into a perimeter around the Troll. Roughly one warrior
for each thousand years the perimeter had gone unchal-
lenged. It was a small force, as Slug forces went, but it
outnumbered the Scouts, Sappers, and artillerymen that
had survived our mountain odyssey ten to one.

The Scouts had borne the brunt of battle from the Red
Line in the sea to the landing beaches. They had been bat-
tered and shifted ever since, as Casus dashed across the
continent. Now, they could barely have forced a temporary breach in the Slug perimeter if Bassin massed them
and hurled them at a single point. Then they would have
been slaughtered.

Only the cannon batteries that the Scouts and Bassin's
Sappers had dragged across the mountains changed the
odds in our favor.

Two hours after Bassin and I first saw the Troll, we looked out across the forest and saw only trees.

I said, "The Scouts are deployed down there in an outpost line?"

Bassin nodded. "If the Slugs patrol these forests, they'll encounter Scouts before they discover our guns. The Scouts could only hold them off for a couple of days, if we're discovered."

Alongside us, Sappers and cannoneers laid our guns.

I said, "We only need a couple of hours more. I can tell you from experience, that incubator's a bomb waiting to happen. Once we start shelling, that thing will blow and take out everything around it, including every warrior on that perimeter. Casus will hear the explosion clear down the valley."

I drew a breath. We were about to win this war with scarcely another casualty.

As Bassin's Sappers reassembled and emplaced our artillery, Bassin and I stood alongside the ammunition carts. The Sappers cut the cords that held the tarps that protected the rounds with which we would shell the Troll.

A Sapper said, "What?"

The first cart was loaded with four-inch cannonballs, not the rifled shot required by the guns we had sweated blood to drag over mountains. The cargo was useless.

Swearing, I ran to the next cart, as a Sapper peeled back its cover. Worse than useless, the cart contained the debris Ord, Howard, and Jude had salvaged from our crashed Firewitch, seemingly a million years ago, which Howard had been toting across Bren ever since. Nobody had checked to be sure these pre-packed wagon loads matched their paperwork.

I squatted on a rock, head in hands, and moaned. "War is a catalogue of blunders."

This operation had been conceived in hours, executed under the most extreme duress of weather and terrain, by soldiers who had neither trained for it, nor trained with each other. Under the circumstances, any fair-minded person would grade it ninety-eight out of a possible one hundred. But, in war, often even ninety-nine is failing.

Checking what was actually in the ammunition carts was exactly the kind of thing that a supernumerary like me should have been doing. But I had been too worried about my next cliff ascent.

Bassin, shoulders drooping, shook his head. "Load manifests must have gotten switched. Where could that ammunition be?"

I stared at the Firewitch debris that some idiot had pack-ratted halfway across this planet, then I stood, and looked around Bassin's HQ camp. "I think I know. Where's your Prick?"

SIXTY-EIGHT

THREE MINUTES LATER, a Sapper set at my feet an olive-drab, twenty-three-pound metal box the size of a case of old aluminum soda cans. A flat three-foot spring-metal antenna like a carpenter's rule poked from the box top. For a second after the Sapper set the AN/PRC-25 radio down, the antenna whipped back and forth.

I bent over the Prick 25, twisted the squelch knob, then held the handset to my ear and thumbed the talk button. "Bear, this is Eagle, over." I released the talk button, and listened. I repeated the call, over and over, for three minutes.

Bren's sky wasn't just grayer than Earth's, it was more transparent to our old radio's transmissions. We had found the old radios' range improved to four times what they could transmit on Earth, better even than our helmet radios. Both Bassin's Headquarters and Casus's Headquarters carried one. Still, I held my breath after each transmission I sent.

No American military unit had been equipped with the AN/PRC-25 radio since the years when Berlin had a wall and the Rio Grande didn't. But our Earthside Advisees had cheerfully used surplus Prick Twenty-Fives eighty years later.

The same could not be said of Casus. My handset burbled with his voice. "—thing!"

I could picture Casus, eyes bulging, standing in his HQ tent, holding his Prick Twenty-Five's corded handset between his thumb and forefinger at arm's length, like it was a talking roach.

Casus's voice grumbled across the gray sky of Bren. "Get Hibble! The tethered insect has captured Jason's soul!"

I muttered to myself, "Goddammit, Casus, take your thumb off the 'talk' button."

Four minutes later, Howard's voice sounded in my ear. "Jason? Where are you?"

I sighed. A full bird Colonel and decorated combat veteran had just identified the Supreme Allied Commander by name, then asked him to transmit his location, and broadcast it all over this operations area in clear, uncoded speech.

We always doubted that the Slugs could monitor our radio traffic, or bothered to, anyway. But a good commander never underestimates his enemy.

I said, "Where I'm supposed to be." A good commander never overestimates his subordinates, either. "Put Falcon on."

"He can't come to the phone right now. Ambush patrol."

Ord would be out of touch for an entire day.

I drummed my fingers on the radio. "Owl, I need you to do something. Fast."

"I'm glad you called. You'll never guess what happened."

I rolled my eyes. "You pulled back the cover on a supply wagon, and found Ordnance Rifle ammunition, instead of your junk."

Silence.

"How did you know?"

"Never mind. Load that ammunition on a Cargo'Bot. Ride the 'Bot to me."

"I hate riding. And you know I can't read maps."

"Just dial the 'Bot to head west twenty degrees north from your location—don't tell me where you are now!—and hang on. Call on your helmet radio at random intervals. Short transmissions. When you get close enough that I pick up your transmission, I'll guide you in."

The 'Bot would beeline Howard and the ammo over thirty miles of mountains, which had taken us days to cross, in thirty-six hours. If we had a battalion of 'Bots, this war would have been won long ago.

"Can't somebody else do it?" Howard's voice quavered.

I smiled at my mental picture of the 'Bot spidering Howard up sheer cliffs, then dashing across mountain ledges, while Howard screamed like a bridesmaid handcuffed to a rodeo bull.

My smile faded.

The journey could kill or cripple even a young, fit Scout, even if the Slugs didn't intercept the 'Bot.

I said, "Nobody but you and Falcon's willing to touch a 'Bot, even if they knew how to program it. You have a helmet radio, and nobody else but Falcon and I do. Pack animal transport is too slow, anyway." I drew a breath. "You can do this. You have to do this."

Howard sighed. "Okay."

I transmitted, "Godspeed. Eagle out."

"Bye-bye."

For the next thirty hours, we all sat hidden in our observation post, and watched newly grown armored warriors pour out of the Troll. They formed into units, then *boom-boom-boom*ed around the low stone buildings. Then they headed down the valley to reinforce the Slugs that Casus's army was painfully, and too slowly, driving back this way. As long as the Troll remained intact, the Slugs were replacing more warriors than Casus could kill.

Jeeb overhead here would have reassured me, but Casus's army needed his tactical intelligence more. Besides, we had a screen of thousands of Scouts scattered through the forest that provided eyes and ears.

On the next cloudy afternoon, thirty-eight hours after Howard departed from Casus's headquarters, I paced a rise two miles further back from the Slug Troll than Bassin's HQ. I checked my 'Puter again, and swore.

Howard should have come within helmet radio range hours before. The rise was overgrown with a stand of redwoods bigger around than silos, and five times taller. From this vantage, I should have been better able to receive Howard's transmissions, and Howard could spot the light of the Marini lantern I carried, so he could guide in on it.

I worried for our missing ammunition, but I worried as much for Howard.

I stomped around the redwood copse muttering to myself.

"Eagle, this is Owl, over."

I grinned. "This is Eagle. How was the trip, over?"

"Fair. Please show your position with colored smoke and I will identify, over."

Howard actually knew how to soldier. Whenever he started behaving like one was when I knew he was dead serious and dead tired. Smoke grenades had been a simple location marker on Earth for a century.

But I wrinkled my forehead.

If Howard was thinking straight, even he would have known we were on a different planet, and we didn't have smoke grenades.

"Sorry, Owl. I have no smoke. I say again, no smoke. I will mark my position with light, over."

I swung the lantern overhead in the gray, fading afternoon.

"Eagle, I do not identify your light. I say again, please show . . . your light again, over."

"Owl, are you okay?"

"Had a little fall . . . on the way."

My heart skipped. "Wait twenty, Owl. I will reposition my light, over."

Howard just breathed.

I roped the lit lantern to my back, walked to the tallest redwood, and craned my neck toward its crown, three hundred feet above me.

Then I popped the wrist and sole-plate crampons out on my Eternads. With my feet together, the tines touched each other and rattled, because I was shaking inside my Eternads.

I took a step back, jumped against the tree, and my crampons nailed three-thousand-year-old bark. I hugged the redwood like I was an armored Koala, shinnied for the sky, and never looked down.

By the time I cleared the shorter redwoods, which the trip altimeter in my visor called two hundred feet, the sun sat low on the horizon. My underlayer was sweat-soaked despite the suit ventilators, and I trembled, more from the altitude than the exertion.

I looked up.

I would shinny twenty feet higher, then call Howard again.

Swoosh.

Something shot past me, behind my back, and I flattened myself against the tree trunk. I panted inside my helmet, my cheekplate against bark.

Neither Slug sniper rounds nor friendly fire went "swoosh."

I inched my head around and peered between branches. A hundred yards away, a forty-foot pterosaur wheeled, then glided back for another pass. It wouldn't be able to bite through my armor—theoretically—but it could sure knock me off my perch. I forgot about climbing twenty feet higher.

I transmitted, "Owl, this is Eagle. Do you identify my light, over?"

Swoosh.

My right arm slipped. I tried to swallow, but my mouth had been dry for a half hour.

"Eagle...I'm not sure. Can you shake your light?"

"Goddammit, my light's been shaking since I left the ground!"

Swoosh.

Something thumped the lantern on my back, as the flying lizard swept past, and I inched around to the other side of the tree trunk.

Howard's voice chirped in my headset. "Eagle, I identify yellow, I say again yellow, light."

"That's me."

"Estimate arrival your position one-zero minutes. Owl out."

Even as I shook, I smiled, and relaxed. The pterosaur, puzzled by an unappetizing intruder, swung into view again, but now two hundred yards out and receding.

Magnificent, free, and soaring, it looked nothing like its cousin's tangled corpse, crushed by our dropped Ordnance Rifle. Collateral damage. Us four Earthlings had, in our short time on this planet, butchered every sort of animal that walked, flew, or swam on it, polluted rivers with alien blood, and forced our enemy to burn the land itself.

War is cruelty, and there is no refining it. Sherman said that to the Mayor of Atlanta, then demolished the city's rail yards, so Sherman's enemy couldn't use them to move troops against him. The rest of the city burned, despite Sherman's contrary orders. The cruel and unrefined collateral damage I had ordered befell a resilient ecology bigger than we were. At least killing animals was better than killing noncombatant humans.

I moved my left foot down, and began descending, when I realized that from up here I could not only see the Troll. I could see the Troll from a different heading and elevation than we got from our observation posts.

In the dusk, I upped the magnification and switched to night passive.

"No."

I zoomed my snoopers, then shook my head inside my helmet.

"No, no, no!"

SIXTY-NINE

MILES AWAY, across the artificial green dusk of my visor display ghosted pale, spindly shapes. They poured from the long, low, windowless ancient stone buildings that surrounded the vast clearing alongside the mountain that was the Troll.

I toggled my threat counter, and it spun into the thousands. I zoomed my optics, and my eyes widened against the surrounds.

The shapes were thin and ghostly. They were hunched and naked. But they were human beings.

I hung back away from the redwood trunk, as though the image I saw had punched me.

We always wondered whether the Slugs took prisoners. We would have taken Slug prisoners, if they had ever let us, just to better know our enemy. It stood to reason that the Pseudocephalopod would be curious, too.

I peered down, again. These people were as often women as men. Their hair tangled shoulder-long, not GI-short, and many seemed curled over with age. Here and there, a robust head thrust above the throng. There might be some of our troops, taken prisoners of war, sprinkled among this population. Some of the rest appeared to be civilians, likely captured at the Great Fair and made to transport Cavorite here. But most of these people had never been soldiers or civilians.

They shuffled on bare, shackled feet.

They had never been soldiers. For countless generations they had been slaves of the Pseudocephalopod.

Two hundred feet below me, Howard's 'Bot whined into the clearing at the redwood's base.

It lurched five-legged, its right center ambulator tucked up against its carapace, useless. Howard, his crimsons caked with dust, swayed and leaned to his right like a drunk.

I attenuated my radio range, and spoke in the clear. "Howard?"

SEVENTY

WHEN I REACHED THE GROUND and dragged Howard off the 'Bot's back, he was conscious, but his right arm hung limp.

I popped his visor, and peered into his eyes. "What happened?"

"Slipped off a ledge six hours out. Damaged the 'Bot. My shoulder dislocated, I think."

I clenched my teeth, and hissed. Thirty-two hours in the saddle pounding a dislocated shoulder.

"You reduce it? And drop Morph?"

He nodded. "Morph's all gone. You wouldn't have a cigarette on you?"

I shook my head, smiled, and slid both of my own MorphTabs under his tongue. He closed his eyes and sighed.

I waited three minutes, until the 'Tabs made him giggle, then slung him back aboard the 'Bot, as gently as I could. I swung up behind him, and moved the 'Bot out at a walk.

The 'Bot could still carry the two of us faster on five legs than I could run.

"Howard, those old stone sheds by that clearing next to the Troll. There must have been people in them. They just came out in the open. Thousands of 'em. Most of them look like they've been Slug slaves forever. What's your hunch?"

Howard didn't answer, he just giggled, then sang, "Ho, ho, ho . . ."

Howard was feeling no pain, so I kicked the 'Bot's speed up.

Howard's head lolled, and he sang again. "Down through th' chim-un-ee comes old Saint Nick."

I sighed.

One MorphTab would have been plenty. Howard had lost all touch with reality.

Or had he?

SEVENTY-ONE

THE FIRST MOON HAD RISEN by the time I got Howard back to Bassin's HQ. Bassin and I lay side by side in the still, cold darkness, on a rock ledge that overlooked the Troll. I flipped out my Elephant Ear so Bassin could see what I saw through my snoopers, showing up in my helmet's external flatscreen.

We peered down at the scene, and Bassin said, "The warriors that were guarding them before? The nearest warrior's a thousand yards away from them, now."

The moonlight lit the thronged slaves now, as they moved into the open space by the Troll, now clearly visible from our vantage.

I nodded. "But nobody looks inclined to run for it. No wonder the Slugs aren't worried about keeping the Stones flowing if they eradicate this civilization. They know how to use slaves, and they can just keep a few more. You all accept slavery, and piling Stones on the devil's doorstep, because it's been beaten into you for thirty-five thousand years."

"It's consistent with our prehistory and our theology."

Had the Slugs trained humans, then turned them loose

on Bassin's side of the wall? Like sheep that the Slugs
came back and sheared annually? Or did humans escape,
breed like lab rabbits loosed in the wild, then get domes-
ticated? It didn't matter. The question was—

Bassin frowned. "The question becomes, what do we
do now?"

I pointed at the Troll. "If we shell that thing like we
planned, we'll kill all those people."

Bassin frowned. "But—"

"Bassin, I hate sacrificing soldiers. There may even be
POWs down there. But I will not deliberately sacrifice non-
combatants. Period. Slugs may be the devil. I won't be."

Bassin was the future king of most of the troops around
us, and they were under his operational command. If he
ordered them to shell those people, they would.

I stabbed my finger at him. "You try it, it's over my
corpse!"

He raised his eyebrow and both palms. "Agreed! Jason,
don't you know me at all, by now?"

My finger trembled, and I lowered it. "Sorry." Physical
stress exhausts GIs, then inattention kills them. The added
mental stress of command exhausts Generals faster. But if
Generals succumb to stress, their slip-ups kill others.

Bassin said, "But every hour that we don't shell that
blue mountain, our enemy grows stronger. The odds that
face Casus have already grown far longer than our supply
lines. The Scouts we have dispersed in these woods could
barely swoop into that position down there, before they'd
be overwhelmed."

Bassin was right. Moreover, if I was on edge enough to
snap at Bassin, all our troops were on edge. We had to end
this war now, or the Slugs would end it for us.

Behind us, a voice whispered, "Holy moly! Right on time."

Howard, lucid again, crawled up alongside us, favoring his right arm. He stopped, then pointed at the sky.

From a foxhole in brush to our right came a soldier's gasp.

I looked up, where Howard pointed, my eyes widened, and I muttered, "Holy moly is right."

A silhouette drifted across the white moon. It was a slow-rotating, bulbous, black scorpion with a down-turned, glowing red stinger and six upturned claws.

The Firewitch half-eclipsed the moon.

Bassin gasped. "So that is a ship that flies among the stars. You arrived in one of those?"

The Slug vessel whispered above us, and its low hum shook the ground beneath my belly. Then the ship settled slowly, tail-first, into the clearing alongside the Troll.

Howard's Santa came down the chimney as he had predicted.

I turned to Howard. "Why—"

He pointed below. A red, glowing human lava flow snaked from the stone buildings toward the descending Firewitch. The human slaves were hauling this year's Cavorite harvest from temporary storage. Bins alongside the Firewitch glowed red like bonfires as Stones by the thousands filled them.

Howard said, "The only reason for the Pseudocephalopod to maintain human stock near this landing site was to handle Cavorite. The only reason for that stock to be released above ground was to load cargo. Cavorite gets harvested by the local population each summer, the locals trade and move it each fall, and a transport calls to pick up Cavorite once each year. Elegantly simple. Of course, this year, the Pseudocephalopod eliminated the middleman, permanently, because we arrived. Now, here's the thing—"

I raised my palm, and the moonlight reflected off my gauntlet. "Howard, I don't need elegance. I need to win this war, without killing those people. And I'm about out of time."

Howard rolled his eyes. "I was getting to that." He frowned. "But we are almost out of time."

SEVENTY-TWO

AT FIRST LIGHT THE NEXT MORNING, I sat on one snorting wobblehead among fifty, in the trees a mile back from the clearing where the Troll rose, and where the Slug's Stone transport ship had parked, perched atop triangular landing gear. Between us and the clearing was what Scout reconnaissance had identified as a sixty-yard gap in the Slug's perimeter, where weather had crumbled an ancient stone wall.

The Leader of the Troop I would ride with reined up his mount alongside me, and held up an empty ammunition sack. "Sir, what do we do with these?" His armored shoulders slumped, and his wobblehead panted.

"Follow me. Do what I do."

There wasn't time to explain the plan that had grown from Howard's hunches, much less time to train Scouts, so exhausted they could barely stay in their saddles, to execute that plan.

More battles have been lost by failure to seize opportunity than have ever been won by caution.

Howard expected the Slugs to start their human laborers moving Stones out of the bins and into the transport ship as soon as the humans had enough visible light to work.

Bassin estimated that it would take an hour, start to finish, for the slaves to shift the Stone volume from the bins into the transport. Once the Stones were loaded into the transport, our opportunity window would close.

I checked my rifle for the fourth time, checked my 'Puter, and chinned my visor display to Jeeb's overhead of the vast battle advancing slowly up the valley. Green bars showed Casus's army, drawn up opposite the red bars of the Slug defending units.

Two hundred thousand men and four hundred thousand maggots boiled in parallel lines, separated from each other by a mile, and waited for dawn.

Since we had left the main body, Casus had defied logistics by force of will, pushing the Slugs back to within thirty miles of us.

I had coordinated by radio, through Ord, what we needed from Casus. His troops and animals had to be dead on their feet, but in a few minutes he would challenge every one of them to throw everything into one more assault toward us. If we failed, they would fail. If we all failed, mankind would forever after exist on this planet only as naked slaves.

My mouth went dry.

Fast, improvised initiatives had throughout history won battles—and wars. But too many "brilliant" initiatives had proven to be almost brilliant instead. Lee hurled Pickett's division against the Union Center at Gettysburg, and his mistake doomed the Confederacy. The Ardennes Offensive nearly expelled the Allies from Europe, but when it failed, Germany's defense collapsed.

Thump.

The first Ordnance Rifle emplaced above and behind us fired. Seconds later, the rest of the battery rumbled.

Six shells screamed by above the trees that hid us, and thundered, not into the Troll, nor into the humans massed around it, but into the Slug perimeter to our front.

I swallowed and shook my head. We weren't going to blow up the Troll, or the transport, and kill those thousands of innocents. But we had better not lose the battle and this world on that gamble.

I checked Jeeb's overhead. Down the valley, Casus's troops responded to our guns' distant rumble, and charged across the mile that separated them from the Slugs.

After three minutes, the guns behind us fell silent, their ammunition expended destroying the Slugs to our front.

The Troop leader next to me raised his rifle, and turned to his Scouts. "Forward!"

We galloped through the perimeter breach before the Slugs could react. Six hundred more Scout wobbleheads followed us, before mag rounds began falling on our column.

I spurred my wobblehead forward, as the lead Troop that I rode with crossed the open space toward the glowing red Stone bins.

Bewildered slaves scattered, but no Slugs advanced to meet us. Howard's Spooks had estimated that Cavorite killed a Slug in thirty seconds from five hundred yards. The little maggots kept their distance, as we had hoped.

Now that we had gotten inside their lines, the maggots could turn their guns inward to potshot us, but they couldn't advance on us, without killing themselves by Cavorite exposure. Individual Slug warriors weren't afraid to die. If the ganglions in them thought independently at all, they probably thought—correctly—that since the overall organism survived they weren't even dying. But individual warriors were smart enough to avoid dying without accomplishing anything.

I reined up alongside a bin, dismounted, then scooped glowing Stones into the empty ammunition bag I carried, until I could barely heft it across my saddle.

My visor display showed the green bars of Casus's army racing forward, now.

As we expected, once the Slugs' main army realized we were in their rear and threatening the Troll, their formations had to fall back to reinforce against our attack. The Slugs beat that retreat so fast that Casus's troops could barely advance fast enough to maintain contact with them.

Once two Troops of Scouts riding behind me had loaded their bags with Stones, I led them at a gallop southwest, down the valley, toward the Slugs retreating from Casus.

As I approached the Slugs' perimeter this time, I didn't bother shooting. I chucked a couple Stones left and right. Slugs scattered or died.

Thirty minutes later, our Scouts had sprinkled their Stones in a belt that spanned the valley, wall-to-wall. The retreating Slugs either had to turn, fight Casus's army, and die, or keep retreating into the Stone barrier belt— and die.

Slugs aren't much for individual initiative, but a few made for the forests at the valley's edge. Casus's cavalry cut them down before they made two hundred yards.

The Slug remnants squeezed between us and Casus could no longer win the war. I wheeled my duckbill, and stared back at the thirty-five-thousand-year-old mountain fortress that was the Troll. The defending Slugs that remained inside it couldn't win the war, but they would fight to the last maggot. Worse, if they blew themselves and the Troll up, they would take the Scouts and the prisoners with it.

I chinned my magnification. Bassin's Sappers had blown a breach in the Troll's hull at ground level, and it yawned big enough to swallow an airliner. But I could see Slugs boiling out of the breach, mag rifles spitting. Beyond them, the Scouts that were supposed to have charged through the breach and secured the Troll before the Slugs could blow it, hunkered, sheltering behind wobblehead carcasses that had been shot out from under them. One of the pinned troops wore old, Eternad crimsons. Howard was attached to those Scouts, to guide them through the Troll. I intercommed, "Owl, this is Eagle, over."

"This is Owl."

Good. Howard was still in military mind-set. "Owl, you need to get those people moving before the Slugs blow your objective to rutabagas."

"You know how it is, Eagle. They send out warriors faster than we can send out bullets to kill them, Eagle. We can't go back. We can't go forward."

"You were supposed to use Stones to drive the Slugs back."

"The Troop with the Stones never got here."

I scanned the battlefield. Five hundred yards from Howard and the pinned-down Scouts lay a bloody jumble of wobbleheads and Scouts, ripped apart by Slug Heavy rounds. Even in daylight I saw red Cavorite glow from Stones saddlebagged among the corpses.

I spun my wobblehead, and gathered a half dozen mounted Scouts.

In thirty seconds, we reached the Stone bags. Two minutes later, we began lobbing them, grenade-style, toward the Troll's hull breach.

Slug defensive fire slacked, but the pinned-down Scouts didn't wait for it to stop before they were up, and charging forward. As they ran, dodging dead and dying Slugs, the Scouts scooped up thrown Stones, to throw again and clear their advance.

The first man through the breach carried his rifle in one hand, and swung his free arm forward, in the follow-me gesture of the infantry. He wore Eternad crimson.

By mid morning, Jeeb's display showed no red bars of organized Slug units. Only scattered Slugs meandered around in the mile-wide belt that remained between our onrushing line and the Cavorite barrier.

Meanwhile, the Scouts had wheeled, returned, and stormed the Troll and the Firewitch.

My helmet radio sang. "Eagle, this is Falcon, over."

I smiled. "Eagle here, Falcon." What the hell. There was nobody left to eavesdrop. I spoke in the clear. "Well done, Sergeant Major. My compliments to Casus."

"You'll be able to deliver them yourself in a few minutes, Sir."

Twenty minutes later, the ground shook as Casus, on his white stallion, rode into view at the head of his cavalry. Rifles cracked no more often than the last kernels in a popcorn popper, mopping up the last Slugs.

High atop the Troll, Scouts crawled out through the tops of the ventilators like summiting mountaineers. They shouted, took off their tunics, and swung them above their heads to announce victory. One of the figures waved a crimson Eternad breastplate.

Howard radioed. "We captured the Stone freighter, too! Jason, we have a way home, again!"

I blinked back tears. We had a ship. But we didn't have my godson to pilot it.

Ord rode up, dismounted, and saluted. I returned his salute, as we looked around the battlefield.

In the acrid black-powder fog, infantrymen searched for wandering comrades that had become lost in battle, found them too seldom, and hugged them. Others bent forward, searching among the corpses, peering into cold faces, and found their comrades too often.

I cleared my rifle, then slung it across my shoulder. "Eisenhower was right. There's no glory in battle worth the blood it costs."

"But blood buys more than glory, Sir."

The thousands of slaves stared wordlessly at all that swirled around them, as blank as newborns. They might never become more. But blood had bought them a chance.

The recent captives from the battle of the Great Fair wept, hugged one another, and hugged the soldiers that had freed them, regardless of Clan. The Clans had shed their blood together, and that bought them the chance to stop shedding it separately.

In the crowds, the soldiers the Slugs had captured during our campaign were easy to distinguish from the liberators. The freed captives wore only occasional scraps of uniform or armor.

"None of it changes what Wellington said." I remembered it after every battle, and I cried.

Ord said, "Sir?"

I raised my visor, and wiped my eyes. "There is nothing so melancholy as a battle lost, except a battle won."

Far down the ragged rows of pale slaves, one pale, naked figure stood, taller than the others, and waved an object at me.

I blinked away the blur of my tears, and stared. Then I ran forward.

The pale, thin figure dropped the crimson breastplate he had waved, then Jude ran toward me, too.

SEVENTY-THREE

I STAND AT PARADE REST on the lecture hall stage, and stare out across three thousand young faces, all eyes staring up at me. The Cadets' uniforms are gray, impeccable, and indistinguishable one from another. The faces, however, are brown, white, and yellow, male and female. Tattoos curl around some faces, jewels dangle from others. They are badges of their human homeworlds, each spawned, and once ruled by, the Pseudocephalopod Hegemony. Some of those worlds I fought to free from the Hegemony. Some I fought to keep in the Union. The names of some I can barely pronounce.

The Commandant stands to my right, then gives me a wink. She's an old friend. Well, more than a friend.

She grips the podium, and her words to her Cadets echo off the arched 'lume ceiling. "I'll keep the intro brief. I know you don't want Assembly to run long. That could shorten morning PT."

Three thousand throats boom a chuckle off the ceiling. Then silence returns.

The ceiling 'lume dims, and a quote fades in on the

flatscreen wall behind the Commandant. She turns, then reads aloud:

> Terracentric it may be to refer to "The Pseudocephalopod War," much less to date its onset from "2037." However, all history pivoted on those events in the Spiral Arm, as undeniably as conventional space folds around every Ultradwarf at every temporal fabric insertion point. Students of that time and place will find no truer account than in the warrior's-eye view of Jason Wander.
>
> —*Chronicles of the Galaxy, The Mobian Transliteration,* Volume XXIII

The Commandant turns back to the Corps of Cadets. "Today's topic is a retrospective on the campaign for the liberation of Bren." She takes a seat in the audience, leaving me alone center stage.

I step alongside the chair placed there for me. My legs ache all the time, these days. So does every other part that the Slugs and the calendar have forced the Army to rebuild.

But I frown down at the chair, and say to the audience, "Everybody provides one of these for me, these days. Deference to rank, or age, I suppose. But infantry doesn't sit."

Whoops and pumped fists erupt from the back rows, where the lousy students stand. When the Cadet Corps draws for Post-Grad assignments, the top students will snatch the glam slots, like Flight School and Astrogation. The back row will become infantry Lieutenants. It's natural selection, I guess. Infantry gets the sharp, dirty end of the stick from the beginning, so it learns to laugh about it.

I smile, and pump my fist back at them. Where they're going, they'll need their sense of humor.

I clear my throat.

PalmTalkers swivel up alongside whispering lips. Personal 'Puter keyboards unfold in hands. A few kids snatch pterosaur-quill pens and sheets of flat paper from hiding places beneath stiff shirt fronts. Different cultures, different study habits.

I wave the devices away. "No notes. You get enough Logistics and Tactics at the Puzzle Factory next door."

Laughter.

I say, "Bren wasn't liberated by so-called military genius."

A kid in back raises his hand. "Then why do our chips teach the Bren campaign, Sir?" He knows the answer. Every kid in the Union does. He's just stretching the lecture.

But I answer like they don't know. "Because it turned the tide of this war. We flew the transport we captured back to Earth, used that ship's power plant for a template, used Bren's Cavorite for fuel, and built the fleets that liberated, then unified, the planets of the Union. My meaning was that wars are won by soldiers sacrificing for other soldiers. And by trial and blunder. And by which side got stuck in the mud least. And by commanders who learned to lead effectively while engulfed by chaos, and lunacy, and their own heartbreak."

Twenty minutes later, I take questions. The kids know the current Commandant wants cadets to speak their minds. I point at the raised hand of a shave-headed kid with indigo-dyed eyebrows.

She stands as straight and as hard as a Casuni broad-

sword and asks, "Sir, our poli sci chips say the real libera-
tion of Bren only came years later, when Bassin the First,
Casus, and the Council of Headmen signed the Treaty of
Marinus and ended slavery on Bren."

I nod. "They're right. The uncivil 'peace' among the
Clans that followed the Expulsion of the Pseudocephalopod Hegemony killed more Marini, Casuni, and Tassini
than the Slugs did."

With those indigo eyebrows, she's Tassini. Probably
second-generation emancipated. I'm guessing she's asking a rhetorical question, designed to educate those of her
classmates to whom *slavery* is just a word. If it hadn't
been for the changes that started on Bren with the Expulsion of the Slugs, she'd be bending over some landowner's
plow or washtub today, like her grandparents did. Thanks
to Emancipation, she's traveled to the stars, here to the
Motherworld, where she's learning things like Astrogation and Comparative Lit.

She asks, "You agree with the chips that say the war
was wrong, then?"

"Creating freedom for people can't be wrong. Even if
some people create wrong out of freedom."

She half-smiles at the kid next to her.

I point at his raised hand, and he says, "Maybe the war
was right for Bren. And for the Union. But on a galactic
scale, since the Expulsion we haven't seen the end of war.
Soldiers are still dying."

"'Only the dead have seen the end of war.' The chips
attribute that quote to Plato. It's still true twenty-five
hundred years after Plato died. The lesson you're here
to learn is this: Never waste the life of any soldier you
command."

He nods.

I say, "Even if you learn that lesson, you'll hate it. Command is an orphan's journey."

The kids milk question time for twenty minutes more, then the applause from the infantry gonnabes in the back rows shakes the Omnifoam floor tiles.

As I step offstage, Jude grasps my elbow and steers us toward an exit.

Jude's a Zoomie now. A better pilot than his father, they say. On invasion morning Jude's buoyant Eternads helped him swim to another boat when that rhind shattered his own. In the melee on the landing beach, Jude caught on with another unit, moved inland, and was captured in the first battle of the campaign. Jude doesn't speak about his captivity much. It changed him. Since Bren, too much else has changed, too. Jude and I have grown apart in too many ways. But we still follow orders, and we still have each other.

He shakes his head. "You gave the same speech last year. They still applaud."

"They applaud because I talk so long that the Commandant cancels PT. What's your hurry?"

Jude slides back his Zoomie-blue uniform sleeve, to show me the red-flashing screen on his wrist 'Puter. "Orders. We lift on next hour's Fleet Orbital. You won't believe what the Slugs just did. Want to hear where we go next?"

I shake my head. "Just so we go together."

Acknowledgments

Thanks to my editor, Devi Pillai, and to Orbit's publishing director, Tim Holman, for support and wisdom in making *Orphan's Journey,* and the series that surrounds it, possible. Thanks also to Hilary Powers for thoughtful copyediting; to Calvin Chu for a cover that pops; to Alex Lencicki for telling the world about it all; to Jennifer Flax for all things great and small; and to everyone at Orbit for their energy and great work.

Thanks also to the readers, whose enthusiastic feedback makes it easy to keep writing.

Finally, thanks also to Winifred Golden, agent *par excellence,* and, always, thanks to Mary Beth and the kids for putting up with me.

extras

orbit

meet the author

ROBERT BUETTNER is a former Military Intelligence Officer, National Science Foundation Fellow in Paleontology and has published in the field of Natural Resources Law. He lives in Georgia. His Web site is www.RobertBuettner.com.

introducing

If you enjoyed ORPHAN'S JOURNEY,
look out for

ORPHAN'S ALLIANCE

Book 4 of the JASON WANDER series
by Robert Buettner

"MOUSETRAP'S VISIBLE NOW, GENERAL." My Command Sergeant Major taps my armored shoulder, points through UHSS *Harmony*'s forward observation blister, and my heart skips. The two of us float shoulder-to-shoulder in infantry Eternads, like unhelmeted frogs in a gravityless fishbowl. Ord has been a jump ahead of me since he was my drill sergeant in Basic.

With my gauntlet's snozz pad, I mop condensed breath off the observation blister's Synquartz, and cold stings through the glove. Fifty thousand frigid miles away spins Mousetrap. In two hours, on my orders, a hundred thousand kids plucked from fourteen worlds will arrive down there, innocent. None will leave innocent. Too many won't leave at all.

The gray pebble Ord points to has just orbited out from a vast orange ball's shadow. In the red sunlight that bathes the gas giant planet and its tiny moon, Mousetrap tumbles as small and as wrinkled as a peach pit.

Ord grunts. "The real estate hardly looks worth the price, does it, Sir?"

"Location, location, location, Sergeant Major." Mousetrap is the only habitable rock near the interstellar crossroad that linchpins the Human Union's fourteen planets.

That's why the Union fortified Mousetrap. That's why the Slugs took it away from us. And that's why we arrived here today to take Mousetrap back, or die trying. "We" are history's deadliest armada, carrying history's best army. My army.

I'm Jason Wander, war orphan, high school dropout, Lieutenant General, Commanding, Third Army of the Human Union. And infantryman until the day I die. Which day is now thirty years closer than when I enlisted at the start of the Slug War, in 2037.

Ord and I push back from the observation blister's forward wall, to head aft to our troop transport. I glance at the Time-to-Drop Countdown winking off my wrist 'Puter. In two hours, Ord and I will be aboard a first-wave assault transport when compressed air thumps it out of one of *Harmony*'s thirty-six launch bays. Kids embarked aboard *Harmony*, and aboard the fleet's other ships, will go with us.

Ord sighs. "A hundred thousand GIs don't buy what they used to, General."

Whump.

Harmony's vast hull shudders, tumbling Ord and me against the observation blister's cold curve.

Hssss.

A thousand feet aft from our perch here at *Harmony*'s bow, thirty-six launch bay hatches reseal as one.

A tin voice from the Bridge crackles in my earpiece. "All elements away."

I turn to Ord, wide-eyed. "What the hell, Sergeant Major?"

Ord turns his palms up, shakes his head.

Through ebony space, thirty-six sparks flash past us, from the bays that ring *Harmony*'s midriff. In a blink, they disperse toward Mousetrap, leaving behind thirty-six silent, red streaks of drifting chemical flame.

For one heartbeat, *Harmony* forms the hub that anchors thirty-six fading, translucent wheel spokes. It is as though we spin at the center of a mute, exploding firework. To our port, starboard, dorsal and ventral, identical fireworks blossom, gold, green, blue, purple, as the Fleet's other cruisers launch their own craft, each ship trailing its mothership's tracer color.

I blink at the vanished silhouettes. The Army I command wasn't scheduled to launch for Mousetrap for two hours. We expect to take lumps by landing with no aerial prep. And more lumps when we start digging the Slugs out of Mousetrap, one hole at a time. But landing without prep is the only way we can avoid killing the fifty thousand human POWs that the Slugs hold on Mousetrap.

But what I just saw fly by weren't chunky troop transports. They were sleek scorpions, their bomb racks packed with liquid fire. The ships that made that fireworks display weren't just an aerial prep force. The formations I just saw were powerful enough to incinerate every living thing on Mousetrap, Slug and human alike, three times over.

Before Ord and I paddled up to this observation blister for a final, weightless look at our objective, I inspected every launch bay myself. One of our troop transports filled every bay. But one order from the Bridge could rotate troop transports out of the bays in fifteen minutes, like cartridges in old-fashioned revolvers, and replace them with bombers.

I'm already torpedoing my weightless body hand-over-hand down the rungs that line the cruiser's center tube, back toward the Cruiser's Bridge. "If those bombers fry Mousetrap, our POWs die." Mousetrap's POWs are infantry, and that swells my throat even more.

But Army commanders are supposed to consider the Big Picture, as well as their kids. I shake my head at Ord. "The Outworlds already oppose this war. If this fleet kills Outworld POWs, the Union's dead. If the Union dies, the Slugs will wipe mankind out. Did Mimi lose her mind?"

Ord paddles up alongside me, so fast that the slipstream seems to flatten the gray GI brush he calls hair. He shakes his head. "Admiral Ozawa wouldn't launch bombers, Sir. She wouldn't even consider it without consulting you, first. But there is a ranking civilian authority aboard this ship. If ordered, the Admiral couldn't—"

The two of us tuck our legs, then swing into the first side tube like trapeze artists. Then we 'frog along toward the Bridge, gaining weight as we move away from the rotating Cruiser's centerline.

"I know. But I warned them, Sergeant Major. That Alliance was a deal with the devil." Lieutenant Generals don't have tempers, especially while commanding invasions.

But Ord and I are alone in the passage tube, so I take the opportunity to punch my fist against the tube's wall until my knuckles bleed.

Not because our allies are cruel and stupid. Thirty years of war have taught me how to beat cruelty and stupidity. I pound out my frustration because my godson has become one of them. Worse, I know my godson is the only officer in this fleet who could be leading those bombers.

Ord closes two hands over my fist, until I stop punching, and I stand panting. "Sir, Churchill said if Hitler invaded hell, Churchill would at least make a favorable reference to the devil in the House of Commons."

I know the quote. I talked myself into believing Churchill had the right attitude, so I could smile while diplomats pattered their white-gloved hands together, applauding a deal that I should have known would bring us to this. An infantryman's life is talking himself into things that may kill him, or kill others.

Crack.

A side-tube pressure valve releases, like a rifleshot, and my heart skips; just like it skipped when this mess started eight years ago.